She knew she should turn around . . .

It was Raven. Charm knew she should turn around and march back toward camp. But she didn't. Standing at the top of a steep bank, she looked down.

In the moonlight, his hair gleamed a deep sapphire color. His shoulders where wide and dark, and from there his body tapered in masculine lines to the taut expanse of his waist. Below that . . . Charm swallowed hard. She shouldn't be there, she knew, and had nearly convinced herself to leave when he knelt to splash water on his torso. The silvery waves lapped lovingly at his buttocks.

Charm grasped a branch in each hand and drew a sharp breath through her teeth. Raven's head turned, like a fine, gallant stallion that had caught a scent of danger. Charm remained motionless, not daring to breathe. Yet, he stood, finally turning slowly to stare in her direction.

Dear God. This was no time to faint, because he'd probably hear her fall, and besides, if she fainted she'd be unable to watch . . .

THE
Gambler

Lois Greiman

JOVE BOOKS, NEW YORK

THE GAMBLER

A Jove Book / published by arrangement with
the author

PRINTING HISTORY
Jove edition / November 1995

ISBN: 0-515-11787-0

A JOVE BOOK®
Jove Books are published by The Berkley Publishing Group,
200 Madison Avenue, New York, New York 10016.
JOVE and the "J" design are trademarks
belonging to Jove Publications, Inc.

PRINTED IN THE UNITED STATES OF AMERICA

10 9 8 7 6 5 4 3 2 1

To Laurette Nelson,
who believed in my talent
long before I had any.

Thanks Mom—for all the times you rocked me to sleep with countless verses of *Stand Up Stand Up For Jesus*—for the frigid nights we linked arms and wandered out to the pastures in search of newborn calves—for the times you told me I was beautiful when I was not. Thanks, Mom, for encouraging me to be different. If I could do it all over and choose any mother in the world, I would choose you.

Chapter 1

Deadwood Gulch, South Dakota—May 1877

He had a pair of queens, but *she* had cleavage.

Not that Raven Scott had noticed.

"You ready to play, boy?" asked his opponent. Jude Fergusson was a wilted frame of a man, well past his prime, and impatient. Behind him, the woman called Charm leaned over his shoulder, deliberately exposing a good deal of smooth-skinned distraction.

She was, without a doubt, a rare beauty, but it had taken little time for Raven to realize she was not the woman for whom he searched. Not Eloise Medina's niece. And that was regrettable, for she could have made the journey to St. Louis enjoyable indeed. But luck was a fickle lady. One could not expect to have both an exquisite traveling companion *and* a fortune at journey's end. Thus, Raven would restrain himself from the luxury of greed—and take the fortune.

"Then you've never heard of a Chantilly Grady?" he inquired now. It was basically the same question he'd asked twice before. He only mixed the words a bit. In his line of work it paid to be thorough. And in any case, he wanted to delay the game. He wanted to build up the old man's edginess and give himself an opportunity to glance now and then at the bounty Charm so generously displayed above her bodice.

"I told you I ain't never heard of no Chantilly," said Jude, making no attempt at civility. "Now, you playin' or throwin' in yer cards?"

A less experienced gambler might easily be distracted by the girl's presence, thereby causing him to do something foolish, Raven knew. But he was not such a man.

Still, she had great . . .

"You ready to play, boy?" Jude repeated, his voice cracking.

All right. So he was a *little* distracted. Lowering his gaze to his cards, Raven checked his composure, making certain he offered his opponent no clue to his thoughts. But no, years of gambling assured a bland countenance. Despite Clancy's irritating and sundry shortcomings, his former partner had taught Raven that much. Damn his hide.

"How many cards?" Without looking, Raven knew Jude's right hand shook slightly as he held the deck, a tremor discernible only to the sharpest eye. A tremor that might be subdued completely if old Burle Dorsey, the inn's proprietor, would bring the man a drink. But Burle was kept busy with other patrons, so exposing Jude's debility to Raven's predatory gaze.

Pity might be appropriate here, but pity was not one of Raven Scott's weaknesses. Cleavage, on the other hand . . .

"How many?" Jude's tone was even harsher now, which meant he held a decent hand and was becoming impatient to win, an idea supported by the fact that he had taken only two fresh cards.

As for himself, Raven was bored with the game. He'd won enough to call it a profitable night. In fact, he'd won enough to have mercy on his rival, for if Raven had made the attempt, he could have imagined himself in the other's chair in thirty or forty years. Yet mercy was as useless as pity to a gambler's way of thinking.

Although Raven didn't actually consider himself to be a professional cardplayer. No. He played for reasons other than money, which made him what? A detective with a weakness for sport? No, gambling was not a weakness for him, either. It was merely a means to obtain an end, as was everything in his life. He'd learned, if nothing else, to be pragmatic, even if it galled him, or perhaps more specifically, *especially* if it galled him.

"You keepin' them cards?"

Raven raised his gaze slowly, knowing nothing but boredom would show in his eyes. It seemed his intentional delay had disconcerted the old man and caused the woman's brow to wrinkle somewhat, as if she, too, were displeased, but too careful to show it more clearly. Who was she? That was the question that had first prompted Raven to enter this game. Even now curiosity held his interest.

Was she Jude's wife? It was possible. Maybe the old gambler wasn't as elderly as he appeared. Though he was dissipated and worn, he was certainly not past the age of needing a woman, if such an age ever came.

Still, the thought of the old piker bedding the charming Charm made Raven's gut clench. Which meant, perhaps, that he wasn't as jaded as he had thought.

What a disconcerting idea!

"Damn it, boy!" growled Jude, rising jerkily to his feet. But already Charm's hand was on his shoulder and her whisper in his ear.

The ruddy color of the old man's face lightened somewhat, and as Jude's attention was diverted by the girl's words, Raven allowed his gaze to settle, just for a moment, on the high, softly mounded tops of her breasts.

It was a mistake, for despite Raven's pride in his single-mindedness, clearheaded thought and womanly charms did poor bedfellows make. Raven mentally grinned, almost allowing the humor to touch his lips as testimony to his clever wit. Or was it for the girl's magnificent bosom, so perfectly displayed above the bright tangerine hue of her gown?

Charm's attention lifted in unison with his eyes, and for just an instant their gazes met. From across the table, Raven could hear her faint intake of breath, as if she were shocked by the boldness of his stare. But she didn't straighten immediately, he noticed, and now Raven allowed a brief escape of his well-confined smile.

"I'll take two," he said, his gaze still locked on her face. Her cleavage wasn't her only spectacular feature, it seemed, for her eyes, too, were riveting. Dark, heavily lashed, and decidedly sultry.

"Two?" asked Jude in a rusty tone, his already shaky confidence rocked a bit more.

"Did I say two?" Raven shifted his gaze smoothly back to the girl's bosom before lifting it to his opponent's reddened face. "I meant three."

The trio of cards was rapidly, if grumpily, delivered. They fit neatly into Raven's hand. Better than neatly, but he kept his gaze casual as he perused the queens.

"I bet fifty." Again the old man's tone was taut.

"And I'll . . ." Raven let his concentration stray to the game. He was lucky in cards. Lucky and adept. Always had been. Maybe it was hereditary. Maybe not. He paused in his betting, his voice dwindling, as if uncertainty had finally set in. "I'll see your fifty and . . . raise you."

It was no surprise that Jude raised, nor that he raised again after that, but Raven doubted his ability to do so a third time, for already he had lost a good deal of money. Though he was a fair gambler, he didn't appear to be exceptionally flush. Raven prided himself on being a first-rate judge of people. A mercenary bastard himself, but a damn fine judge of others.

"Is Charm your real name?" he asked now, knowing he was not above taking whatever the girl was willing to offer him. And according to her eyes and languid movements, that was a fair amount.

Old man Fergusson turned his head to the right, as if not trusting his hearing to his opposite ear. "What's that?"

Raven tightened his grip on his cards, knowing his rivals would notice and think him nervous. "I asked if Charm was her real name."

"What the hell's that got to do with poker?"

It was surprising, even to Raven, how quickly the man became angry, but again the girl's hand appeared on Jude's shoulder, soothing.

"Yes," she said, looking no less stunning when she straightened to gaze down at him from her full height. "My name's Charm."

"The name suits you." He allowed himself one more glance into her eyes, wondering if he'd been wrong about their color. Perhaps he'd been hasty in assuming they were brown. But her hair was as dark as the hide of a blood bay mare, and just as shiny in the wavering light cast by the oil lamps. Her skin was the creamy hue of winter goldenrod and looked flawless. But the fact that he thought so could probably be attributed to his own deprivation of female companionship. Deadwood Gulch was notably short of women. Although it hosted a sort of second-rate gold rush, the gentler sex was mostly absent, including one Chantilly Grady.

Tomorrow Raven would search again for the girl. But tonight he would gamble on games of chance and love, or as close to love as he was willing to let himself get.

"I'll raise you fifty," Raven said distractedly, then waited for the agitated sounds of Jude's agony.

They came just as suspected, beginning with a scratchy clearing of the old man's throat. "I ain't got that much left," he admitted finally.

Raven delayed only a moment before making his offer. "Then I'll accept a night with the girl."

For an aging man with a drinking problem, it was

amazing how fast Jude could reach across the table. But Raven was younger and faster. He tilted his chair out of reach, watching the old man's face contort with rage.

"I killed better men than you for my daughter!" he choked.

His *daughter*! Now there was an interesting twist. Who would have thought the old man could have sired a beauty like her? And what kind of father would allow his own child, well grown and proportioned though she was, to participate in the deprecated practice of gambling? Especially with that scandalous tangerine gown exposing her tantalizing . . . eyes!

"My apologies," Raven said, realizing Jude was *just* such a man. Not bothering to rise to his feet or change his expression, Raven kept himself casually out of the other's grip as the girl called Charm attempted to reel her father back. "I misspoke, of course," he said, using that irritatingly gallant tone he had learned from the other boys at school. "I meant to say I would appreciate her company this evening. For *dinner*. Nothing more."

The older man straightened, his face brick red. "You can go to hell!"

"A distinct possibility," Raven said flatly. "But you've bet your last dollar, or nearly so."

Jude's hand curled to a fist on the table's rough-grained surface, but he didn't lunge again, seeming immobilized by rage.

Charm straightened. Her eyes were slightly narrowed now and her fine body very still as she watched him. Raven returned her gaze. Despite it all, his muscles tightened with anticipation when he allowed himself to look directly at her. She, on the other hand, seemed perfectly focused on whatever it was she wished to determine with her point-blank stare.

A moment passed before she took a deep breath. If that action was meant to distract him, it succeeded admirably.

"It's all right." Her voice was almost inaudible as she

tugged her father back into his chair. He landed with a scowl and a lurch. The seductress was gone for a moment, replaced by a woman Raven had yet to pigeonhole. She didn't look at him when she spoke, but gazed instead at Jude as she pushed a stray wisp of mahogany hair behind her left ear. "I'm certain Mr. Scott didn't mean to insult us."

"The hell he didn't!" grumbled Jude, refusing to be soothed or to look at the girl.

But she tried again, squeezing his arm slightly and smoothing back that gleaming wayward tress a second time.

"Ten years ago I'da beat the tar outta you for less." The old man's hands trembled as he glared at Raven. His voice was gnarled, as if anger taxed his strength.

"You're tired," Charm said. "And I'm certain Mr. Scott would like to get to bed, too." Her voice was sweet, and yet when she raised her gaze to Raven's, he could have sworn her expression was suggestive. But again she brushed her hair behind her left ear and lowered her gaze to Jude's face, finally catching his attention.

It took a moment, but finally the old man relaxed a mite and nodded. "All right," he acquiesced and turned to Raven. "It's a bet."

"Then I call," Raven declared simply.

"Four tens." Jude spread his cards deliberately between them.

Raven raised his brows and nodded in appreciation. "Quite a hand. I'd think you could have dared bet more than an evening with your daughter on those cards, but . . ." He lifted his gaze to the girl's face again, which looked tense. "She is a Charm, after all."

He could hear the old man's relieved exhalation as he leaned forward to scoop up the pot.

"And yet," said Raven, interrupting Jude's movement. "Four queens will still beat a Charm." He laid them down. Two pair of royal women grinned smugly at the ceiling. Raven leaned back, every muscle taut, waiting for trouble. It came without delay.

"Cheat!" Jude roared. Pitching his gaunt body upward, he clutched the table's edge with both hands. "There ain't no one that lucky."

It was pretty much the standard statement and no less than Raven had expected. He watched his rival carefully, every sense aware. "I only cheat when I have to, old man," Raven said. He liked to call out all the trouble at once. No use skirting it with pretty words. More fun this way. "And I didn't have to with you."

"Damn you!" Jude swore and bolted around the table. But the girl was on him like a tick on a hound, dragging him back.

"No! Please." She yanked at him, refusing to let go as Jude pulled her along. "He won fair and square. Remember your condition!"

"Damn my condition!"

"Please!" she said again, then lunged ahead to grab Jude's arms and speak into his face. "It's only dinner," she reminded, nimbly dancing to the side as he tried to escape her hold. "And I'll see you to your room first." The old man gradually relaxed somewhat, watching her eyes. "I'm certain Mr. Scott will understand my wish to see you safely abed, and to . . . freshen up a bit." She turned slightly to gaze at Raven. Her eyes were half-lidded now, her tone marinated with pleasant promise. "Won't you, sir?"

Raven watched her for a moment, letting the tension leave his body. He was quite content to abandon the excitement of impending conflict for another kind of thrill. "Of course," he said. "Take your time."

"Thank you." She smiled, and in that instant he doubted if Charm's luscious body was truly her most seductive feature. It was, very possibly, her smile. A careless man could spend a good deal of his life doing nothing more than trying to coax forth that smile again.

Luckily, Raven Scott was *not* a careless man.

Taking her father's arm, Charm escorted him up the stairs to his room. From where he sat, Raven could see her lean over to speak softly into the old man's ear. For a moment he allowed himself to wonder how it would be to feel her breath against *his* lobe, to let it shiver down every nerve, titillate his senses.

Ahh, women's wiles. They were an intoxicant and a wonder. Raven shifted forward in his chair to collect his winnings. Behind him a saloon girl laughed seductively, spurring on his hopeful thoughts of Charm.

Burle's place still held a lively crowd, though it was late. Smoke hung suspended like a dry fog. But it was an atmosphere Raven had become comfortable with. From his breast pocket, he drew forth a cheroot to light and hold casually between his fingers.

It had been a long while since he'd allowed himself the company of a woman. Impatience burned him, but he hid the fire, making certain it didn't show in his expression. It was a discipline of sorts and usually easily done. But not tonight. Though Charm had tried to hide her feelings from her father, her interest in Raven had been obvious from the start.

Raven indulgently blew out a fat, symmetrical smoke ring. He imagined the girl warm and willing beneath his hands, her sultry eyes heavy-lidded and her strawberry lips parted, waiting for . . .

"Hey, Burle. Them Fergusson folks," called a voice from the doorway. "Was they all paid up?"

"Fergussons?" Burle's voice was deep and distinctive. "No, but the old man's still playing his luck."

"That right?" asked the first. "Guess my eyes is getting worser than I thought, cuz I coulda swore it was him and his girl a runnin' past when I come in."

Chapter 2

"Hurry!" Charm pleaded, trying to drag her father to safety. But already two dark forms were sprinting down the muddy street after them.

"Go on alone," rasped Jude.

"No!" Fighting down the encroaching panic, she remained by his side. "Come on. We'll hide. Just a little farther."

But even a little way was too far for Jude. In a moment they were caught dead to rights with Burle's huge frame planted, legs widespread, before them.

"Seems we got us a bit of a rub, folks." His tone was not what Charm would call friendly—but she'd heard worse.

"Mr. Burle, sir." She gasped, managing to employ her very best expression of helplessness as she clasped her reticule close to her chest. "I'm so glad you're here. My father is terribly ill. We had stepped out for a breath of air when he nearly collapsed." Jude wheezed in accordance to her words. Charm tightened her grip, hoping he was faking. "He needs a doctor real quick."

Burle opened his mouth, but if there was one thing Charm

had learned it was to talk fast and look sweet . . . until things got *really* serious. At which time her tactics would change dramatically. "Please help us, sir."

The big man shuffled his feet, looking bewildered. "Well I . . ."

"I seen 'em running down the street not two minutes ago," interrupted Burle's lanky henchman. "He didn't look real sickly then. And looky here." The man stepped forward, bending so that his balding pate shone in the moonlight as he retrieved the bag Jude had dropped. "Seems strange, don't it, that they tote their luggage about with 'em on their little constitutional?"

Silence blanketed the street as Charm held her breath.

"I'll have my money now." The proprietor's demand came after a brief eternity. "For two nights and four meals."

"But Mr. Burle," began Charm, blinking quickly and wondering if she should have worn something more revealing than her modest traveling suit. "Jude's had a real hard day. He needs—"

"I don't give a tinker's damn what he needs, miss!" interrupted Burle brusquely. Unfriendly wouldn't quite describe his tone now.

"He just needs to . . . ," she began again nevertheless.

"Fred, get Deputy Hackett."

"Deputy!" Charm gasped. "Mr. Burle, I assure you . . ." But Fred had already turned away. "Listen," she said, glancing quickly from Fred's retreating back to Burle's stoic expression. "Jude just needed a little air. We were planning on going straight back to settle up our bill."

"Tell Hackett to hurry on down here," added Burle evenly, not turning his gaze from his newly departed guests.

Charm swallowed hard. "All right," she said. "We're a bit short on cash. But there's no need to involve the law. We've got us a stake left. Tomorrow night Jude'll win for sure. He's a very good poker player. It was just that that black-hearted devil's spawn cheated and—"

"And tell him to bring his gun, case this turns nasty," said Burle to his unseen sidekick.

Charm's jaw dropped a notch, but the thought of repercussions for their planned escape made her words spurt forth with renewed vigor. "I'll find a way to pay."

Even in the darkness she could see Burle's expression change from animosity to cautious skepticism.

"Next week at the latest," she promised quickly. But already Fred was returning with another man at his side. One glance at Jude warned Charm that running would be a bad bet. Still, she had to get away from these men, hide some place where she could breathe.

"Got yourself some trouble here, Burle?" The deputy was a short man, but solid, with a no-nonsense attitude.

"Yeah. Seems like maybe these folks was tryin' to run out of town without paying up."

"No. I assure you, we meant to pay," Charm vowed earnestly.

"I seen 'em runnin' hell-bent fer leather," interjected Fred, waving a skinny arm to indicate the general direction of their getaway. "Straight down the middle of this here street."

Damn Fred and his blasted night vision, thought Charm. "But we had every intention of returning to—" she began.

"And they was carryin' these here bags," added Fred cleverly.

"We weren't . . . ," argued Charm desperately, wishing she could have thirty seconds alone with Fred and a good stout tree limb, but Deputy Hackett was already waving for silence.

"It's late, folks," he said evenly, "and I ain't had my supper yet. So I'll tell you what. I'll give you a place to sleep for the night. It's free and only two of the bunks is spoken for."

"Spoken for?" The world seemed to slow as Charm focused her attention on those two words, but Hackett reached for her arm now, jumbling her thoughts.

"Deadwood ain't hardly big enough for a separate cell for the ladies, miss," he apologized. "But you don't need to fret none, cause the other two occupants is too sauced to give you no trouble."

Charm, however, could imagine a good deal of trouble. Stepping quickly back, she raised a hand between herself and the deputy.

"I won't be locked up with men!" she vowed.

"Now, miss, there's no need to carry on so," assured Hackett, advancing.

"Don't come any closer!" Charm said in breathless desperation, but in that moment another shadowy form stepped forward.

"I fear this is all my fault," said a quiet drawl from the darkness.

The deputy stopped, canting his head toward the newcomer and remaining silent for a moment. "And who might you be, mister?"

"I'm the black-hearted devil's spawn."

"What's that?" asked Hackett, but Raven was certain there was no need to explain his words to the girl. If her wide eyes were any indication of her thoughts, she knew he'd been eavesdropping for quite some time.

"What's your name, son?" asked the deputy again.

Raven shifted his weight and delayed just a moment, letting Charm stew in her juices a bit longer before deigning to pluck her from the boiling broth she'd so cleverly concocted.

"My surname's Scott," said Raven, finally pulling himself from the girl's gaze. "And I fear this is all my fault. You see, these fine people were in a rush and asked me to pay for their lodging and meals." He paused momentarily, then fished out a few of the bills he'd hastily shoved into his pocket. "They did, of course, leave me adequate funds with which to do so." If one tried really hard, one could almost find a shred of truth in that statement. And Deputy Hackett, it seemed, was willing to try.

"So you're gonna pay Burle here?"

Raven met Burle's gaze steadily. "With apologies for my tardiness." After handing forth several bills, he pulled out another. "It appears now, however, that Mr. Fergusson will be needing a comfortable place to spend the night, as he's in no condition to travel." Raven shifted his attention to the girl's wide eyes. "Don't you agree, Miss Charm?"

Jude straightened with some difficulty, and for just a moment Raven thought the older man might repeat his suggestion to spend eternity someplace warm. But he kept quiet, as did his daughter for several seconds before bringing herself to concede.

"Yes." That generous monosyllable was all she offered, and though Deputy Hackett paused for a moment, he finally nodded.

"If everything's fixed up to your satisfaction, Burle, I'll be getting myself some grub and a few hours sleep."

"Sure." Burle skimmed his attention from Charm, to Raven, and back to Charm, doing nothing to hide his befuddlement. "Sure enough."

The deputy departed, Fred shuffled his oversized feet, and Burle cleared his throat. "Well, it seems there's been a misunderstanding. But with Deadwood being what it is, booming with the gold fever and such like, there's all kinds of folks hereabouts these days." He shrugged, abbreviating his apology. "Guess there ain't been no real harm done."

The Fergussons remained silent, causing Raven to wonder if they would bolt off into the darkness once Burle turned his broad back. But Jude was still breathing hard. Unless he was a damn good actor, which Raven doubted, he was in no condition to do much of anything.

"No apologies necessary, sir," said Raven, employing all his considerable charm. "As I said, it was entirely my fault. Had I—"

"I'll be seeing Jude to bed," said Charm brusquely, interrupting Raven's carefully ingratiating monologue as she moved forward to do just that. But Raven was not willing to play the game without a chance at the spoils and stepped quickly before her.

"I'm certain Mr. Burle would be happy to see your father safely to his room," suggested Raven evenly and reached to grasp Jude's arm.

"No!" Charm's response was as sharp and hard as a well-chosen rock.

"I beg your pardon?" said Raven, seeing the nervous glance she immediately shot toward the looming innkeeper.

"I mean," corrected the girl, her voice as soft and sweet as boiled molasses now. "My father's very ill. I'd best see to him myself."

"But I promised to buy you a meal at the first possible opportunity, Miss Fergusson, and surely you must be famished."

For just a moment Raven thought he saw the flash of some flinty emotion light her face, but it was gone before he could assess it. She now graced him with a timid smile, which she soon turned on Burle.

"That's ever so generous of you, gentlemen, but I really must think of my father," she said, tugging Jude toward her.

"But surely you must eat," argued Raven, dragging him back.

Her smile didn't slip a bit, but remained neatly etched on her seductive lips. "We'll have a bite at the inn," she said, reeling Jude in.

"We won't be servin' supper no more tonight, miss," Burle observed, his eyes slightly narrowed. "Was I you, I'd take Mr. Scott up on his offer. Maybe you could have somethin' sent up to yer pa."

She turned her luminous gaze on Burle, but before she could speak, Raven launched himself back into the dispute. "It's settled, then," said he, yanking Jude from Charm's grasp to place him, a bit more roughly than he'd intended, beside the innkeeper's huge form. "Burle here will assist your father to his room, while you and I have something sent up to relieve his hunger. Anywhere you might suggest, sir?"

Burle's expression was open to interpretation, but blatant curiosity would be a fair description. "Wendel's is the only place still servin'," he said, obediently taking a firm hold on Jude's arm.

Raven nodded expansively. "Wendel's it is, then. Shall we, Miss Fergusson?" He extended his arm, but Charm turned her head and seemed preoccupied with lifting her dark skirt, as if suddenly concerned with the mud that encrusted its hem. "Or would you rather dig your own way out of this grave?" he asked quietly.

Her smile, when it returned, could light up the night. Casually ignoring Raven's extended arm, she turned her radiance on the innkeeper. "If you're certain it's not too much trouble, Mr. Burle."

Burle's momentary bedazzlement couldn't be mistaken. It was the strange by-product of Charm's appeal, suddenly turned loose in full force on the innkeeper. Raven watched her hone her allure, and couldn't deny her aptitude. It was possible he'd met his match as a scoundrel.

"No." Burle shook his head, never losing contact with her eyes. "No trouble at all," he said, but momentarily forgot to move from the spot.

The silence was beginning to sweat when Raven stepped into the void. "Then perhaps Fred here could carry the luggage, and you should go, Burle," Raven suggested, "before Mr. Fergusson weakens further."

"Oh." Burle wrested himself from his trance with admirable speed. "Yeah." But now Jude pulled free from the innkeeper's grasp with a wheeze and a shred of dignity.

"Scott." His voice was raspy, but his back was straight. "You lay a hand on her, I'll chew your head off," he said in flat warning. Turning, he hobbled back in the direction from which they had come.

With a nod, Burle followed. Fred, too, turned away,

though he looked regretful of the anticlimax to such excitement.

Raven watched them go. "Tell me, Miss Fergusson," he said, absently reaching for her arm, "did *Jude* name you Charm or is it simply a characteristic you inherited from your old man?"

With a snap, she yanked her elbow from his grasp. "Don't touch me," she warned, her tone low and rushed.

"Well . . ." Raven smiled at her, hoping to achieve the same bright hypocrisy she attained with so little effort. "I guess that answers my question then, doesn't it?"

From a nearby doorway a pair of miners approached them. Raven nodded and held his expression, and Charm smiled, too, matching his toothy insincerity with obvious and disconcerting ease.

"Yes." She dimpled when she answered, causing the moon to cast crescent shadows in the delicate hollows of her cheeks. "I guess it does."

"Then we understand each other," said Raven.

"Perfectly," she agreed sweetly and, grasping her small reticule to her chest, strode primly off.

Wendel's Roadhouse was a modest establishment that had once stood at the edge of town. Deadwood, however, had managed to render up enough gold to cause the booming community to engulf and enliven it, despite frequent and bloody skirmishes with the Sioux.

Inside, Wendel's was illuminated by a lamp placed upon every occupied table, which meant there was little enough light with which to see by. For even the rough-edged inhabitants of Deadwood had to sleep sometime.

"And what would you be wantin'?" asked a man who appeared from the dimness. He wiped his hands on a greasy apron and waited.

Had Raven not already become acquainted with the Fergussons, he might have thought the innkeeper unfriendly. As it was, Wendel's proprietor seemed just about average for the inhabitants of this backwater town.

Finally seated at a small table, Raven and Charm ordered perfunctorily and then sat in silence. Two nearby diners stood and left, followed not much later by a trio of others.

They were alone now, unless one counted the menagerie of gamblers who occupied the adjoining card room.

"You're looking at me!" Charm's words cracked the silence like a dropped egg, but Raven merely tilted his head slightly, pretending not to comprehend.

"What's that?"

"I said, you're looking at me!"

He raised his brows at her and leaned back in his chair. "And is that a crime in these parts, Miss Fergusson?"

"I don't like to be looked at."

"Really?" He almost laughed. "And is this a long-standing attitude or one that changes with your attire?"

She drew herself straighter in the slat-backed chair, pursing her fine mouth slightly. "I have no idea what you're talking about."

He did smile now, grimly and carefully. "Then let me explain. Back at Burle's . . . you were trying to seduce me."

Her eyes widened, and she gasped. "How dare you!"

"How dare I be honest?"

Her lips moved long before she managed to force a sound from between them. "How dare you assume—"

"Oh, I wasn't assuming. I *know*. You were trying to seduce me, make me lose my concentration. Not that I resent it. In fact, I enjoyed it. But now . . ." He shrugged lazily. "You owe me."

"You're crazy!"

"Are you saying you had the funds to pay the good Mr. Burle for his hospitality?" She rose swiftly to her feet, but he merely shrugged again. "If that's the case, I'd be happy to accompany you back to the inn. I'll get my money back, and you can explain the situation. Is that what you want?"

She didn't speak, but stared at him with eyes mean enough to torch water.

"That's what I thought. Then sit down, Miss Fergusson," Raven said stiffly.

She did so, though slowly. "What do you want from me?" she whispered as she clenched her hands into fists.

"I only want what you promised."

"I didn't promise you anything."

"Oh, but you did," he argued, picking up a fork to twirl it between his fingers. "You promised me everything . . . with your eyes."

She drew a deep, sharp breath through flared nostrils and fumbled with her reticule to finally extract a white, pocket-sized book. "'And I stood upon the sand of the sea and saw a beast rise up out of the sea, having seven heads and ten horns, and upon his horns ten crowns, and upon his heads the name of blasphemy,'" she jabbered rapidly. "'And—'"

"I don't mean to be rude," interrupted Raven, "but what the devil are you yammering about?"

"Revelations. Chapter 13. Verse 1," she breathed.

Raven scowled, watching her face in bemusement. "Crazy as a coot. Waste of cleavage," he murmured. "Tell me, Miss Fergusson, are your parents closely related? Siblings perhaps?"

Charm's nostrils flared again as she lifted her chin. "My mind is perfectly sound, but I know your kind. I know about men. Can read them like a book."

Raven ignored both her disdain and her biblical blathering. "It's a clever little scheme, distracting men with your . . ." He raised his hand casually toward his own chest. "Charms," he finished. "Promising them pleasure with your eyes, then running out before you live up to your end of the bargain."

"I make no bargains with Satan's spawn."

"I'm not complaining," he said, easily ignoring her intended insult. "I'm merely stating my admiration and wondering if the deception might work for me. Tell me, if I batted my eyes and showed some chest, would you be distracted?"

Her lips moved again in that strange wordless way she had, and then the Bible was suddenly flipped open to a new page. "'Save me, O God! The water is up to my neck. I am sinking in deep mud, and there is no solid ground. I am out in deep water, and the waves are about to—'"

"Oh, for Christ's sake!" rasped Raven and, reaching out, snatched the volume from her hands. "What the devil is wrong with you?"

"Give me!" she demanded and tried to grab it back as they both jerked to their feet, but their fingers bumbled now, and the book fell, spilling open to the front page where a name was penned in dark, scrolling ink.

"Eloise Medina!" Raven read aloud.

Charm made a wild grab for the book, but before her fingers could touch the white leather, Raven scooped it back into his hands to stare in disbelief at the swirling words on the inside front cover.

"Where'd you get this?" he demanded.

Charm lifted her chin. Her breathing was harsh, and her eyes sparked with anger, but Raven failed to care, for never in all his searching for Chantilly Grady had he come so close.

"Give it back," she demanded hoarsely, extending her hand.

Raven grasped her wrist. "Where'd you get it?" he asked again.

For just a moment an indefinable expression crossed her face, but it vanished, replaced by arrogant rage.

"Where?" he repeated with a tight grip and cool, feigned patience.

"From my mother," she gritted and with an Amazonian effort, yanked her arm from his fingers.

Chapter 3

"You, my dear," Raven said, remembering his gentlemanly demeanor lest he get thrown from Wendel's for improper behavior, "are a world-class liar."

"And you," she retorted with bitter sweetness, still standing and breathing hard, "are the very spawn of Satan."

He watched her, feeling his temper rise, but holding it carefully in check. "For all I know, you may be right, Miss Charming, but I believe we were speaking of *your* parentage. Now . . ."—Raven took a deep breath and narrowed his eyes—"about the Bible. Where did you *really* . . . ," he began, but suddenly a movement caught his eye, tripping his memory with hair-trigger speed. "Take it," he ordered sharply, thrusting the Bible toward her.

Charm's mouth formed a circle of surprise, but there was no time to delay. Pushing her back into her chair, he found his own seat.

"Put it away," he insisted quietly.

"What?" Her eyes were round and her tone breathless.

"Hide it," he ordered, but through his teeth now, for the trouble he'd seen approaching had materialized into a man.

"Well . . . Mr. Joseph Scott," said a familiar voice. Clancy Bodine, damn his hide, spoke with the molasses-slow drawl of the Southern boy he was. "Been a long time."

Charm sat immobile, still staring at Raven as if he'd lost his mind.

Hide the blasted Bible! Raven wanted to yell. But such agitation might cause a bit of suspicion. So instead he rose slowly to his feet, pushed his sleeves away from his wrists, and slammed his fist squarely into Clancy Bodine's handsome face.

Bodine careened backward, crashing into a chair that broke beneath him like a matchstick house. He lay motionless there, momentarily stunned, his battered hat askew.

There was a gasp from Charm and a brief moment of silence from the cardplayers next door. Clancy put a hand to his chin. He grimaced, looking only mildly surprised and waggling his jaw a bit as if to make certain it was still attached. "Can I assume, then, that you're still carryin' a grudge?" he asked, looking up from the floor.

"No." Raven kept his gaze on his ex-partner as he shook the pain from his bruised knuckles. Clancy always did have a hard head. "No. I don't hold grudges," he said, and seeing that Charm had finally stashed the Bible back under cover, he sat down.

"Well . . ." Bodine rose slowly, grimacing again, this time as his back left the broken shreds of the chair beneath him. "It's good to know you learned somethin' from me, Joseph."

For just a moment Charm had hoped she might be afforded a chance to slip away unnoticed, but she saw now that was not the case, for the violence seemed to have come to an abrupt and quite unsatisfactory finish. Watching the man called Raven, though, she saw his left brow dip slightly over his deep-set eyes and wondered if it might not be a sign of anger. Since she had already learned she was a poor judge of the man's thoughts she could only hope—not be sure—such was the case. He should have been holding the

losing hand when gambling with Jude. His every idiosyn-
crasy had indicated poor cards. And yet he had won. Maybe
the man would lose his temper now and provide her a
chance to escape.

Luck was certainly not a lady. It was a man!

"Sure," said Raven now. "I learned a great deal from you,
Bodine. Nothing that wouldn't get me hanged. But a great
deal, nevertheless."

Clancy laughed, wiggling his jaw again and approaching
casually.

Beneath the table, Charm opened the drawstring of her
reticule and slipped her hand inside to let it rest there
unseen. She had difficulty breathing the stifling air. Who
was this Raven, and what did he want? And now Clancy
Bodine! Feeling the panic well up within her, she closed her
hand about a smooth, familiar object, drawing comfort from
its presence. She sat in silence, carefully reading every
nuance of her unwelcome companions and waiting for the
proper moment to escape.

"Now, Joseph, you're bein' unfair," Bodine complained.
"You wouldn't want to give your ladyfriend here the wrong
impression." He turned toward Charm now and removed his
hat as he smiled. His teeth were perfect, his ruffled mop of
hair wheat-toned, and eyes so blue she was certain a host of
women had been lost in them.

As for Charm, she closed her fingers about the hard, cool
handle of her tiny derringer. Remembering every lesson her
father had taught her, she forced herself to breathe regularly.
Her muscles were taut, and in her head she chanted a silent
biblical verse regarding the sins of man.

"Let me apologize for Mr. Scott's rudeness," Clancy said
with a bow, widening his smile slightly. "We must forgive
him," he said, his voice dropping to a whisper that easily
carried to Raven's ears as well as her own. "The boy was
shortchanged in his upbringin'." Clancy nodded, glancing
momentarily at Raven. "But it wasn't his fault. And I did all
I could to help. By the way, I'm Clancy Bodine and happy

t'meet you, miss . . ." He paused, extending his hand and waiting for her response.

Charm remained perfectly immobile, fighting down the consuming terror caused by his closeness. She wouldn't shoot him . . . yet. "The Lord is my Shepherd," she murmured.

"I beg your pardon?" Nonplussed, Clancy drew his hand back.

"Her name is Charm." Raven's voice was flat.

"Really?" Clancy asked, smiling at her again before reaching behind him to pull up an unbroken chair. "Charm? I should have guessed." He spun the spindled back beneath his hand and straddled the thing. "And how did you two meet?"

He was too friendly and too close. She didn't like friendly, and she *hated* close. It made her air passages close up. Made the black nightmares return.

"She can talk, can't she, Joseph?" Clancy asked. "Not that it would matter none, but I was just wonderin'."

"What do you want, Bodine?" Raven asked, finally diverting Clancy's attention from Charm. Air rushed back into her lungs, and her fingers loosened slightly.

"You're so suspicious, Joseph. If I was the one sitting across from a lady like that, I'd be on my best behavior."

Raven shifted slightly in his chair, stretching his legs out under the table. Although she tried, Charm found she could neither read his emotions nor guess his thoughts. It was a disconcerting feeling, as if she were groping about in the dark.

"Your *best* behavior," Raven said. "And how would I differentiate that from your worst?"

"Ooo." Clancy groaned. "That hurt. You've developed a sharp tongue, Joseph," he complained, turning to look at Charm. "Doesn't he have a sharp tongue?" He paused. "Damn, she's pretty! Where did you say you met her?"

Bodine was looking at her again, but more intently now, making the hairs on the back of Charm's neck stand upright.

"What in blazes happened to my chair?" The proprietor had arrived, carrying two platters of food. He sported a dangerous scowl but blessedly drew the men's attention from Charm.

"Joseph here has a hell of a right hook. But," Clancy said with a shrug, "I guess I can't blame 'im. Put the damages on my bill."

The plates were set on the table with a grunt, and in a moment the server was gone, grumbling back toward the kitchen.

Raven cut up his steak, seeming to ignore his companions, but Clancy was not easily disregarded.

"Don't worry about the cost of the chair, Joseph," said he magnanimously. Raven's left brow again dipped almost imperceptibly over those dark, deep-set eyes, Charm noticed. "I've had me some luck tonight," Clancy continued happily. "Course, not so much as you." He turned his gaze on Charm again. "Where did you say you met her?"

"Bodine," Raven said, his voice low.

"Yeah?"

"Get lost."

Clancy grinned. "Thought you said you didn't hold no grudges, boy," he argued mildly.

"I don't." Raven's knife was poised over his plate. "I just don't like to eat with snakes. It turns my stomach."

"Now that one *really* hurt," Clancy said with a dramatic wince. "And after all I've done for you. You wouldn't know it to listen to 'im, Miss Charm, but Joseph and me is really very close. Like brothers. Matter of fact, for all *we* know, we could be brothers," he said, and he laughed.

For a fraction of a moment Charm thought Raven would strike. She saw the tendons in his wrists tighten, felt the tension, but again she misjudged him.

"Oh, come on, boy, loosen up. You always did take things too damn serious."

"And you always thought a lynch mob was too funny, but only if they're after *my* neck," said Raven.

"Hey, they didn't catch you, did they?" Clancy asked, then waited momentarily for an answer. "No. 'Course they didn't, or you wouldn't be here with this stunnin' lady. Where did you say you met her?"

"I should kill you, Bodine." Raven said the words very casually and sat back, causing Clancy to laugh again.

"But you won't, cause I'm so damned charmin'. Not as charmin' as her." He nodded toward Charm. "But charmin' nonetheless."

"What did you do with the money?" asked Raven finally, watching Bodine as one might watch a coiled rattler.

"For that Georgia deal? Oh, I didn't get paid. You think I got paid for that job?" questioned Clancy, looking shocked as his tone rose slightly. There was not, Charm noticed, a shred of honesty in his expression. "I didn't get a penny. The boy got away." He canted his head, studying Raven. "I thought you might've knowed that. Thought it might've been you who helped him escape, once you'd learned the truth."

Raven said nothing. He kept his gaze level.

"Hey. Don't go looking at me like that. I was as surprised as you. Thought they just wanted us to find young Josh so's he'd return some stolen goods. Thirty days in the jug and all that. How'd I know they planned to string him up?" He shook his head. "Guess Southern gents don't like their gals messed with."

Raven's expression remained unchanged. "So you're saying you had nothing to do with them thinking I helped the boy escape?"

"Me?" Shock stamped Clancy's tone again. "No! You still thinkin' I'm holding a grudge since you broke up the partnership? Hell, it's best you went yer own way. You always had too soft a heart fer me."

Raven began to eat again. Charm noticed that he was left-handed like Jude. She stashed that information away.

"And you always had an imagination, Bodine," he said now.

"Yeah." Clancy laughed. "Yeah, that I did. Hey, like to join us in a game of poker?" He nodded toward the open doorway where men still sat around a table. "Been a long time. Maybe I'll let you win. Like I used to. But then, maybe you brought your luck with you tonight, huh?" He turned his smile on Charm. "Damn, she's pretty. Where did you say you met her?"

Raven's wrist tendons were tight again, but he showed no other signs of tension that Charm could discern.

"You out here on a job, Joseph, or still searchin' for your old man?" Clancy didn't turn his attention from Charm when he asked. Raven's expression changed, but so slightly and so quickly that Charm failed to interpret it.

"I'm working," answered Raven. "Was offered ten thousand dollars to find the queen of England. You seen her around?"

Clancy threw back his head and laughed, causing Charm to jump at the sound, though in a moment she recognized it as honest mirth. "Well, it just so happens *I'm* on a hunt," he said with a nod. "Looking for a gal named Chantilly Grady. From St. Louis. You heard of her?"

"I saw the ad," said Raven evenly. "Who didn't?"

"Hey, you want to find her together? Partners again?"

"I'd rather live a couple more years, if you don't mind."

Clancy laughed again, seeming to find Raven's opinion of him quite amusing. "This Grady deal ain't nothin' like that. No risk. Course, there ain't much information 'bout her. She could be 'most anyone." He turned a broad smile on Charm. She shrank away mentally while making certain her physical being remained as it was. "You sure your name ain't Chantilly?"

For a moment she failed to find her voice, but this time Raven wasn't speaking for her. She lifted her chin, remembering to breathe. "No. It's Charm. Charm Fergusson."

"Ahhh." Clancy sighed. "Too bad. Just my luck Grady'll be ugly as a snake-bit possum."

Charm shifted her fingers gently on the trigger of her

hidden derringer and managed again to speak. "Are you a lawman, Mr. Bodine?"

She heard Raven's derisive snort mix with Clancy's chuckle.

"Me? No. I'm a detective. You sure you ain't Chantilly Grady, huh?"

She shook her head, wanting desperately to be gone from here. It wasn't fear exactly, but she had never thought of a better way to describe this horrible tension. And, too, Jude needed her. She shouldn't have left him alone. Not after that loss at poker. But what choice had she had?

"If you'll excuse me." She forced out the words. They sounded surprisingly cool. "I must see to my father."

To her amazement, Raven nodded his agreement and rose. Clancy scowled. "But, Miss Charm, you ain't ate a bite."

She rose, too. "Jude's not well." And if he had found a bottle, she would make Raven Scott sorry. "It's been . . ." She paused. Remembering how the elegant Southern ladies spoke, she tried to emulate their aloof politeness. "It's been utterly delightful meeting you."

Clancy stood, still straddling his chair before swinging it out beside him. "Very delightful." He reached for her hand.

She sucked in her breath and turned, trying to look casual. But now the door was within sight, and freedom loomed before her. From behind came the sound of coins dropping to the table, the rumble of combative voices. Then quick footsteps followed her. She hastened her retreat.

Only one man pursued her. Of that she was certain and grateful, for if she could just get outside, she would lose him.

The door creaked as she pulled it open. She hurried through, feeling fear grip her in clammy hands. Darkness engulfed her. The door groaned closed behind. Without a moment's delay, Charm lifted her skirts and sprinted off down the hard-packed street. Her reticule was clasped in a tight grip, her heart hammering, but even over the sound of her thudding terror, she could hear the door moan open behind her.

"Charm." Raven's voice was a raised whisper. "Where . . ."

There was a moment of silence. Charm used every second, realizing she would not have many, somehow knowing he would follow her.

From up ahead came the sound of approaching horses. It was all the inspiration she needed. The livery stable was near. Suddenly she could smell the tangy barnyard fragrance. A horse nickered. On her right was a broad, open doorway. Light spilled out at a diffused, yellow slant, but she had no choice but to dash through it, knowing that her pursuer would see her. Up ahead, a wagon stood unhitched. Ten more strides and she was past it and out of Raven's sight. Lungs aching, she spurted along the side of the livery, hoping against hope that the devil's spawn would think she had gone on. But still she needed a place to hide. Somewhere unlikely. Pale light spilled from an overhead stable window. He would not expect her to hide somewhere well lit and possibly inhabited.

Adjacent to the barn was a fenced area. Up the side of the building a ladder ran toward a dim square of light. It was a small doorway from which hay could be thrown. Twice, the heel of her boot caught in her skirts as she hiked upward, but finally she was in the safety of the loft.

Last year's fodder lay in mounded piles, tied in bundles or left loose. It was a perfect place to hide and a good soft spot to spend the night if need be. The hay would offer relative comfort, and from the height of the loft, she could watch for trouble. Charm drew a deep breath. She'd finally outwitted him. Lost him. She'd rest for a while and wait, and then when she was certain he would bother her no more, she'd sneak from hiding and find Jude. It would be very simple now. No need to fear. He was only a man, after all, with a man's shallow instincts and very little . . .

"Hello," said Raven and grabbed her arms.

She squealed in terror.

"I'm beginning to think you're more the criminal than I realized," he said, "because you sure know how to lose a fellow." Luckily there was no one in the stable below to take exception to his actions. Not that he planned to harm her, of course. She was just a girl, after all.

It was at that precise moment that her knee slammed into his crotch. Pain blasted through his groin. There was nothing he could do but crumple to his knees. Every nerve ending begged for mercy. There was none to be found from Charm. She lunged for the ladder. But the toe of her boot caught in her hem and she faltered. It was just for a moment, but it was all the chance Raven needed. Anger welled up on the crest of pain, spurring him into action. He leaped after, slamming into her fleeing form and dragging her down.

She wriggled beneath him. He remained immobile and agonized, trying to wrestle his muscles into submission. But that one leap was all he could manage for the moment, and so he lay, heavy as an inert log, sucking air through his teeth and trying to keep her still to lessen the shattering pain that crippled his body.

She bucked, trying to dislodge him. Raven moaned a curse through his teeth, but already she was squirming away. He grappled for a better hold, but somehow she found her feet.

Frantically, he willed his fingers to work. They snagged in her skirt. There was the sound of rending fabric melded with a squeal of dismay as she fell. He thumped his weight fully atop her, hearing her breath leave her in a whoosh of anguish.

For a moment all was silent, and then they were both breathing hard, fighting to do nothing more than fill their lungs with air.

"What the . . . devil . . . is wrong with you, woman?" he finally managed to ask, closing his eyes as he gripped both her arms with his hands and let his upper body crush against her back.

"Get . . . off me," she ordered, her voice tight.

"Not on your life."

"Jude'll kill you!"

Raven drew a deep breath and settled his knees beside her legs to lever his body painfully upward. "Not before I get a few answers."

It was ridiculously difficult to pry the girl over on her back without giving her the opportunity to get away, but finally she was face up on the straw, and he was astride again. Her hair had come loose and spread dark and wild against the golden wheat stalks beneath. Her eyes snapped with temper. One daring wisp of hay projected from above her left ear at a jaunty angle.

Blast it all if Clancy hadn't been right. She *was* stunning. Mean as a cornered cougar, but stunning. He stared at her from only inches away, momentarily forgetting his mission and realizing finally that she had become very still beneath him.

"You're looking at me." Her words were low and sounded rather silly, considering that he was also sitting on her abdomen while he pinned her arms up above her head. Still, the ridiculousness of the situation only barely reached his brain, for despite it all, she fascinated him.

"Who could not?" he asked quietly.

She stared at him, her eyes wide and dark, evidencing an emotion he couldn't quite place.

"Please don't." Her words were no more than a whisper suddenly, barely breaking the quiet.

Raven felt her shiver beneath him and somehow felt like a cad. He almost forgot she had all but seduced him with her eyes, had made promises she'd intended to break. That she'd just kneed him in the groin, for God's sake.

"Don't what?" he asked.

"Please let me go," she pleaded softly.

"I'm not going to hurt you. I just want to talk." All right, it sounded strange from his position atop her, but how else was he *supposed* to talk to her? She was like a blasted race horse. Flighty, long-limbed, and damnably fast. "Lucky for me I saw the livery's open door," he said. He was biding his time and hoping she would relax, although he suspected that was a bit much to hope for, considering their respective positions. "I came up here thinking I'd have a clear view from the loft. Didn't know you were here until I heard you breathing." He waited, watching her, but her expression didn't change. He scowled. "Will you quit looking at me like that?"

No response.

He deepened his scowl, trying to remember her rather deadly habits. "If I let you up, will you promise not to run off?"

A nod was all he got, but he finally slid off her, letting her sit up. She did so stiffly, looking sheepish, and slowly reaching for the reticule she had dropped in her efforts to escape.

"There now. See?" He raised a palm upward toward her as testimony to her continued health and well-being. "I'm not going to harm you." He took a deep breath and ran his fingers through his hair. "I just want to talk about the Bible."

"My Bible?" she asked, blinking once and looking smaller somehow.

"Yes." He nodded, careful to keep his movements slow. "Could I see it?"

She watched him in silence for a moment. Then, nodding, she opened her reticule and reached in. "Stay where you are!" she ordered and yanked the tiny muzzle of a derringer toward him. "Stay right where you are."

Raven scowled. "The devil! Put that thing away before someone gets hurt." He raised his hand, but Charm scooted backward across the hay, waving the weapon between them.

"I'll shoot you. An eye for an eye and a tooth for a tooth."

"What eye? What tooth? I haven't touched you," he pointed out practically.

Charm opened her mouth, ready to denounce him as a liar, but he held up a hand and interrupted. "All right. I touched you. But I had, and have," he hurried to add, "no intention of harming you. In fact, I'll pay you," he said, sounding suddenly inspired and hopeful. "I'll pay you just to *see* the Bible."

She said nothing, knowing in her gut that she had to escape before he turned violent. The edge of the loft was only a few inches behind her, but the ladder was several feet away. She could shoot him, of course, but shooting men had certain drawbacks. Hanging, for instance.

"Here. I'll pay you a dollar just to look," he said, and reached for his pocket.

But suddenly straw was strewn through the air. The gun was knocked from her hand, and she lay flat against the fodder again with him planted firmly on top.

"If I didn't know better, I'd think you liked this position," he said, his face very close to hers.

She fought with everything in her, but it was no use, for he had the advantage of weight and strength.

"Are you done?" he asked finally, watching her as her struggles subsided. He gripped both her wrists in his left hand now.

"Let me go!" she gritted.

"We already had this conversation," he reminded her, shaking his head in a fatherly manner. "It wasn't all that interesting the first time. Let's not have it again."

She glared, hate and fear and bewilderment mixing to a heady potion inside her. Why was he doing this? Why her? Why her Bible? Already he had managed to draw it from her reticule and open it to the first page.

"Eloise Medina." He said the name again, as if mesmerized. "Who is she?" he asked, still straddling her with his knees and pinning his gaze on her face.

She said nothing.

"Who is she?" he repeated, leaning closer.

"I already told you," Charm said, forcing out the words. "But it seems you didn't like my answer."

"That's because you lied, my dear Miss Charming. Now let's try again. Who is she?"

"She's my father's favorite cousin, once removed," she said coolly. "Penny Pritchard. She lives in Pittsburgh with her husband Paul, two pigs and a pigeon named Petunia." Charm forced a cold smile.

Raven smiled back. "I give you full credit for your marvelous use of alliteration and imagination. But let's try the truth, just to be different."

"Maybe that is the truth!" snarled Charm and, yanking her wrists free, grabbed the Bible.

"The devil!" swore Raven and jerked the book away.

Charm shrieked, covering her face with the back of her hand. "Don't!" she pleaded.

The air was heavy with a silence that was disturbed, only for a moment, by the stomp of a horse's hoof.

"Does he hit you?" Raven's voice was very low, revealing no emotion.

Charm pressed her arm against her face and kept her eyes closed. The aftertaste of her shameful terror was bitter. In a moment he grasped her wrist and tugged it gently away.

"Does he?"

She opened her eyes fearfully. His face was lean and dark-skinned, easily showing the rise of his cheekbones, the taut curve of his jaw. His eyebrows were full and low, and his eyes . . . indescribable in their deep moodiness. Was there anger in his expression, or was there no emotion at all, just aloof curiosity? She watched him breathlessly. The two top buttons of his white shirt were open. His neck was broad and dark, with the tendons running in at an angle to converge at the hollow above the slope of his chest. Charm drew in a sharp breath and raised her gaze to his.

"Answer me." His voice was as dark as his skin and carefully controlled. "Does he hit you?"

"Who?" she asked softly.

"Jude." Raven scowled, looking impatient. "Who else?"

There they were. The nightmare memories, called forth again. For a moment she saw the face behind the upraised fist, but it was gone, fading in a bellow of rage. A shiver raced through her, making it difficult to breathe.

"Charm?"

She gasped at the sound of his voice and tried to push him away, but he caught her wrist again. "No one hurt me," she said. "Not until you."

His brows dipped a little lower over his solemn eyes. "If you want to be treated gently, perhaps you should be gentle yourself."

"I know what you want," she said hoarsely.

"Do you now?" He grinned, but the expression lifted only a corner of his full mouth. "And how do you know?"

He was patronizing her. She gritted her teeth. "I know because Jude told me."

His brows raised at her words. Was he surprised? she wondered, trying to decipher his emotions, or was he simply laughing at her? "And what has Jude the Wise told you?" he asked, leaning closer still.

She pushed back into the straw, focusing on his face and forgetting to breathe. "Unspeakable things!"

"Unspeakable?" He leaned even nearer, setting the Bible aside. "Unspeakably bad or . . . unspeakably pleasant?" he asked and suddenly kissed the sensitive underside of her wrist.

The gentle caress ripped a spasm of shock through her terrified system. She forgot his question entirely.

"What?" she asked, hoping speech would distract him, would distract *her*. He kissed her wrist again, causing another spasm to arch like a shooting flame along her arm to her frazzled nerve endings.

"I mean . . ." He drew away slightly, looking into her eyes. "What did Jude tell you?"

"Men are evil." She said the words directly into his face, knowing they were true. He merely watched her.

He'd been wrong about her eyes and wondered now how he could have been mistaken. Even in this dim light he could see they were green. Green like the color of aquatic plants as seen through the shifting waves of a sparkling pool. And wide, so wide and deep there seemed to be no bottom to the emotion there.

"Is this evil?" he whispered as he lifted her palm to his lips and gently kissed its center.

The intake of breath was loud and sharp as she tried to wriggle away from him across the straw.

"Or this?" he asked, easily moving with her and using his tongue to trace an invisible path down her life line to the tip of her pinky.

"Don't!" Again she tried to wrest her hand from his grasp, but he noticed now that it shook like a willow beneath a strong wind. He couldn't help wondering if it was fear or if there was, perhaps, some other emotion that caused her to tremble.

"Maybe it doesn't feel so evil as you had expected. And maybe this will not either," he whispered. Beneath him she was soft and breathless and indescribably beautiful. He leaned forward to kiss her.

He heard a squeal like that of a snared rabbit. He felt the quick, hard heave of her leg. One moment he was anticipating untold sensual pleasures, and the next he was falling. With a curse and a bone-jarring jolt, he landed on the hard-packed earth below.

Chapter 4

Was he dead?

Charm trembled again, watching the darkness from her hiding place. It was black and close where she crouched beneath the fetid, rotting boards of the porch she'd scrambled beneath. No one would find her there. Still, she scrunched farther back. Something slithered from beneath her hand, and she nearly screamed, but no sound left her constricted throat.

Sheer luck had helped her locate her derringer in the dim light of the loft. She gripped it now but found little comfort in the embrace.

Dear God, she hadn't meant to kill him. But he had been so close and so . . . She shivered again, hearing her breath come in rusty gasps.

Minutes ticked away like ragged, nearly forgotten nightmares. Hoofbeats thundered in her head. She crouched lower, covering her ears, trying to hold back the dark tide of panic. But darkness pressed in closer, welcoming terror. It enveloped her in clammy hands as screams echoed within the confines of her aching skull.

There was nothing now but loneliness. Nothing but that

hole in her mind from which evil things crept. But no. She was imagining unreal terrors. And unreality couldn't harm her. Still, the minutes ticked by like shuddering hours.

It was pain that finally brought Charm back to her senses—the pain of her fingers and knees against the sharp, jagged rocks beneath her. She drew a ragged breath. From between the crooked boards of the porch, she noticed a glimmer of moonlight. All was not darkness; all was not hopeless. She took another shuddering breath.

Jude would be waiting for her. If only he had remained strong despite his poker loss. But she wouldn't allow herself to think about the alternative. Not now.

It was time to leave this place. Slowly she crept out. There was blood on her palms, but she ignored it. She should have gone back long ago, but she'd been certain someone would find Raven's body and follow her.

But there was no way of knowing if he was dead. She was letting terror lead her mind. Raven Scott wasn't dead, she told herself firmly. He'd merely fallen from the loft. He was young and strong. Too young and too strong. She remembered his hands on her and shivered again. She had done what needed doing. Anyone would understand that, and now she was safe, for it was not yet dawn and no one had found her.

Slinking from the shadow of the porch, she glanced about. Although she was alone and unthreatened, she was also lost.

The streets of Deadwood seemed twisted and unplanned, but Charm hurried down the rutted roads, breathless and wary, until she saw the inn. Crouching against the corner of a general store, she stared through the uneven darkness, watching for movement, for some sign of trouble. All was quiet. Still, she dared not try the front door. Even if it had been left unlocked, someone might be hiding in the interior.

It was simple enough to find the window of Jude's rented room. It had not been so many hours before that they had escaped that way. A rail fence ran below the slanted roof.

She climbed now as quietly as possible and finally wriggled up a rough post to the rooftop. The shingles were softened from years of rain and grey-green moss. They made only a quiet protest as she crept across them.

The window was open. Charm drew a relieved breath. She'd left a narrow shim there to keep it ajar during their escape, but had worried it might have been removed before now. With one quick glance over her shoulder, Charm slipped into the soothing safety of the darkness within.

"Jude," she whispered, keeping her steps cautious and short. Now would not be the time to crash over a chair and announce her arrival. "Jude." Holding her breath, she bumped against the mattress and felt along its surface to find her father. He was there. Thank God. So her luck had returned after all. "Come on. We gotta go."

"So soon?" asked a voice from the darkness.

Charm shrieked, pivoting about. A match scratched to life. It flickered unsteadily, then illumined the tilted half-smile of Raven Scott.

"You!" Her voice was barely audible. "You're not dead!"

Raven set the flame to the wick of a nearby lamp, then shook out the match and watched her in silence. "Disappointed?" Her face was smudged with dirt and framed by the disheveled, untamed mass of her mane. But it was her eyes that held his attention. They looked like those of a cougar as, wide and shocked and unblinking, they stared at him. "You must have found yourself one hell of a hiding place," he said.

"How did you get in?"

Her voice was very weak, and for an instant Raven wondered if she might faint. But then he remembered who she was. The killer woman. Fainting was unlikely. Murder, on the other hand . . .

"It wasn't difficult." He considered taking a step forward, but every inch of his body ached. If he moved, she would surely see his weakness, something he could not afford to reveal. Not with *her.* "Burle let me in."

Her brow wrinkled slightly, and for a moment it seemed he could see her mind work. "But . . . Jude?" She turned slowly, almost as if she were afraid of what she'd see.

The old man lay unconscious on the bed. His legs were spread, his boots still on, and his mouth ajar. He snorted in his stupor and twitched.

She said nothing. In a moment she turned back to Raven. Her expression was unreadable again, as if she'd found that secret place where she stowed her emotions.

Raven knew she'd see the whiskey bottles strewn beside the bed. Was she surprised by Jude's condition, or had she seen him intoxicated a hundred times before?

She took a deep breath and pursed her lips now. Neither narrow nor frail, her face possessed strong, well-defined bones and an unexpectedly full mouth. "It's your fault."

Her words yanked him from his examination of her. "And how exactly would you go about deducing that?" he asked, intrigued as much by her words as by her brittle self-control.

She gripped her hands tightly together in front of her soiled skirt, and for a moment he thought she would answer. But he had misjudged her, and hardly for the first time. "You have no right to be here."

Raven tilted his head, allowing a hint of a smile. "Burle seemed to believe differently. He seemed to believe you owe me something." Raven took a painful step forward, thinking himself quite an innovative cad for the lies he spread so easily. In truth, he'd seen the open window and crept up the roof just as she must have done. Clancy, damn his hide, would be proud of his deceptiveness. But even without Bodine's careful tutelage in the ways of deceit, Raven would have been inspired by the girl's charming presence to use whatever means necessary to preserve his life.

She backed away now, her eyes shifting from side to side as she rounded the end of the bed. "Go away or I'll . . . I'll scream for the sheriff."

Raven allowed himself to laugh. "Don't you think we've

bothered the good Deputy Hackett enough for one night?" he asked. He knew his words would remind her of her failed escape of some hours earlier.

"Get out," she insisted, tossing her head slightly. Maverick wisps of hair skittered outward, as if fleeing from the sparkling light of her eyes. "I'm not afraid of you."

"Then why are you backing away?"

She stopped abruptly, as if she'd been unaware of her retreat. "What do you want?" Her nostrils were slightly flared.

"I just want to know one thing, darling. What did you do to Chantilly Grady?"

He could have sworn that for just a fleeting moment he saw honest surprise burn across her features. But in an instant it was gone, replaced by her usual, careful veneer. "I have no idea what you're talking about."

Raven lifted his brows and painfully crossed his arms against his chest to study her askance. "Your lies get better and better."

Her nostrils flared again. "You think I'm lying?"

"I *know* you're lying."

"All right." She nodded once and smiled tightly. "Then please tell me what I did to Chantilly Gady."

"Grady," he corrected, volleying with one of his own, patently insincere smiles. From the bed Jude snored a single, snarled note. "Perhaps you didn't have time to learn her full name before you killed her."

"*Killed* her!" The words came out in a hard whisper.

Raven studied her in silence. If she was lying now, he had sorely underestimated her ability. "Where'd you get the Bible, Charm?" he asked, not giving her time to recover her composure.

She shoved one fist into her pocket and eyed him warily, as if she thought he might fling himself at her again. Which, in fact, he had seriously considered doing. Disabling sparks of sundry aches, however, warned him against such foolishness.

"I already told you where I got it," she said tightly.

When Raven was ten years old, another boy had called him a bastard. Even now, Raven could remember the hot rage that had infused him. It had felt so good to hit him, to grab hold of the boy's hair and thump his head against the red Kentucky clay.

Raven took a deep, cleansing breath. Rage solved nothing. Rampant emotion caused only a delay of practical resolution. Besides, there was no need for such anger now. "Yes, from your father's favorite cousin once removed, I believe. Penny Petunia, wasn't it?"

"Pritchard," she corrected tightly. "Petunia was the pigeon."

"I'm getting really tired."

"Me, too. Why don't you leave?"

"I'm waiting with bated breath to hear more about the pigeon."

"It flew away."

He felt a smile curve his lips and was surprised to realize it was real. Turning swiftly away, Raven seated himself in the room's only chair. "All right." He moved to stretch out his legs but winced at the shooting shards of pain. He raised his gaze, rapidly checking to see if she had noticed. But *her* gaze had shifted toward the door, and now snapped back to his face. "I'd catch you," he assured her, though he seriously doubted his ability to capture a hoptoad in a water barrel. In fact, sitting down had been a mistake, for he was entirely unsure whether he could rise again. How embarrassing to be found there in the morning, all alone, with Charm and Jude long gone. But no. It wouldn't be embarrassing, for he would probably be dead, if the lady's expression indicated her thoughts. She hated him, Raven deduced. He wondered at that fact now, for most people didn't hate him until they'd known him for at least a full day.

"I just need some answers," he said now, catching her gaze with his. "Miss Grady wasn't anything to me, you understand. This isn't personal. Maybe she was dead when you found her. You just took her possessions. No one would blame you for that. I just need the truth."

She said nothing, but watched him, her body very stiff. Anger flared in his chest again, but he tamped it down.

"She would be twenty-one this year." He paused, waiting.

"I told you." Charm's tone was clipped. "I got it from my mother."

He drew a deep breath. "All right. What was your mother's name?"

"Eloise."

"And her maiden name?"

"Medina."

"Eloise Medina? Really?" He rose slowly, not thinking to hide the pain now. "Have you told her?"

She eyed him nervously as he paced past. "What?"

It was that fake innocence that made him nearly snap. He turned with a start, barely stopping himself from grabbing her to him. "I said, have you told her yet that she has a daughter?" he asked. "Because when I last talked to her, no one had informed her of the birth. And she's a nurse of sorts; you'd think she'd have noticed such a thing as a baby. But wait. How strange. I'm certain she said she's to be married for the first time in just a few months. No former husbands. No former children."

"You're insane!" Charm gasped out the words, backing stiffly away. "My mother's dead."

"That I don't doubt. But Eloise Medina is very much alive. And she wants her niece back. Her *niece*! Chantilly Grady. Ring any bells now?" he asked, gritting out the words.

"No."

"Damn it, woman!" he swore, but suddenly he remembered the miniature painting. Dropping his hand into his pocket, he pulled out a small leather bag. From it he drew out a tiny portrait that he thrust toward her. "Old lady Sophie refused to change with the times. No family photographs. But I managed to find this." He thrust the tiny oil portrait toward her. "This would have been the girl's mother. There may be some resemblance. Does it look at all familiar?"

Charm's eyes widened. There was something about the frail, peaked face in the oval. Something . . . Eerie silence gripped the room as memories rushed in on her like a dark, consuming wave.

"Was she with Chantilly when you found her?" Raven asked.

A gun exploded in Charm's mind.

"No!" she gasped, certain for the flash of a moment that she herself had been shot. "No!" She was breathing hard. "I don't know her."

"You never saw her before?"

It was hard to breathe. Half-remembered nightmares assaulted her. She dropped the miniature into her pocket. "No," she whispered.

Raven watched her. "You lie," he said evenly. "But blast if you don't do it well. Almost as good as . . . ," he began, and reached for her again.

But suddenly the derringer was in her hand. She backed away a step.

"Touch me again, and I'll kill you," she warned. "I swear I will."

He stopped. His eyes were narrow and shadowed by his dark brows. "Like you killed Chantilly?"

"I told you." Her voice quivered. Where had she seen the face in the tiny portrait? Where? "I didn't kill anyone."

"Then where did you get the Bible?"

"My—"

"Don't say it, Charm," he warned, holding up a hand between them. "I pride myself on my self-control. But I have my limits."

She pursed her lips, trying to think. How was she going to escape? And what about Jude? She couldn't leave him to the mercy of this madman. She longed to glance toward the bed, hoping Jude was awakening, but she didn't take her eyes from the lunatic before her.

"Eloise Medina never married, Charm," he said now, his face expressionless. "Never had a child. She's eccentric, but not so eccentric as to forget such an event. And then there's a darkie named Cora who talks like she knows Chantilly, though she's never seen her. She too is waiting to hear what happened to the girl. You're going to have to work on your lies. You could have said Eloise was a friend. Or even . . ." He chuckled, looking not the least amused. "Even that you had no idea who she was. There's a fortune at stake, you know. But no. You *don't* know, do you? Else you would certainly have planned to take more than the Bible. Or did you? What else did Chantilly have on her?" he asked, and took a step forward.

"I'll kill you!" She drew in her breath, holding the derringer in both hands. But terror made her shake, and doubt gnawed at her, making her fingers stiff. "Leave me alone. What do you want from me?"

"The truth." He stopped. "Just the truth."

"She was my mother," Charm said.

In that instant Raven lunged. She squealed and twisted, but he held the derringer now. They spilled to the floor, crashing down together on their sides. They gasped for breath as they tussled for control of the gun.

"Let go!" he ordered, his tone scraped and hard, but she fought back, trying to tear the weapon from his grip.

"No!" she cried, but he was stronger, and she was losing the battle. Bending her leg, she banged her knee against his thigh. He gasped in pain, and seeing her advantage, Charm struck again. But this second assault seemed to do nothing but enrage him further.

With a grunt, he yanked at her hand. The gun exploded. Charm shrieked, but in an instant she saw his face again, miraculously unscathed.

The gun was suddenly beyond her reach. His hands encircled her wrists in a painful grasp.

"What did you do to Chantilly Grady?" he barked right into her face.

Charm sucked in sharp gasps, trying to control her terror.

"What?" he asked, gritting his teeth and gripping her arms harder still.

"Nothing! I didn't know her. I didn't!"

"Then where did you get the Bible?"

"I told you," she whispered. "My mother."

"The devil!" he rasped.

"It's true."

He ground his teeth, then smiled grimly through them. "Then *you* must be Chantilly Grady."

She stared at him, unable to move.

"Is that it?"

Breathe. She had to remember to breathe. "No."

"But you got the Bible from your mother," he said, his tone bitter. "So it must be. But there's a way to tell." He raised his brows at her, looking like evil personified. "Proof. You want to know how?"

She failed to move, but stared up at him, transfixed, horrified.

"A scar," he said. "Grady had a scar. On her thigh. So let me see yours."

"No!"

"No scar? But surely there must be one. Let me look."

"You're mad!"

"Could be."

"Let me up."

"Show me the scar."

"Get up!" She tried to shove him aside, but he was much too heavy.

"So uncooperative," he spat, "when in the name of fairness, you owe me proof. And Eloise Medina . . . your mother," he scoffed. "She'll want proof that she bore a child. Strange that she could forget such a thing. She'll be grateful when you refresh her memory, I'm sure," he said, and taking both wrists in his right hand, began pulling up her skirt with his left.

Charm bucked against him, desperately trying to dislodge him. He teetered off her hip, and she lurched up, trying to scramble away. But he was on her again, pressing her back onto the floor.

"Blast it, woman! I didn't start this, but I'm sure as hell going to finish it." Grabbing her skirt again, he yanked the thing up. She thrashed wildly beneath him, pummeling him with her knees. He grunted, trying to quell the shattering pain and managing to still her motion with the weight of his thigh across hers. "Tell me the truth," he ordered, staring into her face. It was flushed a bright red. "Tell me," he repeated, but quieter, for even now he felt himself falling into the wide pools of her eyes.

"Please." The single word was soft and pathetic. "Let me go."

Raven opened his mouth. He wanted to swear at her, for she had no right now to appeal for mercy. Not after the kicking, pushing, and shooting she had done. And yet . . . She looked very fragile suddenly, with eyes so wide and frightened they seemed to wound his soul. And here he'd thought he no longer had a soul. No longer needed one.

"Listen." His voice sounded hoarse to his own ears, making him feel foolish. "I'm being paid to find the girl." He took a deep breath, trying to pull himself from her eyes. "She'd been given a Bible by her mother. A small Bible, bound in white leather." He paused, trying to unravel the mystery. "Inside it said Eloise Medina." Their gazes held. He wondered how long it had been since either of them had breathed normally. "There wouldn't be two Bibles exactly the same," he said, answering his own unspoken question. "There couldn't be. But I'm not accusing you of anything, Charm. I won't turn you in. In fact . . ." She looked very young lying there, and he wondered how old she was. "I'm not on the best of terms with the law myself. Just tell me the truth. Where did you get it?"

Her lips parted. They were pink and full and very well-defined, with a strange little upward tilt, even now.

He waited silently for her answer.

"Please let me go."

Raven gritted his teeth. "You're not listening to me. Tell me the truth, Charm, and I'll let you go. I swear I will."

Still no answer, only her wide, frightened stare on his face.

"All right." He nodded once. "Then I'll have to prove it." He felt like a brute. Hell, he *was* a brute. He pulled her skirt up a scant inch.

"I got it from my mother," she muttered. "I promise you."

He shook his head once, momentarily allowing himself to admire her beauty, if not the originality of her lies. "I'd like to believe you. I really would," he said and pulled at her skirt again.

"All right!" She gasped. "I'll tell you the truth. Just let me up."

Although Raven had never considered himself to be a genius, neither did he like to think he was quite as stupid as she seemed to believe him to be. "Sorry," he said simply. "Tell me now. Then I'll let you up."

"But I . . . I can't breathe like this."

Raven watched her face. She did look pale, as if the hot blood had left her cheeks in a rush. But the thought of blood made him think of his own. It would be all over the floor, in copious amounts, if he were so foolish as to release her.

He eased off her slightly, however, still holding her wrists. "Now talk," he said, making his tone hard and pinning her with his eyes.

Her lips formed a circle for a moment, making her appear very innocent.

"The truth," Raven reminded.

Her breath came in a sharp gasp. "You're right. The Bible wasn't mine. But I didn't steal it."

He sharpened his glare.

"I didn't," she repeated. She licked her lips, breathing fast now. "She'd been . . . shot." Her nod was rapid and short. "In the back."

"By whom?"

"I don't know. She couldn't talk."

"And so you stole her Bible? That seems a bit cruel, even for you."

"No! She was badly hurt, and Jude said . . . He said we couldn't leave her, so I tried to nurse her back to health."

"Was she alone?"

"Yes. All alone. We tried to help her. Truly we did. She lived for three days." Charm shook her head, rolling it stiffly against the woolen rug beneath her. "But it was no use."

He watched her very closely. "She died?"

"Yes. But she wanted me to have her Bible."

"Why?"

Her mouth went round again, like a frightened child's. "We had become very close. Like sisters."

"In a week?"

"It was a long week."

Raven tightened his grip on her wrists and leaned toward her face. "You said it was only three days."

Air left her lungs in a whoosh. "I mean—"

"Want to tell me the truth now? Or just a more convincing lie?"

"It's the truth. I swear it."

"What is? The one about your mother, Aunt Petunia, or the fact that you'd become close to each other?" He glared, wishing he could throttle her. "Like sisters."

"We did."

"Think of a better one, Charm," he warned, leaning closer still. "Or I'll have you hauled off to jail."

"You can't do that."

He nodded once, playing his last card. "Suspicion of murder, darlin'. Who shot Chantilly Grady if it wasn't you?"

Her lips moved again, but no sound came. He wondered

curiously if she were praying, chanting something to save her soul.

"I'm tired," he said finally. "But I'm giving you one more chance."

She opened her mouth. He stopped her words with an upraised finger. "Just one."

No sound was forthcoming. He waited. Perhaps now she was beyond speech, he thought, for she looked shocked enough to die.

He shook his head, causing increased pain to shoot along his neck and down to his stiffening body. "I can't disprove the third lie," he said, feeling anger pierce him again. "But I sure as hell can disprove the first," he growled and, reaching down, yanked her skirt above her knees.

Her scream was piercing, and when the lamp hit his head, it was hard and unyielding, sending him into oblivion with a curse for his own carelessness.

Jude Fergusson, it seemed, had not been quite so inebriated as Raven had thought.

Chapter 5

It took Raven four days to walk with a semblance of ease, and exactly two minutes and thirty-six seconds for him to swear revenge.

He knew, because an aging miner with a weakness for liquor had clocked the time span between the Fergussons' clandestine departure and Raven's vow for vengeance.

Unfortunately the miner had failed to note in what direction the villains had fled. But it mattered little, for despite the difficulties, Raven had found her.

He remained motionless now, watching from a shadowy corner of the saloon. Since New Eden boasted only a half dozen wooden structures, the Red Eye was generally well occupied. But it was not yet dusk, and the miners who frequented the place would flock in later.

For now there were fewer than a dozen patrons in the room, five of whom occupied the same table. It was there that Raven's attention was held. Three of the men were large burly fellows who appeared to have been drinking since making enough ore to buy the booze. Or perhaps they were trappers, for they wore hides of uncertain origins draped upon their massive shoulders like trophies of war.

Raven shifted his gaze to the fourth man. Jude Fergusson sat with his brows pulled low, impatiently tapping the table with two blunt fingers. During his search, Raven had been afforded time to craft several possible scenarios concerning that man. None of them was complimentary, but all of them were interesting, and should assure a rise from the old man if properly stated. At the moment, however, Jude's past transgressions seemed insignificant, for Charm was there, too.

Raven filled his lungs with a deep waft of smoky air and waited, savoring the anticipation of approaching her. Gone was the girl's stained traveling suit. In its place was a shimmering gown of scarlet hue. It hugged her bosom with lusty intimacy before sweeping over her hips to fall to the floor in ruffled layers. Raven took another deep breath, knowing he'd forgotten her effect on him. But it wasn't just on him, he realized grimly. On all men. Not one of Jude's opponents was looking at his cards, for Charm took that precise moment to bend over her father's shoulder.

Damn her conniving, luscious, mouth-watering little body.

"You in or out, Henri?"

Raven could just barely hear the giant's husky question. A grumbling response followed as cards were tossed to the table. None of the gamblers, however, took his eyes from the girl. It wasn't long before the game was completed, for, indeed, who could concentrate with Charm looming softly curved and smiling at her father's side?

Anger diffused Raven in hot waves. He stood with slow, well-controlled impatience, quietly pushing himself from the table to cross the dim room. "Mind if I sit in?"

Her expression made it all worthwhile. All the pain. All the searching.

"You!" she whispered in surprise, but Jude's welcome was not so benign.

"Damn you!" he roared, lunging to his feet. But a table and three men occupied the space between them. Raven smiled with smug satisfaction.

"Good to see you again, Fergusson," he said with a nod. "And you, too, Miss Charming."

Her face, he noted with some satisfaction, was as pale as a silver dollar, and her eyes were just as round.

Raven brightened his smile.

"I'll kill you!" Jude growled.

"Seems to be a family custom," Raven said. "In fact . . . ," he began, drawing a cheroot from the inside pocket of his silver-embroidered vest, "that's exactly what I wanted to talk to you about." From a mental file Raven pulled a possible scenario with casual aplomb. "Killing. Randall Grady, to be specific."

Jude dropped like a fallen stone back to his chair. The blood drained in a rush from his face.

Raven raised his gaze to Charm again, enjoying every moment. "I ain't no ghost. Though I can't blame *you* for that fact. Now we have us a little something to clear . . ." But Jude's breathing had become harsh and rattling, interrupting Raven's words.

Charm dropped to her knees beside him, touching his arm as she examined his pasty face. "Are you all right?" she asked, but Jude was beginning to list toward the left. She teetered under his weight, trying to keep him from falling. "Help him! Please!"

There was little Raven could do but assist, for Jude's three large opponents seemed nailed to their chairs, and surely a dead man could give him no answers. So, he rushed about the table to push the failing fellow to the right, balancing him there as Charm rose rapidly to her feet.

"Have to lay him down," she murmured. "Here. Over here." She motioned toward a red settee.

Raven wrapped his arms about the old gambler's torso and followed her, half dragging Jude along. In a moment the old man was propped up on the frayed, red velvet of the once elegant settee.

"There now. You're gonna be fine," crooned Charm, immediately on her knees again. "Somebody get him some water. And hurry."

From the table behind, two men bumbled away to do her bidding. Raven stood idly by, feeling ridiculously out of character and irritably impatient for his carefully planned revenge.

Water was brought in a shot glass, carried hurriedly along by a lumbering grizzly of a man. Liquid sloshed generously across his coarse fingers as he panted to a halt by Charm's side. "Here y' go, miss," he said, pressing the nearly empty glass toward her.

Breathing a word of thanks, she gently urged Jude to take a sip. But even that tiny bit of liquid seemed to be too much for the old man.

"Is it your stomach?" Charm asked, leaning nearer her father.

"I'm all right." His tone sounded ghastly, vividly belying his words. "Just get him the hell outta my sight before I kill 'im." He waved toward Raven, but his strength failed to sustain the lift of his arm. It fell limply over the edge of the settee as his lids dropped closed.

"Jude?" Charm's tone was desperate and ragged.

The old man's lips moved, and she leaned across his chest to hear him. "*My* gal," he whispered, trying to pat her hand. "So sorry. Shoulda learned who he was. Shoulda—"

"Just rest for a spell." She forced a smile. "Everything's going to be fine. You'll see. Just rest. Then I'll get you to your room." Her voice wobbled slightly, and when she reached out, her hand did the same.

Tears? Raven wondered. Were those real tears in her eyes? But no! He was forgetting her identity—and after all the pain she'd caused him. She was an even better actress than he'd realized. Not to mention the old man, who surely deserved some kind of award for his touching performance.

"I'll have some answers first," Raven said. Remembering the pain the Fergussons had caused him, he stepped nearer the settee. "About—"

"Have you no heart?" She looked up from the floor, and, indeed, in her forest-deep eyes there were tears.

Raven stared at her, temporarily forgetting his concussion, his throbbing groin, his aching back. God, she was beautiful.

"No heart at all?" she whispered.

Raven brought himself back to reality with a painful lash of his memory. "No," he said evenly. "None. And I believe we've played this game before. It was amusing, but once is enough."

"Can't you see he's terribly ill?"

"What I see is that you think me terribly stupid."

She pursed her lips. Anger darted in the kaleidoscope recesses of her eyes. "Then you're not completely blind."

Raven gave her a cold smile. "All you need do is tell me the truth about Grady."

"I told you before." Her voice wavered, and her gaze flickered to the trio of men who shuffled about not far away. "I don't know any Grady."

Raven canted his head at her. "Then maybe your father can tell me what happened to the girl. Hey! Old man," he said, shaking the limp shoulder. "That was a good try, but it's time to talk now."

"What are you doing?" Charm demanded, jerking to her feet. "Are you crazy? He needs his rest." She yanked at Raven's arm, but he caught her hand in a carefully controlled grip, pulling it near his chest.

"I've had just about enough of your entertaining lies. Now I'll have the truth."

"I told you the truth."

"The devil you did!"

"This fella botherin' you, miss?" asked a voice from behind.

Charm's wide gaze was trapped on Raven's. "Let me go," she ordered.

"Over your dead body," he said, managing a smile.

"He bothering you?" asked a second man. The first one stepped closer, his movements agitated.

Charm's gaze held on Raven's.

"Yes," she whispered. "He is."

"Let the lady go, mister," said yet another rough voice. Raven knew better than to turn his back to Charm when he spoke to the grizzly men. Despite the damage they could do him, Charm Fergusson could, no doubt, do worse.

"She may be a lot of things, friend," said Raven quietly, still holding her gaze, "but a lady, she's not."

Three large bodies shuffled closer. "You'll be 'pologizing to the *lady* now, mister, or you'll be sayin' adieu to your teeth."

It dawned on Raven, rather belatedly, it seemed, that Charm had found herself not one but three large and well-fermented champions. He scowled mentally and turned while still holding her arm. "My apologies to one and all," he said. If he'd learned anything from Clancy, it was to know when to back away with his hands in the air. The problem was, he only had one hand to lift at this particular moment, for he would not let go of the girl and risk her escape. "But I have a matter of some importance to discuss with Miss Charm."

"We said t'let go of the lady."

Raven tried another smile. Things looked grim. Sober men he could reason with. Intelligent men he could bargain with. These men were neither. But lying he could do with anyone. "The truth is, boys . . . ," he began with a single shake of his head. "She's my sister."

For a moment the three men looked baffled.

"The hell!" exclaimed the closest of them in dubious disbelief.

"God's truth!" Raven swore, simultaneously reviewing the locations of the doors. Good Lord, he'd just regained a modicum of his strength. Now was not the time to be wrestling grizzlies. "She run off with that fellow there," he said, nodding toward Jude. "It broke our mama's heart."

"You lie!" exclaimed grizzly number two, stepping nearer. "That's her pa."

Raven retreated, pulling Charm along and raising an inoffensive palm toward the bulky trio. "Now, think on it a spell. What kind of man would take his own girl into a place like this? And dress her like . . ." He allowed himself one quick glance at Charm's half-bared bosom, then shook his head sadly. "I'm shamed of you, Mary Beth. Plum ashamed."

Her body was stiff, her lips slightly parted, and her eyes very wide. "You're insane," she whispered.

"P'raps Mama shouldn't of married her Uncle Bill after all," Raven reasoned and allowed an honest smile for his own wit and the girl's mien. There was nothing like her frightened expression to improve his mood.

"Let me go," she whispered, trying to pull away.

"We already discussed that, Mary Beth," he said, grabbing her arm with his second hand as well. "And it ain't gonna happen."

"Let me go!" she repeated, louder now. There was panic in her tone and terror in her eyes. But Raven's groin throbbed painfully at the remembrance of her deceit, and he tightened his grip on her.

"We've got to talk."

"The lady says to let her go."

"Back off!" Raven snapped. Momentarily forgetting the wisdom of his patience, he turned to the side.

The first fist hit him like an oak battering ram to the belly. Raven doubled over, cursing his luck, grizzly men, and bountiful bosoms.

"Come on, lady," said grizzly number one, reaching for Charm's arm. "We'll see y' safely to yer room."

"The devil you will!" said Raven. Gritting his teeth against the roiling pain in his stomach, he launched his bent and wavering form toward the three mountains of human flesh.

He would never be certain whom he hit first, or who hit him. Fists were everywhere, flying like wildly flung mallets as men grunted and cursed and threw about miscellaneous body parts. But the battle was too close for accuracy. Grizzly number one swung, but Raven, sober and wary, ducked. The brawny fist landed dead center in grizzly number two's eyes.

There was a howl of rage and agony. Suddenly the two men were tussling like bears upon the floor, grappling, thumping, and cursing.

"Damn you!" exploded the third man. Bent on vindicating his friends' wounds, he swung his meaty fist. Raven ducked again, but the knuckles exploded in multicolored lights against his temple.

The shock of force rocked Raven back on his heels, but from the corner of his eye he saw Charm flee the room. He pivoted, lunging after her, but with a roar the third man was upon him, nabbing him about the waist so that they crashed to the floor like falling trees.

Raven tried to scramble out of reach, but the other held on. Twisting about, Raven slammed a knee into his opponent's jaw.

There was a click of teeth, a grunt of pain, and a momentary chance to flee. Raven grasped it with desperate speed and struggled to his feet. The bear man rose, too, staggering yet undefeated.

"Charm!" Raven yelled, but again the man charged. His impetus was failing, however, and when he tackled, he grasped nothing but a leg. "Charm!" Raven screamed again, dragging the grizzly behind, but suddenly he felt teeth chomp hard against his calf, and his yell turned to a bellow of pain.

From outside Charm heard the yelps of agony, but she dared not stop. "'He leadeth me to green pastures!'" she quoted and sped away.

A thud, a roar, and then staggering footsteps followed her. She could hear them coming, thundering past the sun-bleached tents that lined the street! Trees towered just ahead, huge and dark and concealing. She raced toward them, praying for cover.

Just before she passed the last tent, Raven caught her, dragging her to the ground in a flurry of petticoats and red satin. She screamed, kicking wildly and fighting to break free.

"Hey, what's going on there?" someone yelled. The voice distracted Raven for a moment. She kicked again, causing his grip to loosen for an instant. Squirming, she almost broke free before he encircled her waist and dragged her back down again.

"There he is! Get 'im!" someone shouted.

Charm felt Raven stiffen against her body as he twisted about to look behind.

"Damn it!" he swore. In a moment he was up, dragging her along behind him. She fought frantically, planting her feet and trying to pull from his grip, but suddenly he bent. His shoulder hit her abdomen with enough force to punch the air from her lungs. Turning with a stagger and a lurch, he loped toward the forest at a wavering gait.

It was darker in the woods, though dusk was still some hours away. Trees surrounded them, towering far into the sky. Fallen pine needles muffled Raven's movements as Charm still fought for breath.

"Hey, you! Come on out of there. Bring back the girl."

Charm raised her head, searching for her rescuers. "Over here!" Though she tried to scream, the words bleated out as no more than a rusty croak of sound.

"Shut up!" ordered Raven, still scrambling along beneath her.

"Here!" she called with renewed strength, but suddenly she was tumbled from his shoulder. Even as she fell, her knees kept pummeling and her hands were searching for a weapon. But in an instant he was atop her.

Again her air left with a painful whoosh.

"Quiet," he ordered, but for the moment there was no purpose to his words, for even had she found the nerve, she could not fill her lungs.

"Come on out of there!"

The voice was closer now. Charm opened her mouth, trying to yell despite her debilitation. But Raven's hand made an effective stopper as it covered her mouth and nose.

His face was very near hers. "Shh," he whispered, as if she had a choice. She rolled her eyes toward him and tried to breathe, but it was no use. He was heavy and strong, and though it was possible he wasn't trying to smother her, he was temporarily distracted by their pursuer and forgot her need for air.

Blackness loomed on the edge of Charm's consciousness. She could feel herself falling into the abyss and fought one more time. Her throat squeaked painfully, crying for air.

"Charm?" Raven whispered.

Her eyeballs rolled upward, blurring the vision of his face. He swore in silence and slipped his hand away. Air rushed in through her nose in sweeping, painful drafts and into her mouth in delicious, aching gulps. "Promise not to scream," he whispered, but there was little chance of that just now. "Promise?" he asked, lifting his palm above her face again.

Charm nodded, panting for life.

They lay together, not exactly side by side, but more in layers, with his left hip at the center of her abdomen, and his shoulder pressed between her breasts. Charm remained very still. Off to her right she could hear another man passing. She wanted to yell out, but Raven was watching her, his eyes dark and deadly in the long shafts of light that slanted through the branches from high above.

Perhaps if she waited just a little longer, he would think her too terrified to call out. And perhaps indeed she was, Charm realized suddenly, for again her breathing had stopped.

"What the devil's wrong with you?" he whispered, glancing warily about before returning his gaze to her face. "You damn near got me killed. Again." His eyes bored into hers.

She didn't speak. Couldn't, for fear had again suffocated her senses.

"Blast it, woman!" he snarled as he shook her slightly by the shoulders. "You're turning blue. Breathe, for God's sake."

Air wafted into her lungs. She took it gratefully and shut her eyes, trying to block the thought of him from her mind so that she might continue to do so.

Silence descended over the woods. Whoever was searching for them must have moved on, Charm reasoned. She was on her own. She took another breath, not moving.

"I didn't kill Grady." Her own words surprised her. She could feel his gaze on her face but dared not open her eyes to its scorching heat. "I promise you."

"Tell me what happened," he ordered quietly.

Now would be the time for a really first-class lie, Charm thought raggedly. But the truth was, she didn't have a first-class lie ready. In fact, she couldn't think of a single viable story that might cause this madman to release her. "I never met anyone named Chantilly Grady. I swear it on my father's thigh."

She opened her eyes just in time to see his brows rise toward the dark mass of his hairline.

"On your father's thigh?" he asked dubiously.

"It's a sacred Hebrew vow," she explained earnestly.

He opened his mouth as if to question but finally shook his head. "I don't even want to know. All I want to find out . . ." He shrugged, shaking his head again, as if he asked so little. "All I want to know is how you got the Bible."

Breathe, she reminded herself, but it was difficult indeed, for he would not like the truth, and no believable lies were coming to mind. "I got it from my father." She had meant to say she'd gotten it from her mother, but the truth had made him very unpleasant in the past, causing her to avoid that topic for as long as possible.

His eyes narrowed slightly. "When did he give it to you?"

The lower half of his face was shadowed, while his hair shone raven black in the dusky light.

"When, Charm?"

She let her attention fall breathlessly to his mouth when he spoke. It was close enough to allow her to feel the air of his words stroke her cheek.

"Charm?" he whispered, leaning closer still, so that she could make out each lean, unshaven line of his angular face. "When?"

Fear twisted her gut. It must be fear, she reasoned, for he was too near and strong and dangerous to allow any other emotion.

"I was very young," she whispered. She could feel his heartbeat against her breast, thrumming with his life. "Jude was hurt. Shot." She squinted as the memories rushed painfully at her. For a moment the emotions held her in their grip. "He thought he was dying, so he gave me the Bible."

Raven watched her. A ray of fractured light had found its way between cloud and branch to fall with merciless scrutiny upon her face. Such direct illumination would be harsh to most women. To Charm it was marvelously benevolent. Raven took a steadying breath as he studied her. Good God, she looked like an angel, like a frail piece of heaven, soft, and helpless, and oh so sad. And if the angel had fallen a bit, who could blame her? Surely not Joseph Neil, the man who called himself Raven.

"Why did he give you the Bible, Charm?"

"He said . . ." She paused, lifting her eyes to his. They were huge and bright and so filled with fear and sadness that for a moment he seemed to feel her pain in his own chest. "He said it had been my mother's. That I was old enough to care for it now."

The words fell uneasily into the silence. Raven watched

her, thinking a thousand thoughts. Each had something to do with the softness of her skin, or how the sunlight danced upon the cinnamon streaks of her hair.

"He said she'd wanted me to have it."

Raven brought his thoughts back with an effort. "Your mother's?"

She nodded. The movement was erratic and frightened the shadow of her chin into dancing across the delicate column of her throat.

"Did she look like you?" It was not the question he had meant to ask, for it had little bearing on his search.

"I don't remember her." Charm's words were no more than the breath of a whisper. Raven watched her, seeing the abject emotions in her eyes.

"Not at all?" He could remember his own mother so easily. How she would hum him into dreamland when the world crowded in too close. How she would lift her chin in the midst of trouble and remind him that one must take the bad with the good. But there had been too little good for Abigail Scott, and too damn much bad.

"She died giving birth to me," Charm whispered.

Good God! Such a beauty, with no one but a drunken father to protect her from the harshness of the world. "I'm sorry." Raven's words came unbidden and unwanted. He reached his hand up to gently push a few dark, wild wisps of hair from her neck. A pulse beat there, strong and rapid, like a frightened doe's. For a moment, Raven allowed his fingertips to remain on that delicate spot, feeling the steady, sensual throb.

"It wasn't Jude's fault," she murmured. Her lips were slightly parted, and she breathed rapidly, with her gaze pinned on his while her soft, half-bare bosom rose and fell against his chest. "He couldn't have known what would happen. He couldn't have guessed."

"Charm . . ." Raven said softly, and finding he could no longer resist her, pressed his lips to hers.

They were soft and full and very like a brief touch of

heaven. He moved his mouth, feeling the warmth streak through his system like a thousand fingers of flame. Shifting sideways slightly, he skimmed his hand beneath the dark silk of her hair to cup her neck as his tongue caressed her upper lip.

There was so little warning. One minute she was soft and warm and yielding beneath him, and the next she was gone, simply gone. His hands were empty, his groin ached, and he was lying on his back, feeling sick to his stomach and looking up the ugly barrel of a sawed-off shotgun.

Chapter 6

It was not unheard of to hang a woman molester—not in these backwater western towns. Of course, New Eden wasn't a town in the technical sense. It was a mining camp, ravenously short of women, manners, and entertainment. Lynchings were considered damn good amusement.

Raven stumbled down the muddy street, not feeling particularly amused or amusing. An unknown man was behind him. Henri and the other two grizzlies had either gotten themselves lost in the woods or had passed out somewhere near at hand. But it mattered little, for it seemed every other able-bodied man had turned out for the festivities.

"Charm!" Jude's voice was no more than a croak as he hurried from the saloon toward them. "You all right, gal?"

She didn't answer, Raven noticed as he watched their meeting. The old man's face was pale but no more so than the girl's.

"Did he . . ." Jude's words faltered momentarily as his gaze swept up his daughter's disheveled person to light on her dirt-streaked face. "Did he touch you?"

Her lips parted slightly, as though she were searching for words. Raven held his breath and remained motionless. Now might be a damn good time to learn to pray.

Blood infused Jude's face in a sweep of angry color, and his fists clenched at his sides, where, with great effort, he kept them as he went on, his voice low and raspy. "Did he disgrace you, child?"

Her full mouth formed soundless words, her shoulders lifted, and her head moved, but whether it was a nod of affirmation or a shake of denial, even Raven couldn't tell. But now he saw that *her* face, too, had reddened, and that her gaze dropped from Jude's to the ground.

Raven swore mentally just as Jude erupted into action.

"I'll kill you!" he roared, charging toward Raven. But someone caught the old man's arm, dragging him to a halt before ducking beneath his fist and catching him about the middle. Jude struggled wildly, throwing punches and curses and trying to break free, but now two others were on him, holding him back with obvious difficulty.

"There now, mister," said a man who had just joined the fray. "We ain't savages here in Eden. We got us some rules."

"He disgraced my daughter!" Jude snarled. The veins in his neck were throbbing with rage, but his thrashing had subsided. "I'll kill him if it's the last goddamn thing I do."

"There now. Just you simmer down," said the newcomer. "I didn't say we wouldn't be just. We'll have us a fair trial first." He nodded perfunctorily. "Then we'll hang 'im."

Charm stood wordlessly at the edge of the crowd. Somehow she'd expected a trial to be different. Perhaps she'd even thought it might take place indoors or on another day. But tempers had been at the boiling point, heated up by Jude's ravenous oaths. There had been no delay. It all happened so fast. One moment she was trying to meet her father's gaze, and the next a lanky man called Judge was firing questions at her.

Had Raven hurt her? Had he touched her? Had he *shamed* her?

She'd stood like a mindless fish, trying to think, trying to gasp an answer. But there were men on all sides. Angry men who crowded in and made it impossible to breathe, much less sort her scrambled thoughts, or proclaim the truth.

And what was the truth? He *had* hurt her. Touched her. Shamed her. For, indeed, she was ashamed—so deeply humiliated that she felt surely she would die from it.

Hadn't Jude told her a thousand times that men were not to be trusted? Still, she'd allowed the kiss. Fear coursed through her, for she'd not only allowed it, but for the briefest of seconds, she'd *enjoyed* it.

"All right." In a matter of minutes, Judge's voice broke into her frantic reverie. "Guess we're ready, then. You got the rope, Fritz?"

"Hell, no. It's Mason's job to bring the rope. You know that," answered the other.

Charm's gaze snapped from the Judge to Fritz. This couldn't be happening. Someone would stop it. Someone must.

"Mason!" yelled the judge.

"Yeah. Yeah. I got it. Keep yer shirt on." A man with a paunch and a slouch hat pushed his way through the mob. He held a worn Bible in one hand and a rope in the other. "Where you wanna do this?"

"Same as usual," said Judge. Suddenly the crowd was parting like the Red Sea, and the prisoner was prodded down the aisle of men toward the general store.

"Wait," Charm said, but her voice barely carried to her own ears. "Wait," she repeated, barely louder, but the crowd either did not hear or did not wish to listen. "Jude," she called out hoarsely, and though her voice hardly worked, her legs managed to stumble up to her father's side. "Wait." She nabbed his sleeve, breathing hard. "You can't let them do this."

"It's this or I kill him with my bare hands," ground out

Jude, not looking at her. His tone was tight and hard. Charm swallowed.

"He didn't . . . He didn't do it."

If possible, Jude's gaze sharpened. "He didn't what?"

"He didn't . . . force me."

She could easily hear his sharp inhalation before the pause as he stared at her, his expression surprised, almost frightened. "Do you mean to say you wanted him, gal?" he whispered.

Despite everything, Charm's jaw dropped in abject surprise. "No!" she said, trying to straighten out her own thoughts enough to make Jude understand.

"Get that noose up there," someone yelled. "By God, Mason, you're as slow as a parson's mother."

"Then he deserves worse than he's gettin'," Jude growled and turned away, his face a mask of raw anger.

She stared at his back as he pushed his way through the crowd.

"All right. Bring up the accused," shouted Judge, and suddenly Raven was pushed onto the boardwalk that ran the length of the camp's six wooden structures. He stumbled but caught himself on his palms.

"Didn't you tie his hands?" came an exasperated question. "By God, you can't have a decent hanging without binding him proper. Fritz, you lay-about, tie up his hands."

Fritz moved forward. Charm shook her head, trying to break free of this nightmare.

"Put yer arms behind yer back, mister." She could hear Fritz's voice as if through a deep fog and watched mesmerized.

"You boys ever heard of the Denver Rangers?" Raven's voice was barely raised but somehow managed to carry over the din of the shuffling crowd.

"What's that?" asked Judge, bending his scrawny neck to the side.

"The Denver Rangers," Raven repeated. "We been looking for the girl for eight months now."

"Put yer hands back here now," Fritz insisted. Miraculously, Raven did so without a fuss.

"Just hold up there, Fritz," said Judge. "What's this about a girl?"

"Silver Sally." Raven held the judge's eye in a steady stare. "She's been working miners for years now. Didn't know she'd come this far north. But of course she would." He shifted his gaze to Charm's, and she caught her breath, temporarily stunned by the half-shadowed malevolence in his eyes. "Where there's a sucker with gold, there's Silver Sally."

"Sucker with gold!" someone said, sounding immediately offended. "What's that?"

"Such a sweet face," Raven said softly. "It's sure too bad."

"What's too bad?"

Raven shook his head as if saddened by the truth. "You mean to say you ain't heard what happened in Rockerville?"

There were murmurings and shufflings before the miners silenced to listen intently. They were simple men who would protect a woman in danger, but how much quicker would they protect their own gold?

"'Course you wouldn't have heard," Raven reasoned. "It just happened." He shook his head again. "When she left there was twenty men dead. And guess who had the gold?"

"Why, you goddamn son of a bitch!" swore Jude, sweeping forward. Two men stepped in front of him, blocking his path.

"I ain't believin' a word you say," warned Judge, though his voice lacked conviction. "Not about a lady like that!"

"Known her long, have you?" asked Raven.

"Well . . ."

"Well, no!" said Raven, finally raising his voice. "And her accomplice, either. Jude Fergusson. Better known as Knife Angus in Texas."

"Knife . . ."

"She looks sweet," said Raven, "but if you check her

pockets you'll find her gun. The same gun with which she killed Jimmy Tanner and all the rest."

"He's lyin'," said someone, but his voice was quiet and uncertain, and several men had already turned jaundiced eyes in Charm's direction. She backed away a step, feeling her throat close up.

"Lying?" asked Raven. "Do I look smart enough to fabricate this entire story? Would I spend eight months of my life tracking her down if she hadn't killed Jimmy?"

More murmurings. Charm backed away another step, but suddenly she felt her back bump against someone's chest. She swung her gaze to the man's impassive face before looking hurriedly to Jude. But he, too, was now surrounded.

"Go head," Raven urged. "Search her. Unless you don't care for your lives . . . or your gold."

Suddenly the crowd was moving away from Raven and toward her in a solid, volatile mass.

Panic welled in Charm like a dark tide, threatening to drown her. Dear God, she was surrounded, she thought and fumbled for her pocket, but just then a voice stopped her.

"He's a lyin' skunk!" boomed Henri, pushing his gargantuan body through the crowd.

Every man stopped in midstride, and every voice hushed, waiting breathlessly. All eyes turned toward the speaker. "Wasn't a hour ago he says he was her brother. He's a lyin' lowdown weasel," Henri proclaimed, jabbing a thick forefinger at Raven. "I say he deserves t'hang!"

The crowd swung away from Charm like a pendulum, and Raven swore. His luck was running decidedly short, and he was fresh out of believable lies and ready artillery.

He'd have to make a dash for it. But before he'd taken his first full step, a double-barrel shotgun was pressed into his torso. He came to a shuffling halt, hands raised, mind spinning.

"String 'im up!" someone yelled, and the crowd surged forward to do just that, but suddenly there was the clatter of hoofbeats on timber.

Two horses thundered down the boardwalk with Clancy Bodine bent low over the first animal's neck. Men scattered in every direction, shouting and cursing as they were slammed aside by the horses' crashing impetus. As it was, Raven himself jumped away just in time to escape being trampled and throw himself at the empty saddle that rushed past. He missed the horn with his first hand, but the second caught hold. He swung aboard as the spotted horse half reared, grazing Raven's head against the roof above.

A gun exploded near at hand. The horse snorted, launching itself from the boardwalk into the crowd as Clancy tossed back the reins.

Raven leaned from the saddle, grappling to catch them.

Clancy's horse was still running, tearing straight down the boardwalk to leap from the end and thunder off. But Raven spun his mount in a circle now, searching the crowd for Charm.

Another gun exploded, close at hand, and loud. Where was she? He spun the horse again, knowing it would be suicidal to give the good citizens of New Eden a stationary target. Men were running toward him now, leveling weapons.

He found her suddenly, at the edge of the crowd, frozen with shock. From the corner of his eye he saw a man fire, but already he'd kicked his mount into a gallop. They raced through the throng. Men leaped from their path, momentarily forgetting their weapons as they strove to save their very lives.

Raven knew the moment Charm realized his intent. Even from his place aboard the heaving horse, he saw her eyes go wide and heard her startled squeal of dismay. She began running, but too late! Raven bore down upon her like a vengeful demon, pushing his mount alongside her fleeing form.

For a moment her face lifted. She gasped something inaudible and plunged to the right, but the horse followed like a well-trained cow pony. Raven abandoned the reins and, leaning from the saddle, snatched Charm from the ground.

The effort was neither easy nor graceful. Charm screamed as she felt her feet leave the earth. She scrambled wildly, pummeling the air with her legs and nearly ripping Raven from the saddle. Her feet hit the ground again, but only for a moment, and then she was wrenched upward and dragged across his lap.

From behind, men cursed and fired. The horse stumbled, slamming his knees into the earth. Charm screamed, and Raven swore, certain the animal had been shot. But in an instant the gelding heaved himself back onto all fours and thundered into the woods with the heart of a champion.

They hit a downhill slide going full speed. There was nothing the riders could do but hold on and pray the horse kept his feet and avoided collision with the trees that rushed past.

Level ground met them with a jolt. Raven drew his mount to a shuddering halt, glancing around him, assessing the possibilities. In that moment, Charm acted, squirming wildly to break free. With a curse, Raven yanked her back onto his lap, urging his mount into a gallop again.

"You got a choice. Under his hooves or across my lap," Raven growled ferociously. But just at that moment, Charm pried her knees against the horse's side and pushed herself free.

Raven yelled, nearly pulled from the saddle. She hit the ground with a gasp of pain and escaping air. Behind her was a rivulet, and if they traveled down that they might never be found. But freedom loomed before her, dragging her to her feet. She was running within a heartbeat of time itself, scrambling uphill, knowing her advantage lay there, for the horse would be slower on the steep grade.

The footsteps that followed her were not hoofbeats. She chanced a frantic look over her shoulder and gasped. Raven was on foot and no more than thirty feet behind, grasping tree limbs as he scrambled after her.

Something grabbed at Charm's hair. She shrieked, fighting off the branches and scurrying uphill before she could be snared like Absalom and captured by the madman behind.

Breath burned down her throat. A rock slipped beneath her skittering feet, and she fell, catching herself on her palms just before her face hit the earth. Pain shot through her hands and lungs. She pushed herself up, but suddenly something hit her back, and she was forced to the ground.

"Here we are again," Raven's voice was scratchy and his breathing harsh, but the hand that covered her mouth was steady as the first rider topped the ridge above.

Charm tried to scream in frustration and pain, but the sound was pushed down her throat. She could not see their pursuers, for her view was blocked by foliage and rocks, but she could hear their sliding descent.

They passed within fifty feet of her, a stream of five or six riders who yelled questions to each other as they scrambled downhill. At the bottom they stopped. Charm could hear their horses milling, could hear their voices rise.

"There! Heading east, along the creek!" someone yelled, and they were running again, spurring after the horse Charm had just abandoned.

She lay now in last year's rotting leaves and fragrant pine needles, listening to the sound of retreating hoofbeats and feeling Raven's substantial weight across her back.

"Do you always have such interesting relationships with men?" he asked, his lips very close to her ear.

"Get off me."

"And let you think of some new and creative way to cause my death? Not likely, Miss Charming. I've become rather fond of living."

"It wasn't my fault," she whispered, still finding it hard to breathe for the weight of him spread across her back.

"The hanging?" he asked, sounding sarcastically surprised. "No. Of course not. The miners just didn't like the look of me. Decided to string me up on principle alone." He eased off her an inch, allowing a little more air into her lungs. "Happens all the time."

"It wasn't," she said.

"Listen, my charming little murderess," he began, and suddenly she found herself flipped over onto her back, so that she was staring into his eyes. "I don't give a damn if you want me hanged. I don't give a damn what you think of me, because the truth is I probably think even less of you. I want one thing and one thing only."

Despite the lack of pressure on her lungs now, Charm found her air stopped up again. She shifted her gaze frantically to the side. He was much stronger than she. She couldn't fight off his advances. She had no choice now but to shoot him. If only she could reach her pocket.

"Blast it all, woman, don't flatter yourself," he said, seeing the panicked look in her eyes. "I'm not interested in your person. I want to know about Grady." He leaned closer, staring directly into her face. "And I want to know now."

"Well, hell, Joseph," called a voice from behind, "if you'da just told me you had good-byes t' say, I'da never busted into your party back there."

Charm watched as Raven gritted his teeth before twisting about to face the source of the words. It was Clancy Bodine, casually sitting his horse as he watched them with a grin.

"You planning on leading them back to me?" Raven asked, nodding in the direction the impromptu posse had taken.

"Me? 'Course not. We're partners. Wouldn't make no sense to go through the trouble of saving your hide just to turn you in later. Joseph . . ." The man paused, *tsking* softly. "You got no faith in my good sense."

Raven drew a deep breath. Charm could feel his chest expand.

"It's not like you to lose a good horse like that, Joseph. I'm afraid he's long gone." Clancy *tsked* again. "Looks like you'll have to walk. But the girl . . . she can ride with me."

Charm hadn't planned her escape. But the man named Clancy had a knife strapped to his waist while her own small weapon lay trapped beneath the weight of her body. The thought of her defenselessness spurred her into panicked action. Jerking her right arm from Raven's grasp, she swung with all her might. Her knuckles rapped hard against his skull.

For just an instant, his body went slack, and in that condensed span of time she scrambled backward on hands and feet. But already he was marshalling his senses.

She felt his hand grab her skirts, and she shrieked in rage and frustration as she tried to wrench free. But the movement foiled her balance, and she fell, still fighting as her back and buttocks hit the ground. Grappling wildly at branches and rocks above her head, she tried to lose her attacker, but he'd found her leg beneath the layers of petticoats and reeled her in.

It was bad enough being caught again, but now her garments were being pressed away as he worked his way up her increasingly bare legs. Charm shrieked and kicked at his face. He ducked, catching her foot and continuing to drag her downward, pushing up gown, petticoats, and drawers.

"Let me go!" she cried, forgetting her anger in her terror. But instead he gave her leg a final yank.

"Not until you tell me . . . ," he said slowly, levering his way up her body, "what you did with . . ."

She heard his breath catch in his throat. Momentarily forgetting her battle for a weapon, she looked down to see what had startled him. Her leg was bare—except for the knife strapped to her thigh.

She tried to grab it, but he jerked as if drawn from a trance and snatched the knife from the sheath himself. They lay still, breathing hard with the sharp bowie between them. "Are you going to kill me?" she whispered.

He didn't answer, but stared at her, his expression inscrutable. "What else have you got hidden under your skirts?"

She caught her breath, suddenly remembering her worst fear. Frantically she tried to push the gown back over her knees, but before she could, he yanked her garments back into place. "I meant weapons," he explained dryly. "What else have you got?"

"Nothing."

"You lie," he said, and suddenly his hands were everywhere, patting around her person until he'd found and extracted the derringer from her pocket. "You're a deadly little thing. Any other weapons I should know about?"

"No."

"That's what you said last time. Tell me, my charming one, if I searched your bodice, what would I find? A small canon, or just the usual?"

She cowered, but instead of attacking, he grabbed her wrist and jerked her to her feet.

"Are you ready to go, then, Joseph?" asked Clancy from atop his waiting horse.

"Quiet!" ordered Raven as he hurried her along. "And give me something to bind her hands."

Chapter 7

Charm sat immobile upon the rotting log. They'd made a meal from the supplies found in Clancy's saddlebags. She'd forced herself to eat, knowing she'd need the strength. But now her hands were tied with a strip of leather cut from the back of Bodine's saddle, and she was scared. Her heart thumped wildly in her chest, but she dared not let them see her fear. It had been dark for several hours. Had the men of New Eden given up looking for her? Would Jude come? Or was he too sick to follow? She shoved her fingers between her knees and tried not to worry about him. Surely she had enough troubles of her own.

Raven rose and strode toward her. He looked very large in the darkness, long-legged and lean, made of hard sheets of muscle that gave her little hope of defeating him in a test of strength. Or in a test of sheer nerve, she thought, but forced herself to look defiantly up at him.

"You thirsty?" His voice was low as he thrust a tin cup toward her.

She shook her head, watching his face.

"Listen, Charm," he said, pointing a blunt finger at her. "I haven't done any worse to you than you have to me. In fact, not nearly so bad, if you count the hayloft. So I'd appreciate it if you'd quit stabbing me with your eyes."

From some fifteen feet away, Clancy cleared his throat. "What's this 'bout a hayloft?"

"Don't you have somewhere else to be?" Raven asked, pivoting abruptly about to face the other man. "Isn't there anyone chasing you? A husband maybe? Or an irate father?"

"Now don't go sayin' such things around Miss Charm," chastised Clancy. "She'll think you're serious."

"Get lost, Bodine."

"Get lost," Clancy repeated, rising to his feet to join them by the log. "Don't hardly seem possible for him to be so ungrateful after what I done for him, does it?" he asked, looking at Charm. "Damn, you're pretty. Any idea why he's got you tied up?"

She shook her head, but Raven answered, not bothering to look at either one of them.

"She knew Chantilly Grady."

"Grady?" Clancy's tone lifted an octave as he stared at her in the darkness. "The Grady from the advertisement? So where is she?"

"She's dead," Raven said evenly.

"Dead? How do you know?"

"Even working with you I learned some about detective work, Bodine," Raven answered. "Suffice it to say I know."

Clancy pulled a scowl. "Damn. I had me a plan to find the girl myself. Maybe marry her. Settle down. Make babies."

"And I had a plan to fly like a hawk," Raven said, his tone flat. "But it hasn't happened yet. Some folks think it never will."

"You scorn my sentiment," deduced Clancy, sounding offended. "But the truth is, I feel a . . ." He put his fist to his chest and narrowed his eyes as if searching for the perfect word. "I feel a cosmic sort of pull for the girl. An irresistible attraction."

"You've never met her," reminded Raven.

"Yeah," agreed Clancy, dropping his fist and becoming matter-of-fact, "but I know she's rich."

"*Was*," Raven corrected dryly. "She was rich. Now she's dead."

"Ain't that the way it goes?" Clancy said, shaking his head. "The good—they die young. My heart may never mend."

"You're demented," Raven declared.

"He's not the romantic sort," explained Clancy with a shake of his head. "I fear I found him too late to teach him the gentler sentiments. You'd be far better off as *my* prisoner." He faced Charm in the darkness. "Why *are* you a prisoner?"

"I don't know," she said, finally finding her voice. It was impossible to be sure just how dangerous Raven was. But she knew one thing: he was tenacious. Perhaps, though, she could turn these two men against each other and somehow escape while they quarreled. "I've never met anyone named Chantilly Grady. I swear I haven't," she said, managing to put a good deal of emotion into her honest denial before looking up through her lashes at Clancy. She knew she looked bedraggled and worn and hoped it would be to her advantage at this point.

Clancy stood close enough to look directly down into her eyes. He watched her in silence for a moment before seeming to snap himself from her gaze with an effort and a deep inhalation. "She says she doesn't know the girl, Joseph."

"She says a lot of things."

"Hmm. But why would she lie? She doesn't look capable of lying. Pretty little thing like her. She's got those eyes and all that . . ." He waved vaguely toward his own chest. "You know."

"You didn't learn a great deal from the girl in Nashville, I see."

"Ahh. Sweet Irene." Clancy sighed nostalgically. "You're just jealous because she liked me best."

"Ever recover any of the money?"

"Money is an insignificant thing in matters of the heart. I thought I'd taught you at least that much," said Clancy staunchly. "But you're skirting the issue. We were talking about *her*."

"Maybe *she* killed Grady," Raven said, turning away as if the topic bored him.

"Her? Don't be ridiculous. She wouldn't hurt a rabid skunk!"

"Then *you* should be safe enough," Raven said.

"You wound me deeply."

"Go away, Bodine."

"You, Joseph, are an ungrateful boy, and I think she's cold," Clancy said, wagging a finger before turning toward Charm. "You cold, honey?"

Tears were not hard for Charm to come by, for these two were driving her to distraction. Why didn't they just kill each other and get it over with? She'd hoped they were arch enemies, but now she feared they were just light-weight sparring partners, used to the pattern of jab and duck. "J—just . . . just my hands," she said, trying to increase the chasm of difference between the two. The quiver in her voice sounded good, she thought, and she lowered her eyes. Squeezing a few precious, salty drops from between her lids, she kept her muscles steeled for action and her mind alert for any eventuality. Now was not the time to be caught napping. Not when she'd found someone to watch her cry.

"Well, damn, she's crying, Joseph. I'm surprised at you. Thought I'd taught you better. Come on, honey," Clancy said, pulling his oversized knife from the sheath on his belt. "I'll cut you free."

"It's been a long time since I've hit you, Bodine," Raven said, not stepping nearer or raising his voice.

Clancy turned. "Three days at least."

"A long time," repeated Raven.

Clancy grinned, the expression lopsided. "You always

was one for a ruckus, wasn't you, Joseph? Still no guns allowed?"

"It's healthier that way."

"Knives?"

Raven shook his head. "Too messy."

"Ain't he somethin'," said Clancy. "He don't mind beatin' the tar outta a fellow, but he don't like gettin' his hands dirty. You sayin' you're lookin' to go a few rounds now, Joseph?"

"I'm saying if you set her free, I won't be responsible for the burial fees when she sticks that blade through your heart."

"He's not romantic, but he's very dramatic at times," Clancy commented to no one in particular. "If you're not going to set her free, what are you planning to do with her?"

"Just pry out a few honest answers."

"You need to tie her up for that?"

"I need a crowbar and a good solid string of threats for that," corrected Raven.

"If you know the Grady girl's dead, what's the point of keeping Miss Charm here trussed up?" asked Clancy.

Raven remained silent for a moment before answering. "Say it's for my own peace of mind."

It took a moment before Clancy laughed. "You're plannin' to collect bounty just fer information, ain't you?"

"It's none of your affair, Bodine."

"Huh! That's my boy, Joseph. All them years I thought you wasn't learning nothin'. But it looks like something soaked into that hard head of yours after all. Money! There ain't nothin' like it to make a man feel like a man. Except a woman. In which case money is"—he waved vaguely, quoting his former statement with less enthusiasm—"an insignificant thing." He looked at Charm and shook his head once. "Damn, she's pretty. Well, go ahead. Shoot off them questions."

"Not tonight." Raven said, seating himself on a nearby log.

Clancy turned to face him. "That's the thing about you, Joseph. You always was a patient one. The first time I saw you I said, now there's a patient boy. He'll make a fine detective. It'll be a hard task, but I'll teach him all I know."

"The first time you saw me you said, now there's a sucker. I'll work his ass off and feed him to the crows."

Clancy threw back his head and laughed. "Ahhh, Joseph, such bitterness. And after you bein' just like a son to me."

"You're only five years my senior, Bodine. Even with *your* morals, paternity would be a hard thing to believe."

"Well, you was just like a brother, then," Clancy said impatiently. "Hey, I'm just tryin' to help you out."

"Was that what you were doing in Georgia?"

"No. In Georgia I was trying to make a bundle of money by turning in thieving white trash. Same as you."

"*We're* white trash, Bodine."

"See. I'm impartial. It's a great quality for a detective."

"The fact that I had decided to go off on my own didn't cause you to set me up?" asked Raven. "Teach me a lesson?"

"Don't be ridiculous."

"And the fact that they thought I was aiding the boy's escape instead of turning him in?"

"I had nothin' t'do with it."

"You know, you've always been a supreme liar, Bodine. Not as good as her," Raven said, nodding toward Charm. "But supreme, nevertheless."

"Oh, come now," Clancy said, looking offended. "I must be better. She's so young. Hardly had any time to refine it," he added before changing the subject. "I didn't know they was plannin' t'kill the boy just fer kissin' Miss Annabell Fancypants what's her name."

"Supreme," Raven repeated.

"It's true," said Clancy, then laughed. "Had I known I'd have insisted on more money. And to get *you* killed . . . That would have cost them a fortune. Did you get the kid to safety?"

"Feeling guilty after all these years, Bodine?"

"Don't be ridiculous. It's always been obvious who's the honorable one. You know, I think my old man did me a favor. Didn't leave me any illusions. But yours . . . left too damn soon for you to find out what a bastard he really was. Made you think you might be one of the good guys. Should be a law against it."

"Shut up," said Raven evenly.

"All right. I know how sensitive you are. It's time to discuss the really important things anyhow. Like, how do we get out of here with only one horse? What about food? Who does the girl sleep with?"

Charm's breath caught in surprise.

"Back off, Bodine," he said.

"But she don't like you," Clancy said, seeming to address the issue he felt most important. "And who could blame her . . . the way you've acted. I'm older. A father figure. She'll feel safe with me."

Charm shifted her gaze nervously from one man to the other. Raven frightened her, but Clancy frightened her more. Maybe simply because she had some history with Raven. Lots of running, pouncing, and tortured breathing. But better than what might happen with Clancy. She'd been reading men's faces for as long as she could recall, and although she usually had the uncertain protection of Jude and a card table between herself and them, a few facts remained constant. You couldn't trust men, and you certainly couldn't trust a man who would tie you up. And she couldn't read Raven's face, unlike Clancy's. So perhaps Clancy was a safer bet.

He was from a poor southern family. Chances were good he had a very sensible, and possibly life-preserving, reason for leaving, for he didn't seem to be particularly law-abiding. From conversation she knew that he was a detective of sorts, but unlike his former partner, he was interested but not particularly obsessed with the idea of finding this woman called Chantilly. It was a characteristic she suddenly found most appealing. And, too, he trusted her. Or at least he trusted her more than Raven did. Perhaps he was even sane, and certainly he would be easier to escape from than Raven had proven to be. So despite her gnawing fear . . .

"I'll go with *him*," she said, nodding breathlessly at Clancy while holding her gaze on Raven.

The woods were absolutely silent before Raven spoke.

"No." His tone was perfectly even and cool. "You won't."

"You heard her," said Clancy, sounding delighted, though Charm dared not look toward him. "She's made her choice."

"The choice is not hers to make," Raven said, holding her gaze.

"Are you angry, Joseph?" Clancy asked hopefully. "Jealous?"

But Raven eyed him levelly, showing no emotion whatsoever. "You willing to find out?"

"Damned if it wouldn't be worth it. After all these years to see you not just fightin', but fightin' mad. Might be worth a busted nose."

"You've made your decision, then?" asked Raven, watching him.

"Well, if I wasn't so pretty I'd . . . " Suddenly Clancy's words broke off, and his fist slammed forward.

Everything happened in a heartbeat. Raven ducked, smoothly avoiding Clancy's fist before planting his own in the other's middle. Charm, jarred from her seat on the log, launched into action.

She managed to make it a full fifteen feet before he tackled her. Then she fell in pretty much the same position as all the other times. It wasn't comfortable, but at least it was predictable. Still, she tried to scream.

"I just need one thing." His voice was a whisper. His palm covered her mouth. "Lie," he said, and moved his hand away.

Despite everything, Charm didn't scream. The man was

certifiably insane. "What?" Her own voice was no more than a breathy murmur.

"We've only got a few seconds before Clancy gets his wind, so listen. I'm giving you tonight to think up a first-class lie about Grady's death. Say you found her, took her Bible, then lost it."

"I did lose it, you blackhearted devil," she said. "In the livery."

"Good. Tell him that. But stick to your story. No matter what. You hear me?"

"You're crazy." Her words came out in a windy gasp.

"Could be. I'm giving you one chance and one chance only. Got it? Tell your story. Stick to it. Make it good, and I'll set you free."

"What—"

"Damn it, Joseph," Clancy said, limping up to them in a bent position. "You didn't have to wait for me to jump you."

Raven rose slowly from Charm's aching body before pulling her up alongside by her bound wrists.

"It was more fun this way, Bodine."

"Well, hell," said Clancy, bending over slightly and wincing at the pain in his stomach, "far be it from me to spoil yer fun."

"Good," Raven said, turning back toward the logs they had just abandoned. "She sleeps with me."

Charm didn't mean to stop, but her knees locked up, freezing her feet to the earth on which she stood. Despite all her efforts to look heroic and brave, she couldn't budge them. "I won't," she said softly.

"You will," he countered, and jerked her toward him, but still her knees wouldn't bend, causing her to fall toward him like a toppled pine.

"Couldn't wait to be in my arms?" he asked, catching her against his chest with a grunt.

"I'll send you to hell first!" Even to her own ears, the words sounded melodramatic, but his devilish dark face was only two inches away, prompting melodramatics and much more.

"You already put me through hell, killer woman," he said and yanked her after him.

"And now you'll make me pay," she said through her teeth as she stumbled along behind.

"Oh, for Christ's sake. And Bodine thought *I* was dramatic. Listen, you," he said, pulling her into what might loosely be called their camp. Scowling, he thrust her down onto the log again. "I haven't had a woman in . . . hell . . . I haven't had a woman in half a lifetime. But you couldn't pay me enough to take you. I promise you that much. Even I," he began, but suddenly he stopped talking and toppled her over the log with a firm thrust to her shoulder. She was on her back with him on top, hand over her mouth, as usual, and legs tangled in her skirt.

Stunned as she was, she still managed a few good solid kicks to his shins. His low grunt of pain made her feel slightly better, but now he pulled her closer to the log, palm still clasped over her mouth as he peered over the rotten wood. A horse's low nicker of welcome greeted them.

"Look at that," Raven said, letting Charm rise to her knees to peer into the darkness. "The horse came back."

In a moment the gelding had his neck stretched over the log to gently nudge Charm's shoulder.

"Amazing!" Raven said. "Somebody likes you. But then, you haven't tried to kill him yet." He rose to his feet. Even in the darkness he looked stiff. "Watch your shins, old man," he warned, moving to the back of the saddle. The gelding shuffled a step closer to the log.

Charm looked into the big equine eyes and tentatively reached up with her bound hands to rub his brow. He lowered his head and seemed to sigh.

"What's his name?" she asked.

"How the devil would I know?" Raven worked at something behind the cantle. "You think he's *my* horse?" He glanced sideways now, studying the animal's head. He was white except for brown spots splashed randomly about his raw-boned body. His head was large, and had one ear that had been torn in half, so that it drooped pathetically. "You sure he's a horse at all? Leave it to Clancy to find the ugliest animal in the territory."

"I think he's pretty," Charm said softly.

"Yeah?" Raven looked at the horse before shifting his gaze to her. "Well, you're a sick woman."

Charm scowled. All right, the horse wasn't exactly pretty, but he had heart, and he liked her, which was all that was necessary to endear him to her. "Why did you buy him if you think he's so ugly?"

"I told you he's not my horse!" Raven stormed. "You think I had Clancy stashed away somewhere holding my mount, ready to save me from the eventuality of a lynch mob?" He snorted. "You think this is the kind of animal I'd choose if I had? I thought you knew all about men. Not that I want to crush your esteemed opinion of Bodine, seeing how you want to sleep with him and all, but he stole the animal, decided he hadn't made my life miserable enough yet, and came riding in . . ."—he waved vaguely into the darkness and spooked the gelding with his movement— "came riding in to remedy that fact," Raven finished. "It was just blind luck that the horse came wandering back here. And with the blankets tied behind." He threw one at Charm, spooking the animal again before moving away from the gelding.

"Aren't you going to take his saddle off?" she asked. "You should."

"Why?"

"He'll get sore. What if he wants to lie down?"

"*I'm* sore!" Raven said with a scowl. "Why shouldn't he be?"

Charm scowled. "Because *he* didn't tie me up. You have to take his saddle off."

"You want it off, you take it off," said Raven.

Charm struggled to her feet. Her hands were still tied,

making it difficult to scramble over the log to the gelding's side. He wasn't a big horse. Fourteen hands maybe, but he was built for endurance with solid bone and a well-sloped shoulder. She had always liked horses and had learned as much about them as her lot in life had allowed.

Now she ran her hands down his neck, feeling the sinewy strength there before attempting to free the saddle. Her fingers, however, refused to cooperate, for they'd become stiff and unwieldy. She fumbled for a while, catching her inner lip between her teeth and frowning.

"Oh, for Christ's sake," said Raven, pushing her hands aside. "Let me do that."

The saddle was removed in a matter of moments.

"You should take his bridle off, too."

"You know, for a killer woman you're awfully concerned about this horse," said Raven, facing her in the darkness. "Or are you hoping that bridling him up again will delay us long enough for old Jude to ride down and skin me alive?"

"He saved your life," she said tersely, referring to the horse. "The least you could do is let him rest comfortably."

"And how am I going to rest comfortably?" Raven asked. "Knowing you're ready to slip a knife between my . . ."

"Hey. Look at that," he said suddenly, his eyes falling on the saddle he'd just removed. "A lariat to tie up the pretty lady."

Charm stiffened even more. "Don't you think I'm trussed up enough?"

"No. Actually, I don't. Lie down."

Panic flooded up in a sudden tide of cold. "I'll die first!"

Raven stopped to stare at her through the darkness. "I consider myself a lucky man, Miss Charming, but no one's *that* lucky."

"Leave me alone! I told you before I don't know anything about . . . ," she began, but before she could finish her inflamed denial, his hand was plastered over her mouth again.

"I told you my terms," he whispered. "One good lie and you go free. Got it?"

There seemed nothing she could do but nod.

"Good. Lie down."

"Not—"

He held his hand up, stopping her words. "I'm very tired, and my back hurts. My head hurts. Hell," he said conversationally, "everything I own hurts. But I'll tackle you again if that's the way you want it."

She glared at him, finding that she, too, was exhausted. "Promise on your mother's name you won't touch me," she demanded.

"Leave my mother out of this."

For just a moment, Charm thought she heard a flash of emotion in his tone. Beyond all sense, it intrigued her. She craned her neck, trying to see his face in the darkness. "Why?"

"She's gone." His voice was matter-of-fact again, but perhaps if she concentrated she could hear just the edge of bitterness in his tone. "No need to insult her further."

"I didn't mean to—"

"Just leave it alone," he said quietly.

"But I didn't mean to . . ." She ran out of words. "Is she dead?" Charm asked softly, still trying to see his face.

"Yes."

"Oh." Only an idiot would allow herself to feel any kind of a bond with this strange man, of course. But she'd thought herself an idiot before. "Mine died just after birthing me."

"No, she didn't." His voice was very low, and she canted her head, certain she'd not heard him correctly.

"What?"

"Listen, girl," he murmured, turning abruptly toward her, "I don't know what you're playing at, but the game's up."

The sound of Clancy approaching through the undergrowth drew his attention. "If you want to go free, you'll lie there and come up with a damn good fib," he whispered, his face suddenly very near hers.

Breath caught in a tight knot in Charm's throat. His eyes were steady and narrowed, his expression deadly.

She swallowed hard, nodded once, and lay down.

Chapter 8

Charm remained silent. Her hands and feet were bound, and her back was against a log. She was chilled and cramped, and she longed for sleep but dared not try to find it.

How had the world gone so insane? Why was this black-haired devil tormenting her? She studied Raven's form in the darkness. He, too, was lying down, though she doubted if he slept. In the moon-shadowed quiet, she couldn't tell whether his eyes were open or closed. The possibility of his watching her discouraged any attempt at escape. So she remained, sleepless and unmoving, fighting off her own private demons and wondering what to do.

"Lie," he had said. But why? For Clancy's benefit? It was the only possibility she could think of. Though she couldn't make sense of it, Raven had promised to set her free if her fabrications were believable. It was crazy, but it was the best offer she'd been given.

Despite the discomfort and dampness, sleep finally threatened to overcome Charm's senses. She fought back the brief bouts of unconsciousness and finally assembled the skeleton of a lie concerning Chantilly Grady. Her eyelids drooped languidly, allowing the darkness to seep from the outside world into her mind.

A woman's scream brought her painfully awake. She jerked, attempting to sit up as she gazed wildly about, breathing hard and trying to find the danger. But there was none, except for that which her memory had again brought forth in the small hours of the night.

"What's wrong?"

Raven's voice surprised her. She started, trying to calm her nerves as she brought her gaze to bear on his shadowed face. "Nothing!" she said, then realized the terror that was obvious in her tone. "Nothing," she repeated, softer now, but already he was moving through the darkness toward her.

"What is it?"

As she managed to get into a more upright position, she struggled for a haughty tone to drive him back to the blanket he'd just abandoned. "I said nothing's the matter."

Despite her best intentions, he moved closer still.

"You're not getting sick, are you?"

"Of course not," she said, but he raised the back of his fingers to her cheek nevertheless.

She jerked away as best she could. "What are you doing?"

"Checking for fever. You feel warm."

"I'm not. I just . . ."

"Just what?"

"I had a bad dream, that's all," she said, and held her breath, her body tense.

From somewhere in the woods an owl called. Silence fell again, and then the call was answered by the eerie note of another bird from far away. Somehow the sounds made Charm feel more alone. She shuffled her blanket higher up toward her neck.

"You were scared." Raven's words were not a question, but a quiet statement bearing a light tone of surprise.

"I didn't say I was scared."

"No. You didn't."

They stared at each other for a moment. The moon had sunk lower but still illumined Charm's face. Raven watched her in silence. A thousand questions burned his mind, but he pushed them back, pulling patience from the fray of emotions with a steady hand.

"Tell me your dream," he said, settling back on his haunches.

"No!" she cried, then scowled, as if surprised by her own vehemence. "I mean, I never remember it."

"You've had it before?"

Her lips moved as if to answer him, but she shook her head instead. "Why are you doing this to me? Let me go."

"I can't."

"You mean you won't."

"That's right." He nodded. "I won't. For your sake as well as mine."

Her scowl deepened but did nothing to decrease her beauty. It was a disconcerting realization. "Was it about Jude?" Raven asked.

"What?"

"Your dream. Was it about Jude? Does he hurt you?"

"No." Her answer was breathy and hard to be disbelieved, for her eyes had gone round and her lips soft, but perhaps it was all part of her act. Still, why would she want to deny the old man's abuse?

"Who, then? Who hits you, Charm?"

"No one."

"Then why are you afraid of being touched?"

"I'm not."

"Really?" he asked and, lifting his arm, brushed his fingertips across her cheek.

Her gasp was sharp as she jerked away. Raven dropped his hand and watched her, waiting for an explanation. Her gaze dipped to her wrists, which were bound in her lap. Silence settled in again.

"Well?" he asked finally.

"I'm not afraid," she said quietly, then picked at the wool of her blanket and refused to look up. "I just know men, can read them like a book."

"And what do you read in me?"

"You?" Her tone sounded surprised as her gaze hurried to his face. He said nothing, but watched her. "You?" she repeated, more softly now. Her gaze skimmed his features, and she drew a deep breath, as if not discovering what she searched for. But she answered nevertheless. "You can't be trusted."

The words were surprisingly short of conviction, Raven thought, for in truth, he *couldn't* be trusted. Not where anything but his own survival was concerned. "How can you tell?"

"Because." She shifted uncomfortably. "You're a man."

"No other reason?"

"Isn't that enough?"

Who was she? Who the devil was she? "Yes," he said finally. "I guess it is." He turned, needing to think in silence, but stopped in an instant to look at her again. "If I cut your hands free, could you sleep?"

It was rather like asking a red vixen if she would eat the chickens if allowed the comfort of the coop. She would be a fool not to try to convince him to untie her hands, and though Charm Fergusson might be a lot of things, a fool was not amongst them.

She shrugged, watching him and making him wonder if she had stopped breathing again. He'd like to believe his masculine allure was so powerful that she couldn't draw an even breath in his presence. Unfortunately he believed she simply hated him so intensely she sometimes forgot to inhale. Now, however, he wondered if it was fear. Another disconcerting thought. It was easier to keep his head and his distance when he'd simply thought her murderous. The belief that her dangerous side might be awakened by pure terror made things stickier somehow.

"Could you sleep?" he asked again.

"No."

The honesty of her answer surprised him, and despite years of training, Raven failed to hide that fact. "Too cold?" Perhaps it was hope that made him guess that. Perhaps it was the thought of shared body heat that prompted it.

"I don't sleep."

"What's that?"

She shrugged. "I just . . . don't sleep."

"Ever?"

She scowled, seeming to think him ridiculous. "When men are around."

"Around? As in what? Within a few feet? A couple of yards? Fifteen miles?"

She smiled. It was only a small, tentative expression of budding humor, and yet Raven tensed. No woman should smile like that, he thought distractedly. Not when the moonlight caressed her face like a lover's gentle touch. Not when her eyes were wide and brilliant, and her hair gleamed in touchable disarray. Not when he'd been celibate for damn near half an eternity! Oh, for Christ's sake, now *he* was forgetting to breathe.

"What'd I say?" he asked against all good sense.

"What?"

"To make you smile. What'd I say?"

"You make me sound very foolish," she said. One corner of her smile drooped slightly as she dropped her gaze to her lap again.

There were perhaps a thousand questions he'd like to ask her and more things he'd like to do with her. Raven tightened his fists, gritted his teeth, and tried to keep his distance. "No. Not foolish. That much I know." With some disgust he lost the battle to remain at a distance and rose to cross the small distance between them.

Her smile disappeared as he squatted before her, and though she winced when he reached for her wrists, she didn't pull away. The knot was surprisingly tight, but he forced it open before pulling the leather from her arms.

"Don't run away," he said, his voice low, as if it came from somewhere deep inside. "I'd have to tackle you again." Her hand, where his fingertips touched it, was very soft, and her eyes as wide and round as the moon above. "We wouldn't want that," he whispered. "Would we?"

She shook her head. Her lips were slightly parted, tilted up at the corners, and so damned tempting it made his teeth hurt.

"You gonna just stare at her all night?" Clancy asked from behind.

Charm jumped. Raven wished he had hit Bodine harder. Keeping his movements fluid now, he eased back, trying to look nonchalant.

Clancy smiled, raising his brows at Raven before skimming his gaze to Charm and back. "Pretty, huh? I wouldn't stare at her if I was you. Not if you're ever planning to set her free." He laughed and shook his head. "Goddamn, this is gonna be good." Against all probability, Clancy walked away, chortling out of sight.

Silence settled in, making Raven feel even stupider. Surely there were clever things he might say, but they weren't bursting from his lips, impatient to impress the silent beauty before him. "Get some sleep," he ordered ridiculously, and turned away to find his own blanket.

"So, it's morning," declared Clancy.

He looked refreshed and so damned cheerful that Raven considered throttling him. Besides, it wasn't morning. It was barely past dawn, which was still practically night to his way of thinking. It was the longest night Raven had ever experienced. He hadn't slept a wink, not a minute, and each second of lost slumber was weighing heavily on his head just about now.

"Let's hear them questions," Clancy persisted. "You ready, Charm honey?"

Charm. Raven had kept a watchful vigilance over her all night. It had been foolish to untie her hands, of course, but he couldn't trust her to stay put even if she was caged, bound, and hung from a cottonwood bough, so he'd determined to stand guard. She sat up now, slowly, looking wary and instantly alert. Had she slept at all or had she merely closed her eyes to keep him from watching him watch her?

"I suppose we don't have any coffee," Raven said, not quite managing to take his eyes from the girl as he spoke to Clancy.

"Coffee? No. Listen, Joseph, I spent one hell of an unfriendly night in this here wilderness. It ain't my usual style, and I didn't do it just to see how you look in the morning. Though I have to say," he admitted, glancing at Charm, "*she* looks a damn sight better than you. Anyhow, I'm ready to find out what happened to the Grady girl."

Caution nagged at the worry in Raven's mind. It wasn't a good sign that Clancy had waited around as he had. Raven had hoped he'd up and leave during the night. The only predictable thing about Clancy Bodine was that he was unpredictable. Even if his former partner had taken both horses, Raven would have preferred that to Bodine's continued presence. Despite everything, Clancy was a damned good detective, and if he'd set his mind on finding Chantilly . . . Well, Raven could only hope he'd not overestimated Charm's ability to lie.

"You won't be taking credit for this one, Bodine," he said now, playing his part with careful ease.

Clancy smiled. He was a good-looking rogue of a man, with a long string of conquests to show for it. "'Course not, Joseph. I'm just curious. No more. All the advertisement said was 'substantial reward for the girl's return.' Leaves a lot to a man's imagination."

"Well, you can quit imagining. I've done the work, I'll take the credit."

"Sure, Joseph, sure. But them New Eden boys can't be all dolts. Sooner or later they're gonna find us. Now, I know how you enjoy a good scrap, Joseph, but me, I prefer better odds than—Hey!" he suddenly whispered, his left hand motioning for quiet as his right whipped a small pistol from some hidden place on his person.

Raven allowed himself to jump. Every trick would be needed to fool his old mentor.

Silence remained unbroken for just a moment before Clancy grinned and hid his gun away. "Sorry. False alarm. You sure are jumpy. Never seen you so fidgety."

"You sure there's no one there?" Raven murmured, still staring into the woods where Clancy had pointed his derringer.

Bodine's brows raised. "One would think her *father* was hot on your trail with a shotgun and a parson."

Raven forced a deep breath and straightened his back as if stiffening his pride. "The old man did seem rather fond of her. But I've got my doubts he's got matrimony in mind."

Clancy barked a harsh laugh. "Tell me you didn't take her from her pa, Joseph."

Raven rose to his feet, saying nothing.

"You did! By God, you've got stones. I'll give you that. Stole her from right under her old man's nose. Tell me, was he the one thought you was too short?"

"What the devil are you talking about now?" Raven asked, sounding perfectly irritable.

"Wanted to see you stretched," Clancy explained, making a jerking motion above his head with one closed fist. "By your neck."

"I spent a long time on this case," Raven said, facing Charm finally and hoping she was ready. "I was a mite upset when I realized she'd killed the girl."

"I didn't kill her!" Charm exclaimed, stumbling to her feet. Her eyes were wonderfully wide with fear, and her body seemed stiff. "I swear I didn't. I found her. That's all. It wasn't my fault."

Her words came out in a hurried tumble. Raven forced a blank expression, silently praising her efforts. He'd maybe exaggerated when he'd said she was a better liar than

Clancy, but it was damn close. Unless she wasn't lying. But, no, he knew better now, Raven reminded himself.

"Found her where?" he asked, taking a step forward.

"We were headed to Kentucky. Jude said there was a place there for us. That we'd settle down. Be a family. But when we came to the river . . . There she was. Half in the water. Half out. I thought at first she was dead. But when I reached her I found—"

"Where was her horse?"

"Wh–what?"

"Her horse. She must have had a horse. Else how did she get there?" he asked, taking another step toward her. Charm widened her eyes even farther. Bless her.

"I didn't see a horse. Honest, I didn't."

"Were there hoofprints?"

"I don't know. I didn't notice."

"You didn't notice because you're lying," he said flatly.

"I'm not."

"Then were there hoofprints?" he asked.

"I don't—" she began, but he stepped closer and she held up a quick hand, her face pale. "Yes. There were."

"One horse or more?"

Her lips moved soundlessly, but she recovered in a moment. "One. Just one."

"Then how had she been shot if there was no one else there?"

"I didn't say she'd been shot."

The girl was sharp.

"But she was, wasn't she? You shot her."

"No!" She drew back her shoulders. She was not a small girl, or a fragile one, and possessed a strong spark of life and spirit. "I didn't. You can believe me or not."

"All right." Raven let his muscles relax. "We'll assume you're telling the truth. How did she die?"

"She'd hit her head. On a rock."

"So she was unconscious?"

"When we found her, yes. But when we carried her into the shade she woke up."

"And then you killed her."

"You're crazy." Charm's voice was very steady now, her chin slightly raised, the dark, gleaming mass of her hair flowing over one sturdy shoulder. "Why would I kill her?"

"Because she was a very rich woman, Miss Fergusson. How much money did she have on her?"

Charm pursed her lips. "Two dollars and two bits."

"And you—"

"Yes," she snapped. "I took it. It was in her bag. As was the Bible."

"Which you also took."

"What Bible?" Clancy asked.

"I could have you incarcerated for theft. You know that?" Raven asked coldly, but Charm only tossed her head and laughed, causing her emerald eyes to flash and her hair to dance like glistening waves in the early-morning sun.

"For stealing two and a half dollars and a Bible from a dead woman? Go ahead and try."

"The devil take it!" Raven said, but there was no emotion in his tone as he turned away from her. "Where's the Bible now?" he asked, pivoting rapidly back.

"I lost it."

"Lost it?" Raven said. Barely raising his voice, he let his left brow drift low and his tone go gravelly.

For a moment he actually thought he saw tears in her eyes. She clenched her fists, managing to look terrified and defiant all at once. Damned if she wasn't a better liar than both he *and* Clancy. Another disconcerting thought.

"How the devil did you lose it?"

"What Bible?" Clancy asked again.

"It's none of your blasted business, Bodine," Raven said without turning. "Where did you lose it?"

"It was in my reticule when you attacked me."

Raven tensed his jaw but didn't swear. "In Deadwood?"

"It's hard to remember. You've attacked me so many places."

"Was it in Deadwood?" Raven asked with barely contained impatience.

"What do you care?" she asked, sounding frustrated and wonderfully close to hysteria.

"Charm," he said, his tone warning.

"Yes. It was in Deadwood."

Raven took a deep breath and stared at her with cold steadiness as he nodded toward the north. "You can go."

She moved her lips and raised one shoulder, which was nearly bare and tantalizingly smooth. "Just like that?"

"Yes," he said, and turned to stride away.

"Don't that beat all," Clancy said, half to himself. "Already dead." He shrugged and with an amazed shake of his head turned to follow Raven with his eyes. "You're not gonna make her walk back all alone, Joseph."

"I'm not?"

"Where are your manners, boy? It's miles to New Eden. She needs an escort."

"Then you take her," Raven said, not stopping.

"Where are *you* going?" Clancy asked, but Raven didn't answer and soon disappeared into the woods.

"He's crazy," Charm said softly, stunned and breathless and barely able to hope it was all over.

"Yeh." Clancy nodded. "Crazy like a fox. By the way, honey, where *did* you lose that Bible?"

Charm scowled at him. "Why?"

Clancy grinned, nodding toward the woods where Raven had disappeared. "Want to make him suffer for what he's put you through?"

She nodded, feeling strangely numb.

"Then tell me where you lost the Bible."

"The livery in Deadwood," she murmured. She had no more strength to think of lies, but apparently it didn't matter, for already Clancy was on his horse. In a moment he was gone, spurring toward the north.

"They're both crazy," she said, watching him go.

"You're even better than I thought."

Charm caught her breath audibly and turned quickly toward the sound of Raven's voice. He stood not far away with his fist curled about the reins of the gelding behind him. He'd removed his jacket and vest. The top two buttons of his white shirt were open, and his sleeves were rolled up, revealing the broad-boned expanse of his dark-skinned wrists.

"He left." There was numb surprise in her tone.

Raven smiled. "He went to look for the Bible."

She shook her head, baffled. The movement felt stiff.

"Your Bible," Raven repeated. He didn't approach her, not yet. "He plans to collect the reward for information about you . . . Chantilly."

Chapter 9

The nightmare continued. Charm tried to take a step back, but her feet were still bound. She toppled toward the log behind her. But Raven was there in an instant, steadying her with his hands until she found her balance and shrugged out of his grip.

"I'm not Chantilly." The words sounded as if they had come from someone else.

His eyes held hers, deep and dark before shifting to the ground. "Here. Let me get rid of that rope."

She failed to kick him when he bent to untie her bonds. A moment later, she regretted her negligence, though he looked surprisingly harmless when he straightened again to watch her.

"My name's not Chantilly," she said again. The lack of food and sleep and sane companionship was beginning to wear on her own lucidness. She stared at him. Was he crazy, or was she?

"You must be tired. Please," he said, motioning to the log behind her, "sit down."

His new deference toward her didn't improve her sense of

stability. He hadn't tackled her for several hours now, and she was uncertain how to respond, so she sat with a plop, feeling dazed and silly.

"I'd like to apologize for my behavior," he said. Dropping the gelding's reins, he paced a few strides. "I didn't know."

She considered asking what he didn't know, but in a moment he stopped pacing to look at her again, and he spoke again without being asked.

"I'm an inquiring agent."

He was a nut case.

"I find missing persons. For pay."

Charm had heard this all before, just before Jude had popped him on the head with a bottle, but she waited, listening nevertheless.

"Several months ago I saw an advertisement in a Missouri publication. It offered a reward for the return of a young woman, someone named Chantilly Grady."

Charm opened her mouth. Now seemed a likely time for another denial, but he lifted his hand, quieting her.

"Please, just hear me out. It's important, to your future as well as mine. This woman, Chantilly, it was suspected she would be found with a gambler." He nodded once and paced again. "And gambling, it's a sort of . . . habit of mine."

He turned and looked at her. In the morning sun, his hair was blue-black, his expression intense. Surprisingly so for a man who had been so carefully devoid of showing emotion; he seemed incredibly open now. Or was it an act? A ploy to force her to react a certain way?

"Do you understand me so far?" he asked.

Yes, she understood him. He was, beyond a question of a doubt, insane, and she had to escape. Soon. "You like to gamble," she said.

"Well, no." He paused, running his fingers through his hair. "I don't *like* to gamble. But I need . . . I just do. I gamble, and so I thought this job might be a perfect way to make an income while still keeping me close to the gaming tables. I contacted the person who had placed the advertisement." He paused, watching her closely again as if he feared she might dart from the log and flee into the surrounding woods. "Her name was Eloise Medina."

Charm didn't move. They'd been through all this before. She was no longer shocked by his delusions. "Strange, isn't it, that the woman would have the same name as my mother. But . . ." She forced a smile, hoping to keep him calm. "There may be dozens of women with the same name."

He looked for a moment as if he would object, but then continued on. "This Eloise Medina, she's a very wealthy woman, the only remaining child to the family fortune. But she'd had a sister . . ." He paused, watching her as if waiting for a response. "Her name was Caroline."

Charm kept her gaze on his face and her expression carefully bland, but the name Caroline tripped in her mind, momentarily stalling her thoughts.

"Does the name mean anything to you?"

"No." She smiled again, though the effort took its toll. "Should it?"

"She was the one in the portrait I showed you. Eloise's elder sister. When she was fifteen she met a man named Randall Grady. He was a gambler. A handsome man, I was told. Dashing. She became enamored of him, but her mother, Sophie, the old matriarch, refused to let them marry. So Caroline decided to run away with him. Eloise found out and tried to convince her not to go, but Caroline was determined. All she left with were the clothes on her back . . . and the small white Bible Eloise begged her to take."

Despite her best efforts, Charm could feel her strength drain. "It was my mother's," she said faintly. "Jude told me so." Her voice sounded very weak, and she hated herself for it.

"It *was* your mother's," Raven said softly. "It was Caroline Medina's."

For just a moment, for just one fantastic instant, she believed. "But why would Jude tell me her name was—"

"He's not your father."

Charm felt her jaw drop, felt her gut clench and her world tilt.

"I found a woman who helped bring you into the world. She remembered it well, despite her . . ."—he scowled—"despite her affection for whiskey. She'd been working on a steamboat when Chantilly was born there. Said the baby's father was a good-looking man named Randall Grady. He was jovial most of the time, but moody when things weren't going his way. Caroline, the mother, had a hard time with the birth, but she came through all right. I was able to learn about the next five years of Chantilly's life. Found people here and there who had met her, commented on her beauty. Her vivid green eyes." He caught her gaze. "And always she was with her parents. But suddenly she disappeared, and I could find no trace of her family or her. Until now."

Charm had difficulty breathing in the heavy silence.

"Jude lied to you, Charm. I've seen a picture of your father, and Jude's not him."

No. Reality seemed to slap Charm like the splash of a cold rain. *Raven* was the liar. He'd proven it more than once. Jude had warned her that men weren't to be trusted. He'd told her time and again, and yet she'd fallen for the wild fabrications of the first man who came along. But only for a moment. She had to get away.

That was the only clear thought in her mind as she took her first steps toward the horse's dragging reins. He had remained standing, and lifted his head now, watching her approach.

"Chantilly?" Raven said. But she didn't turn toward him. There was empty distance between herself and her ride to freedom and sanity. "Charm?" he said, and in that moment she bolted.

The reins were in her hand, the horse already moving. She took a few running steps, grabbed a hank of mane, and swung her right leg desperately over the horse's bony back. Aided by terror and impetus, she was aboard and thumping the animal's sides before she had a plan formed in her swirling mind.

"Charm!" Raven yelled, but already the animal was running. "Charm!"

She had to get away. Ahead the woods thickened. To her left the meadow sloped downhill, dotted only with scrubby trees. The horse turned on his own accord, avoiding the woods and jolting into a trot. Charm clung with her knees and hands and leaned toward the turn, but suddenly Raven was beside her, grabbing a handful of mane.

"Why would I lie?" He was panting as he lifted his face to hers.

"Because you're Satan's spawn!" she spat, and thumped the horse back into a gallop.

Raven raced along beside, keeping up for several strides before his grip weakened and slipped.

Seeing her chance for freedom, Charm reined away, trying to pivot to the right, but somehow Raven's hands did not completely falter, but tangled in her skirt. She felt the tug and screamed, trying to stay aboard, leaning away from him, but already she was slipping.

"Stop the horse!" he yelled.

"Let go!" she shrieked, tipping sideways.

"Stop the—" he began again just before the weight of her body slammed against him, "horse," he finished with a grunt as his back struck the ground.

The gelding thundered away. Charm knew she had no chance of reaching him before Raven caught her, so she did the only thing she could. She grabbed a broken branch from beside his neck, thrust it up against his throat, and snarled, "I've got a knife. Move and I'll slit you from ear to ear. I swear I will."

"Ahh, for Christ's sake," Raven groaned, still fighting to regain his breath. "Where did you have this one stashed? In your blasted teeth?"

"Quiet!" she growled, pressing her impromptu weapon

harder against his jugular. "Now it's my turn for some answers."

"Could I sit up first?"

"You want to die young?"

"Not particularly," he croaked.

"Then stay put and start explaining."

He raised his brows at her. His neck was broad and dark, she noticed, and his chest, where she gripped his shirt in one hand, was hard and wide. "What exactly do you want explained?"

Charm drew a sharp, exasperated breath. "Everything."

He shifted uncomfortably beneath her, managing to get clear of a sharp rock that was lodged beneath his left shoulder. "Could we narrow it down a bit?" he asked. "Just for the sake of my well-being?"

" 'Oh, Lord, how much longer must I wait?' " she asked, quoting biblical verse. "I want to know why you've concocted this whole outrageous scheme," she said, thrusting upward with her stick again.

"What outrageous scheme might that be?" he asked, shifting his gaze toward the weapon just below his eyesight and going very still.

"You think I won't do it?" she asked, certain the stick was out of his view and lightly jabbing him a third time. "You think I won't kill you?"

"I didn't say that," he said, raising one hand as if to soothe her.

"Well, I will." She needed him to believe her threat, for at the moment it was her most potent weapon. "Maybe I *did* kill the Grady girl," she growled, making her voice go low.

He hesitated, but only for a moment. "Now, that I doubt, because . . ."—he turned his head slightly, almost apologetically—"you *are* the Grady girl."

"I am not!" she shrieked, poking his neck again. "Why do you keep saying that?"

Both his hands were raised now, palms upward as if he were frightened, though his expression suggested no such thing. "It's not that I favor the truth when a good lie will suffice, but . . ." He shrugged. "Every clue leads to you."

"What clues?"

"You've got the Bible."

"There must be hundreds of similar Bibles. Maybe thousands."

"Boasting Eloise Medina's signature?"

"It's not an uncommon name."

"How old are you?" he asked suddenly.

She delayed a moment, eyeing him warily. "That's none of your affair." She sensed that he was surprisingly relaxed beneath her—lean and hard and long, but not tense. The realization stoked her anger.

"But why not tell me anyway?" he asked.

"Because then you'd say it just happened to be the same age as this Grady person."

One corner of his mouth lifted ever so slightly, and he nodded, moving his head only a fraction of an inch, as if admitting her point. "Chantilly Grady is twenty."

Charm remained very still, neglecting to breathe but finally coming up with a viable excuse for his words. "You could have guessed my age and made it hers as well, in an attempt to fool me."

"When's your birthday?" His tone was deep and quiet.

"I'm *not* Chantilly Grady!" she insisted, tightening her fist in his shirt.

"When's your birthday?" he asked, quieter now.

"I don't know," Charm snapped, and though she planned to drop the topic, found herself hurrying to add, "Jude was gone when I was born. When he returned, Mother had already taken ill. He never knew the exact date of my birth."

He watched her like a bird of prey or perhaps like a black raven.

"It's true," she spat, feeling suddenly uncomfortable. She'd always regretted not knowing when her birthday was.

"October 6," Raven said softly.

"What?" The word escaped on a breath.

"Chantilly Grady was born on October 6 on a steamboat called *The Belle*."

"Not me," she whispered.

"Your mother was only sixteen when you were born. She had black hair, like *her* mother. Green eyes. Cora, your darkie, said they were like spring leaves."

"Her eyes were brown," Charm insisted, her voice stronger now. "Her hair fair, like corn silk."

"You remember?" he asked.

"Jude told me. He told me all about my mother. Said she had eyes like an angel." It was true. Jude had said those words more than once, but only when he was drunk. It was then that the melancholy moods would take him, and he would rave against the undiscriminating hand of death, the weaknesses of men, and his own folly. "It wasn't his fault," Charm murmured. "How could he know?"

"Know what?"

Charm noticed Raven again. For a moment he had faded as she became seeped in memories and thought, but now she looked into her tormentor's eyes, which were like an angel's, though he'd inherited the soul of a demon. Perhaps her mother's had been that lovely speckled brown.

"He was only planning to be gone a few days. He would never have left her for long. Not when she was about to give birth. Not when he loved her so. No one would do that." Her voice, she noticed, had dropped again. She cleared her throat, feeling foolishly near tears.

"Bullshit!"

Charm stared at him incredulously, forgetting her archaic weapon for a moment. "What?"

"I said that's hogwash," Raven explained, and for an instant his emotions were obvious. Anger—as clear as the morning sky. But why?

"You know nothing about it," Charm said, her chest suddenly aching.

"On the contrary," said Raven, and with a suddenness that was almost frightening he smoothed away his angry expression, replacing it with one of cool unemotion. "I know much more about it than you know. I've been living a bastard's lie for twenty-six years."

Despite herself, Charm scowled, intrigued by this man who could feel such anger, yet hide it on a whim. "What do you mean?"

He shrugged dismissively and didn't answer. "How did you get the scar on your thigh?"

Charm drew in a sharp breath and pulled back, letting the point of her stick ease away from his neck slightly. "How—"

"In the woods," Raven interrupted. "When you dropped from the horse and I pulled you down the slope." He paused, but something in her expression must have made him continue. "I would have liked to examine you more closely," he said softly, "but then Clancy arrived. Always did have the damnedest timing."

They stared at each other, point blank.

"You have very nice legs, Chantilly Grady."

"I'm not—"

"Very long."

She couldn't catch her breath. His eyes were mesmerizing, the warm russet color of a floating autumn leaf.

"And shapely," he added.

Her grip on his shirt loosened a bit, but she reminded herself to take a breath and tighten her hand again. This was her enemy. Her *crazed* enemy. But his eyes made her forget, and his slightly parted lips looked almost boyish against the masculine backdrop of his rough-whiskered face.

"It seems you have me completely at your mercy," he whispered.

They were hip to hip and belly to belly with her legs firmly cradled between his. She moved her lips, trying to speak, to remember why she was there, and who she was.

"You wouldn't take advantage of me now, would you?" he asked.

Something coiled sensuously in the area of her stomach.

It was true; he was at her mercy, and if she wanted she could touch him where she would without fear of repercussion. Could discover the mysteries of his maleness that suddenly disturbed her. Kiss him full on the mouth. There was nothing she couldn't do. The coil tightened. She would be a fool to let him touch her, but the same could not be said if *she* touched him. Just a little. Just for a moment.

Against all sense, she found herself lifting her weight slightly to learn forward, drawn to him like an enchanted moth.

Beside her thigh something pulsed and shifted. Charm felt the hard movement of his desire and jerked herself back to reality.

"Lord save me!" She cried out, but Raven's hands were still held warily palm up.

"I won't move," he whispered, his voice like a dark, haunting dream. "You've no need to fear."

For just a moment she was drawn back under his spell, but the vivid memory of Jude's acid warnings awakened her wariness. "What do you want from me?"

He actually sighed, as if he had been achingly close to something wonderful before it was ripped away. "Where did you get the scar on your thigh, Chantilly?"

"I'm not Chantilly Grady!" she objected.

"How did you get it?"

The scar was halfway between her knee and hip. He should never have seen it, but somehow the knowledge that he had only intensified the raw ache of these new and terrifying feelings. "I don't know," she murmured.

"You don't remember?"

She shook her head, letting the loosed ends of her hair brush his chest. "I was very small," she said, and noticed how a few of her stray locks had remained at the top opening of his shirt, spread against his tanned flesh there. The sight of it captivated her somehow. She remained frozen in place, staring at the sight of her dark sienna tendrils against his skin.

"It was a burn." Raven's voice was very soft, very seductive. She felt transfixed by it, captivated by him. "Your grandmother, old Sophie, didn't receive many letters from your mother, but one of them told of the burn. Caroline didn't say how it happened. And she never admitted her regret over leaving home."

"What?"

"It must have been hard, going from such wealth to a life of travel. With a young child. And a husband who gambled."

"But I . . ." She tried to breathe, to think. "But Jude said . . ." Her hands were shaking, she realized suddenly, and she felt strangely cold.

"It's all right now," Raven said quietly. "I'll take you home."

She listened to the tone, neglecting the words. How long had it been since she'd been held in someone's arms? Surely, sometime in her past, there must have been someone. But who? Suddenly it was difficult to imagine Jude comforting an infant.

"Relax now. We have to take the bad with the good," Raven soothed, as if he himself had quit listening to his words. But the phrase reminded her of Jude, who when he was drunk would sometimes say the same thing. Charm stiffened, trying to regain her decorum.

"There now, just relax," Raven continued, pressing her gently against the firmness of his chest. "I won't hurt you, little Chantilly Charm. Why don't you drop the stick?"

Chapter 10

"Stick?" Charm said the word softly.

"Put it down."

"You knew all along it was a stick?" she asked.

"It was a good trick," he said. "Worth a try."

"You mean you never doubted your safety?"

Raven heard a strange note in her voice. He thought it odd that despite everything they'd discussed, she was inclined to talk about the blasted stick that still remained poised at his throat.

"You weren't in the least bit worried."

Her voice had risen another notch. She was either even more bloodthirsty than he'd realized, or she was thinking something he didn't like.

"Don't get me wrong," he said, still flat on his back and trying to pacify her. "I don't doubt for a minute that you could kill me with that stick." Her expression was unreadable. He hated unreadable expressions; they made life so confusing. He much preferred it when every emotion showed on his opponent's face. "No, sir, if there ever was a woman who could kill me with a stick, it would be you."

Women loved to be complimented, Raven reasoned. Clancy, damn his hide, had told him so.

"I don't believe you." She rose stiffly to her feet, drawing her archaic weapon away from his neck with a jerk.

"I beg your pardon?" Raven said, propping himself on his elbows.

She pursed her mouth with the corners still turning up slightly. What a lovely thing she was, even now when she was obviously upset. Not that she shouldn't be upset, of course. After all, he *had* tackled her, tied her up, dragged her over the withers of a running horse, and insisted that she lie. Which, by the way, she had done a bang-up job at. What was surprising was that she seemed, after all this, to be distressed only because he hadn't been sufficiently terrified.

"You never doubted your safety for a moment," she said. "You thought you were perfectly safe."

"With a killer woman like you?" he asked, easily managing to make his tone sound dismayed, for in truth, he knew better than to think her harmless even under the most clement circumstances. "Never." He sat up, still watching her face.

"You knew you were safe," she repeated. "And so you saw no reason to tell the truth."

"What are you getting at?"

"Lies!" she stormed suddenly. "You tell nothing but lies."

"Now wait a minute." He rose warily to his feet, not certain if he should expect her to charge him with that damned stick, or if she were more likely to make a wild dash for the forest behind her. The terrain that surrounded them was marked with huge, dark-needled pines and towering cliffs of stone. If she bolted, he wouldn't find her in a thousand years. "Why would I lie?" he asked mildly.

"I don't know." Her tone was, at best, uncompromising. "And neither do I care. You promised to set me free."

Well, for Christ's sake, after all he'd said, she still didn't believe a word he'd told her.

"You said if I lied to your friend you'd let me go. Never

bother me again." She paused, holding him with the piercing flame of her emerald eyes. "Were you lying then, too?"

Absolutely! Most definitely he'd been lying. But it wasn't supposed to matter, because she was now to believe she was an heiress, and therefore willing, hell, *eager*, to travel with him to receive her inheritance. "No," he lied quickly. "Of course I wasn't lying."

"You must think me terribly stupid."

Stupid? No. Strange? Yes. "Hardly that," Raven said, trying to make his tone soft and inoffensive. "It's all true. I spoke with your Aunt Eloise and Caroline's old wet nurse, Cora. I read the letters from your mother to *her*. They told about the burn on your thigh, about—"

"Quiet!" she shrieked, but her voice warbled with the single word, and the stick quivered with the force of her emotion. "You think I wouldn't remember such a thing? You think I wouldn't remember my own father and mother? She died, I tell you. She died when I was born."

Raven remained silent for a moment, watching her, grappling to gain some sense of her thoughts. "What is it you're so afraid of?"

"Leave me be!"

"Why?"

"Why?" Her voice was high-pitched and hysterical. Her laughter accentuated the wild tone.

"Why not go with me? Meet Eloise. She's not what you would expect. She's . . ." He shrugged. The truth was, Raven himself had been surprised by Eloise Medina, when, in fact, people rarely surprised him anymore. She must have met a hell of a man to fall in love at this late point in her life. "Come to St. Louis. Meet her. Judge for yourself."

"You're insane."

"What would it hurt?" he asked. "Why not do it?"

She paused, staring at him, looking breathless, but she found her voice in a moment and turned her expression to haughty disdain. "I know what you want from me."

"Oh, for Christ's sake! Not that again!" he groaned, turning away before swinging rapidly back. "Please, tell me anything but the wearying theory that I lust for your body!"

For a moment she was silent, then, "You're a degenerate! Dung! Deceitful spawn of Satan."

"Yeah, yeah," Raven said, gritting his teeth and feeling anger rise against his will, carefully trained though he was to hold back the tide of rage. Emotion was a luxury he could ill afford. "But you know what else I am?" he asked, stepping up close in front of her, barely containing that clear, awful passion within him.

He could hear the gasp this caused, and knew that she was suddenly afraid. Damned if his anger hadn't reached the forbidden level where it showed on his face. Damned if he hadn't frightened her.

"I'm sole possessor of your mother's Bible."

"No." She made the denial softly, like a hopeful prayer.

He waited a moment, assessing every nuance. "Do you have it, then?"

She blinked. It was amazing how she could look suddenly very innocent and pathetically vulnerable. "It's lost in the hay at the livery."

He shook his head slowly.

"Yes. I sent a letter to the stable owner, telling him to save it for me. I'll go back after . . ."—she swallowed—"after you're gone."

"No need to go back," he said with quiet finality.

They stared at each other, face to face, without breathing. "You lie."

Raven allowed himself the slightest smile and dipped his hand toward his pocket. She gripped her stick in both hands, pointing it at him as if it were a bloodied bayonet held by a trained and deadly soldier of fortune.

"Don't move," she ordered tersely.

He considered laughing, but one look at her expression made him think better of that idea. Instead, he lifted his hands upward, palms out, remembering how she liked him to think her to be quite deadly. "Get it yourself, then," he suggested evenly.

Her eyes went wide and her body tense. Suddenly he realized her thoughts. She would have to touch him to retrieve the precious Bible herself. She hated to be touched, and she hated touching. He almost smiled.

Charm drew a deep breath, making her bosom rise slightly above the deep neckline of her gown.

Damn! The thought of grinning swiftly fled from Raven's mind. This situation could not possibly be considered arousing, he told himself sternly. It could not, not even under the most celibate living conditions. And yet his body seemed to be blatantly disagreeing. He could feel the hard edge of desire unfurl within him, tightening and erupting, making him angry at his own weakness. "Get it yourself," he repeated.

"I'll get it!" she snapped, then nervously licked her lips.

Raven watched the pink, sharp tip of her tongue dart out. He felt ridiculously tense at the thought of her touch. Maybe she did deserve to be taught a lesson, but he would be a fool to be the one to teach her. If he was aware of anything, it was the limits of his restraint. "Fine," he said nevertheless.

She took a stilted step forward. "Wh—where is it?"

"My pocket." He remained very still. Desire was a great deal like anger; it made fools of men.

Charm shifted her stick nervously into her right hand. She seemed suddenly aware that his present clothing had only two pockets, both of which happened to be in his pants. "You're lying," she whispered, but the now familiar words were weak and faint, as if she believed his statement more than she believed her own.

"No, Miss Charming," he countered, watching her. "I'm not lying. It's in my pocket."

She gave a disbelieving shake of her head, then darted a furtive glance down past his abdomen to his pockets. Raven waited, only watching her eyes as they lifted rapidly back to his.

"It's not there," she denied, but all the color that had drained from her cheeks rushed back now in a sweeping tide of hot blood.

Raven allowed himself the freedom of a half grin. "I'm flattered, sweetheart, that you think me so well-constructed, but I fear you overestimate my . . . appeal. The Bible *is* in my pocket."

Her eyes were round as goose eggs and her jaw dropped. A gentleman would have mercy on the fairer sex, he thought dryly. Thank God he wasn't one. "'Course if you're afraid—"

"I'm not afraid of you," she said quietly, her face red.

There was something in her tone that made the grin slip from Raven's face. He tried to convince himself this was a bad idea, for he could feel his *own* hot blood surging, albeit in different places than *hers*. For a moment, good sense flooded back to him, and he moved slightly, intent on retrieving her Bible before things got out of hand. But again she thrust the stick toward him, making him stiffen with anger.

"Which . . . which pocket?" she breathed, not looking down, but holding his gaze with her own.

"Oh for Christ's sake, woman, let me get it," he said. Apparently, his better sense hadn't completely abandoned him after all, and the ache in his nonthinking parts hadn't driven him past the point of reason. But he made himself a promise. The first town he came to, he would find himself a woman. Someone willing and soft, with no particular proclivity toward deadly weapons.

"You may think me dense," she said, "but I'm not so foolish as to let you get a hand on your gun."

Raven raised his brows in wonder. "*That's* what you're worried about? You think there's a *gun* in my pocket?" The ridiculousness of the situation was not lost on him, and yet he felt frozen in place, waiting.

She scowled, apparently not willing to answer. "Which pocket?"

"Left." Raven tried to keep his tone normal, but what was considered normal to most of the world was not applicable when one was dealing with the killer woman. His words came out low and gravelly.

She swallowed. He could see her throat contract. Despite the circumstances, he thought it a lovely throat, slim and graceful, running smoothly downward toward . . . heaven. Oh, hell! He had to get a grip on himself, he reasoned, but just then she stepped up close, took a deep inhalation, and reached for him. Raven felt her knuckles graze his waistband and slip lower, down along the taut length of his abdomen with nothing separating him from her but the thinnest bit of cloth. He closed his eyes and clenched his fists against the rampant sensations. It was a snug fit. Raven could feel the slight tremble of her fingers as she thrust them into his pocket, searching. There was a moment of breathtaking anticipation.

"That's no Bible!" she exclaimed and snatched her hand away.

Breath rushed back into Raven's lungs.

"Where is it?" she demanded.

"You were a little too far to the right," he said, his own voice hoarse.

They stared at each other, unspeaking. But finally Raven shrugged, grappled for nonchalance and turned to stride back to the vest he'd left upon a log. Dipping his hand inside the breast pocket, he pulled forth her Bible to hold it aloft. "Quite a bit too far to the right," he added.

"You!" The single word came out on a windy gasp, with anger, frustration, and embarrassment all mixed together to procure a neat little package of shame.

Raven watched her, trying to enjoy the obvious show of her emotions. "I only said it was in my left pocket," he explained soberly. "Surely you can't blame me if your own uncontrolled . . ."—he smiled—"lust . . . made you assume it was on my person."

Upon later consideration, Raven thought his smile quite

foolhardy, and though he knew he'd intentionally provoked her, he doubted if she had planned to lunge for the purloined Bible. But lunge she did, causing him to sweep it quickly up over his head as she dove on past. She stumbled, coming to a careening halt near the log and turning like a cow pony.

His smile became more honest as he continued to heft the coveted volume. She was breathing hard, which caused her lovely breasts to rise and fall rapidly with each inhalation. The movement caught his attention, galvanizing a hard core within him.

"Give it back," she said, but he barely heard her.

Raven drew a deep, steadying breath. "What'll you give me for it?" he asked quietly. It was the last thing he had meant to say.

There was a moment's silence, then, "What do you want?" she whispered.

Her response startled him even more than his own had, for had he not known better, he would have sworn there was the trace of desire in her tone. He found himself lost in that thought, in her eyes, in the hard, gripping feel of physical need. "What are you willing to give?" The question was barely audible to his own ears and yet she seemed to hear it for she answered in a convoluted sort of way.

"It's all I have of my mother's."

Except for the miniature portrait she'd taken from him, Raven thought, but other ideas quickly nudged that fact aside as he tried to decipher her meaning. Was she suggesting what he thought she was? That the Bible was irreplaceable, and therefore worth a great deal? Lust gripped him a bit harder, squeezing out the remnants of his practical sense.

"If I did . . . it . . . ." Her voice was as soft as autumn thistledown. "Would you let me go?"

Raven mentally frowned. He'd *already* promised to let her go. It had been a lie. She knew it. So why now would she be prepared to believe he would change his ways and set her free if she gave herself to him? Could it be that she wanted to do it? Could it be she felt the hard grip of desire just as strongly as he?

"Would you let me go?" she asked again and blinked.

It was the blink that brought Raven back to reality, for he'd seen that provocative innocence before. Hell, they'd played this entire game before. And not so long ago. Somehow, even at their first meeting, she had made him believe she wanted him. Look how *that* had turned out. He'd been lucky to escape with his life, much less his manhood. He thought himself experienced, even jaded. But next to her he looked like a babe in swaddling.

"You *are* Chantilly Grady," he said, stifling the scream of his desire and keeping his tone hard and flat. When in doubt, sound businesslike . . . or lie. But in this case, the truth was not only more practical, but more unbelievable than a fabrication. "I owe it to your aunt . . . to you." He pushed her small Bible into his pants pocket, though it was a tight squeeze. "I promised if you were alive, I'd return you to the home of your mother." He drew a deep breath, trying to calm his nerves. "I promised."

She blinked again, looking disoriented for just a moment before the spark of fire returned to her eyes. "Why do you keep spouting such outrageous lies? Do I look so dense as to believe your fairy tales?"

For a moment he'd found a semblance of calm. But he'd learned the hard way that she could raise his anger like no one else. Raven gritted his teeth. "What if I paid you?"

"What?"

"Come with me," he said, keeping his tone carefully even. "When we reach River Bluffs, if you find you don't want to stay, if you find it's all a lie, I'll pay you, just for your trouble."

For a moment words failed her. "I don't want your filthy money. I want to return to my father. He needs me."

Raven took the two strides between them before he could stop himself, and though he felt like shaking her, he only allowed himself to grab one arm and hold it in a steady grip.

"Jude's not your father," he said, teeth clenched as he glared at her.

She gasped and tried to pull away, but he refused to loosen his hold, though her haughty expression had fled, and terror now ruled her face.

"You still expect me to believe that?" Her words were no more than a shaky whisper. "You expect me to believe *you* and not Jude who's cared for me all my life."

"Not *all* your life," Raven said. "What about your mother? What about the woman in the portrait? Caroline Grady. She had eyes like yours. Bright as an April morning, Eloise said. And her hair was long, like yours."

Perhaps he imagined it, but it seemed she paled a shade. "I don't believe a word you say. Not a word," she said hoarsely as she tried to jerk away.

Raven held her fast. "I don't give a good God damn if you believe me or not!" he rejoined. "You'll come along. If I have to shackle you like a runaway slave and carry you every step of the way."

But with a twist and a jerk she was free and running. He reached her in a dozen strides, but as he dragged her about, she turned wildly and stabbed him.

Pain slammed through Raven's chest. He staggered, stunned by agony and shock. Charm drew back the branch with a gasp and stared at the bloody end in horror.

Chapter 11

Charm backed away, dropping the stick, feeling her limbs go numb and cold with fear.

Raven gazed at the tattered, bloody hole in his shirt, then swore aloud and advanced. Terror screamed through Charm's system and she shrank back. Ready to feel his wrath in the power of his fists, she weakly raised an arm to ward off his blows.

But the attack never came. Instead, the arm she'd raised for protection was wrenched from her face, and suddenly she was dragged toward the leopard-spotted gelding who waited in the distance.

The hours passed like an endless nightmare. Charm rode in front of Raven, with her knees on either side of the saddle horn and her back to his chest. Despite the double load, the gelding moved quickly and freely beneath them, and yet each step was agony for Charm. Though the unnatural position burned her thighs and bottom, it was Raven's frightening wrath and proximity that made the journey most unbearable.

Where were they going? And what would he do to her when they reached their destination? She hadn't meant to stab him, but the old, familiar terror had seized her and she had struck out without thought.

The day wore on. Raven had found a small cache of food in the saddle bags. They ate sparingly, taking a little bread and chewing on the dried jerky as they rode. It tasted and looked rather like salty leather and caused them to stop several times at fast-flowing streams where they slaked their thirst and watered the horse. Even at these times, Raven didn't speak.

The sun was hot, the air still. Fatigue weighed heavily on Charm. She'd slept very little on the previous night and found now that she was losing the battle to stay awake and alert. She knew better than to trust the man behind her, but finally the tune of *Old Dan Tucker* eased her tension. It was Jude's favorite ditty. Although he sang in a husky, out-of-tune voice, she had always loved to hear him sing, for it made her feel secure. Charm snuggled deeper under her quilt, but found suddenly that there was no quilt, and that the voice was not Jude's. It was Raven's. Fear and memories sparked and converged. She caught her breath and lifted her gaze to the dark, solemn eyes of the man behind her. With a start, she jerked her weight away from his chest, hearing his half-concealed groan of pain caused by her movement.

To her horror Charm realized that her knees were bare. Her grubby, scarlet gown and all three petticoats had worked their way up as she slept. She jerked them rapidly down, her heart pounding, but Raven made no move and said nothing.

Charm rode on in uncomfortable, bemused silence, feeling her pulse slow with the passing of time. Who was this man who sat behind her? He didn't fit into Jude's description of men, for regardless of how she'd treated him, he had not raised a hand to her. And while these facts should have comforted her, Charm only felt more confused and uncertain.

The woods ended abruptly, making way for a level bit of grassland beside a rapid stream.

"We'll stop here."

She drew her breath in sharply at the sound of Raven's voice and found a hundred frightening scenarios crowding in on her. "Why?"

"We can't make it to Red Rock tonight," he said. The words seemed more for himself than for her as he swung stiffly from the gelding's back, taking one rein with him. Charm darted her gaze to the surrounding woods. She wondered if she could make an escape now, but when she looked down from the horse, Raven was watching her, his expression hard, suggesting no leniency.

"I'm not going to escape," she said.

He watched her in silence, then turned, leading the horse to the stream where he slipped the bit from its mouth, leaving only the leather halter beneath. Walking a few strides away, Raven knelt, seeming to ignore Charm as she slid from her uncomfortable perch on the pommel to the hard, worn seat of the saddle.

It didn't take her long to begin to feel silly, for the gelding was now free to roam at will, and soon did so, wandering from the water's edge in search of grass. Eventually, Charm jolted to the ground to find her legs even more cramped than she'd expected. For a moment she was immobilized by the pain that shot from her back to her shins. But finally her muscles loosened and she straightened, rolling back her shoulders and taking a few experimental steps.

With the coming of darkness and some semblance of agility restored, Charm again considered escape, although she refused to turn her gaze toward the woods, lest Raven see her thoughts a second time. In the end, it was not only the lure of fresh water that drew her, but Raven's blatant disregard. Slowly approaching the stream, she finally squatted down, letting the water wash over her sunburned hands as she stared at the moon-gilded crests of the chattering creek.

Some twenty feet downstream, Raven drew the shirt from his body. Charm quickly turned her face away, feeling a hot sweep of blood color her cheeks. Jude had warned her about all of this. Lustful men, wanting only one thing, forcing themselves on poor innocent women.

Only . . . Raven didn't seem to be lustful. In fact, his movements were slow and pained, and he certainly wasn't forcing himself upon her. In the quiet darkness, she saw him lean toward the swift-flowing water and caught the sight of blood, dark even against his tanned skin.

As for calling herself an innocent woman, the thought suddenly seemed rather ludicrous. Charm grimaced, feeling a surge of confusing guilt for her actions.

"Does it hurt?"

Her question surprised them both.

Raven turned his head to find her in the darkness. "Wasn't that the intent?"

"No." Her answer came out as a breathy denial. "I only wanted to escape."

He turned his gaze back to the water. "Same thing."

"No, it's not." Why she felt any compulsion to explain herself, Charm didn't know. Nevertheless, she rose to stiffly take a few stilted steps toward him. "Why are you doing this?"

For a moment he was silent as he splashed water against his bare torso. "You're a smart girl. You figure it out," he said finally.

Her bemusement was almost a palpable thing. He wondered if she would take this opportunity to escape. Some weakened and battered part of him almost hoped she would. Good God, this couldn't be worth it. If exposing himself to the company of the killer woman wasn't bad enough, there was also the risk of being caught and accused of abduction—an offense he could be hanged for. As if she were an innocent babe that needed protection. When in truth, it was *he* who needed protection.

"Does it hurt?" she repeated.

He hadn't heard her approach, but found her nearness surprised him considerably less than her tone. If he hadn't known better he would have sworn she sounded distressed. Raven gritted his teeth and reminded himself of her deadly ways. If he said no, what would she do to remedy the situation? "Excuse me for saying so," he said, staunchly trying to ignore the ripping pain causing by the washing of his wound, "but that's one of the most idiotic questions I've ever heard."

She stood very still, looking down at him, her face shadowed in the moonlight. Something tightened in Raven's gut. He swore mentally. This was, he reminded himself, another unstimulating situation—defiantly unstimulating— so why did his body insist on disagreeing when all she was doing was standing there? There was nothing seductive about standing there. Hell, a *rock* could do the same. He shifted his weight slightly, condemning the foolishness of the male form.

"Did you come to gloat?" he asked finally, his tone purposefully flat as he watched the play of moonlight on the water.

"I came to . . ." She paused and thrust her hand into a pocket of her gown, as if in search of some kind of security. But the pocket was empty of weapons. "I used to . . . tend my father sometimes."

Despite his discipline, Raven couldn't quite hide his surprise. Was she offering to help him, or was he losing his mind? A thousand possible comments mingled with a menagerie of questions, but Raven kept them all to himself, though he turned finally to watch her in silence.

"I'll . . ." She exhaled softly, as if even the simplest conversation with him was difficult. "I'll get the blankets."

In a matter of moments she was back and spreading a bedroll on a grassy spot not far from the bank of the stream. Raven waited, knowing better than to take anything for granted or to rush her. But also, there was the nagging question of his own safety. Was she offering a modicum of

kindness in the hopes of doing him even further damage?
Did she think him so weakened that she could now rid
herself of him forever? Maybe her pockets weren't empty.

That thought made Raven's breath catch in his throat, for
even the simplest of weapons could be deadly in the girl's
hand. He'd learned that much, and yet when she motioned
to him, he stood, feeling pain rip downward from his chest.

"I could build a fire to heat water for your wound."

Again her words surprised him, but in a moment he
realized how a blaze might bring her rescuers, or other
undesirable visitors. Indians for instance. "No fire," he said
flatly.

She drew a deep breath. The inhalation sounded shaky.
"Lie down."

He examined her in the darkness. When he was a boy, his
mother had read him stories of Samson. He wondered now
if Delilah's hair was the color of burnt sienna in the
moonlight, gleaming with highlights of red and gold to
brighten the wild mass of tresses.

"If you're going to shear me, I'd rather die standing up,"
he said, and though he couldn't see her expression in the
darkness, he wondered why he'd said such an idiotic thing.
He shuffled his feet, feeling uncharacteristically foolish
before explaining in one nonsensical word, "Delilah."

For a fraction of a moment, he thought he saw the fragile,
curved semblance of a smile.

"Are you saying I can't be trusted, or that you have the
strength of Samson?" she asked softly.

"Right now I don't have the strength of the sacrificial
lamb, so it must be the other."

Now he couldn't tell if she smiled or not.

"Lie down," she said.

He took a deep breath and after a pause did as he was
told, lying on his back to gaze up at the vast constellations
in the inky sky. The sound of ripping fabric made him jump.
He turned to Charm, forcing his muscles to relax, though he
was certain, for a moment, that she was grinning at his fear.

"I hope you're enjoying yourself?" he said through clenched teeth.

She didn't answer. Turning away, she walked to the babbling stream to soak a rag in the water. But in a moment she returned. "You forced me away from my father and stole my Bible," she reminded him and plopped the rag to his wound.

Raven sucked air through his teeth and caught her gaze. "He's not your father. And . . ." She scrubbed at the dried blood on his chest, making his words rasp to a halt, but he'd be damned before he'd admit his weakness. "Let's just say I'm *holding* your Bible for you." For a moment he thought he would lose consciousness, but he fought back the black tide and weakly added, "For safe keeping."

"It was safe with me . . . before you came along."

Although Raven tried to think of a rejoinder, her ministrations seared any clever response from his mind. "Good God, woman, can't you find a gentler way of killing me?"

She settled back on her heels. "My father never complained." Though her response was brusque, he noticed her face looked pale. "'Course, he was usually dead drunk by the time I got to him."

Raven relaxed somewhat against his blanket as he watched her face. "He isn't your father, Chantilly."

"Quit saying that." Her words were no louder than a whisper.

"Because you know I'm right?"

"No!" she answered vehemently and jerked to her feet.

It was sheer instinct that made Raven lunge up to grab her, yanking her to a halt. "Listen to me," he said, holding her arms with both hands and gritting his teeth against the surging pain in his chest. "Listen. Jude's not your father. Your father's name was Randall Grady. Jude lied to you."

"No!" she shrieked again, and jerking one hand free, flailed it wildly against his chest.

It hit his wound dead center. There was the sound of breath scraping through Raven's teeth before his hands fell away. Charm delayed not an instant but pivoted wildly about to charge into the surrounding woods. Her breath was loud in her ears, and her heart hammered against her ribs, but still she ran on until her toe snagged against a root and she fell, crashing against the earth. She lay stunned for just a moment, then marshaled her senses and dragged herself behind a rock to listen.

It was very dark under the shelter of the trees. And quiet. Surely she could hear him approaching if he were near. But he was tricky. She held her breath, listening.

There was no sound, except the dry rustle of a field mouse in last year's foliage. For a moment, Charm was certain it was the noise of Raven's feet against the dead leaves, but she covered her mouth with her palm and finally began to breathe more normally when she realized the source of the sound.

She'd lost him. Somehow she'd gotten away, but she couldn't trust to her luck for long. She'd have to move on before it was too late. It took her several minutes to dredge up enough nerve to peek over the boulder. There was no one in sight, and no noise of pursuit. Spying a small, sharp rock, Charm thrust it into a pocket and waited. The minutes marched away. Still no noise. Finally she crept out from behind her shelter. It was time to leave, to escape while she still could. Luckily she had a good sense of direction, honed by years of traveling and her own scalding fears. She knew what approximate direction they'd been traveling. She turned now, determined to hike back from whence they had come.

But they had ridden a long way. She stopped, thinking of the horse. It seemed a pity to leave such a nice animal with a madman. And besides, if she took the gelding, she not only would reach her destination much faster, but she would prevent Raven from following with any speed. Clenching her fist around the stone in her pocket, Charm considered the circumstances.

He was out there somewhere, searching for her. But

where? He'd assume she'd go as far as possible, which made doubling back the logical ploy.

It took some time for Charm to force herself back toward the stream. But finally she did so, creeping to the edge of the trees to gaze out into the relative brightness of the clearing.

In a moment she saw the horse. His spotted coat was like a beacon in the surrounding wilderness. But suddenly another form caught her attention. It was dark and still and crumpled, lying near the blankets.

Her breath caught in a hard inhalation, for she knew without a second thought. The crumpled form was Raven Scott.

Chapter 12

It was another of his tricks. Charm stayed very still, barely breathing as she watched the silent lump. Nothing moved, except for the horse, which wandered to the water's edge to splash in the stream and finally lie down to roll in the coarse sand. But his saddle was still aboard, and he stood, flipping his tail in vexation before dropping his head to graze again.

Surely Raven would get up now, go to the horse, remove the saddle. But he did not. In fact, he made no move at all. Perhaps it wasn't a trick. Perhaps he was dead.

Somehow the thought failed to thrill Charm. In fact, fear and dread strangled her. But no. He couldn't be dead. She'd thought that before and had been frightfully wrong. If the man could take a fall from a fifteen-foot loft and live, surely he could survive a little jab with a stick. After all, she was only a girl.

A mean girl, true, but a girl nevertheless. Of course he wasn't dead. But he was very still.

Finally something propelled her forward, her conscience or her fear, or her curiosity. Who could say which? But creep forward she did, slowly and cautiously, making very little noise upon the dry foliage. Coming to within an arm's length of him, she stopped, breathing hard, watching him with an unflinching gaze.

"I know you're awake." Her tone was unnaturally high-pitched. He would laugh at her for her obvious fear, she thought, but he didn't move. "Raven," she said, and finally calling forth all her courage, reached out to touch his shoulder.

The night was long and still and haunting. Raven Scott's skin was damp with sweat, and yet he shivered. Against his wishes and perhaps her own better judgment, Charm had built a fire over which to heat water.

She sat now, hugging her knees and listening to every sound. She'd heard stories about the Sioux's hatred of whites. It was said they were so quiet, you couldn't hear them move until your scalp was gone. It was said they made whistles and signals like birds.

A killdeer called and Charm jumped. She should leave. She'd done all she could. She had soaked the remainder of their bread in hot water and bound it tightly against his wound in the hopes of drawing out the poison.

It had not been an easy task, for he was heavy, packed with lean taut muscles, and much larger than she. She'd been somewhat surprised by his bulk in the dancing glow of her small fire. Around his neck, she'd found a chain, upon which dangled a strangely crafted ring, made of three strands of fine, interwoven wire. It intrigued her. She'd run her finger along the simple design before letting her hand slip along the rows of Raven's firmly fleshed ribs. But now he lay alone, wrapped in a crisscrossed petticoat bandage, dressed in his blood-encrusted shirt and covered with all the blankets they had between them. She could now leave with a clear conscience. In fact she rose to do just that. But somehow Raven had pushed a blanket aside, and she bent to pull it closer to him.

"Chantilly?"

She straightened abruptly. "No. It's Charm," she said, prepared to flee.

"Charm," he murmured. The moonlight stroked his dark features, gleaming on his blue-black hair. For a moment he looked painfully vulnerable, like a small boy with a fever. Yet his voice was husky, as Jude's was when she cared for him during a bout of sickness or after a drinking spree. But he wasn't Jude and she owed him no allegiance.

Their gazes met in the darkness.

"You're a hell of a fighter," he said softly, then lifted a hand to his chest, feeling the poultice and bandage through his shirt. "Your doing?" His tone sounded mildly surprised. Charm narrowed her eyes and allowed a single nod.

He drew a deep breath, looking weak. "Thank you."

She didn't remind him that if it hadn't been for her, he would never have been wounded. He was looking vulnerable again, and she didn't like that. After all, she knew better than to be weakened by sympathy. And he wasn't her responsibility. He'd abducted her and deserved any injury she could inflict.

"You lit a fire," he said quietly.

She pushed a fist into her pocket. "Needed warm water," she explained, gesturing toward his chest, "for the poultice."

"Not afraid of Indians?"

She didn't attempt to hide her fear, but pushed a stray wisp of hair from her face and scowled. "I was . . . afraid you were dead."

Not a sound disturbed the small clearing as they watched each other. His expression was very solemn, but she could not read his thoughts.

"Take the horse, Charm."

"What?"

For a moment he was quiet, then, "Take the horse and go. I'll make sure Clancy doesn't bother you."

What did he mean by that? And why was he setting her

free now? Of course, she owed him nothing, she reminded herself, and yet . . . She tightened her fist. "Get up."

His eyes narrowed, though he smiled shallowly. "You're not challenging me to a fist fight, are you?"

She scowled. "Get up," she repeated, and before she could change her mind, she hurried to fetch the gelding.

Charm slipped from behind the saddle, speaking softly to the horse as she did so. She had named him Angel, for he had been like a celestial guardian during the dark of night, and had brought her here, to the dubious safety of Red Rock. She patted the spotted neck, glancing at Raven as she did so. He was conscious now, and had been, at times, lucid enough to help her find the town. It was, like most communities in the Dakota Territory, little more than a transient camp. Yet, it had a few dozen wooden structures lining its packed-dirt streets.

After a few inquiries, Charm found the man she was looking for in the livery stable tending a mule.

"Steady, Angel," she said, addressing the horse as she led him into the livery. Mounded piles of straw lay on either side of the aisle. Angel moved placidly along, proving the appropriateness of the name she'd given him.

Up ahead a man was splashing water onto the side of a gargantuan mule.

"Are you Doc?" Charm asked wearily.

The man that turned to face her was well past middle age, slightly stooped and greying. "That's what they call me." He wore round, gold-rimmed spectacles, and looked like a mild-mannered man, one to be trusted, Charm decided. One to relieve her of Raven's care.

"This is Raven Scott," she said breathlessly. "He needs your help."

The old man stepped forward. "What happened to 'im?"

It was, Charm knew, a likely question. The answer, however, wasn't so simple. "He, ahh," she began, and winced. "I think he fell."

The doc reached up, moving Raven's shirt aside to study the bandage. "You do that?"

"Yes. But he needs professional help. And I can't . . . I can't stay."

"Can't stay?" Doc asked, stepping back to study her over his small wire rims.

"No! I have to get back to my father. He needs me. He's very . . ."

There was a movement to her left, and then, like a rock just pried from its lofty perch, Raven fell, plummeting to the straw at their feet.

"Ill," Charm finished weakly.

"And he ain't likely to heal up real quick if'n he keeps fallin' on his head," Doc proclaimed.

"I didn't mean *him*," Charm argued, hurrying forward.

But Doc was already bending over Raven and failed to notice her words. "Do you have any money?"

"I . . ." She shook her head, shocked and weary. "No."

"Does he?"

"I don't know," she said, and suddenly realized the man's miscalculation. "I'm not his—"

"Well, check his pockets," Doc interrupted as he opened Raven's shirt.

"But . . ."

"If you can pay, you can stay at the boardin' house. If you can't, you can most likely stay here in the stable, but the house would be healthier fer him. Check his pockets."

But Charm already knew what he had in his pants. Her Bible, and . . . other stuff. Stuff she shouldn't be touching.

"Really, I'm not his—"

"You want him to die here and now, lady?"

"Uhhh. No."

"Then find some money and we'll get him settled in someplace decent."

Perhaps it was Doc's understated authority that made her

finally comply. Whatever the reason, Charm did as told, pushing her hand tentatively into Raven's front pocket.

"What's going on?" he asked, suddenly opening his eyes.

Despite it all, she blushed. Once again, here she was with her hand thrust deep into places where it shouldn't be. "I . . ." Words failed her as she yanked her fingers from his pants. "Just . . ."

"Good. You're awake," said the doc, studying his patient's face with a calculating eye. "You got any money?"

"What's that?"

"Money. You'll need some to get a room. Widder Worth don't keep nobody for free."

"Money. Yes," Raven said weakly.

"Good. Now what happened to you?"

"Well . . ." Raven shook his head and slowly brought his fingers to his brow as if it ached. "It's rather blurry," he said, raising his gaze to Charm's.

She trapped her breath within the tight confines of her throat and waited.

"I think I fell," Raven deduced, holding her gaze.

"Looks t'be one hell of a wound for a fall. Course it's hard t'tell for sure, till I get a proper look at y'."

"Am I going to be all right?"

"Well . . ." Doc shook his head and settled stiffly back on his heels. "I hope so cuz I got Herbert t' worry about too."

"Herbert?" Raven asked.

"The mule," Doc explained, jerking a finger over his shoulder. "He's got mud fever."

Doc convinced two young men to carry Raven to Widow Worth's Boarding House. The room was scrupulously clean but seemed small when packed with four men, Mrs. Worth, and Charm.

"These here are the rules," said Worth, hands on her broad hips as she turned her scowl on Charm. "It'll be four bits a day, paid in advance. No smoking. No drinking." She frowned at Raven's bandaged chest, then back at Charm. "And if'n he dies, the widow pays the burial fees."

She was gone before Charm could deny being a bride much less a widow. In a moment Doc had stripped off Raven's bloody shirt and bandage, pushing the ring chain aside as he worked. The bread poultice came away in soggy pieces.

"You done a good job here," Doc said. "You had any nurse's training?"

"No."

"Want some?"

"No. I just want to get back to—"

"Well, he won't be traveling for a few days nohow." Doc pursed his lips and lifted his chin to stare through his lenses at Raven's exposed chest. "Though it don't look so bad as I thought it would. You been sick?" he asked, raising his gaze to Raven's face.

"No."

"Hum. You say you fell?"

"Yes," Charm said, then realized she shouldn't have answered. She drew a shaky breath. "Yes. Perhaps on a branch?" She paused. "There was a bloody one there. Maybe he fell on it, then rolled away."

"Could be," said Doc, but he looked dubious. "Still it don't seem like a fall on a stick would make a strappin' young man like him black out. How you feelin' now, boy?"

"My left arm is numb. Other than that, I'm fine," said Raven, but his weak tone belied his answer.

"Well." Doc frowned. "Maybe we'll find the hole goes deeper than it looks once we get it cleaned up good. Sometimes that happens. Now, someone'll have to ask the Widder fer hot water, bandages and soap. Who's gonna do it?"

It was amazing how fast the two hulking men could find work that could not be delayed another instant. Their exit was hurried and clattering.

"Guess that leaves you," said Doc. He didn't seem

surprised by the others' rapid exit as he continued to study Raven's wound while speaking to Charm.

"He's not my—" she began again, still trying to explain her lack of kinship to Raven, but Doc merely shook his head and interrupted.

"I'd ask her myself but . . ."—he slid his wire frames back up his nose—"she scares the hell outta me."

Charm planned to object, but just then Doc tentatively touched the wound. Raven emitted a gut-wrenching groan of pain, and retreat seemed the best of a series of lousy options.

True to Widow Worth's reputation, she was not pleasant to deal with. Nevertheless, she finally handed over a pitcher of hot water and a hard, chipped bar of lye soap. Bandages, she said, would have to be supplied by someone else. Charm hurried up the stairs, and Doc took the proffered items with a grunt of thanks.

"Old bat wouldn't give y' nothin' fer bandages?" he guessed, digging about in a carpetbag that he'd deposited at the bedside.

"She said she didn't have any."

"Mean as a snake-bit badger. I'll need your petticoat."

"But . . ." Charm scowled, thinking she'd donated enough of her personal garments to the well-being of a man she didn't even like. "You must have bandages. You're a doctor."

The chuckle that escaped Doc sounded rusty and wry. "I ain't really, girl. The folks in town here just call me that cuz I'm the closest thing they got. And it makes 'em feel more progressive t' give me the title, y' see."

"Oh." Her gaze slipped cautiously from the old man's face to Raven's. But that one's eyes were closed, though his expression looked pained. "Oh," she said again, suddenly finding a serious shortage of words in her repertoire.

"Listen, honey," said Doc softly. "If'n you don't want me carin' fer yer man, I'll sure nuf understand. I don't make a whole lot of compensation for this kind of work nohow. Mostly vegetables and the like. Though Mrs. Ellingson gives me a pint or so of strawberries every time little Amy comes down with the croup."

Charm decided that the past week had simply been too much for her, because despite everything, she could not come up with a single, intelligent thing to say. "Oh," was all she managed, and that rather weakly.

"He's gonna mend, honey," Doc said gently, tilting his head back to better peer through his spectacles into her face.

"What's that?"

"You're lookin' mighty peaked. But y' don't need t' worry so. Big strong fella like yers, he'll sure nuf heal up fine."

Now it wasn't a lack of words that kept Charm silent, but rather an uncertainty of what to deny first. That he was her husband, that she didn't care a whit if he lived or died, or that she was not peaked. In fact, she considered telling the old gentleman that she was the one who had caused Raven's wound in the first place, just to prove that very point, but already it was too late, for he was talking again.

"Well, what do you think? I have t' be goin', cuz I still got Herbert t' worry about, and that mud fever can be a real pig t' get rid of. Y' see, the clay, it builds up on the animal's bellies. Then they cain't sweat, and then they . . ." He tilted his head back again. "Suppose yer not interested in Herbert. But anyhow, I left Frank watching him, and he don't know spit."

For a moment Charm stood dazedly wondering if it was Frank or the mule that was short of wits. Probably Frank, she deduced, because Herbert had looked quite intelligent. On the other hand . . .

"Honey." Doc broke her reverie. "Am I gonna get them petticoats or not?"

"Oh." She considered refusing, but, after all, her petticoats were little more than shreds anyway. In a few minutes they were bandages.

What Doc may have lacked in medical training, he made up for in efficiency. Miraculously, he even managed to raise a few suds from the hard lye soap. In a matter of just a few more minutes he had Raven's wound absolutely clean. A brown, glass bottle was uncorked and an oily substance poured into the lesion.

Though Raven's eyes didn't open, his fingers clenched the blanket beneath him and his body jerked.

Charm winced. "What is that stuff?"

"Kerosene?"

She crammed her fist into her pocket, reminding herself that Raven deserved worse. "What'll it do for him?"

"Don't know," Doc said, quickly trussing Raven in the petticoat bandages. "But it does wonders for pus in the hoof. Now." He finished up and stood, pressing his knuckles to his back. "Y' gotta unwrap him once a day, douse 'im with that stuff, and bandage him up again."

"But . . ." Charm scowled at the bottle. "It must sting like the devil."

Doc raised his chin so as to study her through his narrow lenses. "If'n y' didn't want 'im t'hurt, honey, y' shouldn't a stabbed him," he reasoned, and retrieving his carpet bag, left Charm to stare after him in utter bemusement.

Chapter 13

Raven woke with a start and lurched upright. His chest burned like fire, and he was ravenously hungry, but his first concern was the whereabouts of his quarry. Chantilly. Where was she?

"What's wrong?"

Her voice came, quick and startled from beside his bed. Raven calmed, finding her in the darkness. He must have scared her, he deduced and mentally smiled, hoping he had paid her back a small whit for all she'd put him through. But no. That would take a good deal more. Pretending he'd fainted had been bad enough! But getting kerosene poured in an open wound! He shivered, remembering the pain.

"Charm," he said in a soft tone perfectly groomed for the occasion. "I was afraid you'd left."

She rose, and he wondered if she'd been sleeping in the chair, though she seemed to possess her usual alertness now. "I'm here." Her stance was stiff, as was her tone.

"Oh." He sighed heavily. "I thought I was alone." A pause, pressing her for a response.

"No."

One thing about this girl, he thought wryly, she was full of warmth and caring. Rather like a grizzly with a toothache.

"I didn't mean to frighten you," he said softly.

"You didn't," she lied and he chuckled, making sure the sound was self-deprecating rather than insulting.

"Foolish of me, I suppose, to think everyone's afraid of the dark."

It took her a moment to speak, but she did finally, her tone, thank heaven, surprised. "You're afraid of the dark?"

"Terrible thing for a grown man to admit." He leaned back slightly, as if expecting support to be behind him. But there was none, so he sat upright again with a quiet groan of pain.

It took her a moment, but she stepped forward finally to brace two plump, down pillows against his back.

"Thank you." The words sounded marvelously breathy, he thought, as if he were unworthy of her unexpected kindness. God, he was good. "I, um . . ." He looked away from her face, partly because it would prove his embarrassment regarding the subject, and partly because the sight of her distracted him from his mission, even in this dim light. "When I was a boy, I was left alone a lot at night."

She was absolutely silent. He could feel her watching him.

"My mother worked while the rest of the world slept. Don't get the wrong idea. She did nothing immoral. Ever," he added quietly, then almost scowled. He shouldn't have said that, for such words called forth too-real memories, and too much truth was a bad idea. "She was a scullery maid of sorts." He paused, seeing, against his will, his mother's face, and his own lean, hawkish image as a boy. Raven, the other children had dubbed him, for he'd possessed the dark, hungry visage of a predator.

His mother, on the other hand, had been beautiful, even when she died, still too optimistic, too soon, too damned young! "Cleaned house for the wealthy. Businesses, that sort of thing," Raven said softly.

The room was very dark, with a single, slanted rectangle of moonlight falling over the foot of the bed. He could hear Charm shuffle her feet. "Where was your father?"

Raven pressed his teeth together and narrowed his eyes in the darkness, glad she couldn't see his expression. Although the girl was playing directly into his hands, her question still raised emotions that should have been long dead. "He left."

He could hear the soft intake of breath. "I'm sorry."

Now why would she say a thing like that? But, of course, he wanted her to be sorry. He'd soften her with her own feminine emotions, woo her with sensitivity and melancholy, then let her spill her troubles upon his broad shoulders. Women loved to talk about themselves, to have someone to tell their sorrows to. She would come to trust him, and then she would agree to do whatever he wished her to do. It was a good plan. Much better than force, which he'd tried. It had gained him little more than the original and irreplaceable sensation of kerosene in a stick wound.

Appealing to her feminine side was an idea that had been slowly hatching, but now, after all he'd been through, he was committed to the plan. She must have a feminine side, he'd deduced. After all, she was decidedly and unarguably female. Thus, when she'd raced off into the woods, he'd let her go, though he'd felt like a first-rate fool, lying on the hard ground like a dying dog and waiting for her to return. It had seemed like hours, and for some time he'd been certain she wouldn't come back, but she had. And she'd brought him here, which was proof of something, though he wasn't sure what.

"How old were you when your father left?" she asked now, her voice very quiet.

"Less than two." The truth again. Raven reprimanded himself sternly for his honesty, but sometimes it was simply easier than fabrications.

"But . . . why?" She sounded shocked, as if such things

were unheard of, when in fact, he could have assured her, they were not.

"It's a funny thing." Raven leaned against the bed's headboard, feeling the cool, smooth pine against the back of his skull and drawing a deep breath through his nostrils. As the air swelled his chest, he was reminded of the ache there. "She never gave up hope."

"Your mother?"

He nodded once, noticing how the narrow frame of diffused light washed the far wall to a pale creamy white. "Her name was Abigail." He scowled at nothing in particular. "She could have married again. She was still young, though I guess I didn't realize it at the time. But she was pretty. Even as a scrawny, troublesome kid I knew that."

"Black hair?" she asked quietly. "Like yours?"

"No. It was the color of wheat straw. I remember her brushing it out. Very long and so soft. It would fall against my face sometimes when she kissed me good night." He laughed, though he could still feel the scowl imprinted on his face. "Always smelled like lye." Raven paused, steadying his nerves. "She used to sing me to sleep."

"'Old Dan Tucker'?"

Raven turned toward her in surprise but realized in a moment that it had been a mistake, for the moonlight stroked her features like a lover's hand. He pulled breath through his nostrils again, but the ensuing pain failed to remind him to distrust her. "How'd you know?"

"You were singing it while we rode."

Ahh yes. He'd sung yesterday to keep himself awake and lucid.

"My father used to sing 'Dan Tucker' to me sometimes."

She looked smaller in the darkness, and less deadly. Very like a young frightened woman, actually. Which, he supposed, was exactly what she was, when she wasn't trying to dismember him. "Really?" he said now. "Jude?" He didn't say again that the old man wasn't her father. So far that sort of statement had done very little to endear him to her. "He doesn't seem like the singing kind."

For a moment, Raven wondered if she smiled. He wished suddenly that the room was better lit, so that he could tell for certain. Not that her smiles were important to him, but every man enjoyed the sight of a beautiful woman, even if she was apt to kill him in the next moment.

"He isn't," she answered finally. "But sometimes he reminisced and . . ." She shrugged.

"Tell me about your childhood." Though Raven made the request very softly, he saw her stiffen.

"Why?"

"Because I'm interested." The answer came too easily and too low. Raven scowled mentally, retracking his thoughts and disciplining his words. "I'm sorry," he corrected, turning calculatingly away. "I have no right to ask. Not after what I've put you through."

Utter silence settled over the place, until it seemed he could feel her thoughts.

"Do you still think I'm this Chantilly person?"

He waited before responding, turning toward her again and drawing out the quiet. "It doesn't matter now. In your heart you're Charm Fergusson. Jude's daughter."

"I *am* Jude's daughter," she said, but quietly now, so that he wasn't certain if she tried to convince him or herself.

"Yes, well . . ." He turned abruptly back toward the wall, momentarily losing control of his words and emotions. "He's been a hell of a lot more father than I've had."

Bleak silence again, unbroken and dark.

"Did you ever imagine him?"

"What's that?" Raven asked, drawn quickly from his sullen reverie.

"As a child, did you ever imagine what he would be like?" Her words were almost inaudible now, as if she'd reached into her soul for them. "I used to imagine my mother."

Her hands were clasped before her as she spoke, and the

moonlight splashed across her knuckles. The sharp ridges looked very pale, he thought.

"She was beautiful, of course. And she laughed a lot. And . . ." Her voice trailed off.

To Raven's abject horror, he found he was holding his breath as he waited for her to continue. "And?" he finally prompted, his voice no louder than hers.

"And she adored me," Charm finished weakly, trying to laugh a little at her own silly sentiment, but emitting the sound on a shaky note. She shuffled about a little, as if wishing to escape, but in the end her movements stilled and she drew a soft breath. "Did you ever imagine such foolish things?" she whispered.

"All the time," he whispered back. His throat felt curiously tight.

"When you were alone at night?"

"Yes."

It was quiet again, but now the silence felt different, comfortable almost, soothing.

"Jude used to leave me alone." The words came, as if unbidden.

"I'm sorry."

She sighed. "It's a foolish thing, I suppose. I mean . . . You might have noticed, I'm not real . . . Well, I'm not real good with people."

Raven smiled, just a little, supposing her propensity toward murder might indeed make her less than desirable at most social gatherings.

"I mean, people make me nervous. Men especially. But I . . ." She shrugged again. "Being alone is very . . ."

"Frightening?"

She didn't answer, and he felt her draw away emotionally, as if the admission of fear might somehow endanger her.

Raven swiftly turned aside, wanting to reconnect with her for more reasons than he dared admit. The realization was sobering, making him stare at the wall in silent thought for a moment.

"Perhaps I was a little afraid. When I was young," she admitted warily.

He turned back toward her very slowly. It was as if she'd offered him a thread of trust. Despite everything he was, he felt unable to do anything but hold that trust gently, as one would a wounded sparrow. "I don't see how the old man could have left you alone."

It was her turn to look away now, throwing the slanted light across her face at a different angle. "It was hard for him to fit me into his way of life. He did the best he could. But still sometimes I felt . . ." She stopped her words, as if feeling guilty for suggesting Jude to be less than perfect. "He was all I had."

Although Raven heard her words, he also read her meaning. Jude was all she had while she was a girl, and things had not changed. He was all she had now. Somehow that single statement seemed to cast a different light on her actions. The old man was her security. Without him she had no one. Little wonder, then, that she would fight to return to him.

"Did he always gamble?"

She hesitated for a moment. "Always."

"Mine too."

"What?" He could almost hear the scowl in her question.

"My old man. He left to play the riverboats. Promised to be back in a month or less. But he never meant to return." There was acid in his tone again. And he wondered, with less concern than necessary, whether Charm could hear it.

"How do you know that?"

"Because he didn't come," Raven said flatly.

"There could have been a thousand things that kept him from returning."

"Nothing would stop me," he said, holding her gaze with his own. "Not if I promised." It took him only a second to realize his mistake. He'd already told her he'd promised to return her to her aunt, and now he reiterated his obsession with fulfilling his vows. It wasn't smart. Not when he wanted her to forget his mission, at least for the night. But if she was disturbed by his words, she gave no sign. In fact, she shifted her weight slightly, as if she were weary and unconcerned with his slipup.

"I'm sorry." His tone was a little more sincere than he had planned. "You must be exhausted. I didn't mean to wake you."

"Oh." He heard her draw a deep breath. "I don't really sleep."

"Ever?"

"Snatches."

"Were you snatching when I scared you?"

Miraculously, she didn't deny her fright now, but hedged quietly. "I'm not, ahhh, accustomed to sleeping in strange men's bedchambers."

Raven could think of a good dozen clever rejoinders for that statement. He squelched them all. "The chair must be uncomfortable."

"No. It's fine."

Considering what a marvelously talented liar she was, he thought she could do better. "You could sit here," he said softly, "on the bed."

She backed away immediately, as if slapped.

He took a slow breath, trying to keep quiet. The words came nevertheless. "I wouldn't touch you. I promise."

She laughed. The sound was unnatural. "That's insane."

"Yes." There was little he could do but agree. For the situation was indeed insane. "But perhaps it's not our fault." And perhaps he'd thrown her off guard with his statement, for he could hear the perplexity in her voice when she next spoke.

"What do you mean?"

"Me raised by a mother who refused to disbelieve in the good of the bastard she married, and you with no mother to care for you. Who could expect us to be normal?"

"Who could even *identify* normal?" she asked softly.

It was the most honest thing he'd heard her say. "I

wouldn't touch you," he repeated, the words coming of their own accord.

If the hand of God had reached down and plucked him from the mattress, Raven couldn't have been more surprised than when she actually complied. She moved one foot slowly in front of the other until she sat, stiff as a rock upon the straw-filled tick.

It was the strangest sensation. As if he'd never had a woman in his bed before. But of course, this was different. She wasn't actually *in* his bed. She was on it. And just barely that, for she was perched at the very edge of the thing, making him afraid to sneeze, lest he project her right through the wall. Perhaps it would be best to talk in order to ease her nervousness. But suddenly he was fresh out of words and felt like an idiot. Like an untried boy, dazzled by the proximity of a beautiful woman.

"I . . ."

They both said the word at the same time, then laughed nervously.

"Go ahead," Raven suggested, watching her carefully and noticing with appreciation that she was positioned directly in that single, kindly shaft of moonlight.

"I was just wondering how you came by the name of Raven."

He remained silent for a moment, then, "Why?"

Apparently the redundancy of their conversation wasn't lost on her, for she answered exactly as he had. "Because I'm interested."

Raven remained silent. He'd meant to appeal to her emotions, of course, had meant to soften her with gentle words, but he'd never intended to dredge up his entire past. He didn't like dredging. Never had. Despite the discipline with which he surrounded himself, the past still gnawed at the dangling ends of his memories.

"We were very poor." He wasn't sure where the words came from. He hadn't intended to say them, but she was very close, within inches, and watching him with those

forest-green eyes. Talking seemed like the wisest and safest
option open to him. "Without a man to support us, Mother
had to work very hard just to keep us alive. Only . . ."
He glanced toward the window, reminding himself not to
grind his teeth. "Only just staying alive wasn't enough. She
said my father was an educated man. She was always so
proud of his schooling. His intelligence. 'He'll come back to
us,' she'd say." He paused now, feeling his gut wrench and
hating himself for this childish weakness. Good God, he
was a full-grown man, not some sniveling whelp. "'And
when he comes back I ain't gonna have him find you
ignorant like your mama,' " she used to tell me. He paused,
taking a deep, slow breath. " 'You got to take the bad with
the good,' " he murmured, momentarily forgetting his audi-
ence to visualize his mother's weary smile. " 'We'll just
have to do the best we can until he returns. He'll be so proud
of you, Joseph.' " Raven's throat burned, as did his chest.
"She must have said it a thousand times."

"You were so lucky."

"Lucky!" Raven canted his head in disbelief. "Lucky?"
he breathed.

"She loved you," Charm whispered, as if there was
nothing in the world more important than that.

Raven stared at her, seeing the stark pain of her expression and feeling the sight burn into his soul. He filled his
lungs with air, trying to shake the raw emotions. But it
was no use. He took another deep breath. "I'm very tired."
It was a lie, of course. He was wide-awake. He was just a
coward. "I'd best sleep," he said, and waited for her to move
away. But perhaps she knew he was lying. Perhaps she
could read it in his expression.

"You haven't explained your name."

No, goddamn it. He hadn't, he wanted to snap, but
something stopped him. He could only hope it was his need
to groom her sympathy and trust. He settled his head back.
"It cost Mother everything she could scrape together to keep
me in school." He smiled, feeling the grimness of it curl his

lips. "I was a big kid. Could have worked. Never was sure how she convinced the schoolmaster to keep me around. I was a troublemaker." He looked out the window again, thinking. "She always seemed so mild-mannered and gentle, but when she set her cap on something . . ." He shook his head. "She'd set her cap on my education."

She still watched him closely, but said nothing.

"School was easy enough, but I didn't fit in. They all had rich daddies," he explained simply. "For a while they called me Bastard. Raven was a big improvement. They commented on the darkness of my skin and hair, and speculated about my heritage. Thought maybe my father had been a darkie. An unforgivable sin, of course," he mused, then straightened slightly, drawing himself from his reverie. "They called me Raven just to remind me of my place in the world."

"I'm so sorry," she whispered.

Please don't be sorry, he wanted to plead, for her pity made his chest ache and his resolution crumble.

"So very sorry."

The ache in his chest was too low to be associated with his wound. He swallowed once. Hadn't he planned for her to talk about herself? "Get some sleep," he said gruffly.

"I don't sleep," she reminded him.

Then come here and let me hold you. Let me wrap you in my arms and cuddle you against my heart. Let me kiss your funny little turned-up mouth and stroke your hair until you relax in my embrace. Let me . . .

Good God! What was wrong with him? He was losing his edge. Hell, he was losing his *mind*! Raven tightened the muscles in his jaws until his teeth ached. He had to get himself under control. This was a job. A very lucrative job. And she was a murderous little . . .

"The dreams always find me, sooner or later," she went on.

She certainly didn't *look* murderous, and she didn't sound murderous. In fact, her tone was so soft and earnest that he almost reached for her. But he wouldn't. He ground his teeth again. He would play his scheme and play it well. And that scheme did *not* include frightening her away with his own painful desires.

"I'm sorry," she said quietly. "You need rest. I shouldn't have—"

"The bed's big enough for two." He didn't know what possessed him to say it, except that he was a half-witted idiot who thought with his crotch. He refused to let himself believe he also thought with his heart. He couldn't afford feelings.

Her mouth opened a small bit, and she stared at him, her eyes very wide. "I—"

"You're safe with me." No! She wasn't! She wasn't safe! Good God, it had been half an eternity since he'd had a woman, *any* woman, in his bed. He'd be a simpleton to think he could resist *this* one. "I won't touch you. I promise."

"All right," she breathed, and Raven ground his teeth.

Chapter 14

They lay side by side, like two oaken planks, not looking at each other, not speaking, barely daring to breathe.

"Aren't you cold?" Raven asked finally.

"No!" She'd answered too quickly, Charm thought, berating herself. There was nothing to fear. The man was wounded—by her. She winced. It made practical good sense that she share the bed. After all, she was exhausted. She tried to relax, but it was impossible.

"Are you sure?"

She jerked at the sound of his voice, almost as if she'd forgotten he was there, though she most definitely had not. "What?"

"Are you sure you're not cold?"

"No. I mean . . . yes!" She nodded stiffly at the ceiling. "I'm sure."

Though she didn't look at him, she could hear the grin in his voice. "You know, I'm completely dressed."

"What?" she managed to ask again, but the word sounded ridiculously breathy. What was wrong with her? She was a grown woman, and though it was true that such behavior would ruin a lady's reputation, her unorthodox life had already done that. It was a fact she'd easily learned to live with. Hence, there was no reason for her to be so terrified. After all, he'd promised not to touch her, and for whatever reason, she believed him to be a man who kept his vows.

"I'm clothed," he repeated. "You could come under the covers."

"Not cold!"

He was staring at her. She could feel his gaze but refused to turn to meet it.

"Have you ever . . ." He paused as if searching for the correct phrase. "Have you ever been wooed, Miss Fergusson?"

"Wooed?" Her voice sounded pathetically squeaky. She swallowed and lowered the tone. "I've been busy. Taking care of my father, you know. And traveling about. And . . ."

"Little wonder you're afraid of men. They must come crawling out of the woods, clambering for your attention."

There was a slight groaning of bed ropes as he shifted his weight. Charm took a deep breath and woodenly turned her head toward him. His proximity made her start back in surprise, for he was not two feet away. And he wasn't *fully* dressed. There were whole inches of his chest exposed above the stark whiteness of his petticoat bandages.

"Jude is probably wise after all." His voice was very soft.

For a moment she said nothing, but finally curiosity won her over. "Why?"

"To keep them all at arm's length. Being near you—it could drive most any man past the point of restraint." He said the words very sincerely, as if he, too, might feel some temptation to do more than just talk, and yet, surprisingly, his admittance didn't increase her fear. In fact, it did the opposite. She drew a deep breath.

"Perhaps my father's impression of men is colored by his own failings. He never forgave himself for my mother's death. Said if he hadn't . . . hadn't touched her, she would have been far better off."

"Maybe he's right."

"But then I would never have been born," she reasoned softly. It was an argument she had often waged in her own head, wondering if Jude regretted her birth, regretted the responsibility of caring for her for all those years. The thought had stung her in the past and did so now. She turned her body slightly toward Raven, feeling the old pain and worry assault her. "Do you think he wished I'd never been born?"

Raven lifted a hand from atop the coverlet, reaching toward her before slowly pulling it back. "No man could wish that," he murmured.

Charm remained very still, feeling his words warm her like hot buttered rum. "If you had a wife," she whispered, "would you want a daughter like me?"

He stared at her, his gaze steady and unmoving.

"With or without a wife," he murmured, "I'd give my life for a daughter like you."

Raven awoke first. She was still atop the coverlet, her emerald eyes hidden by dark-fringed lids. Was she sound asleep or just snatching? He moved the slightest bit, and his question was immediately answered.

Her eyes were instantly wide. In a fractured second, she was on her feet beside the bed, but in a moment her surprise turned to silent wariness. Raven remained as he was, careful not to move.

"Good morning." Even his tone didn't waver. It was flat and smooth. He deserved some credit for that, he thought, not to mention his astounding self-control during the night. For though one could argue that it was his weakness and fatigue that allowed her to remain untouched, the hard-edged readiness of his body would vociferously disagree with that argument.

She blinked at him and tightened her narrow hands into fists. Her long hair was tousled and shone in gleaming hues of chestnuts and browns as it caught the slanted rays of the morning sun through the window. Raven studied her in silence. He was naturally skeptical and conservative in his estimations of others. He decided quite pragmatically that she was, nevertheless, the most exquisite creature ever to grace the earth.

"Did you sleep well?" he asked softly.

She swallowed, as if afraid to speak, but finally managed a single word. "Snatches."

He grinned a little, because seeing her thus, it was impossible to do otherwise. "Did you snatch well?"

Good God, she smiled back! Raven held his breath, watching as her curved, strawberry lips lifted momentarily into a whimsical, heartrending expression of humor.

Her fists unclenched to push her long slim fingers through her rumpled curls. "Are you feeling better?"

For a moment he couldn't speak. It was foolish, he knew. But when she looked at him like that, with her eyes morning bright and her manner soft as a lover's sigh, all words disappeared from his mind. "Much better," he managed finally, his voice a bit too husky. For a man who had spent most of his life carefully regulating how the world perceived him, she certainly had the ability to cut him to base honesty. It was, once again, a disconcerting thought and one that caused him to say more, perhaps in an attempt to fluster her. "I think sleeping with you has healed me."

To his surprise she didn't back away, but stood her ground though she blushed a rosy hue. As if seeing her tousled and soft wasn't enough. Tousled and soft and blushing was almost more than he could bear. Raven clenched his teeth, fighting for self-control.

"Are you . . ." She drew a deep breath. "You must be hungry."

He could eat her whole, right down to her tight-laced shoes if that was what she meant. "You still have them on," he said, nodding toward her feet. "I think I could have controlled myself, even had you made so bold as to expose your toes."

Her blush deepened, spreading down the smooth expanse of her throat toward her breasts. "Or . . . perhaps not," he admitted reluctantly.

There was a long moment of silence before she made any response. "Are you teasing me?"

What would happen if he moved very slowly from the bed? If he took her ever so gently into his arms and kissed her? How dangerous could it be? "No." He remained exactly where he was. "I'm flirting with you."

"Oh." She said the word very seriously. "Why?"

"Haven't you ever flirted, Miss Fergusson?"

She bit the inside of her lip, looking philosophical. "My conversations with men have rarely lasted very long in the past." She paused, blinking. "And usually involve weapons."

Raven laughed, knowing he was foolish to allow himself to be charmed by her. "If I sat up, would you run screaming from the room?"

"Probably."

"But how would you explain your actions to Widow Worth?"

Charm scowled. "She thinks we're wed."

Raven didn't resist the smile that tugged at his lips. "I realize that. But I have a cramp in my leg. Sooner or later I'm going to have to move."

The smallest hint of a grin appeared at the corner of her lovely mouth again. "All right. I won't scream."

"How about the running part?"

"I'll try not to."

Raven sighed. "A man can't ask more than that." He turned slowly over. Feeling pain rip through his chest, he winced and levered himself up against the headboard. "I think it would have been less painful if I'd allowed you to keep your gun."

She scowled a question.

"Of course, I'd be dead," he explained quietly.

She stared at her shoes again, looking guilty. "I've never actually shot anyone."

Raven was surprised to discover that he didn't especially like her to look ashamed.

For a moment he almost laughed, but she looked too mournful for him to allow a guffaw. "Really?" Even without the laughter his question sounded humorous, he thought, but she took his words at face value.

"Really." Her expression was absolutely earnest. "But I'm a very good shot," she assured him rapidly. "Jude taught me."

"I'm certain he did."

She was watching him point-blank, with her mesmerizing eyes such a deep emerald shade that he felt he would drown in their wide depths.

"Are you flirting with me again?" she asked, her voice low and husky.

The way Raven saw it, he had two options. He could drag her into bed and satisfy the raging lust that consumed him. Or he could demand that she leave the room right now. He did neither, but sat in rigid, characteristic self-control. "Yes, Miss Fergusson, I am flirting with you."

"Oh," she breathed. "And how am I supposed to react?"

"You might smother me with kisses." God, what a stupid thing to say! "I didn't mean it, Charm," he said quickly before she could back away. "It's just that you're so . . ."

She stared at him, waiting.

"So . . ." Irresistible. Dangerously alluring. "You're fun to flirt with."

"I am?" For some reason he thought she'd quit breathing. "Why?"

It would be wise not to answer, he knew. "Because you're beautiful and charming and innocent."

She scowled. "I stabbed you with a stick."

Raven tried to grin, but it didn't quite work. It seemed hot in the room and rather stifling, as if something were consuming all the air. "I didn't mean that kind of innocent."

"Oh. You mean that I haven't . . ." She winced, seeming to work very hard to find the proper words. "I haven't . . ."

He watched her struggle and would have helped if he could, but there wasn't a single word he could come up with that wouldn't make the ache in his lower body burn even brighter.

"That I haven't . . . ," she repeated.

"Charm?" he said, trying to clench his teeth while still maintaining self-control. "I think I need something to eat. Right now."

She stared at him, as if not understanding his plea for mercy from her suggestive admission, but he could not tolerate even her innocent stare a moment longer.

"Could you get me something?" he asked.

"Definitely," she whispered and escaped the room with whatever dignity she could muster.

It didn't take Charm long to return with his breakfast. It seemed Widow Worth had already served the morning meal to those who were inclined to sit at her table.

"Can you feed yourself?" Charm asked, staring over the two plates at the man who was presumed to be her husband.

Raven could imagine her feeding him, sitting close to his side, with her thigh pressed up against his. "Yes. I think that'd be safest . . . wisest," he corrected quickly. "I can manage with my good hand."

Charm released a shaky breath, not sure if she was more relieved or disappointed. That uncertainty worried her as she handed him his share of the meal. Rounding the bed, she sat in the room's solitary chair and did her best to concentrate on her breakfast. Finally, when her plate was empty, she could find nothing more to occupy her attention and raised her gaze to Raven.

He was staring at her.

"What?" she asked, startled by his dark gaze.

"Go back to Jude, Charm."

She watched him watch her, feeling ridiculously warm.

She should run out of there and never look back. But he was wounded and it was her fault. "It wouldn't be right. I mean, not until I know you're going to heal."

His voice was very low when next he spoke. "If I was any better than the men Jude warned you against, I'd insist that you go."

"But?"

"But I'm just a man."

Charm curled one hand into a loose fist but couldn't quite contain her smile. "You look . . ."—words were not her forte—"better." Shockingly, frighteningly alluring, would have been more honest.

She watched him swallow and realized that he looked pale as he tightened his fist around the handle of his fork. "Better than what?"

Better than anything. "Better than . . . yesterday."

He opened his mouth to speak but paused for a moment, as if changing his mind about which words to use. "You need a new gown."

"Oh." He always managed to surprise her. She glanced down at her battered, scarlet dress, trying to hide her bewilderment. "Perhaps I can repair it."

He actually winced as his eyes strayed to her low neckline. "It's not that. I just . . ." He drew a careful breath through his mouth. "I think maybe we'd both be better off if you wore something more . . . concealing."

"Oh." Her face flamed. She could feel the heat of it and shifted her gaze quickly off to the side. "I don't usually dress like this, except when Jude's gambling."

"To distract the opposition?" he guessed. She nodded. "Well, I'd say that'd . . ."—he nodded in turn—"that'd work all right. But maybe . . . um . . . if I want to stay alive, and you don't want to kill me, maybe you'd better make this a little easier on me."

She wasn't sure why his words made her feel giddy, but she was quite certain it was a bad sign. Dangerous. This flirting stuff was very scary. Or *was* he still flirting? She wished she knew. "I'm afraid I don't have any money to buy a new one."

"I do." He said the words very quickly, as though unable to spew them out fast enough. When he grinned in self-deprecating humor, she could not help but do the same. "I'll pay," he said, more slowly now.

"I can't take your money."

He raised his brows at her. "Afraid of owing me, Lucky Charm?"

"Maybe," she admitted softly.

His smile widened. "I can't say I'm not the kind that wouldn't usually take advantage of that. But in your case I won't. Promise. I owe you that much at least."

"I . . ." She lowered her eyes. "I can't."

"Please." His tone was throaty and quite desperate, and when she glanced up, he laughed out loud, as if he found his own weaknesses rather comical. "For my peace of mind," he said, "and continued survival."

She couldn't help but smile back. "All right."

"And I'd like to pay for . . ." He touched his petticoat bandages. "Replacing these."

Now, that was going too far, becoming too personal. She opened her mouth to object, but he raised a hand and interrupted. "Please, go on. Buy what you need. Take your time." He drew a heavy breath, which sounded weary. "Believe me, little Charm, the more layers between us, the safer I'll feel."

Chapter 15

Raven paced the rented room, flexing his chest and lifting his arms to test the tightness caused by his wound.

To his surprise, Widow Worth had sent up the noonday meal without prompting. He'd eaten it with relish, finding his appetite unimpaired by his small, inconvenient injury. In truth, however, it wasn't inconvenient at all. Nothing less than a blessing really, for look what it had accomplished. Charm's acquiescence.

He paced again. Lying in bed had caused him to stiffen up and become lazy. He could afford to do neither, for though his little Charm had indeed been quite charming of late, she was apt to change at any moment, making it necessary to have all his wits and strength.

Thunder rumbled, drawing Raven's attention to the window. The sky was dark, swollen with ominous charcoal clouds. Charm had been gone for several hours. He frowned now, stopping beside the window, well out of sight from the street. What was taking her so long? Perhaps he'd been a fool to encourage her to go. Perhaps she would flee.

Worry suddenly twisted in his gut, but the sudden rap of

footfalls on the stairs startled him from his thoughts. In a few quick strides he was in bed. He lay on his back with his mother's small ring resting atop his petticoat bandages and the blankets just so, exposing some of his chest and abdomen as he waited.

The footsteps reached the landing. Raven closed his eyes, hearing her approach. Charm had returned. Not that he cared on a personal level, of course. He imagined how she would look by his bedside, how her eyes would shine down at him, and her impish mouth would purse in that so serious expression of hers. Not that he cared on a personal level . . . of course.

She opened the door quietly. He heard the soft shuffle of her feet as she turned to close it behind her, carefully, so as not to wake him. Although Raven would have liked to surreptitiously watch her, he didn't dare chance it, for she was a bright girl, not one to take undue risks with. So instead he moaned quietly and pulled his eyelids up as he reached achingly for his chest with his right hand.

"I didn't mean to wake you." Charm stood by the door, holding a plate of food and a brown paper package he assumed contained her old dress. She looked repentant, but Raven had little enough time to notice her expression for his attention had latched onto her new dress and the priceless treasure stashed inside it.

Good God, she might just as well have kept the red thing. He swallowed hard, realizing with half his mind that he was forgetting to act ill and was staring as if she were a succulent leg of lamb. For a moment he hoped she hadn't noticed, but when his head cleared, he found that her eyes had gone wide and she had already raised one arm, as if to ward him off.

He closed his eyes with a great effort, cursing himself as a thousand kinds of fool. Though they both remained as they were, Raven could feel hot desire diffuse him. Why had he thought a simple change of attire would affect his ardent feelings for her? She was irresistible, no matter what she wore, for though the new gown rose modestly to her throat, it did nothing to calm his desire. In fact, the gentle way in which it hugged her breasts and waist only made him want to do the same, and he'd come too far to take such a foolish risk. He clenched his teeth and kept his eyes resolutely closed, hoping she'd relax.

"Are you feeling poorly?" Her voice came eventually, and when he finally allowed himself to open his eyes, he found that she was watching him with gentle but wary concern.

"No," he said. Looking into her emerald gaze, he paused just long enough to let her think he was lying as he kneaded his left arm with his opposite hand. "I'm feeling fine."

"Are you sure?" She took a single step forward.

Where on earth had she found that gown? Perhaps she *was* a lucky charm, for in a town this size it seemed highly improbable that she would find something ready-made that would fit so well. Too well! He forced his eyes closed again, but still he could visualize her. The dress was green, very much like the color of her eyes and fit her with the casual intimacy of a cotton glove. This wasn't good.

"Raven?" Her tone sounded concerned as she stepped closer. "Should I call the doc?"

"No." He said the word a bit faster than he'd planned, the sharp reminder of kerosene pushing him to speak. "I'm certain the feeling will return to my arm."

She looked pale. "Your . . . arm?"

"You worry too much. I'm healing well. Just tired."

"Are you certain?"

Definitely. "Of course. Don't worry." He opened his eyes slowly, hoping he looked weary and not allowing his gaze to stray immediately to her. "Where did you find the gown?" He hadn't meant to ask exactly that, but the words were out now.

She shuffled her feet nervously, warning him not to look at her yet. But there was little else to see in the room, so he made his eyes fall closed again and wondered if it was time to pray for strength. He had two options; he could keep his control, and probably, in the end, gain a fortune. Or he could throw in his hand and seduce the girl. Maybe. If she didn't kill him first. Still, even considering possible death as a side effect to one of the options, it was a hard choice. One best made with his eyes closed.

She cleared her throat. "Do you like it?"

Raven's eyes almost popped open with surprise, not only because of her words, but because of her tone, which was husky and quiet. Damn it all if she wasn't testing her wings, flirting with him, teasing him. He clenched his teeth, careful not to let her notice his tension as he lifted his lids.

Her radiance filled the room like a light that drew his eyes. "It's very nice," he said with just the correct amount of casualness. Thank God he was covered with a blanket or she would realize just how nice it was.

"I found it at the mercantile," she said, her tone nervous. "It just needed a few alterations."

He could imagine where. Across her breasts. God help him. "Good." He was beginning to sweat.

One of her fists clenched and unclenched while her other still held the plate. "I suppose I might just as well discard the old one."

He nodded, though he couldn't help thinking it a shame to never see that scandalous scarlet gown on her again.

"Does your chest hurt?"

Raven drew a deep breath. He must remember to play this game well, for a fortune depended on the roll of the dice. "You've no reason to feel responsible for this. It was my own greed that caused my plight."

"Greed?"

He watched her eyes. Her heavy lashes were dark but sprinkled with a deep cinnamon color, as was her hair, which was pulled up in a heavy knot at the back of her head. It was dappled with the evening's first drops of rain and very shiny. "I was promised a great deal of money if I returned you . . . I mean, if I returned *Chantilly* to her aunt. I fear I gave little thought to *your* feelings." He expelled a soft sigh and narrowed his eyes. "I was raised as a pauper among the wealthy. In the past there has seemed nothing more grand than being affluent. It never occurred to me that you might already possess everything you wish for. Jude is a lucky man."

He noticed that her right hand searched unconsciously for a pocket, but there seemed to be none in the new gown. Somehow, that knowledge allowed him to breathe easier. No pockets, no hidden weapons. He hoped.

"Why?" Her voice was very soft.

"Because." He paused, trying to remember his line of thought. The world somehow seemed very still. As if there were not another human inhabitant within a thousand miles. "He has your trust. And your love."

Utter silence held them as Raven's heart thrummed steadily against the framework of his ribs. It seemed every fiber of him was trilling with excitement.

"I . . ." Her lovely lips parted, but for a moment she said no more, merely staring at him, as if lost in some thought she refused to share. "I brought your supper."

"I'm not hungry." Though it was, quite suddenly, the truth, it was also, Raven realized, the perfect thing to say, for sickness often dulled appetite, didn't it?

"But you must eat. You'll only weaken if you don't. And you had no breakfast or lunch.

"You mustn't concern yourself," he said, gladly allowing her misconceptions.

"Are you feverish?"

"Of course not." Only when he looked at her.

She bit the inside of her lip, staring at him before setting aside his meal. "I'd better see to your wound."

Goddamn if he hadn't forgotten his wound. "It's fine. Really it is." Really it *was*. But he'd hate for her to believe him.

She looked as if she did not. "Doc said to change the

bandage." Her voice was firm, though she didn't move forward to follow the old quack's advice.

Raven watched her. She looked terrified; apparently the thought of touching him was almost too much to be borne. "You needn't," he said quietly. "It'll heal fine on its own." He felt he could actually see her relax as she absorbed his words.

"It's my responsibility."

By God, yes it was. He almost smiled. He'd done his duty as a decent person, which he wasn't, and as a scoundrel, which he was. He'd allowed her the opportunity to shirk the job of touching him. He couldn't be expected to do more to discourage her.

"Well . . ." She drew a deep breath. "I'll get started."

He said nothing, and in a few moments she was perched on the edge of the bed, looking scared enough to faint and flighty enough to fly.

"Shall I sit up?" he asked quietly, knowing better than to move without her permission. Widow Worth would indeed wonder about their relationship if his charming little wife went scampering from their room because Raven had taken it into his head to sit up without warning.

"I suppose you had better."

He did so, slowly sitting erect before sliding back to rest against the headboard. It wasn't an easy task with only one arm to support him.

Charm stared at him as if he were somehow more dangerous now, but he didn't move farther, and finally she reached out to touch his bandages. The knot came loose in her fingers. She bit the inside of her lip again.

"I'll need you to . . . lean forward a bit."

"I can care for myself, Charm."

"No," she said with surprising speed. "I'll do it."

He nodded before fulfilling her request, putting the bare flesh of his chest very near her torso.

"Be merciful to me, O Lord!"

"More Scripture?" he asked quietly, entranced by the intensity of her face.

"Job." She swallowed hard. "Chapter 9. Verse 13."

"Why?"

"What?"

"Why do you quote Scripture?"

"Oh. It makes me feel better. The people in the Old Testament, they were . . ."—she shrugged—"they were . . . less than perfect, but God took care of them. Kept them . . . safe." She eyed his bandaged chest as if it might jump forward and consume her.

"You seem to know it very well," he said, trying to keep her talking, to calm her nerves.

"Jude thought it important that I learn to read." One hand was formed into a loose fist in her lap. "He wanted to teach me himself." She smiled weakly. "Said he could. I was almost ten when I learned the truth. He can't read a word. He was terribly ashamed, though I never understood why, because it never mattered to me. But in the end he hired Mrs. Billet." Charm nodded as if remembering. "She was, ahh . . . addled with strong drink most of the time."

It took Raven a moment to realize she meant "drunk." He found it rather amusing that she sometimes used biblical terms.

"She taught me enough to get me started, but we've never had access to many books," Charm said. She shrugged, looking a bit more at ease. "But I've always had Mother's Bible. At night, when Jude was asleep, I'd read."

"You've memorized the Bible."

"Just portions." She lowered her gaze. "Mostly the begging for mercy parts."

Raven remained silent, watching her down-turned face. "Mercy from what?" he asked finally, the words very quiet.

"I don't know." Her answer was no louder.

"Who has frightened you so?"

"No one," she said quickly. She lifted her gaze sharply to

his, but in a moment her expression softened and she sighed. "Everyone."

"But why?"

She shrugged, looking very young. "The fear—it's just inside me. In my head. My dreams."

There seemed to be nothing he could do to keep from touching her. His hand simply moved of its own accord. "I won't hurt you, Charm," he whispered and let his fingers drift to her cheek.

She didn't move away. But she sat very stiff, her eyes suddenly clamped shut and her breath coming hard.

"I won't hurt you. See?" He drew his hand back. "There's nothing to fear. Not from me."

Her eyes opened slowly. He raised his brows and smiled at her. "You can touch me, Charm. I won't bite." But she looked as if she expected him to do just that, and so he reached out, taking her hand very gently in his own. "See?" He longed to kiss it. As never before in his life, he wanted to feel her skin against his lips. Instead, he pulled her hand nearer, finally resting it against a hale portion of his chest. Her breath came to a halt, but she didn't pull away.

"You can touch me," he repeated quietly. "I won't hurt you. In fact," he whispered, caught in her wild, green gaze. "I won't even touch you back. You're safe to do whatever you wish with me."

Chapter 16

She could do whatever she wished with him, he'd said. But what was it she wished to do? Charm stared at him in silent uncertainty. He remained very still. His shirt was removed, and the hard slopes of his chest rose slightly with each breath.

She kept her gaze carefully planted on his face. He had deep-set, brown eyes. Not a solid generic brown, but a mesmerizing warm tone, swirled with highlights of gold and green. Fascinating eyes, she thought, when she looked closely at him. His hair was black, as were his brows, which were cast in a straight solid line, and though his expression could be intimidating, it was not so now. In fact, at this moment, he looked quite innocent and rather shy.

"You can leave," he repeated softly. "Anytime you want."

The knowledge that she didn't want to leave hit Charm like the blow of a fist. She winced, wondering what had come over her, knowing she should remove herself from his presence immediately.

Instead she simply murmured, "But Doc said I should change your bandages."

"Doc never saw you in that gown." Raven's tone was deep and quiet, and though Charm would have liked to ask what he meant, she found she lacked the nerve.

Nevertheless, her hands reached out to untie the bandage. Neither of them spoke as he leaned forward, allowing her to pull the fabric from behind him once again. For a moment their faces were inches apart. Their gazes caught. Their breath halted in unison. Beneath the bandages, Charm could feel the warmth of his living flesh. Stark, raw sensations assaulted her. But what they were she couldn't tell. Excitement? Terror? Excruciating anticipation?

His lips parted. She heard the sharp rush of his breath returning, but as for herself, she failed to inhale, failed to think, to move, finding herself only able to feel as she stared at him.

He leaned back stiffly, seeming to force his body to comply with his commands. His chest was rising and falling more dramatically now, as if he'd run a hard race and won. "I think perhaps I should see to this myself, Charm."

The words were soft, so soft, in fact, that she found she could ignore them, as if they were never said. She drew a deep breath. Her hands were shaking. She should hide her fear, she thought, but didn't, for he looked no more certain than she felt. Somehow that knowledge reassured her, causing her to continue on, to unwrap the remainder of the bandage from his chest, letting her fingers brush against his skin now and then, and feeling the sparkling sensations lick her like flames against bare flesh.

Finally the dressing was completely removed and his wound exposed, but still she couldn't speak. The flesh near his injury was reddened and inflamed, while the center of the thing looked even worse. Charm swallowed hard, feeling sickened by what she had done.

"I'm sorry." Her words were a mere whisper, and suddenly her fingers reached out as if to touch him. But she snatched them back, raising her gaze to his at the same time.

As for Raven, his expression remained unmoved. He

watched her steadily, his lips parted, exposing neat rows of teeth as he drew breath through his mouth.

You can touch me. I won't touch you.

Though he didn't say the words again, it seemed they still reverberated in the room. Slowly, ever so slowly, she reached for him. The skin near his wound was warm and certainly must be painful. Nevertheless, he didn't flinch as she touched him. Neither did he move.

Charm again drew a deep breath and pulled her hand slowly back. Their gazes met again. She closed her fingers into a fist and exhaled, feeling shaky.

"Does it hurt?" she whispered.

"No. It feels like heaven."

She scowled, thinking he was teasing, but as she studied his face, she realized he was not talking about his injury but about her touch. She shivered now, feeling his words sear a thousand hot trails to the core of her being. For a moment she wanted to flee, wanted to run away, like a child from a thunderstorm, but she remained as she was, feeling the electricity crackle around and within her.

"Please." His voice was so low it seemed that she felt rather than heard it. "Touch me again."

Her hand moved like a separate entity. Slipping from her lap, it lay finally against the hard, hale slope of his right pectoral. His flesh didn't feel like her own, but was very solid. She could hardly breathe, and she didn't raise her gaze to his but held it steady on her hand. Her fingers looked pale against his dark skin and beside the slim rope of gold that held his ring.

Below her thumb, his nipple was a small dark pebble surrounded by a circle of creamy brown. Charm exhaled. Her body felt stiff. From somewhere, inside or out, thunder crackled a warning, but she didn't respond. Her fingers slipped lower. His aureole was as soft as an old scar. She lifted her hand away slightly, all but her ring finger, which drifted around the small target of brown.

The muscles of his torso jerked. Charm gasped. Frightened by the quick movement, she yanked her hand away as her gaze fled to his face. Raven's nostrils flared and his lips parted. He was breathing hard, and every muscle looked tight, including those in his broad, dark throat. The tendons there stood out in sharp relief, making him look predatory, dangerous. And yet it was a danger that enticed her now.

She raised her chin a notch. "Did I hurt you?"

He remained silent for a moment, but finally he spoke, his tone as rich and dark as black coffee. "I think you know better."

She swallowed hard, wanting to ask more. But she found now that it was easier to touch than to speak. Her hand drifted hesitantly out again, and she held her breath, waiting to see where it would land. His cheek was stubbled with unshaven whiskers. They felt rough and somehow alive beneath her strangely sensitized fingertips.

When was the last time she had touched a man's face? As a child? She couldn't recall. In fact, she couldn't remember ever willingly touching anyone but Jude. Somehow that realization frightened her, made her feel less than human. For a moment she wanted to draw away, wanted to find a place in the dark to hide.

"I won't touch you," he said. The words were real now, though very quiet and rather forced, as if he somehow understood her need to hear them, yet found it hard to press them forth.

Her lips parted and she breathed through them, watching his for a moment. Could he read her mind? Or could she read his? Or was it simply the terrifying magic of touch that was affecting her so?

She wanted to ask, but no matter how she worded the question, it would sound foolish. Taking a deep breath, she skimmed her fingers down his cheek to the corner of his mouth and across his smooth lower lip. She felt his shiver transferred from him to her. Lightning flashed, illuminating the world outside their window but failing to draw her attention from his face.

With her middle finger, Charm traced a path over the precipice of his lip to the small indentation below, and from there to his chin. It, too, was stubbled with dark, unshaven hair, like nothing she had ever felt, but below that his throat was smooth. A trio of her fingers rippled across a taut tendon of his neck before following the ridge downward to fall finally into the deep hollow between his collar bones.

Life beat there in a steady thrum of vibration. Charm breathed to the rhythm. Resting her fingers in this little valley, she noticed again how light her skin looked against his.

"Have you met your father?" Charm had no idea why she asked the question, but it came nevertheless, seeming somehow pertinent to the moment.

She could feel his warm gaze on her face. "No. I've never found him."

His chosen words, as well as his tone, told her something. She lifted her gaze to his, trying to discern what it was. "You've been looking for him?" she asked. "All these years?"

He drew a deep breath, making his nostrils flare more dramatically. "Since Mother died."

She wanted to delve into his past, to draw their similarities into the coldness of light. But she lacked the strength, or whatever it was that allowed two people to share their frailties.

"Since I was thirteen," he added. In that moment, Charm wondered if he was so much stronger than she, that he could speak of reality with such seeming ease.

She dropped her gaze to her own fingers, where they still rested in the warm depression of his throat. "Why?" she asked softly.

He didn't answer. She shifted her gaze to his face, narrowing her eyes and asking again, "Why have you been looking for him?"

There was another pause, but he answered finally, his tone harsh but carefully controlled. "Maybe to kill him."

She held his gaze, seeing there the deep well of his soul. There was nothing between them now. No artifice. No lies. Only the open, aching wounds of the past and the unhidden reality of what they were.

"I don't think so," she said softly, but he shook his head quickly, as if loath to allow her kind misconceptions.

"I *did* plan to kill him, Charm." His expression was hard and intensely honest. "For leaving her . . . us."

Still she watched him. "And *now*?"

Raven drew a deep breath and let his heavy shoulders relax against the headboard behind him. She could see the tight tendons in his throat soften a bit. "It's not that I hate him any less," he said, as if warning her of his lack of soul. "Maybe I've become complacent. Still . . ." He looked at the jagged flash of light against the blank blackness of the window. "She deserves vengeance."

He was very handsome, Charm thought in that moment. And very lonely. Her throat felt tight. Again she thought of fleeing, but she did not, for he looked so sad, like a lost boy.

"She had such an ability to believe in goodness. In truth. In loyalty." He laughed, but the sound was strained. "Her naivete used to make me angry. But now I miss . . ." He shrugged, looking weary, letting the lines around his mouth and eyes soften. "Maybe she needed something to believe in. Maybe it was her weakness." He shifted his gaze solemnly to her face. "Maybe it's one of mine too."

The room was very quiet but for the thunder that grumbled from afar. "Maybe not," Charm whispered and shifted her gaze away.

"What?"

There was an image in Charm's mind. An image of a mother with her son upon her lap. His hair was raven black and his eyes were closed in slumber. "Did she hold you?"

She knew he shook his head in bewilderment, though she didn't glance up to see. "Did she hold you in her arms? Did she rock you to sleep?" The boy in her mind stirred, snuggling closer against his mother's breast, and the woman smiled, showing such tender adoration that it made Charm's chest tighten and her heart ache. "Maybe it's not a weakness at all."

Thunder rumbled quietly again before letting the room fall back into silence.

"I'm sorry, Charm."

She shook her head, still staring at her hand against his chest. "For what?"

He was quiet for a moment, as if searching for words, then, "For making you cry."

Charm meant to shake her head in denial again, but suddenly she felt the wetness on her face and lifted her fingers to touch it. She drew them away, able to see the sparkle of moisture by a diffused flash of lightning. How long had it been since she'd allowed herself to cry over her past?

Not long enough, said the cynical, wary part of her mind. But the cynical, wary part had no needs, no desire to touch another human being, to share that which made her flesh and blood. She swallowed, perhaps only now fully realizing the risk she took by being here.

Charm swiped the knuckles of her hand across her cheek and pulled a shaky breath. "You must look like your father," she said quietly.

Raven's inhalation was little different from hers. "Why?"

"Dark skin." She swiped her other cheek, then ignored the wetness as her opposite hand moved of its own accord, sweeping across his hale pectoral and down to where the muscles lay taut and rippled across his abdomen. His next inhalation was sharper. "All this dark skin. He must be dark, like you?" She lifted her gaze to his face.

"Charm," he said and raised his right hand, but she jerked away and he forced himself to draw back, flattening his fingers against the linen sheet beneath him. "You don't look anything like *your* father."

Though she could feel her heart hammering a terrified rhythm in her chest, she refused to flee. There was something here to be discovered, if she only had the nerve. Raven watched, his dark gaze steady, his body unmoving.

Lightning crackled close at hand.

"I'll go with you." She had fought with every demon she knew to force the words past her terror, and still she was surprised when she heard herself speak.

Raven moved nothing but his head, which turned slowly, as if he had not heard her correctly. "What?"

She raised her chin slightly and very slowly forced herself to place her left hand against the bare flesh of his chest. "I said, I'll go with you."

His first impulse was to pull her into his arms. His second was even more foolhardy. But he did neither. Instead, he held a tight check on his reactions and felt some pride in his well-honed self-control. "To St. Louis?"

Her expression was one of sheer terror. "Is that where Eloise Medina lives?"

Raven tightened his fist against the coverlet and wondered if she had quit breathing again. "Yes."

"Then that's where I'll go."

Suddenly, and for some peculiar reason, Raven felt like arguing. He wanted to ask, why now? What had finally convinced her that he spoke the truth? But he dared not question her motives. He must get her far from this place as quickly as possible. He must head south and east before it was too late. Jude might be following. Clancy certainly would be, for he was not the kind to pass up the opportunity of a small fortune, even if it was someone else's. Leave immediately, said his good sense, but her hand was still on his chest. The slim tapers of her fingers were just below his mother's ring. They felt warm and gentle, and indescribably needy.

Transfixed, Raven stared at her hand now, then cleared his throat and tried to think clearly, to remind himself of his mission, of his need for haste. He opened his mouth, intending to speak, but when he saw her face he stopped.

Her eyes were downcast, and upon her cheeks remained the evidence of her tears.

Something twisted in his gut. Get her to St. Louis before she changed her mind, practicality insisted. Retrieve your reward and get out, good sense demanded.

"We'll stay here tonight," his lips said.

She didn't respond but remained very still, as if she were too frightened to move and too uncertain to question.

He cleared his throat, feeling the light touch of her hand burn through his skin to what used to be his soul. He'd been a fool to encourage her to touch him, he realized suddenly, for it only made his own desire more fierce. But what was desire? Nothing but temptation. Temptation to be used to sharpen his self-control. And she was only another temptation. Something he could not have. Something to be used to gain the greater prize—but only if she trusted him.

"I'll sleep on the floor," he said, though the words sounded harsher than he'd intended.

"No," she said quickly but didn't lift her gaze from his chest. "I mean. Last night worked out all right. I think . . ." She swallowed, sitting very still. "I think the same arrangement would suffice again."

Well, she was wrong! Dead wrong. The same arrangement would definitely not suffice tonight, because he knew his limitations, and one night was it. His limit! "I'll sleep on the . . . ," he began again, more forcefully this time, but in that moment her gaze lifted to his. Emerald emotion smote him with the impact of her gaze and he drew back, feeling the force of her need like a physical blow. She had given him this fleeting gift of trust. A gift she had, perhaps, never given another man. A gift a wanderer like himself might never receive again. "Bed," he finally said with a single nod, though he mentally berated himself as a thousand kinds of fool. "I'll sleep on the bed." He cleared his throat again. "Right here." He nodded, still holding her gaze. "Right . . ."—he tapped the coverlet with a forefinger that he'd just pulled from the tight grip of his fist—"here."

She continued to stare at him, but the inside of her lower lip was now caught between her teeth and she was breathing again. He could tell because her chest was rising and falling slightly.

Damn! The only thing worse than her not breathing was her breathing.

Raven pulled in a light draught of air and raised his brows, trying to relax. "You could sleep there." He nodded vaguely toward the opposite side of the bed, though he didn't quite manage to break eye contact. "On the other side." But her hand didn't move. Damn again. He could feel the effects of her touch clear down to his toes, for every inch of him ached now, as if something had given his body the false impression that now was the time to be aroused.

Now was not the time. In fact, now would be a first-rate time to pull away from her—to turn his back and go to sleep. He almost snorted at such a ridiculous thought, for he was anything but drowsy. "Tired?" he asked, then noticed that his tone was a bit high-pitched. Good God, he was acting like an idiot again.

Her hand slipped slightly lower, toward his abdomen. He drew a sharp breath through his teeth and began to sweat.

Her gaze rose quickly to his face. Her eyes were very wide, and for a moment he thought she might beat a hasty retreat, but she did not, though he could feel her tension.

"I am." He nodded, staring straight into her face and doing his best to make his lie believable. "Tired." He nodded jerkily. "Really tired." He yawned. It was, he was certain, not even remotely credible and made him look like a braying jackass.

He watched her swallow. Her throat was slim and fine, her lips slightly parted and bright as wild strawberries.

"Do you want to sleep?" she asked in a whisper.

Good God! What were the options here? Was this a test? What if he said no? What if he admitted he wanted to peel that damned modest gown from her body and lick her belly button? What then? Would she impale him with some as yet undiscovered weapon, or was she hoping he would admit his desire? Was she wanting him as much as he wanted her? Perhaps that was it. Perhaps she found him irresistible. Perhaps she was as randy as . . .

"Because you haven't eaten yet."

Her words shattered his illusions. God damn, she was worried about his meal getting cold, and he was worried about beginning to drool, like a hound on a hot scent.

Somehow the knowledge of their differences made him angry.

"You have to eat or you'll never mend. A healthy appetite is the first sign of healing." She straightened slightly, pulling her hand slowly from his chest. Its absence made him feel suddenly bereft. "Aren't you hungry?"

"No." The lie came fairly easily, spurred on by disappointment. Knowing she was suffering too would have somehow made celibacy easier.

She frowned. "I'll get Doc," she said and turned to rise.

Raven caught her hand without thinking, and though she jumped, she didn't pull away.

"No," he said, softening slightly. "There's no need."

Her scowl deepened. "You haven't eaten for days. I'm worried you'll—"

"You're worried about me?" His voice was quieter than he'd planned. If he was going to lie and play her for a fool, he should do so with some panache, he thought, but he failed to correct his mistake.

"It's just . . ." Her face was very tense. "It's my fault."

"Then I'll eat."

"What?"

"If it'll make you feel better, I'll eat."

She blinked once, looking very young. "Thank you."

Thank you! Raven almost smiled. It was the first time he'd ever heard those words from her lips. And there was nothing more gratifying than hearing them for something he wanted to do anyway.

But, he realized suddenly, in order for him to eat, she'd

have to move away, and despite all his better judgment, he didn't want that.

"If you help me," he said quietly.

"What?" She sounded surprised. And there was certainly a good measure of terror thrown into the wild expression on her face.

"My left hand. It's . . ." He winced, as if trying and failing to move it. "I'm certain it will recover soon."

He watched her gaze shift guiltily from his arm to his plate. "All right." Her acquiescence was soft.

She moved away only long enough to retrieve the platter, and then her soft hip was nestled up against his leg again. It was comfortable having it there.

The meal consisted of pork roast and cooked potatoes. Charm balanced the plate on her lap and cut up the meat. Her cheeks were slightly pink, Raven noticed, and her lips pursed as she worked. It made a charming picture.

Finally the first forkful was raised to his lips. Raven dutifully opened his mouth. The meat was cold, but tender, and very tasty. He ate several bites, feeling ravenous. Perhaps lust increased his appetite, but he dared not give up the slight edge he'd gained by playing on her sympathy.

"That's enough," he said quietly.

"But you must eat."

"You worry too much," he complained.

"You fainted and fell off Angel," she countered.

He grinned, lifting only one corner of his mouth. "I'm not even going to ask what possessed you to name that mule-headed beast such a celestial name. Maybe I just fell off."

She scowled, looking sweet enough to eat, which was very confusing, considering the girl could be called a number of things, sweet not being amongst them. "He was standing still, and you fainted," she insisted.

"Maybe it's got nothing to do with the injury. Maybe I faint all the time," he countered, intrigued by her look of concentration. "Maybe I'm just sickly."

To his surprise, she lowered her gaze to his chest, letting it settle there for a moment before skimming it back up to his face. "You don't look sickly."

He'd meant to make a joke, to lighten the mood. Charm's husky tone, however, brought everything back to base reality. Which was that he was as horny as a bull moose in autumn, and she was too damned close.

Pull back. Pull back, caution warned, but suddenly he was taking the plate from her hand and setting it unceremoniously aside.

"So I fainted," he said dismissively, not admitting even to himself that he'd staged the whole thing to gain her sympathy and keep her from leaving. Besides, at this moment it seemed quite possible that her presence could cause a man to swoon. "Maybe I was overcome by your nearness."

She bit the inside of her lip, looking scared. "Are you flirting again?" she asked, her tone breathy and barely audible.

Raven stared at her, and indeed, her presence did make him feel faint. "Damned if I know!" he admitted.

She tilted her head, looking quizzical.

"You make it hard to think when you . . ." When she what? When she breathed? When she sat? When she looked at him? None of these things seemed wise to admit. Still, she watched him with that unique, childish stare, as if she were trying to find the answer to some mystery that continued to baffle her. "It's hard to think when you're you." His explanation didn't seem to answer the unspoken question that lingered in her eyes. He sighed, pushing his fingers through his hair. "You're very tempting, Charm," he admitted. "No use pretending otherwise."

"Tempting how?" she whispered.

His smile had long since fled. "I think you know."

She shifted her gaze swiftly to the window, which was black and blank now. "What if we kissed?"

For a moment, Raven couldn't quite believe he'd heard

her correctly. He drew a deep slow breath, trying to think, to delay any foolish reactions. He shoved the splayed fingers of his right hand through his hair again, feeling the tension galvanize his muscles.

Her gaze returned jerkily to his face, where their eyes met with a jolt.

Charm held her breath and remained motionless, afraid to move. "I didn't . . . I didn't mean it." She tried to shake her head, but her neck felt wooden. His fingers were still embedded in the raven blackness of his hair, while his upper arm remained parallel with the bed. The muscles stood out taut and rigid under his dark skin. Charm's gaze caught there, where his biceps flowed into his muscular shoulder. Beneath his arm, she glimpsed a bit of silky black hair. Below that was a slight hollow, and then his ribs began, row after row of lean muscled bone, curving down toward his abdomen. She swallowed, feeling very weak. "I didn't mean it," she repeated.

He lowered his arm very slowly, and though she tried to ignore it, she didn't fail to notice the tight ripple of muscle through his torso as he moved. "You're frightened again."

"No!" she denied, and found the ability to shake her head.

Raven watched her face in silence, making her feel foolish. She drew a deep breath and straightened her back, wondering if it would be wise to deny it again.

"Afraid of a kiss?" he asked softly. "Or what you think it would lead to?"

"I'm not—"

"Did Jude force you to help him?"

"What?"

Raven settled his arm against the coverlet. It looked no less powerful now, she thought, but somehow less dangerous, without the muscles standing out in such stark relief. "Why did you dress so . . . provocatively, when you fear men's attention as you do?"

Charm's stomach lurched and she stood, pacing rapidly away. "We didn't cheat!"

He watched her closely, though his expression was innocuous. "I didn't say you cheated. I just want to understand. Why the gowns? Why the seduction when it scares you so?"

She hurried to the far side of the room, putting a few more feet between them. "It worked. Men, they're . . ." she shrugged. Though she tried, she feared she did not quite contain her disdain.

"Trash?"

"Easily distracted," she corrected, though she found it hard to disagree in theory. "I've studied gamblers ever since I was a child. For years." She shrugged again, feeling the familiar terror nibble at her senses. "Jude says I didn't talk." She bit the inside of her lip and scowled, thinking herself foolish for admitting such intimate details of her past to this man whom she barely knew.

"Didn't talk?" he asked now, tilting his head slightly to the side. Lightning flashed, highlighting his hair in shades of blue and black. "Why?"

"I don't know why." She turned rapidly away, wishing she hadn't spoken.

"For how long?"

"I don't know."

"But he must have—"

"I don't *know*," she repeated, turning again, though she could barely see him in the darkness now. "But he was afraid to leave me alone. So he took me to the gambling tables with him. I had nothing to do but study men's faces."

He was quiet for a moment. "So you began to guess what cards they held."

She nodded stiffly. Her shoulder pressed against the door, giving her a modicum of security.

"How did you let Jude know your opinion?"

She swallowed, glad he couldn't see her in the darkness. "We had signals."

"Such as?"

She knew she would be a fool to tell him, and yet she did. "Like pushing my hair behind my ear."

Silence again, then, "Ahh, so you thought you knew what I held."

In all of her life, she had never spent this much time in conversation with a man. It was wearing, she thought, and yet she felt herself relax, for she was near the door and he had not tried to stop her from leaving. "You have a very good poker face," she said softly, at the same time thinking that he simply had a very good face.

Lightning flashed again, gently illuminating him.

"But why the gowns, Charm, if you could read their expressions?"

"I told you, it distracted them." She tried to keep her tone steady, but somehow that particular question wrenched her gut.

He was silent for a time, as though not believing her; then, "Have you ever kissed a man before?"

She backed up sharply against the door, finding the handle smooth and cool against her palm in the darkness. "I didn't mean it," she said, hearing the frantic tone in her voice and wishing to heaven she had never opened her mouth.

"I was only wondering," he assured her softly.

"Well . . ." She tested the handle, pushing it downward, making certain it wasn't locked. It was not. "It's none of your affair."

He was silent, as if debating her point.

Charm straightened her back, immediately defensive. "I never said I wanted to kiss you."

Her words fell into silence as black as the room. She squinted, trying to discern his thoughts. Though it was too dark to see for certain, she was sure he was smirking at her with that all-knowing expression of his. She drew her hand from the handle, curling her fingers into fists.

"I've never wanted to kiss any man."

From the bed came a soft snort. Her fists tightened.

"I *haven't*," she insisted.

There was silence now, but the quiet seemed even more derisive than the snort, so she tightened her fists and paced swiftly forward to confront the scoundrel face-to-face.

"I haven't!" she repeated, leaning aggressively forward, but when the lightning flashed again she saw that his eyes were closed and his lips slightly parted as he rumbled a quiet snore.

He'd fallen asleep. Well, damn it all! How dare he? How dare he fall asleep while she stood there not wanting to kiss him?

Chapter 17

It had been another hard night. Charm remained motionless, watching Raven as he slept. He lay on his side facing her. His right arm cushioned his head and his left fell across the taut, mounded muscles of his exposed chest. His dark hair was tousled. In the early morning light, he looked quite harmless.

Why was she here, lying with a man who terrified her? Or was it simply that he *should* terrify her, but didn't? Not quite. Not anymore.

She sighed, letting worries and uncertainties wash over her for a moment. In that instant Raven awoke. She saw awareness return to his features, saw his mahogany eyes flicker open, and there she was, caught in his gaze once again.

"You've changed your mind."

"What?" She had expected him to be surprised by her presence. After all, in his last waking moments she'd been squashed against the door like splattered berry juice.

"You've decided not to go to St. Louis," he said, lifting

his right arm to prop the heel of his hand against the rough stubble of his cheek.

Sometime during the night, Charm had realized she'd not only neglected to bandage his wound, but to apply the kerosene as well. She pushed the guilt from her mind and made a conscious effort to relax. "No. I haven't changed my mind. I'll just . . ." She broke eye contact nervously. "I'll just tell Jude my plans, then I'll go."

Raven remained very still, though when she shifted her gaze back to his face, she could now discern the faint signs of tension: the tightness in his jaw, the way the tendons stood out in sinewy ridges on his wide wrist.

"He'll try to kill me." His words fell flat and hard into the quiet of the room.

Charm scowled, and though she immediately understood his meaning, it seemed immensely safer to pretend she didn't. "What?" she whispered, needing time to consider the danger element she had somehow failed to think of earlier.

"He'll never let you go, Charm."

"You're being ridiculous."

"*I* wouldn't."

She remained lying on her side, very still, with every article of clothing still buttoned and tied in place. Nevertheless, she felt somehow undressed. "What?"

"I wouldn't let you go, if I were Jude."

She bit her inner lip, wildly wondering for the first time what she would tell her father. How would she justify her plans to travel to St. Louis? There was no way of explaining without accusing him of deceiving her about her heritage. Indeed, there was no way of explaining her plans at all, not even to herself. Why was she here? Why had she agreed to go with this man whose bed she so cautiously shared? Why? she asked herself desperately, but found she was unwilling to delve for the answers. So, she shut off the nagging queries and let the expressionless vizard cover her face, holding the world at bay.

"He won't try to stop me from doing what I want," she said softly.

Raven's brows raised slightly. "My relationship with the man has hardly been one of undying friendship, Charm. Since the first moment, he thought me the devil incarnate." He paused for an instant, watching her face. "How do you think he'll react now, after I've forcefully abducted you? After we've spent whole days and nights together?"

She opened her mouth to speak, but he stopped her words. "No matter how platonic the situation, think how it will look."

She felt trapped. "I'll tell him nothing happened between us. I'll convince him I want to go, that you were a perfect gentleman."

Raven almost smiled, then shook his head, slowly, the movement very slight against his supporting hand. "Whatever the man's shortcomings, Charm, he'll do what he can to protect you, and in his opinion that will mean eliminating me from the picture."

Uncertainty squeezed in, threatening to smother her. "I won't let him," she said, but her voice was a mere whisper.

Raven smiled now, but the expression was a cheap imitation of true mirth and failed to reach his eyes. "I appreciate that, Lady Charm, but you may not be able to stop him, and in my present condition, neither will I."

"But I have to tell him that I'm safe. Tell him where I'm going."

"He won't allow it." Raven's words were very quiet. "But it's your choice. I'll take you back if that's your wish. And I won't fight him. You have my word."

She stared at him. "You'd do that for me? Risk your life?"

He did nothing more than nod.

She began breathing again, feeling somehow lighter with the decision made. "If we ever became separated, I was to meet him a week later in the exact spot where we last saw each other." She paused, pushing aside her fear and uncertainty. "I'll send a letter to New Eden. I'll tell him I'm safe, that I'm going to St. Louis, but I'll be back."

"He'll follow you."

She frowned. "How do you know?"

"Because that's what I'd do."

"Why?" she whispered.

One corner of his mouth lifted into an expression she couldn't quite read, but he refused to answer. "If you tell him where you're going, he'll follow. You know he will. And he's not a well man."

"Then what do I do?" she asked finally, needing guidance in a maze of options she had never trod before.

"Send the letter. Tell him you're safe and that you'll write again soon. Or . . ." He almost frowned now, though not quite. "Tell him you'll return, if you like. In a month. Or two. It's your choice."

Every second seemed a lifetime. Was she safe? Or was she crazy for trusting this man? "All right. I'll tell him I'll return."

The town of Red Rock boasted no stagecoach line. In fact, Raven felt lucky to be able to buy a few provisions and an extra horse. Although the thought of riding double with Charm was appealing, the heavy load would slow their progress. He felt now a burning need to move on as quickly as possible, for the number of people following them could be multiplying by the moment: Clancy, Jude, Angel's owner, if he had a particular attraction for truly ugly horses, and any number of the men in New Eden who felt it their responsibility to complete their effort of hanging him.

They headed south and east, traveling parallel to a narrow stream. It would lead them to Jordan where they could get a coach.

"Are you all right?" Charm asked now. She sat the split-eared gelding very well and somehow managed to look poised, even while trotting.

"I'm fine."

"We could stop if you like."

It still fascinated him that she worried about his well-being, making him realize yet again how tenuous he felt his hold on her was. As far as he could tell, there was little enough that kept her near, besides her guilt over what she believed to be a nearly deadly wound. He hated to think how she would react if she ever learned the truth. But if he played his cards well, he could, perhaps, convince her of her true identity, therefore causing her to want nothing more than to meet her Missouri relatives and learn the truth of her heritage.

"No need to stop," he said, remembering to put his right hand weakly to his chest and wince. "I'm fine."

They rode throughout the day. Although they traveled as quickly as possible, it was not nearly fast enough for Raven's peace of mind, for the country was rugged and rocky here.

Sometime after noon they stopped to eat. Although Raven had hoped to reach Jordan before nightfall, it was clear now that such was not to be the case. Camp was made near the sheer slope of a yellow bluff. Not far from the stream they'd been following, it was sheltered by a million towering pines. Their fire would be well hidden, the smoke dispersed by the branches overhead. Despite the rain of the previous night, they were able to find dry wood and soon had a small blaze flickering in the hollow.

Charm sat, watching the flame rise and dwindle, thinking her own thoughts and sharing none. Raven cut and fried strips of bacon, distributed cold biscuits on tin plates, and tried not to stare at her. But it was difficult, for in the fickle glow of moonlight and fire, she looked like a lost, enchanted princess, sad and untouchable. And still he longed to touch, longed for it more than he dared allow himself to contemplate. Finally, he smoked his last remaining cheroot and tried to think of other things until the cigar was only a stub of a thing that he crushed into the earth.

"Tired?" he asked.

"Yes."

It seemed to Raven in that instant that this was the first time she had admitted a weakness without blanching, without a second thought. "I'm sorry to make you spend the night here in the woods." He watched her as he spoke, knowing he was a fool to do so, for looking at her had a tendency to weaken his best intentions.

She said nothing, but continued to watch the flames.

"There's a good soft spot beneath that bent pine," he said, nodding toward a gargantuan tree that leaned toward their blaze, sheltering a small alcove beneath. "Years of fallen needles. Fairly dry. Probably the most comfort to be found until we reach Jordan."

She lifted her face to stare at him. For a moment, Raven felt the air trap in his lungs as the firelight illumined and shadowed the fine hollows of her face. "What?"

Realizing that she hadn't been listening, he longed to know what it was she considered so deeply.

"I said, there's a good spot for bedding down beneath that tree," he repeated. "Like a natural . . ." Why was it that he lost his train of thought when he looked at her? It wasn't right. Wasn't smart and certainly wasn't safe. He lived by his wits. Had for years. "Like a natural tent," he finished abruptly, pulling his gaze quickly from her to unwrap the blankets.

"You sleep there."

Her words surprised him. He foolishly raised his gaze too abruptly, shocking himself with her numbing beauty once again. "I like to think I'm not a completely unredeemable bast . . . scoundrel," he said, trying to concentrate on his words. "You take that spot."

She was silent, looking very serious and watching him. "I suppose . . . I mean, we could . . . share that shelter. After all, it might rain."

But there hadn't been a cloud all day. Raven stared at her, transfixed, knowing he should draw away and find a really first-rate reason why he couldn't share that particular piece of ground. For, in fact, he had one. Lust! Hot, deep burning, and nearly out of control.

"I really think it would be better if we—"

"You might catch a fever," she interrupted quickly, then slowed her words to add, "if you get wet."

Her expression was soft as the night air, as hopeful as a child's. But hopeful for what exactly?

"Charm, I really think . . . ," Raven began again, but paused now. Seeing some vulnerability in her eyes, he pushed his fingers through his hair and fought to remain strong as the silence lengthened.

She bit the inside of her lip and watched him. "I wouldn't molest you, if that's what you're worried about."

Nothing she could have said would have surprised him more. He laughed aloud, startled by her rare show of humor.

"Well . . ." He lowered his arm slowly. "That surely does ease my mind, Miss Charm."

He couldn't quite tell if the shadow of a smile tilted her lips or if it was merely the natural curve of her bright, delicious mouth. But whatever the case, she continued to watch him, her gaze ultimately steady.

His own smile dropped away. "It's not that I don't appreciate your trust." It was simply that he didn't deserve it. "But I . . ."

She was holding her breath again. He could tell, even from where he sat. "All right," he heard himself say. How was it that she thwarted all his best intentions?

After dousing the fire, Raven spread a single blanket and sat down upon the cushion of needles he had admired earlier. Then he waited, raising his brows and gazing at Charm. She stood not far away, looking unreasonably shy, considering this had been her idea. Raven leaned back on the heels of his hands, watching her through the slanted boughs of the ancient pine.

"It's all right if you've changed your mind," he said softly.

Apparently those were the words most effective for

allaying her fears, Raven realized. But whether that was desirable or not was now debatable. For regardless of his own misgivings, she came. Carrying her bedroll, she bent beneath the leaning branches and sat stiffly near the slanted trunk.

"So tell me, Lucky Charm," Raven said finally, unable to hold back his curiosity. "Do you think you can trust me because I'm too weak to be a threat, or is there another reason?"

The moonlight was refracted by the branches, gently shadowing her face. She said nothing.

Raven waited, watching her as she remained upright and stiff. "Guess you don't trust me enough to remove your shoes," he said finally.

Her gaze lifted, like the startled, wide-eyed stare of a doe.

"Still afraid the sight of your feet might be too much for my shaky self-control?" He considered laughing, but she dropped her eyes nervously away, and he held back his humor. "Take a risk." He hadn't meant to say it, for they were already taking too large a risk, being together as they were.

"What?" The question was breathy.

"Take a risk," he foolishly repeated. "Remove your shoes."

"But . . ."

"Better yet, let me."

Her mouth fell open, as if he'd asked her to run naked through the pines with him. But he ignored her expression and crept slowly forward to sit near her feet.

"It's just your shoes, Charm," he reminded softly, watching her face and seeing that she was just about ready to scramble away. "I really think I can resist the sight of your feet."

From somewhere far away came the haunting sound of a coyote.

"What do you say?" he asked quietly.

"Why?" The single word sounded very tense.

"Why not?"

She swallowed. "That's no reason."

"Do you need a reason for everything? Don't you ever just . . ."—he shrugged—"do things?"

"No."

Raven drew a deep breath. "Neither do I. Perhaps we're missing something. You're so serious."

"But I'm still alive."

It was immediately clear she hadn't meant to say those words. He watched a look of regret and confusion cross her face. He fashioned a grin, not moving, trying to make light of the situation. "I don't think it'll kill you if I take off your shoes, Charm."

They sat in silence. Her knees were pulled to her chest and her eyes were like bright emeralds as she watched him.

"Tell you what. I'll take off my boots first. To prove my good faith. If I'm struck dead, you can keep yours on."

He wasn't positive, but he thought he saw a whisper of a smile lift her lips. It intrigued him and somehow made his heart ache. "All right, here goes. Pray for me," he said and placed his hands above the heel of one boot. There he stopped, screwing up his face and closing his eyes as if afraid lightning would somehow find and sear him to cinders.

"You're teasing me."

Very soft now, her voice didn't seem to hold resentment.

He opened his eyes. "Yes, I am," he said and saw now that she was smiling shyly. The pain that had begun at his heart swept outward, making it difficult to speak. "You are an extremely beautiful woman."

Her expression faltered slightly, leaving the frightened doe look again.

"Now you say, 'Thank you, Joseph,' " Raven coached.

The smile brightened slightly. "The name Joseph seems quite . . . personal."

"Ah, but you forget." He pulled off his first boot with a flourish and held the thing aloft for a moment. "We are now

at a very personal stage in our relationship. The . . ."—
he tugged his other boot free—"shoe removal stage." He
raised his brows at her, and, wonder of wonders, she
laughed.

"Now you're making fun of me."

"No, I'm not." He set the boots aside and searched her
face for fear. It was still there, though mostly hidden by
other emotions and shadows. "How do you sit like that?"

"Like what?" She hugged her knees more closely to her
chest, so that her chin was just above them.

"Like that." He watched her.

"I just do." She shrugged, looking nervous.

He sighed. "Can't do that," he said, making a feeble
attempt before settling back onto one palm. "Men must be
made different."

Surprisingly, she responded, though slowly. "Entirely
different species, I think."

"You're doing very well here, Charm," he said with a
smile. "Carrying on a ridiculously inane conversation and
still breathing. I think you could manage the shoe thing."

A long, burnt-cinnamon lock had come loose from her
knot of hair. She pushed it back. "You think I'm a dolt."

"Hardly that," he said seriously.

"You think I'm a frightened little mouse."

Raven clenched his teeth, suddenly feeling inexplicably
protective of this young beauty before him. "I think I'd like
to kill whoever has hurt you."

He had not intended to be so blatantly honest. He found
suddenly that they were both silent, waiting.

"All right." She said the words very suddenly, as though
she had to chase them out before they became trapped in her
throat. "I'll take my shoes off."

"Oh no," he said on a smooth exhalation. "That wasn't
the deal. Either *I* take them off or those things stay on."

Her laughter could light up the night and seemed to do
just that.

"Is there something I should know about your strange affinity for feet?"

He laughed now too. Who would have thought the girl had a sense of humor? "Feet? No. But elbows!" he said and shot her left arm a lascivious glance.

She drew her knees in more sharply, as if she might crawl within herself. Raven sighed mentally.

"Tell me who it was who has scared you so, Charm."

Silence settled between them.

"Are you going to take off my shoes or am I going to have to sleep with them on again?"

How did one attempt to breach the emotional wall Charm had so effectively erected? Raven wondered, but now hardly seemed the time to discuss it. Reaching slowly for her laces, he tugged the first one free. Her full skirt and petticoats made an effective barrier between him and her legs and fell full-length down to her shoe tops. Still, there was an intimacy somehow that baffled and exhilarated him. Easing the lace loose in its holes, he slipped his hand behind her heel to gently pull the shoe away.

"There." He set it aside and watched her face, wondering if she looked pale. "That wasn't so bad was it?"

"Almost . . . bearable," she said, and he grinned at her before reaching for her second foot.

This time he made so bold as to touch her ankle as he tugged the shoe free, and now they sat, staring at each other like two errant schoolchildren.

"Well . . ." He took a deep breath, remembering a time when he had actually touched a woman's bare skin, had felt her move beneath him. Yet somehow it seemed that those times had held no more excitement for him than this. He was a sick man, Raven deduced wryly. "We'd better get some sleep.

"Would you kiss me?"

He was quite certain his heart stopped beating. For a moment he considered giving his chest a good hard rap to start it up again. "No." It was amazing how a person could sometimes force himself to say almost anything. "I won't."

"Why?" Her voice was nothing if not surprised.

"Because you'd hate me. Not to mention the fact that you'd probably kill me."

"What if I promised not to?"

"Not to hate me, or not to kill me?"

"Both."

He ran his fingers through his hair, wondering how fast he could saddle his horse and get the hell out of there. But he couldn't decide which was more cowardly, staying or leaving, so he stayed. "You're a very confusing young woman, Charm. First I can't touch your shoes, now you want to be kissed."

He could hear her draw a breath. "You think *I'm* not confused?"

On the contrary, he thought, she was very confused. She was confusing him with someone who had the strength to kiss her and go no further. All he'd bargained for was shoe removal, and that was stretching his limits. "Why?"

She hugged her legs more tightly against her chest, looking very small. "Why what?"

Oh for God's sake! he wanted to yell, but he kept rigid control and asked, "Why do you want me to kiss you?"

"Well . . ." Her voice was tight. "The usual reasons. You know."

He wanted to laugh, but every fiber in his body felt taut as a bow string, from his throat on down, making it impossible. "No. I don't."

She swallowed. "Neither do I," she finally whispered. "What *are* the usual reasons?"

Why not just kiss her and get it over with? Raven wondered rather wildly, but good sense made him answer instead, for rushing the girl would be a bad bet. "Oh . . . desire," he breathed. "Lust." He frowned, wondering if she had meant to make him think this hard. "Love maybe. Curiosity."

"How about fear?"

"Fear? No. I'm afraid people don't kiss out of fear."

"I hate being afraid."

"Forgive me for not following your line of reason."

"Maybe I'll get over it . . . if I kiss you."

Raven frowned again, thinking he should, perhaps, be insulted. "So it'd be a kind of experiment?"

"Yes."

"And I'd be nothing more than a sort of lowly, ignorant test animal."

She blinked, looking young and sweet and chagrined. "Well, rather like that, yes."

Raven shrugged. "That sounds reasonable."

Chapter 18

"But . . . no hands," Charm said.

She could see Raven watching her in the darkness. "What?" he asked.

"You can't . . . touch me." She knew she was crazy, and yet, never in her life had she felt it was so possible to overcome her fear of men. "Can you do that?" Her question was little more than a breath of uncertainty to her own ears.

It took him a few seconds to answer. "Of course."

"All right."

Neither one moved.

"How . . . um . . ." She felt as if she might faint and half hoped she would. "How do we go about this?"

"Well," he began, raising his brows slightly, "folks usually trust their instincts in the heat of the moment."

She blinked. "Oh."

"It's not usually discussed to death beforehand. Usually a passionate embrace, that sort of thing."

"Oh. Then you mean we can't—"

"I'm sure we can," he interrupted swiftly, then grinned in

that self-deprecating manner she had almost learned to expect from him.

"Then . . ." Though she tried, she found she could not finish the question.

"Lie down."

"What?" Her tone was panicked and her throat felt tight.

"I'm not going to hurt you, Charm. Not ever."

She remembered to breathe, and she nodded mutely.

"Lie down."

She did so finally, lying flat on her back and feeling very like a piece of lumber ready for the mill. Just as stiff, just as breathless, just as doomed.

Raven eased down beside her, keeping almost a foot of space between them and staring into her eyes. "Nervous?"

"No!"

He laughed, very low in his throat. "Oh, come now, you can lie better than that. Let's try it again." He paused, still watching her. "So, Miss Charm," he began slowly, "are you nervous?"

Why didn't he just kiss her and get it over with? But he seemed determined to play games, so she took a deep breath and said, "No," in a voice that almost sounded seductive in its breathlessness. "Why should I be?"

He laughed again. The sound felt strange, like the rough stroke of a kitten's tongue, shivery, yet gentle. "Very good. I decided when you lied to Clancy for me, right after the lynch attempt, I decided you could lie with the best of them. Maybe even better than Clancy, damn his hide. May I touch your hair?"

She opened her mouth to deny his request and his assessment of her abilities, but he interrupted smoothly.

"I wouldn't actually be touching *you*. No skin, of course. Just hair."

Somehow he made it all sound very silly, and she could do nothing but nod.

He reached for that wayward lock that always escaped bondage. It lay across her left breast, and though she held her breath, he was true to his word and avoided contact. His fingers connected with the hair where it touched nothing but air near her neck.

"Very soft." He caressed the lock between his thumb and fingers. "Like living water in cinnamon hues."

He was a poet. Who would have thought?

"May I take it down?"

"What?" Her inhalation was sharp.

"Should I take that as a 'no'?"

"Take what down?"

"Your hair. It's coming loose."

"Oh." Her breath came slightly easier now, for in her frantic imaginings, she had thought of all sorts of things that could be taken down. "Well . . ."

"No skin," he promised. "And just one hand." He replaced the wayward lock to lift his right hand as evidence. "Surely you can't sleep with those pins in anyway."

"I don't sleep," she reminded him breathlessly.

"I could help you."

"What?"

He remained absolutely silent, watching her. "Nothing. How about the hair?"

"All right."

He was lying on his numb arm and reached for her with his right hand. She felt his fingers brush her scalp, felt a pin tugged free. The knot loosened at the back of her head. His hand appeared again to place the pin between their bodies before returning for a second, and then a third. It was a breathless sort of endeavor. His fingers just barely caressed her hair until all the pins lay before her, and the heavy mass of her tresses was set free.

"You should wear it down all the time," he said, and reaching behind again, drew it gently forward to stroke the ends against his face. "Can I come a little closer?" But before she could answer he was already a few inches nearer. "This is a hard job to do from back there." He grinned, reminding her of his promise to kiss her. "Are you ready?"

Charm almost pulled away, almost jerked to her feet. Instead she remained as she was, feeling panic swell around her like a wild tide. He moved nearer, his gaze boring steadily into hers. Breath knotted in Charm's throat. His eyes were sleepily seductive. His lips were parted. He moved nearer still—and kissed her cheek.

"Good night, Charm," he said casually and turned his back.

"You cheated."

Raven woke to the sound of Charm's voice. Opening his eyes, he found her staring at him from only inches away. It was a shock to his already shocked system. After all, who would have thought he would actually have the strength to kiss her cheek and draw away? It was amazing what he could do when he set his mind to something: pretend to faint to prevent her from leaving, pretend to sleep to prevent her from leaving, pretend to be content with kissing her cheek to prevent her from leaving.

"Do you realize it's the dead of night?" he asked quietly.

"Yes."

"You really don't sleep, do you?"

"Only . . ."

"Snatches," he finished for her and sat up wearily. "Was there something you wanted?"

"A kiss."

He was immediately wide-awake and cursed himself for it, trying to feel sleepy. "I already did that."

"But you cheated."

"Explain or go away," he said, feeling impatient frustration ride him with more force than he thought possible.

"It wasn't a real kiss."

"I beg to differ."

"It wasn't even . . . frightening."

"You want to be scared, take your clothes off." He hadn't meant to say it, but the words were out. He could see the fear in her eyes and cursed himself again, but fatigue and celibacy had made fools of better men than he. "Let sleeping dogs lie, Charm," he said more softly.

She drew a quiet breath. "You're not sleeping."

He frowned, wondering if this conversation was making as little sense as he suspected. "Are you calling me a dog?"

"You don't know what it's like, living with this fear."

"Is that why you don't sleep?"

She looked away. "I have dreams. Had them as long as I can remember. Of a big man with blond hair. He wears a hat . . . cocked . . . to one side. He's very handsome." She took three full breaths, doing her best to fight the fear. "He wakes me up. Smiles. Always smiles. And then . . ." She shook her head, knowing the motion was jerky. "He hurts me. He wakes me up. And . . . hurts me."

"Charm . . ."

"Once . . ." She interrupted him quickly, though for a moment words failed her. "When I was about twelve a man came into my room. He was so big . . ." She paused, remembering his hands on her, remembering her consuming fear. "And he was wearing the hat."

"The source of the nightmares."

"No!" She shook her head wildly. "I dreamt of him before . . . before I saw him! It was as if . . . as if I had conjured him up in my dreams." Her voice was a whisper. "I can't afford to sleep."

"What happened that night?"

Although she heard his question, she refused to answer. "Can't afford to sleep," she murmured again.

"What happened, Charm? Did he hurt you?"

She swallowed, feeling as if she would surely die. "Jude came. Saved me. Killed him," she whispered and nodded. "With his bare hands. Beat him to death." A strange sobbing sound rattled from her throat, surprising her. "Left him dead. All beaten . . ." Her voice broke as her eyes closed and Raven caught her in the strength of his arms.

"Shh," he whispered, holding her against him.

"Jude killed him."

"Are you sure he was dead?"

She closed her eyes, remembering. "No one could have lived through that."

Raven's jaw tightened. "Good."

She drew a sharp breath between her teeth and drew abruptly away. "What if it was my fault?"

Raven scowled and reached for her again, but she shook her head and drew back.

"What if I created him in my head? Called him in my dreams?"

"That's crazy."

She sat very still, feeling sick to her stomach. Never had she spoken of that night. "I *am* crazy," she whispered.

"No." Raven's expression was somber and hard. "You're not crazy, Charm. You're just a survivor. It doesn't make you guilty."

"But the man in the hat—"

"Deserved to die," Raven interrupted. "You did the world a favor."

She tightened her fists, trying to allow the relief he offered.

"I wish I could make it better for you, Charm. Take away all the pain. But—"

"But maybe you can," she said softly. "I mean, I'm a grown woman, Raven. There's no longer any reason for me to fear men as I do."

"Most men are . . . aren't to be trusted," Raven said quietly.

"Trust!" She laughed shakily, then swallowed and paused a moment. "I'm not talking about trust. I'm talking about . . ." She shook her head. "Sleep. About being able to sleep. To breathe. Just to be . . . normal."

"You're better than normal, Charm," he whispered.

She studied the intensity of his face. "Kiss me," she whispered back.

He shook his head. "I don't think a single kiss will—"

"You asked me why I wore the gowns."

"What?"

"You asked if Jude made me wear those gowns. Well, he didn't. I did it on my own, and you know why? Because it gave me power. Because when men look at me, I can feel their lust." She paused. "I know I have something they want but can't have. I feel the derringer in my pocket. The knife in my garter. And I know I can kill them if they touch me. It's a power," she said more quietly, "that's all mine."

He said nothing, and she wondered numbly if he hated her now, after admitting something she hadn't known herself.

"I want to get over it, Raven," she whispered.

There was a moment of absolute stillness, and then he reached for her. She squeezed her eyes closed and waited. His touch was very soft against her cheek, and when he leaned closer, she could smell the tangy fragrance of woodsmoke and sweet tobacco.

The kiss was gentle, very soft and very brief. Yet, it ignited sparks of something other than fear. They flashed from her lips to her breasts and downward in curling flames of surprise. She could sense him leaning back and opened her eyes to find him watching her.

"So what do you think?" he asked quietly.

"That's it?"

One corner of his mouth lifted into a wry smile. "'Fraid so."

"Well . . ." She sighed, not sure if it was relief or exhilaration. "That was almost . . . bearable."

His laughter was a beautiful thing. "You're very hard on a man's self-esteem, Lucky Charm."

She smiled, feeling suddenly as if she could fly, as if she had stood the test of fire. "And you're very cautious."

"How's that?"

She bit the inside of her lip, wanting to laugh. "I think you can kiss better than that," she said, and turning her back to him, lay down.

*   *   *

The little imp! Raven remained awake for the rest of the night, staring at her back and wondering if she were snatching sleep. She was driving him insane, of course, tempting him, threatening him, wounding him, tempting him again, and then smiting him with the tender emotions raised by her fears and memories. And if *that* wasn't enough, she had begun teasing him.

Yes, teasing! Who would have thought? He smiled despite himself and waited for dawn.

By the time they reached Jordan, the only stage had already left, and Raven decided to use the time to purchase a few supplies and find them a room. His worrying over Charm's preference to spend the night with him or alone turned out to be a moot point, for there was only one room available in town. Calling them Mr. and Mrs. McBain, he rented it with a mental smile that he knew should shame him. Supper was a simple affair. Afterward, he accompanied his pretend wife up the stairs, noticing the other men's glances and feeling a strange swelling in his chest that he feared might be pride.

The door closed quietly behind them. Charm turned to watch him.

"There was only one room." Raven knew he had told her that before, but it seemed worth repeating. He hoped she wouldn't consider the fact that he *could* conceivably spend the night in the stable with the horses. "Would you like a bath?"

"What?"

"A bath." He grinned, knowing he shouldn't tease her. "I could wash your back."

Her lips parted in silent astonishment.

"Or not," he said, widening his grin. "But . . . you must feel gritty. I wouldn't look. In fact I could—"

"All right."

His jaw dropped slightly, and his eyes narrowed. Surely he hadn't heard her correctly.

"You did say you wouldn't look."

He *had* heard her correctly, for Christ's sake. For a second Raven was certain the world was coming to an end. He stood waiting for a bugle call, or something that would signal the termination of life as he knew it. But nothing changed, so he closed his mouth with an effort. "I don't think you understood me correctly."

"You said you wouldn't look if I took a bath."

By God, that was what he'd said, so why was he still living? Surely there was some kind of weapon close at hand with which she might attack him. "Maybe I lied."

"I don't think so."

The realm of unreality seemed foggy. "What do you mean, you don't think so?"

"When you lie you tighten your right fist."

Raven tried to think of something to say, some clever rejoinder, but no words came. It was as though he had broken through the floor and was now floundering for footing. What the hell should he do now?

"I'll, uh . . . order the bath," he said, and turned numbly away.

In a short while, the tub was filled by an Oriental woman with a quick smile and a limited use of the English language. Raven eyed the oval vat longingly, not because he felt dirty, but because he could imagine Charm in it, looking charming . . . and naked . . . and unarmed.

"I'll wait downstairs," he said, and using every bit of the self-control he thought he didn't possess, left again.

He wandered about town for a bit, checking on the horses before finding a poker game. But in the end, games of chance seemed unappealing, partly because he thought it wise to remain as unseen as possible, and partly because of his thoughts of Charm. Damned if she hadn't been flirting with him, and damned if he hadn't run out of there like a hound with a broken tail.

Finally he found his way back to the room to knock twice on the door. He knew he should wait for an answer. But he didn't, and when he stepped inside he found it impossible to think he had made the wrong choice.

Charm was there, standing in the middle of the room. Her long, mahogany hair was wet and slick, her sweet luscious body wrapped in a white sheet that she'd apparently yanked from the bed in the seconds before he'd entered.

"She took my clothes!"

Raven raised his brows and tried to think coherently. She had very nice shoulders. They were the color of rich cream and were smooth, not hidden by the sleek hair that was pushed behind her ears. "What's that?"

"The Chinese woman." Her voice sounded fairly panicked. "She took my clothes."

He almost laughed and would have, but . . . she was naked beneath that sheet. It was a sobering thought. "Don't worry," he said. "They won't fit her. She'll bring them back."

"She didn't steal them!" Charm sputtered, and Raven wondered for a second if she would add "you idiot" to the end of that sentence, but she didn't. "She took them to the laundry."

"Oh." Raven nodded, still trying to think. "Good idea."

"I have nothing to wear."

"Then why did you tell her to take them?" He raised his brows higher, pausing and realizing the humor of the situation with some difficulty. "Are you trying to seduce me?"

"I didn't tell her to take them," Charm choked. "She said, 'want wash' or something and I . . . I just . . . I didn't know she meant my clothes."

For a moment he actually wondered if she was going to cry. He eased back against the door, remembering to give her room to breathe.

"I thought you trusted me."

"I didn't say that," she said, shaking her head.

"Yes, you did."

"No." The sheet made her look like a mermaid with an ungainly tail. "I said, I think I *can* trust you. Not I *do* trust you."

"Ahhh. And there's the difference."

"All the difference in the world."

"She'll bring the dress back, Charm."

"But what will I do until then?"

He could think of about . . . oh, a thousand different and intriguing ideas. "Stage leaves at eight o'clock. Why don't you get some sleep?"

"But I—"

"Go on. Go lie down."

She took a deep breath, seeming to try to act rationally. "You're not going to . . ."

"To what?"

"You know."

"Seduce you?"

She nodded stiffly.

"Could it be done?"

No answer. He swallowed hard, holding to his self-control with all his might.

"You know what they do to men who force themselves on women in this part of the world?" he asked quietly.

She bit her inner lip.

"I don't want to think about it," he said, "and you, I hope, don't want to hear about it. But one scream from you and my chances of survival would be severely reduced. Remember New Eden?"

They stared at each other in the waning light.

"Go to sleep, Charm."

"I don't sl—"

"Well then, go snatch!" he almost yelled, frustrated to distraction by her nearness, her near nudity, and his own near insanity.

She drew another deep breath. "All right." She shuffled about, dragging her tail with her before turning back to stare at him suspiciously. "What are you going to do?"

"I'm going to take a bath."

Chapter 19

Raven thought Charm's jaw couldn't possibly drop lower. And her eyes could get no wider.

"You are not," she said.

"Not what?" He watched her with an innocuous expression.

"Going to take a bath."

"Yes I am."

"I'll scream. I swear I will."

He actually laughed now, but very quietly. "Screaming is only allowed for molestation and lewd advances. Besides, I didn't scream when you bathed."

"You can't bathe in here."

"You're being silly. What are you afraid of?"

"You know what I'm afraid of."

"Why am I more threatening with my clothes off than on?" He waited for an answer which didn't come. "I'm not. Less, in fact. You run out that door, I can't follow you."

"How could I run out the door? I have no clothes."

"Then stay in here. Watch even. I don't care. But I'm

taking a bath for Christ's sake," he said and began to unbutton his shirt, remembering to use only his right hand.

She remained as she was, staring at him as if he'd lost his mind.

Raven cleared his throat and loosed his fourth button. "Are you really going to watch?" Somehow the idea was a little more disconcerting than he'd expected.

"You said you don't mind."

Well, God damn it! He'd lied. Call it a habit of his. Wasn't she supposed to be shy or something? Raven scowled. "You are the most unpredictable woman I have ever met."

"Do you need help with that shirt?"

"Good God, woman, what the devil's come over you?"

Her cheeks were pink. "I'm just trying to be helpful."

They stared at each other, both becoming suddenly quiet and deadly serious.

"Yes." He nodded once, soberly calling her bluff. "I do need help."

Though fear and uncertainty sparked in her eyes, there was something else as well. Spirit. Alive and flaming within the beautiful framework of her body.

"All right." She lifted her white tail and walked toward him. He noticed without really meaning to, that the sheet was wrapped twice around her body, and the corner was tucked snugly into the upper edge. She stood before him, her eyes wide, her hands unmoving.

Raven watched her. "Breathe," he reminded softly.

"Oh yeah." She did so, failing to notice the strangeness of his statement. "Now what?"

He smiled at her, feeling an unknown emotion flood him in soft waves. "Now go to bed."

"I don't want to." Her words were whispered and now it was Raven's turn to forget to breathe.

"I suppose . . ." He tried to stop the words before they escaped, but it was no use. "I could try to improve on that last kiss."

Her nod was almost imperceptible and completely unnecessary, for he felt as though he could read her thoughts. The distance between them evaporated. Their lips met, shocking them both with intensity and warmth. He opened his mouth, touching her with his tongue. He felt her shiver against his chest before he pulled back.

"Well?" he asked softly.

"Almost—"

"Bearable," he said and tried to grin, but there was a suspicious ache in his lower body, an ache that boded ill for sleep and continued celibacy. "Go to bed, little Charm."

"I . . ." She touched her top lip with her tongue. Her teeth were very white, he noticed, and her tongue pink and pointed.

God, he wanted her! The ache turned to a burn!

"I need to help with your shirt."

That was the last place he needed help, Raven thought, but he couldn't afford to admit the extent of his weakness, not after he'd come so far. Her hands shook when she reached for him. Raven watched his buttons fall open, watched the dark ridge of hair become visible against his torso.

Her knuckles brushed that hair. The touch was like velvet, soft as a sigh. Raven closed his eyes, unable to watch any longer without reacting. For just a moment more she touched him, and then she was at the next button. It eased open. He gritted his teeth, feeling her fingers again, feather soft upon his flesh as he pressed his shoulders against the door behind him. She tugged his shirt free of his pants. He felt it scrape against the sensitized skin of his abdomen and drew breath through his teeth in a ragged gasp.

Now would be a damned fine time to leave, he thought, but there was really no hope of it, for every nerve ending was waiting for her next touch. Every breath was pinned on the hope that she wouldn't quit. The last button fell open. There was a moment's hesitation before her hands were pressed lightly against his chest. His muscles tightened in heart-stopping anticipation and then, like the proverbial forbidden fruit, she was kissing him, her lips sweet and soft against his.

Raven moaned, keeping his hands at his sides and his shoulders pressed hard against the door behind. Every living fiber of him ached for her, but he dared not touch, lest he frighten her from her timid exploration.

"Raven . . ." Her voice was thistledown soft and breathy against his ear. "What now?"

Now he should carry her to bed, his gut said. He should peel her from that silly sheet and kiss every inch of her body. He should cover her with his hands, feel the life and loveliness of every inch of her luscious form, stoke her desire like a small precious flame, and bring her to ecstasy in his arms.

"Now you go to sleep," his lips managed.

She was very close and breathing hard. "What about you?"

"Is the water cold?"

"What?"

Raven closed his eyes and wondered dismally how things had come to this. Surely he didn't deserve such temptation. All he wanted was the reward. He'd never bargained for such a beauty. And yet they'd barely begun their journey together. How would he ever stand the test of hundreds of miles with this woman at his side? But he must, for Chantilly Grady's kin would surely not take her defilement kindly. "I need a bath," he said, but his teeth were clenched, and if she asked if he needed help with his pants, that was it! All bets were off. She was his! In that bed. Right now!

Unfortunately, she didn't ask. Instead, she backed away a cautious step, looking shaky. "Can I really watch?"

Raven tried to ease his fists open but they wouldn't be loosened. If she watched him undress he would burst into spontaneous flame. He was sure of it.

"God, woman!" was all he could manage.

"You said I could." Her voice was small as a child's. "You promised."

No, he hadn't, but he was past the point of making any coherent arguments. He pulled the shirt from his shoulders, easing it down his arms until it fell to the floor in a heap.

Charm swallowed. His chest was very wide. It was sculpted with valleys and hills of muscle and marred by the wound she had given him. His arms were thick with rigid strength, and his ribs were visible in lean rows that ended at the flat expanse of his belly.

His right hand dropped to his buckle and her gaze nervously followed. Turn away! her mind screamed. But she could not and stood transfixed as his belt was eased open and the first button slowly undone. The waistband loosened, exposing more rippled abdomen and a slight increase in the narrow mat of black hair. His fingers moved lower. Another button succumbed. There was a notable bulge to the left of the opening. Had it shifted slightly? If so, it definitely wasn't her Bible.

"If you're going to faint, try to hit the bed."

She was breathing through her mouth, which was, she thought, better than not breathing at all. A decided improvement.

"Charm?"

Had it moved? Did it move on its own? Like an extra arm?

"Charm!"

"What?" she all but shouted, startled from her reverie and snapping her gaze to his face.

"Go away."

She puckered her lips, trying to speak. Nothing came out. "Did you hear me?"

Her knees were shaking. An interesting side effect. "You said I could—"

He gritted his teeth at her. "I don't care what I said."

Charm scowled, thinking hard. "Are you . . . shy?"

"No!" he said, sounding immediately offended.

She wondered why he would consider shyness a fault. "Embarrassed?"

He jutted his chin out toward her slightly, looking increasingly offended, plus aggressive now. "No."

"Ashamed?"

"Ashamed!" he nearly shouted, and then his fingers were on his buttons. They fell open in one quick sweep.

Charm dared one rapid-fire glance at the burgeoning life that sprang into view and then dove for the bed. In less than a heartbeat her head was covered.

Where was her derringer? Where was her knife? But Raven made no attempt to ferret her out, and finally she felt silly, smothered under all those blankets. She heard him splash into the bath. Gradually, she relaxed. Her breathing returned to normal, and finally she removed the blankets from her head to stare into the pillow.

Well, she'd certainly handled that cleverly, she thought. Like a mature woman. She almost snorted. Dear God, what was wrong with her?

Minutes ticked away. Half an hour passed, during which time she kept still, refusing to look up, though she had turned over onto her back now. She could hear Raven exit his bath. She felt a blanket being pulled from the bed, but didn't dare move, much less raise her gaze to him.

"Really, really hard on a man's self-esteem," he said quietly.

She remained as she was, thinking. The bed dipped beneath his weight. It was dark now. She screwed up her courage. "What was I supposed to do?" Her voice was very quiet. Still, that was no reason for him to pretend he hadn't heard her, she thought. "Raven?"

Still no answer. Very timidly, she reached out to touch his arm. "What was I supposed to do?"

"You're an heiress!" He sat up very suddenly, startling her with his movement and the intensity of his tone. "You're Chantilly Grady. A lady of wealth. You did exactly what you're supposed to do—finally."

She stared at him in terror, but he didn't move and said no more. "You're making no sense," she whispered.

"*I'm* making no sense!" he stormed, suddenly out of bed and pacing, one blanket wrapped loosely about his shoulders. "*I'm* making no sense? *You* make no sense. Good God, woman, first you . . ." He raised one hand, motioning wildly. "Then you . . ." He waved again. "And now you . . ." His gesturing became more frenetic, and finally the blanket abandoned his shoulders to disappear onto the floor. "Now you watch me! Watch me! Well, damn it all," he said, making no move to retrieve his impromptu garment and placing his fists on his hips. "I give up. I can't resist." He strode back toward the bed. "You win. Or lose, or whatever. Get ready for a first-class seduction, woman, because I—"

The door swung open as if blasted with dynamite.

"Lay a hand on her, I'll blow yer brains from here to hell!"

"Jude!" Charm gasped.

"Jude!" Raven groaned.

"Say the word, gal, I'll kill him right now."

"No need to kill him!" said Clancy, stepping in with a lantern and raising his brows as his gaze swept up and down Raven's naked form. "Joseph, I'm surprised at you."

"Get dressed, goddamn it!" Jude growled. "Or there won't be enough left of you to send home to yer mama."

"Damn, she's pretty," said Clancy. "That really your daughter?"

"Get out, Charm," Jude said. "Unless you want to watch him die."

"Jude," Charm began.

"Get out!" Jude yelled, but in that instant Raven lunged.

His left fist slammed the gun aside while his right smashed into Jude's face. There was a crash as the old man fell backward into unconsciousness, but already Raven was atop Clancy. The lantern fell, bursting into sparks of glass and light as it struck the floor, but the men didn't notice as they struggled for supremacy. From the bed, Charm watched in horror as Raven sent Clancy into slumber beside Jude's still form.

"Help me tie them up," Raven gasped.

"Jude!" Charm called. Raven stopped, watching her.

"You said you wanted to come with me."

"Jude," she said again, dragging a sheet with her as she rose.

"He's fine. We have to hurry, before they wake up," Raven said, but she was already kneeling beside her father, her fingers on his cheek.

The last spark from the lantern flickered and went out, leaving them in darkness.

"You hit him," she said quietly.

"Of course I hit him," Raven reasoned. "He was going to shoot me."

"There's nothing wrong with your arm, is there?"

The silence was enough of an answer.

"Get out!"

"Charm," Raven began softly.

"Get out!" she spat.

"He's not your father, Charm. Believe me."

"You lie!"

"*He* lied. He's been lying all these years."

Somehow she found the gun in the darkness and fired without thinking. But before she could correct her aim, Raven was upon her. He wrestled the gun from her hand and pinned her to the floor. Bare legs tangled in linen as Charm thrashed and swore.

"God damn it, woman, hold still!"

"Get off me!"

"So you can kill me?"

"Yes!" she snarled, bucking again.

"I don't think so. You're coming with me."

"Like hell."

"A lot like hell!" he said, and pulled her to her feet as she grappled with the sheet. "Get dressed."

"Never!" she exploded, draping the linen before her quivering body. "I'll never go with you."

He stood very still, staring at her shadowy figure and still holding her wrist. "Then I'll call the law in myself and tell them everything."

She narrowed her eyes, hating him. "What are you talking about?"

"I'll tell them Jude killed the man with the hat. Randall Grady." He paused, letting his words sink in. "Your real father."

"You're mad!" she breathed.

"Maybe, but I know the truth, Charm, and they will, too, unless you come with me."

From down the hall, footsteps hurried toward them.

Charm tried desperately to think. "You won't hurt him if I come?"

"You have my word."

"What's going on here?" A light appeared with the voice.

Raven pulled his attention from Charm to aim it at the newcomer. "These . . ."—he waved wildly, hoping he looked near hysterics—"these brigands broke into our room."

"Thieves?"

"Just damn drunkards," Raven countered, sounding outraged. "Raving mad bastards. Thought my sweet Emily was some floozy named Charm. Scared her near to death," he added, pulling Charm close. "Does this town have a sheriff?"

"Say, you're . . . you're naked, mister."

"Damn it, man!" stormed Raven, thrusting out his chest and scowling darkly. "These no-accounts nearly scared Mrs. McBain into apoplexy, now do you have some place to keep these two till they sleep it off or not?"

"I'll . . . I'll get help!" squeaked the man, and taking one last look, fled down the hall.

"Get dressed," Raven ordered.

"She took my gown," Charm pointed out.

"Wear your old red one. It's in the bag."

"You . . ."—Charm drew herself straighter—"you had it all along?"

"Just say I became attached to it," he said. "Put it on and keep quiet or I'll tell everything I know about Jude, and it's not good."

Chapter 20

They rode hard all night. Although Raven kept a hold on Angel's reins, he was never sure if it was necessary or not. Charm was absolutely silent, giving no clue to her intentions. But her thoughts were clear to him. She hated him. And why not? He'd lied to her, hit the one man she trusted, and forced her to leave him while he was still unconscious, bound and gagged.

Yes, she hated him, and would probably murder him if she got half a chance. The killer woman was back.

The black-forested hills had been left behind, making way for a sea of grasses that seemed to stretch on forever. Although the horses had plenty to eat, human rations were low. The midday meal consisted of nothing more than the remainder of bacon and biscuits, but it seemed like a feast in comparison to supper.

No fire was lit that night. The horses were hobbled to prevent their escape, and camp was made in a small, rare copse of cottonwood near a shallow pond.

"I'm going to have to tie you up." Raven's voice broke the silence. Charm didn't move. She remained as she was, dressed in the frayed elegance of her seductive gown and seated on a rotting log where she stared at nothing in particular. He watched her. Not one word had she spoken for the forty or so miles they'd traveled that day. "I hate to do it."

Still she didn't move, didn't speak, didn't raise her gaze to his. Raven gritted his teeth.

"He's not your father!" he spouted suddenly, unable to hold back the words. "Your name's Chantilly, and you're a wealthy woman. You have an aunt who wants you back. A mansion, River Bluffs. Servants. Old Cora."

The silence was as heavy as the darkness.

"Eloise is paying a great deal of money to get you back."

The frustrating thing about the woman was that she could pretend not to hear him. But he knew she heard. She was sitting only a half a dozen feet away, and she was trying to drive him insane. That's all. But it wasn't going to work. She could remain mute from now until hell froze over. He didn't care. He'd just keep feeding her information, and if she didn't believe his story now, she was sure to by the end of their journey.

"Eloise gave your mother her Bible before she left. Caroline ran away to be with your father, Randall Grady. Your grandmother didn't approve. Then, ten years or so later, she gets a letter from Grady that says Caroline died in an accident. But their daughter, Chantilly, is alive and well and can be brought to River Bluffs if old Sophie will pay the expenses."

Though Charm didn't speak, she was watching him now, very tense and silent.

Against his will Raven softened his tone. "I don't know what the old lady's response was. All I saw was Grady's letter. But I know nothing came of it. As far as I can tell they never heard from him again, and Chantilly never showed up. Finally old Sophie died, and Eloise found the letters, Caroline's and Grady's." He paused, running the splayed fingers of his left hand through his hair. "You'll have a home, Charm, real family, security."

She didn't so much as blink an eye, but he knew she had heard. And that was all he asked. There was no need to react, no need for her forgiveness. After all, he was only doing it for the money. Raven relaxed his jaw with an effort. The silence was very loud.

"All right, goddamnit, I lied about my arm!" he shouted, and she jumped as he strode angrily before her. "I lied because you were so damned scared of me. I knew you'd feel better if you thought I was half dead. And it sure did work, didn't it?" he asked, leaning forward from the waist to speak directly into her face. "Damn right it did, because all of a suddenlike you were flirting, teasing, watching me undress, for Christ's sake."

Her gaze had met his, and though he searched, he could find nothing but the aloof indifference she had learned to show the world.

"Talk to me, goddamnit!" he shouted, but she said nothing, merely extending her hands to be tied.

This was, without exception, the most miserable night Raven had ever spent. He had indeed tied her. First her wrists, then her ankles. Then, however, she couldn't move her arms, which, of course, had been the purpose. But it had bothered him, somehow, for who could sleep on the hard ground without at least an arm to cushion her head on? In the end, he had cut her hands free and bound her to his own body.

It was now long past midnight, and he was about to go insane. "God damn it, don't you ever sleep?" he asked miserably.

She stared at him from twelve inches away, her expression absolutely unreadable, saying nothing.

Raven gritted his teeth again. "At least close your eyes. For Christ's sake, woman, I'm not going to eat you."

She didn't even blink. His teeth ached with the increased pressure he applied.

"Close your eyes," he said again, "or I'll . . . have to kiss you."

At least that news warranted an expression of some sort, though he couldn't quite read it in the darkness. He could, however, see that her eyes remained open. So he kissed her. Her lips were soft and warm, her breathing rapid, but she didn't try to pull away. She tasted like heaven, and for a moment he thought he imagined her kissing him back.

"Charm." He breathed her name, feeling her heady appeal to the depths of his bones. He wanted nothing more than to pull her into his arms and beg to be forgiven, but when he looked into her face, he saw that her eyes were closed.

By morning, Raven felt as though his eyelids were made of sand and his mouth of sawdust. The sun was just beginning to rise and the killer woman was staring at him from such close proximity that he felt he could feel her think. Good God, the reward couldn't possibly be worth all this. In fact, an Indian raid was beginning to look more and more desirable. Maybe they'd take the girl. Or maybe they'd just kill him and deprive Charm of that pleasure.

They saw buffalo that day. Not the huge herds reported years earlier, but several hundred, moving slowly and raising dust. A little past noon, he shot a rabbit with the gun he'd found in Angel's saddlebag. He hadn't told Charm of his find, of course, fearing she'd think to put it to better use than the delivery of a meal. The killer woman, however, seemed unexcited by the sight of the gun, unimpressed by his marksmanship, and downright disdainful of his cuisine, which consisted of charred bunny accompanied by muddy water.

"I'll cook."

"What's that?" Raven raised his head to stare at the girl he'd been sure had forgotten how to speak. It was almost dark, and the small cooking fire had been cautiously extinguished, lest they attract unwanted visitors.

"Is there a town nearby?" she asked, not looking at him.

"We should reach it tomorrow morning."

"If you buy supplies, I'll cook."

He stared at her. "Why?"

She stared back, giving him that prim little smile she reserved for cutting a man to the quick. "Because I don't want to starve . . . before I see you hanged."

The town they reached was little more than four buildings stuck together in the midst of nothingness, but it had a mercantile, and a saloon. Which was all Raven wanted. He accompanied Charm into the store, bought her a dowdy dress that would, he hoped, disguise her figure. He let her choose supplies before hustling her into the saloon where he bought two bottles of wine, which were a rare find in this part of the world.

Once again the prairie stretched out before them, and this time, made nervous by thoughts of those who must be tracking them, Raven pushed along well into the night. For a few miles the terrain became slightly rolling, and finally they came to an area of small rocky bluffs, dotted with scrub trees and boasting a trickle of fresh water.

"We'll camp here," Raven said, dismounting stiffly, still holding Charm's reins in one hand. He'd felt like an idiot leading the girl's horse through town, but he didn't trust her, not for a moment, though she seemed docile as a kitten. "You still want to cook?"

She nodded and he grimaced. Perhaps he shouldn't trust her with the cooking utensils, he thought, but how much damage could she do with a cast-iron pan? Upon further thought, however, he realized he didn't truly wish to know.

"All right. We'll build the fire under that tree. Keep it small and make sure it burns clean." Actually it would be virtually unseen there, even from close range. "Can I trust you not to run off while I take care of the horses?"

She smiled. It was wonderfully executed, beautiful in its insincerity. "Of course."

Raven frowned. "You really want me here hounding your every move?" he asked, scowling at her. He was tired. Tired of the endless miles, the constant worry, but perhaps most of all tired of the frustration of her perpetual distant closeness. Which of course, didn't make any sense at all. He was losing his mind.

"I won't run away." She dropped the smile and said the words flatly. "I'm waiting to see you hang, remember?"

He watched her expression, which couldn't be called an expression at all, then turned the horses toward the stream. Maybe she was lying and would run at the first opportunity, and maybe that was just as well.

Although Raven had seen and approved everything they had purchased, he still looked warily at the food she placed before him. He found it a bit hard to trust her after she'd admitted to wanting to see him die. Such a statement tended to put a damper on a potential romance. Still, the meal looked good and smelled better. "Is it poisoned?" he asked taking his gaze from the unexpected cuisine to watch her smile.

"Yes." She dimpled slightly when she spoke. "It is," she said, and took a bite from her own plate.

He watched her chew.

"But only your portion," she added as she took another forkful.

In the end, there seemed to be nothing he could do but taste it, and once he'd sampled the first bite there was no turning back. It was truly delicious, and though he could not quite determine how such simple food stuffs had been convinced to become ambrosia, he ate every bite before raising his gaze to Charm again.

Surprisingly, she had changed into the dress he'd purchased for her. It was a nondescript color with long sleeves, a blessedly high neckline, and enough fabric to fit Angel. Still she looked lovely. God damn it. "Where'd you learn to cook?"

For a moment he thought she would refuse to answer, but she didn't. "Jude was a horrible chef. Not as bad as you," she added, "but horrible."

He sighed. "If I weren't so full, I'd be insulted. Hold up your cup, I'll pour you some wine."

"I don't drink."

"Neither do I, but I'm making an exception. Hold it up."

"No."

Raven reminded himself not to grit his teeth and honed his patience to a sharper edge. "Don't think I'm not flattered by your inability to take your eyes off me, Charm, but if I wake up once more and find you staring at me, I won't be responsible for my actions."

"Which means what exactly?" she asked, her tone perfectly level.

There was not the slightest bit of fear in her voice, Raven noticed. Three days ago he would have been thrilled by that fact. But three days ago she had asked to watch him undress, now she asked to watch him hang. Things were progressing nicely.

"Have a drink, Charm, maybe it'll help you sleep. It sure as hell will help me."

She remained silent and unmoving.

"It's just wine."

The little copse was quiet. The horses grazed not far away, stamping their hind feet now and then to ward off mosquitos.

"You're scared to let down your guard, aren't you?" He watched her closely. "Still think there's not a man alive that can resist you?"

She knew he was trying to goad her into drinking, and she almost smiled to herself, for he was playing right into her hands. It was true, liquor did cause sleepiness. She'd seen it happen a thousand times. It was, in fact, one of the reasons she didn't allow herself to drink. Because she couldn't afford to relax. But this once she would chance it, for she was an insomniac and certainly wouldn't fall asleep now, not when her enemy was so near. Raven, on the other hand, was accustomed to getting a full night's sleep. Sleep he'd been deprived of lately. So she'd drink and encourage him to drink. Soon he'd be unconscious and she'd be gone.

"I think there's not a man alive that can resist anything," she said coolly, not wanting to give in too easily, lest he become suspicious.

"Well, you're wrong, my dear girl. Again. But I see you're too scared to take the challenge."

She held his gaze to the count of ten, then lifted her tin cup.

Charm had never tasted wine, and though it didn't particularly appeal to her, it wasn't repulsive either. She drank slowly, taking small sips while she kept on planning. "So what are you going to do with the reward money?"

His brows rose as he lowered his cup. "Does this mean you believe you're Chantilly Grady?"

"No. I just think you're deluded, and that *you* believe I'm Chantilly Grady. But let's pretend I am, for argument's sake."

Jude often had visions of grandeur and would talk for hours about the things he would do when he became wealthy. And as he talked he would drink, until finally there would be no more words and he would fall into a drunken swoon. She had loved him even then, hoping that some day he would care enough to leave the liquor and talk anyway. "Will you build a grand house and live in style?"

Raven snorted softly and gazed into the rosy liquor. "I have no spectacular plans, Charm," he said and took another draught of wine from the metal cup.

"Not like Jude then. Not in that way at least."

Raven drained his portion and watched her. "Are you saying we're alike in other ways?"

"There are similarities."

Raven raised the bottle, pointing the top toward her. "More?"

"No. But go ahead."

He raised one brow. "Not unless you do."

Well, hell. She pursed her lips, wanting to give him her well-trained, sweet smile, but knowing he'd be suspicious. "All right. Just a little more." She was a nonsleeper. No matter what. A little wine wouldn't affect her, while a lot of wine would certainly affect him.

He filled her cup. "You were telling me about the similarities between Jude and myself."

She shrugged, wanting to keep him talking, keep him distracted from his impending drowsiness. "You sing."

He drank again and canted his head. "Most people sing, Charm."

"I don't."

"Never?"

"No."

They took a sip in unison.

"Anything else? Maybe even *more* significant?"

He was mocking her. "You both have black hair."

"Jude's hair is grey."

"Well, it used to be black. And his skin is dark like yours." Charm scowled. "Or used to be. When he was healthy. Liquor!" She turned her frown toward the contents of her cup. "It's an evil thing."

There was a momentary silence, in which Raven watched her face. It was beautiful with silly upturned lips and a pointed chin that boasted a tiny dent in its center. "Was he good to you, Charm?" he asked softly.

Her gaze lifted. "He saved my life." Her answer came quickly, as if she needed to say the words before he disputed them.

Raven was quiet, watching her. "Saved you from the hat man?"

She was on her feet in an instant, her eyes wild and her nostrils flared. "He wasn't my father! He tried to kill me! Broke into my room!"

Raven raised his gaze to her face but remained seated. "Some men deserve to die, Charm. Even fathers. I didn't say he wasn't one of them."

Her lips moved, and though Raven thought she would question him, she didn't.

"The hat man wasn't my father." Her tone was perfectly controlled.

She might be right, of course. Raven couldn't be sure his suspicions were correct. But he'd seen a brown tintype of Randall Grady. He had a lady-killer smile, fair hair, and a hat, tilted to the side. He'd been young and handsome and cocky when he'd given the photograph to Caroline. But how had he looked ten years later, when he'd written old lady Sophie concerning Chantilly's well-being?

Perhaps Raven was wrong, for it was all speculation, but the timing was right. Couldn't it be that Jude had somehow found Chantilly and taken her into his care? Then ten to twelve years later, Grady learned of Chantilly's whereabouts, tried to take her back, but was killed by Jude instead? Wasn't that possible?

"Do you know anything about the man Jude killed, Charm?"

"I know he wasn't my father," she snapped. "Jude wouldn't kill my father. Jude *is* my father!" She sounded near panic again and ready to flee.

Raven shook his head slowly. "There's nothing here to hurt you. No one to raise a hand to you. Sit down," he urged quietly.

She watched him, realizing with her gut as well as her mind that he was being honest, at least about that. He had never hurt her, despite all they'd been through. She returned stiffly to the log but sat on the ground now, with her back to its smooth expanse. "Sometimes I think I'm insane." She dared not look at him, for what if, in his expression, he showed that he agreed with her assessment and thought she truly had lost her mind?

"Show me a man without fear and I'll show you a lunatic." He stood slowly to pace the short distance between them and finally squat down before her. "You're not crazy, Charm. The world is. Sometimes. Crazy, and inexplicable and frightening. But you've no reason to fear *me*."

He was very close, only a few feet away, with his warm mahogany gaze steady on her face and his strong hands holding the cup and bottle. "Here." He raised the wine. "Let's drink to peace."

She sighed. Peace sounded good. Even temporary peace. In the moonlight, Raven's hair shone with a deep sapphire gleam while his broad throat looked dark and smooth in the opening of his white shirt. "To peace," she said, and raised her cup.

He filled it and they drank together.

"All I want is to get you to St. Louis." Raven took another swig and, watching her face, knew he was lying, knew he wanted much more. "Then it's your decision. To stay with your kin there, or to return to Jude."

Her gut twisted and she tightened her grip on the metal cup. "It can't be true."

Silence. Deep and secret as the night.

"Jude's my father," Charm whispered into the quiet. "He said he was." She raised her gaze to Raven's, wanting the truth, yet terrified by the possibilities. "Why would he say that if it wasn't true?"

"Perhaps everyone needs someone to love."

His eyes looked to be a rich russet brown in the flicker of the firelight. For one undisciplined moment, Charm wondered if he spoke of himself. "He does love me, you know," she murmured, "in his own way."

Raven's gaze remained level.

"He does," she repeated, softer still, but he merely nodded

and she scowled. "But how . . . I mean how . . ." Her voice cracked and she felt her throat bind with tension. "How . . ."

"Shhh," Raven whispered.

"I want to know how! How?" she cried in anguish, and suddenly Raven abandoned the bottle to wrap her in his arms.

For just a moment, panic swelled, but then her head dropped against his shoulder, drawn there by the incredible appeal of his quiet strength.

"I don't know what to believe," she whispered and shivered.

"Shhh, Lucky Charm."

She felt his hands on her back, and though she told herself to draw away, she failed to do so. "Was he really my father?" she asked hoarsely.

"I shouldn't have said that," he murmured, brushing his breath against the sensitive skin of her neck. "But back at the inn, when Jude and Clancy, damn his hide, busted in, I needed to get you out of there. Needed to leave right away. I knew you'd do anything to save Jude . . . even leave with me if I threatened his safety. But I was only guessing at the truth."

Charm could feel herself relax somewhat, which, perhaps, made no sense. "You lie all the time," she sighed.

"I know." He reached up, caressing her neck with gentle fingertips, brushing back her hair. "It's a gift."

"How do I know you're not lying about Eloise Medina? About everything?"

His lips grazed her ear.

She shivered and let her eyes fall closed. "Why would I do that?" he asked.

"I don't know. But you might have a reason."

"Like what?"

"I don't know."

"You must have thought of some possible scenarios." His

fingertips traced the rim of her ear, raising goosebumps on her arms.

"Maybe you're going to . . ."

His lips replaced his fingers, making her gasp silently for breath and causing her mind to lose its line of thought.

"Going to what?"

"To take me to a . . . You know."

"No." He drew away slightly, watching her. She could feel his gaze on her face.

"To a . . . you know." She still couldn't quite say it. "To sell my body," she whispered.

"This body?" His left arm tightened around her back, pulling her slightly closer, while his opposite hand skimmed, feather soft, down her throat. "There are a thousand things I could do with this body, little Charm. Selling it wouldn't be one of them."

She knew it was true. The idea had seemed ridiculous, even in her most terrified moments.

"Maybe you're a bounty hunter."

His fingers traced the outline of her homely bodice. "Have you done something for which a bounty would be warranted?"

She drew breath through her teeth, feeling his touch burn her soul. She'd had no way of knowing how a man's fingers would feel against her skin. "I stole a peppermint stick once. When I was six. I didn't mean to," she added quickly, feeling as if she had somehow slipped from her body into another dimension. "I thought Jude had paid for it, and . . ."

"That's pretty serious," Raven said and ever so gently, like the soft caress of a spring breeze, kissed her throat. "But the posse's probably given up the chase by now."

He was very close, pressed up against her, in fact, with his hard chest warm and his lips heavenly against her neck.

"Any other possibilities?"

"What?" She could barely force out the single word.

"Have you thought of any other reasons why I might want to abduct you?"

"Oh." The word was no more than a sigh, for his kisses had slipped downward and found the sensitive hollow between her collar bones. "Perhaps you're trying to seduce me."

His kisses ceased. She could feel him draw away, but only far enough to look into her face. Charm opened her eyes, finding his gaze warm and steady on her.

"Would I do that?" His voice was husky, his eyes fathomless.

Her nod was very stiff, and his kiss, when it came, was full force and hungry.

Charm could do nothing but answer back. Too many years had she been starved. Too many nights had she been lonely. Their lips slanted across the other's, their tongues touched and caressed. Sparks seemed to be ignited at every point of contact.

Breathing was harsh, hands shaky. His kisses hurried downward again, over her chin to her throat, where they spread out in a hot rain of sensuous stimulus.

"Charm, we should . . ."—his breath was warm against her neck—"we should stop."

"Please." Her arms tightened about him of their own accord. "Please don't stop. Please don't."

Somehow her buttons came open. She didn't know how and neither did she care. All she was certain of was that suddenly his hands were against her skin, and now the fire that he had ignited was spreading wildly lower, like a tide of pleasure.

Sleeves slipped from her arms, followed by his kisses, hot and exhilarating and breathtaking. Laces were loosened, straps eased downward and suddenly, inexplicably, she was naked, but for the blanket he had pulled about her shoulders. Her fingers reached for the buttons of his shirt. They fell open, revealing the hard, sloping planes of his chest.

Charm touched him with breathless reverence. She marveled for a moment at the beauty of him before he groaned and kissed her again, easing his body down upon hers.

They were hip to hip and heart to heart now. Everything from Charm's breasts to her loins ached with a burning need. And she could feel *his* need, could feel the hard shaft of his desire even through the unwelcome barrier of his pants.

Her arms were wound about his bare torso. Every inch of him felt hot—hot and sensuous and so lovely that she felt she would surely die of sheer ecstasy. His kisses were running wild again, leaving her lips to blaze new trails down to her shoulders and beyond. But her grip on him was too tight for them to go far, and so he returned with a groan to reclaim her mouth.

"Charm . . ." His breathing was very harsh. "Really, we must quit."

"No!" She pulled him more tightly against her, lifting her hips in an attempt to ease the burning ache there. "Please. I've never . . ." She pushed up again, then caught her lip between her teeth as the pleasure of this new pressure momentarily overcame her ability to speak. "I've never felt like this before. It feels so . . . good." She pushed up again, feeling the heat of his desire press just so against her need.

Her moan came in perfect unison with his, and suddenly he had pulled from her grasp and was unbuckling his belt.

Fear came to her like a sudden stab of conscience, sharp and quick.

"Charm?" His hands had gone still and his voice very low. "Are you all right?"

"Yes." She swallowed, still ridden hard by desire. "Don't stop."

His gaze held her face for a long moment, and it almost seemed, even in her fuzzy state of unreality, that he was fighting some battle she didn't quite understand.

"Don't stop," she said again, and reaching up, placed one palm on the hot expanse of his bare chest. "Please."

He groaned. The tone was deep and needy and somehow sounded pained.

"Please," she whispered again, no longer feeling fear, but only the achy need to be his. "Touch me. Don't quit."

"No," he said, his tone perfectly level now. "No, I won't quit. Roll over."

"What?" She heard the wariness in her own tone.

"Trust me, Charm," he said quietly. Leaning down, he kissed her.

Though the caress was ever so gentle, she could feel him tremble. "All right," she whispered, and when he'd moved aside, she rolled onto her abdomen, feeling suddenly foolish, and naked and stiff with fear.

His hands were very warm against her shoulders when they massaged her there. She remained as she was, barely breathing, waiting. He kneaded gently, down one arm, rolling the aching muscles in his strong palms.

Charm let out a sigh, beginning to relax, absorbing the lovely feel of flesh against flesh. Raven's hands worked up again, toward her shoulder and then down along the length of her back. His kisses felt like warm liquid against her spine, his hands like magic even when they massaged the intimate tenderness of her buttocks.

She noticed with rather dim surprise that a blanket was beneath her and that her body felt very limp and warm, as though it had been dipped in tepid water and had been lying in the sun to dry.

Raven's kisses followed his hands, over her buttocks, down her legs. Her eyes fell closed. His hands kept moving, across her calves now, easing away the ache there and finally kneading the soles of her feet.

Charm shivered as his lips touched her toes, but she failed to open her eyes as she pressed her hips weakly into the blanket below.

The kisses were traveling upward again, over every yielding curve of her body to finally stop at the nape of her neck.

"Please," she whispered, forgetting everything but the soft waves of darkness that welcomed her. "Don't quit."

"No," he said, and kissing her shoulder, gently folded her into the soft comfort of sleep.

Chapter 21

Raven watched her awaken. It had been a new experience for him, watching her sleep, watching the shadows be replaced by light upon her lovely features. He had helped her find rest, had lulled her with his hands into slumber. It was a heady feeling, this one night of owning her trust.

But she sat up with a start now, looked down in wordless awe at her shocking nudity, and grasped the blanket close to her chest with one shaky hand. "How dare you?" she gasped, looking like nothing more than a wild-eyed wood fairy caught in a compromising state of undress.

"How dare I what?" he asked, keeping his tone steady, though he felt tense and starved for something he could not quite define.

"Where are my clothes?" Her question was breathy, her hair tousled and glistening in the early morning light.

Without a word Raven handed over her garments. Their gazes caught and their hands touched, shocking them both with the contact. She yanked away as if seared, but her gaze remained on his. Her expression showed a mosaic of confused emotions before she turned her face rapidly away.

He felt he could see her thoughts, could read them as though they were his own. "We didn't do anything wrong, Charm," he said softly. He wanted to take her into his arms and cradle her against his chest, to smooth away her fears, to do the very thing he had disallowed himself to do last night. But it would indeed be wrong. For all she had wanted was to be touched, to be held, to be loved. Whether she knew it or not, it was true. While he wanted much more . . . or was it, in fact, much less? "There's no need to be ashamed."

She swung her gaze wildly toward him again, and then, like a fragile doe leaping away, she fled, hugging blanket and clothes to her bosom and scurrying into the cover of the trees.

She was silent again that day. What had he done to upset her so? True, he'd gotten her drunk. Well, not drunk exactly, only slightly tipsy. And besides, he hadn't done *it*. Hadn't . . . Words, even mental words, always failed him at this point, for the thought of making love to Chantilly Charm Grady Fergusson made his hands sweat and his throat go dry. Perhaps he'd been a fool to resist her. But . . . His gaze traveled sideways, finding her wide eyes again. She still looked frightened.

"We'd best stop for the night," he said, feeling weary. It was an unreasonable fatigue, he thought, for in the past, he'd been known to gamble through several consecutive nights without undue strain. But her reticence, her fear, her very presence, was wearing on him. "Angel threw a shoe."

They'd come to another break in the prairie, a rocky knoll with a smattering of trees and a small, precious water source.

Again she made the fire and again he unsaddled the horses before leading them down a sandy decline to drink. It had been a hot day, and still the air hung heavy and unmoving. Raven's horse drank before sampling a few sparse blades of grass that survived the current, but Angel splashed in the stream, playfully tossing his homely head as the water sprayed up to douse his face and chest. Raven watched his silly antics, but he thought of Charm, how her lips parted when he kissed her, how she arched her breasts against him and set his being on fire.

Angel's water play became more subdued, and finally he buckled his knees to slouch into the water. Raven watched— and thought of Charm, how her breathing escalated when he touched her, how she begged him not to stop.

The spotted gelding rolled now, sloshing water in every direction before clambering to his feet to collapse on his opposite side. Raven watched, and still he thought of Charm.

"Christ's sake," he finally said aloud. Disgusted with himself for his perpetually wandering imaginings, he clamped his teeth shut, as though that might force the girl from his mind.

Refreshed by his impromptu bath, Angel finally stood and shook, spraying water over the pair on the bank before pulling on the reins in an effort to reach the nearby grasses. Raven moved along with the geldings for a few minutes, watching as they grazed, and finally he hobbled them in a sheltered spot where the turf was deep and green. In a moment he went back to the stream where he filled the canteen before returning to Charm.

Her top two buttons were open!

It was the first thing . . . no . . . it was the only thing Raven noticed. His gaze riveted to that space where her gown separated to reveal a modest vee of flesh. It was no more than nine square inches of skin, and yet . . .

Raven's feet dragged to a halt. Their gazes met. Charm straightened slowly, looking dazed and stunning. Their breath stopped in unison.

"Charm . . . I . . ." He took one unconscious step forward. She lifted her chin slightly, not breathing, her eyes wide. "I need a bath," Raven murmured on an exhalation and, turning stiffly about, fled toward the stream.

*   *   *

Charm chopped the potatoes into small bits. They were old and wrinkled and would cook quickly amidst the bits of beef jerky broth that boiled over the fire. Putting water in a small kettle, she hung it, too, over the blaze, and then she sat, wringing her hands and biting her lip.

It wasn't as if she had any desire to watch Raven Scott bathe. No. That would be indecent. She bit her lip again and found, however, that her gaze had strayed in the direction of the stream.

The sun had set, and her fire burned clean. She wouldn't be needed to watch the meal. Her hands separated nervously. She tapped her fingers on her thigh, still kneeling by the blaze and thinking.

It was hot. Cool water would feel wonderful. Not that she wanted to watch Raven bathe, of course. But it sure was hot. She stood and paced a circular path around the small fire. The evening's bumpy clouds, alight with tangerine and scarlet hues, had faded, only to be seen as tattered grey ghosts over the besieged moon.

Maybe it would rain. Was Raven in the stream now? Completely naked? She paced again, chewing her lip. It sure was hot. A bath would do her good. Not that she wanted to watch Raven bathe but . . .

"Oh hell!" she breathed suddenly and found she was already striding toward the stream. Off to her left, the geldings were grazing. Angel raised his head and bobbled his massive roman nose at her as if in greeting, but Charm barely noticed, for through the leafy, low branches of a cottonwood she caught a flash of movement.

It was Raven. Without having to give it any thought, she knew she should turn around and march back toward camp. But she didn't. Her feet were silent on the sandy soil. The semidarkness and the muted colors of her gown hid her approach, and suddenly she was poised in the spring-green foliage of the trees. Standing at the top of a steep bank, she looked down.

The moon, perhaps battling with the clouds for an unobscured view of the scene beneath its bald yellow head, shone full force now. It glistened on the silvered peaks of the magical waves and fell without modesty on the bared posterior of the man called Raven.

His hair gleamed a deep sapphire color. His shoulders were wide and dark, and from there his body tapered in masculine lines to the taut expanse of his waist. Below that . . . Charm swallowed hard. She shouldn't be there, she knew, and had nearly convinced herself to leave when he knelt to splash water on his torso. The silvery waves lapped lovingly at his buttocks.

Charm grasped a branch in each hand and drew a sharp breath through her teeth. Raven's head turned, like a fine, gallant stallion that had caught a scent of danger. Charm remained motionless, not daring to breathe. Yet, he stood, finally turning slowly to stare in her direction.

Dear God. This was no time to faint, because he'd probably hear her fall, and besides, if she fainted she'd be unable to watch . . .

What was wrong with her? He'd lied to her, taken her mother's Bible, *abducted* her! And yet . . . as he turned his attention back to the water, she could not forget the feel of his hands on her skin, the quick hard beat of his heart against hers. Charm's breath came in quick spurts now. She should leave immediately. This very instant. But . . . Well, didn't she need to learn about men in order to overcome her fear of them? And wasn't this the most practical way to do so—without his knowledge, from the safety of the trees?

God, he was beautiful! She released her hold on the branches, easing forward a scant half inch to see better. Yes, he was constructed like a wild stallion, with every muscle tight as a knot, and every line sleek as a running steed's. And his . . . his . . .

Suddenly, Charm's foot slipped on the exposed root of a cottonwood. She grappled wildly for a hold, scrambled for footing, and then gasped in dismay as she slid down the sharp bank to land with a slithering thud not four feet from where Raven bathed.

Even by moonlight she could see the shock stamped on his face. His mouth moved soundlessly. Charm could do nothing but stare up from her soggy position in wide-eyed horror.

"You were watching me!"

"No!" she squeaked in denial. But there was no hope of being believed, for she lay like a beached trout, gaping up at him.

"You were . . ."—he waved a hand indicating the immediate area—"you were sneaking around *watching* me."

Her lips moved. Everything else remained immobile.

He strode forward, his fists lightly clenched. Even now, she could not help but notice the fine, fluid movement of his glistening form.

"What do you want?" His words were a mere whisper but seemed to reverberate down to her very soul.

"You." She thought she had only said the word mentally, a shameful admission of her own weakness, but suddenly she realized she had verbalized her scandalous desire. "I want you," she whispered, no longer attempting to stop the words.

His fists tightened, as did his jaw. "No," he said hoarsely. Turning with stiff resolution, he marched out of the water and away.

Why was she doing this to him? Raven sat alone in the darkness. He had retrieved the remaining bottle of wine and was now determined to drink himself into oblivion. Lots of people did it. It couldn't be that hard, and yet he felt stone-cold sober.

Perhaps she would run away. Perhaps she'd go back to Jude. He'd let her go. He would! In fact, he'd have himself a little celebration. He must have been crazy to drag her halfway across the Dakota Territory. The reward wasn't worth it, because he was losing his mind.

He could think of nothing but Charm. She troubled his days, haunted his nights. He'd lost track of his main goal in life. Hell! What *had* his mission been? To find his father? Why? To make him pay for leaving his mother? But he knew none of the circumstances. He didn't know why his old man had not returned, and now things seemed so much more complicated. Love for a woman changed everything.

Love!

Raven stood abruptly. Love! With a wild toss, he smashed the empty bottle against a tree and swore. The girl was driving him insane, but who was to say his own mother hadn't done the same to his father? Perhaps Raven's old man had left to gain a fortune just as he had told his young bride. Perhaps he had had every intention of returning, but when his mission failed, he lacked the nerve to return empty-handed to admit defeat to the woman he loved. Love changed a man.

There was that word again! Love! Raven gritted his teeth and paced. The last thing he needed was to be tied to a woman, and especially to the killer woman. He snorted wildly, but his gaze had turned unconsciously toward camp. *She* would be lying down with the moonlight painting soft shadows across her perfect features. Her eyes would be closed and her lashes would be like dark chestnut down against her cheeks. He could go to her now. He could take her in his arms and kiss her and tell her of his love.

God damn it! He didn't love her! He lusted for her! He was just goddamn randy. Raven paced again. He was just randy and he could prove it! He could go and take her up on her offer. He'd make her sorry she'd ever tempted him, sorry . . . for everything.

To his own inebriated mind, Raven's passage through the woods sounded quiet, even stealthy. When he reached camp, however, she was already on her feet, staring wide-eyed in the direction of his approach.

His chest was heaving as he breathed, and his shirt was open, but that didn't mean he wasn't thinking clearly. He would give her what she wanted, would take her to the pinnacle of pleasure and drive her from his mind. To hell with tenderness! To hell with her fear! She'd said yes and yes it would be!

"Raven?" Her voice was very soft.

Something tripped in his chest. To hell with love! he reminded himself sternly.

"Are you all right?"

"I'm . . ." He took two staggering steps to the left, realizing suddenly that his stance was not quite what it might be. "I'm drunk as a st-stunk. But I'm still ready."

Her eyes widened, he noticed, and he was certain she was impressed with his ability to perform.

"Ready for what?" she whispered.

He grinned. So she had decided to be coy after all. "Ready for . . ."

The tree limb was as wide as his upper arm and hit Raven dead square across his chest. He was slapped backward like a bug on a stick, and he hit the ground gasping for breath and explanations. "What the—"

"I'm gonna kill you now, boy!" roared a voice.

"No! Jude! No!"

Good God! Jude again, Raven thought foggily. But there was no more time for thinking, for now the end of the tree limb was planted against his chest and the business end of a .45 pointed at his left eyeball.

"Are you breeding?"

"What?" Raven croaked, but realized now that his question had synchronized with Charm's.

"I said, are you breedin', gal?"

"No!" she gasped. "Of course not."

"Good!" Jude said through his teeth. "Then I can kill 'im!" He cocked the .45.

"No, Jude! Don't!"

"Don't! Don't!" the old man yelled. "I been goin' crazy tryin' t' find y'. This bastard took the only good thing in my life when he took you, gal! He deserves t' die, and by God he will!" he said, raising the gun.

"No!" Charm grasped his arm in desperate appeal. "I think I love—"

"I'll kill him, by God," Jude growled again.

"I think I . . . I'm . . . in the family way!" she gasped wildly.

The old man went deadly still. "What's that you say, gal?" His tone was tense, his gaze steady on Raven, who remained unmoving.

"I said . . ." She swallowed, then nodded with jerky resolution. "I am. I'm carrying his child. You can't kill him!"

Chapter 22

"Did he force you, gal?" Jude's voice was guttural and strained.

Charm stared at Raven. He was flat on his back, his shirt open and his broad chest marred by the wound she herself had inflicted. "No." She shook her head, feeling short of breath and strangely numb.

Jude's gnarled hands tightened on the branch as he pressed harder against Raven's chest. "Did he hurt you?"

"Listen. Jude, I—"

"Did he hurt you?" Jude demanded, his voice rising with his wrath.

"No. No," she breathed. "He never did."

The branch was slowly removed from Raven's chest, though the .45 didn't waver. "Tie him up, Clancy, then get him on a horse."

Until this moment, Charm hadn't noticed the other man's presence.

He cleared his throat now. "What are you plannin'?"

"Tie his hands," insisted Jude, keeping his .45 aimed at Raven's head. "Or get the hell outta my way."

*　　*　　*

"You got a preacher in this here town?" Jude asked, his voice harsh, but not raspy, as if his mind and body had become clear of the liquor that had poisoned him for so long.

They'd been riding for hours. Raven's head felt as if it were a strong man's overused anvil.

"A preacher?" asked the skinny man who descended the steps of the general store. "Yeah, Father McMurt. He's a preacher. Sort of." Skinny scowled, not bothering to hide his curiosity. "What you want him for?"

"Bring 'im here," Jude ordered, and Skinny scurried off down the hard-packed street, his curiosity making him hurry.

"You're plannin' to marry them up," deduced Clancy with sudden exuberance.

Raven lifted his head. The clanging got louder, threatening to drown reality.

"You are," said Clancy happily. "Ain't you?"

There was a momentary pause; then, "Goddamn right I am."

"Hell," said Clancy joyously, removing his hat to wipe his brow. "Wouldn't it be kinder to shoot him? Not that I got nothin' against yer gal."

"I hear you're in need of a clergy?" All gazes turned to the two men who had approached on foot and now stood not far away.

"That's right," said Jude.

Beside the skinny man stood a rumpled-looking fellow with a squashed hat and an unsteady stance. "I am such a man."

Jude straightened slightly, tightening his hands on his own reins as well as on the reins of Raven's mount. "You're drunk."

"'Tis the sad truth," the Scotsman agreed without a trace of regret.

Jude scowled. "Can you perform a wedding?"

The preacher lifted his chin. "Can you purchase a bottle?"

Raven tried to quiet his cerebral clattering. "I won't be forced into marriage, old man," he warned.

Jude turned his head. "It's your choice, boy. You can marry her. Or you can marry her with a leg wound. Truth is, I prefer the latter."

"I didn't sleep with her."

"You callin' my gal a liar?" Jude's hand was on his gun again.

Raven winced at the pain in his head, wondering if his cranium was about to explode. "Maybe she's mistaken," he suggested, but quietly now, lest his eyeballs desert the rest of his body.

"Goddamn you!" Jude's gun was all the way out. "The child won't be raised without no pa. You hear me? Not after the hell *I* been through fer the past twenty-six years."

Raven scowled, vaguely aware that Jude was making no sense. A small, silent crowd had gathered about them.

The priest cleared his throat. "Are we ready then, or would you be plannin' to untie the groom?"

"We're ready," growled Jude, gun held level.

McMurt patted a pocket, then another, but finally lifted his face to scowl. "Might there be someone with a Bible?"

"I'm gonna shoot them both," Jude warned. "Where's yer mama's Bible, gal?"

Charm's face was pale. "It's . . . Raven's got it."

Clancy fished it from Raven's vest pocket to hand it to the priest who cleared his throat and lifted his gaze to the prospective groom. "Do you have a ring, young man?"

"What do you think this is, a goddamn garden party?" snapped Jude. "Get on with the—"

"There's his mother's ring," said Clancy, his tone becoming merrier by the moment.

Raven swung his head about—a bit too quickly, for it seemed to continue pivoting far past its normal range. "Back off, Bodine," he managed to order.

"Come now, Joseph," said the other, pushing his mount

closer and reaching for the chain about Raven's neck. "If you're gonna get yourself wed you might as well do it right. Besides, she's damn pretty. If I was gonna get hitched . . . which I ain't . . ."—his grin widened as he lifted the ring from the other's chest—"I'd want it to be to someone just like her."

"Remind me to kill you when I can see straight," Raven requested.

"Certainly, Joseph," Clancy said and loosened the ring from its simple chain to hold it in his palm. "We're ready."

"Would you care to dismount?" asked McMurt.

"No, he wouldn't," growled Jude. "Just get on with it."

In the end the cold hard muzzle of Jude's gun was held to Raven's temple, prompting the appropriate vows. When it came Charm's turn to speak, however, the ceremony came to an abrupt and breathtaking halt.

"Say the words, gal," urged Jude. Her lips moved, but no sound came forth. "What is it? You scared of him?" he asked quietly.

Her answer took a moment to come, but when it did it was surprisingly clear and honest. "No, I'm not scared."

"Then say the words, Charm, cuz I won't have my grandbaby raised without no pa."

The silence was as heavy as sin.

"He won't mistreat y', gal," added Jude quietly. "I'll see t' that."

"But—"

"It's too late for second thoughts now. He'll marry y' or he'll die."

"I do," she said faintly.

Clancy slipped Raven's ring onto her finger, Jude led them toward a building that boasted baths, and Charm's head spun.

"You stink like cheap liquor," Jude said. Although Raven was tempted to ask whether that was an insult or compliment coming from that front, he kept silent and dismounted with a lurch. "Charm, you go ahead to the boardinghouse.

We'll meet you there in an hour's time for supper, if I can scrub the stench from this bast . . . from your husband here."

There seemed little for Raven to do but follow Jude's orders. The bathhouse was quiet, the water warm and soothing, giving Raven time to plan. Of course he would have the marriage annulled once Jude and his ever present .45 disappeared. The bastard couldn't stay with them forever. Eventually he'd have to break down and get a drink. Except that he appeared healthier now somehow, and sober, and God knew a sober man was apt to cause more trouble than a drunk one. Raven shaved and lathered and soaked until finally Jude appeared from outside the door where he had been standing guard, lest the bridegroom decided to slip town.

"Get out. I'm thinkin' you're clean as you're ever gonna get."

"Where did you find her, Jude?" Raven asked, looking up into the man's brown eyes.

"What's that?" Jude asked, tilting his head slightly to hear better.

"Where did you find Chantilly Grady?"

There was a slight pause as the man stared at him; then, "I don't know what the hell you're talkin' about."

"I'm talking about Charm. She's not your daughter."

"Damn you." The .45 was out again and surprisingly steady. "She's my own, so don't think I won't protect her like she ain't."

Raven lifted his brows slightly, allowing no other expression. "I just want a few questions answered."

The old man took two quick strides to stand tense and still beside the tub. "When I see the house you build her, when I see the home you make for her. When I see you makin' my Charm happy, then you got a right to ask me questions," he growled. "Now get out, cuz I'd sure hate for my granddaughter t'be an only child."

There were several possible meanings to that statement, Raven thought. None of them was good. He got out.

"Put on them clothes," Jude said, pointing to a pile of garments brought in earlier.

So, the old man had given him a wedding gift, Raven mused wryly as he shook out the clothing. They fit surprisingly well. Raven couldn't help wondering if, perhaps, Charm had helped estimate the size.

The walk to the boardinghouse was short, and yet it was almost dark by the time they passed the door. They were shown immediately to the dining table. Charm was there. Her gaze rose nervously when they entered. Raven drew in his perceptions quickly, wondering at her agitation and realizing it had been quite some time since he'd seen her look so edgy. But then, Clancy, damn his hide, sat quite close to her left side, and Clancy, with his easy, phony charm, made Raven nervous too. Bodine smiled. Raven clenched his teeth, and Jude nodded him to a seat.

Charm was wearing a new gown. Though that fact was, in truth, irrelevant, Raven noticed anyway. It was ivory, with two ruffles of lace starting at her shoulders to form a vee that ended at her tiny waist. Somehow it irritated him that he hadn't bought it himself.

The meal was ordered and eaten with barely a word spoken except by Clancy who could speak about nothing at great lengths.

Charm sat unmoving. Raven's hair was still damp, she noticed. It was drying now and curled away from his white starched collar like blue-black feathers.

"So . . ." Clancy leaned back in his chair and grinned. "What now?"

"Have you got any money, boy?" Jude asked brusquely.

"Why do you ask?" Raven's expression was as blank as it had been during that first poker game. But now Charm could read some of the signs of his smoldering emotions. He was thinking and planning as he waited with hard-won impatience. But thinking and planning what?

"Her and the baby will need a home."

Charm held her breath. She must have been crazy to declare herself pregnant, but the options had seemed so poor at the time. She sat very still, feeling the tension swell around her and aching with a sharp need for security. She slipped her butter knife into her pocket.

"I see." Raven leaned back slightly, stretching his long legs under the table and keeping his gaze on Jude. "And you expect me to buy her a house?"

Jude was immediately aggressive. "Damn right I do."

"I see *you* never afforded her such a luxury?"

"It wasn't me got her breedin'," Jude growled.

"Maybe it wasn't me either," Raven countered.

"Goddamn you!" roared Jude, lurching to his feet. "Watch what you say about my gal, or I'll—"

"Please," Charm said, trying to pull Jude back down. "Haven't we caused enough scandal?"

For a moment she thought Jude would attack, but he gritted his teeth, and fought for control. "Hard work will do you good, boy."

Raven's face was still impassive, though she had finally acquired the ability to read the tension in it. "What's that?" he asked coolly.

"I still got me a little land in Kentucky. You'd make a pisspoor farmer. But at least my granddaughter will have a home."

"Granddaughter?" Raven leaned back in his chair, holding Jude's gaze. "Maybe it's a boy."

"It ain't no boy," growled Jude, leaning across the table. "It'll be a girl, like her mother, I tell you."

"Are you psychic then, as well as your other fine qualities?" asked Raven. "Such as alcoholic and child abductor?"

"Quit it, both of you!" Charm ordered. "This is insane."

The men remained silent for a moment, looking slightly chagrined.

"He don't deserve y', gal," Jude sulked, "but he'll stay

with y', and he'll treat y' right. I'll see t' that." He drew a deep pensive breath. "Tomorrow we'll start heading south. Maybe I should a took y' there a long time ago."

"We'll be heading south, all right," agreed Raven. "But only so far as St. Louis. She has . . ." He smiled, showing a good many teeth and no good humor. "*We* have relatives there."

"I've been to St. Louis," Jude said, his face stern. "It's no place for a gal like my Charm. You'll take her to my farm in Kentucky or you'll be sorry you didn't."

"Jude, please," Charm begged, placing her hand on his arm. "Not now. Can't I have a moment's peace?"

Jude's brow wrinkled as he put his hand with slow uncertainty on Charm's slim fingers. "Peace. That's what I want for y', gal," he murmured, then patted her hand, sighing as he noticed the difference between her pale skin and his. "Such a pretty thing." His tone was guttural with sudden, unexpected emotion. "You always was pretty, Charm, since the first day I seen . . ." He lifted her hand in his gnarled one. His fingers grazed Raven's ring, drawing his attention there, and he noticed the unique, unforgettable design for the first time.

Charm felt his pain even before she heard him gasp.

"Jude?" She leaned closer. "Jude! What is it?"

His face had gone pale. His gaze remained downcast as if he lacked the strength to lift it to her eyes. He rose stiffly, however, and with a tremble, finally turned to stare at Raven. "You mistreat her, boy, I'll kill y', no matter who the hell you are," he said hoarsely. Turning with a jolt, he stumbled away.

"Jude," Charm called, rising quickly, but Raven, too, had risen.

"What the hell was that about?" He turned to follow, but Clancy was behind him, and without a breath of warning, crashed him into unconsciousness with a bottle across his skull.

Chapter 23

"What—" Charm gasped, but Clancy was across the floor in an instant, grabbing her from behind and pressing his palm across her face.

"Sorry to spoil your weddin' night, Miss Charm, but we gotta go," he said and pushed her toward the back door. Before she could move, a gag was tied about her mouth and a coarse rope around her wrists. "Sorry. Sorry again, but there's a bundle at stake here, and this ain't nearly so bad as it might be. Come on now, up on yer horse."

It all seemed to happen before Charm could draw a breath. One moment she was watching Jude depart from the room and the next she was prodded into Angel's saddle. Her bound hands gripped the horn, and her reins were, once again, out of her keeping. They rode at a walk at first, staying at the softest footing until they'd passed out of town, where they picked up to a trot and then a canter.

But where were they going? Charm wondered frantically. And why? Panic threatened to swell up and drown her, but suddenly, in the back of her mind, she saw Raven. His expression was impassive, but the tendons in his dark throat stood out in sharp ridges and in his mahogany eyes was the glint of rage as he followed their trail.

She drew a breath, calmed her nerves, and waited.

It was well past midnight when they stopped. The waving green of the prairie stretched endlessly away from them in the darkness, but they'd finally come upon a small oasis. It boasted fewer than a dozen stunted trees.

"We'll rest here for a couple of hours," Clancy said and threw a leg over the pommel to dismount.

She couldn't help but notice the nervousness in his tone. "Damn this nothingness. There ain't enough brush t' hide a flea. I should have tied him up. Shouldn't a . . . Oh," said Clancy, seeming to notice Charm with a start. "Get down. Get down, and don't worry," he said, reaching for her arm.

She pulled her elbow from his reach, feeling some of her old terror return. Angel tugged at his reins, reaching for grass and moving her a few inches farther from Bodine.

"I'm not gonna hurt y'," Clancy said. "You're too damn pretty. 'Sides . . ." He glanced over his shoulder, then chuckled, seeming amused by his own nervousness. "Joseph would kill me if I did. You know . . ." He placed his hands on his hips to gaze up at her and keep the horse's reins within his grasp. "He ain't the killin' kind. But fer you . . . Now me, I'd like to believe it's just the reward, but it's damn hard, cuz . . ." He paused. "Damned if it ain't fun to see him riled. Come on now, get down."

He reached for her again, and she allowed him to help her. In a moment the gag was removed. She turned abruptly to face him. Her breathing was a bit ragged, she noticed, and she knew with some chagrin that it was caused by her old, hated fear of men. But Raven was a man, and Raven hadn't hurt her, and Raven would come. She raised her chin slightly, hoping to look brave. "Why are you doing this?"

He stared at her. "Damn you're pretty. But . . ." He shrugged. "I can't tell you."

"What do you mean, you can't tell me?"

Another shrug. "Just can't."

"What are you planning to do with me?"

"Plannin'?" asked Clancy. "Nothin'. I'm just gonna keep you out of trouble for a few days. Wishin' . . ." He looked into her eyes again and sighed longingly. "That's a different story." Pacing over to Angel, he pulled a bedroll from behind the saddle before tossing it to the ground. "Now get some sleep."

"I don't sleep."

He turned toward her again, his surprise obvious even in the darkness. "Ever?"

She was remembering to breathe, even when he stared at her. "Hardly ever."

"Damn, that'd give us a lot of time wouldn't it?" he murmured with a shake of his head. "If only . . . Well, you better lie down at least. But hell . . . if you don't sleep, how am I gonna trust you to stay put?"

She backed away a step, knowing his thoughts. "I'd promise not to run away."

Clancy chuckled. "I seen a fresh scar on Joseph's chest. And somehow I don't think it was made by Injuns. No, I think I'll tie you up, just to be safe. Sorry."

Charm sat very still upon the blanket as he tied her ankles. There was fear again, just on the edge of control. She closed her eyes and breathed slowly through her nose.

"You all right?"

"Yes."

"Good. Now try to get some sleep," he said, retrieving his own bedroll and tossing it to the ground next to her. "Unless . . . you wanna do other things?"

Her throat closed up with fear, but she managed to shake her head.

Clancy sighed. "Pity," he said, and untied his blankets before stretching out atop them. "Good night."

She remained as she was, watching him for quite some time. But after a while her breathing came more easily, and her muscles relaxed. She lay down, closed her eyes, and waited.

It took less than fifteen minutes before she knew he slept. The butter knife was still in her pocket. She could feel it against her hip and eased over just enough to grasp it with her bound hands. It was no easy task to reach it, even harder to pull it from her pocket, and when she finally had, it slipped from her tingling fingers to fall to her blanket.

She stifled her gasp and stiffened, snapping her gaze to Clancy's face, but he only grunted in his sleep and twitched once. The knife handle was warm from her body's heat and smooth against her fingers when she retrieved it. She held it tightly now and carefully turned it so that the serrated edge was against her wrist bonds.

Clancy twitched again, and she jerked, but again it was a false alarm. She bit her inner lip, and then in a moment's decision, rolled silently to her other side. This new position was somehow worse, because she could no longer see her captor, no longer watch his face and read his intentions, but it also hid her movements.

She lay immobile for a few minutes, waiting to hear Clancy awaken behind her. But no sound came, and so she quietly pulled her knees toward her chest, pried the knife handle between her feet and began to saw at the binding on her wrists.

It took almost an hour to cut through the first rope. The coarse hemp eased away from her arms, but she remained very still, waiting and listening. No sound came from behind her. She finally pulled the knife from between her feet to cut her ankles loose. She was free! But she kept her breathing steady and soft, praying Clancy would continue to sleep.

He did so. Charm thrust the knife back into her pocket and rose silently. She wanted desperately to turn to make sure Clancy was still sleeping but forced herself to creep quietly toward the scrub trees. The horses remained saddled and were grazing not far away. Charm chanced a deep breath and lengthened her strides. It was then that Angel raised his head and nickered.

Behind her Clancy awoke with a start. "Time to . . . Damn! Hey!"

Charm could hear him scrambling to his feet, but already she was running.

"Hey. Come back here. Don't do that, Miss Charm. Hell, I ain't gonna hurt you."

Angel skittered sideways, frightened by Charm's quick movements and dragging his reins.

"Come on!" Clancy shouted again. "We don't have time fer this. I gotta find us a good hidin' spot. Joseph might be here any minute."

"Wrong," said Raven. Stepping from behind a bent cottonwood, he slammed his fist into the other's face. "Joseph's already here."

"Damn!" swore Clancy, crashing to the ground where he lay, feeling his jaw before rising cautiously to his feet.

"I haven't hit you for a long time, Bodine," said Raven, advancing.

"Yeah." Clancy retreated. "How'd you track us?"

"I followed a three-shoed horse and a snake in bastard's clothing. And now . . . I'm going to enjoy this."

"Hey!" Clancy shouted, peering past Raven. "She's getting away."

Raven turned a fraction of an inch. In that moment Clancy struck, but already Raven was turning back. The blow glanced off his chin.

With a twist and a jolt, Raven jabbed his fist into Clancy's abdomen. There was a whoosh of pain and surprise from Bodine. Charm had caught Angel's reins, but stood now, watching while the emotions roiled within her.

Though she couldn't see where Clancy's next blow fell, she knew it connected. She heard Raven's grunt of pain and watched as he slammed his fist forward in a rapid uppercut that struck Clancy squarely beneath his jaw. Charm heard his teeth clink, then saw him fall liked an axed pine, straight over backward.

Raven braced his feet, wanting to see if the other would rise, but he did not, and so Raven staggered forward to lift the downed man by his shirt-front. "Damn you, Clancy," he swore. "Thought you could claim the reward yourself, didn't you?"

"Can't blame a man for tryin'."

"Oh yes I can. You've made a regular practice of taking credit for my work. It's just like you." Turning, he dragged Clancy back toward the blankets.

"Now don't go fergetting we're pals, Joseph."

"I'm not forgetting anything, Bodine. Nothing at all. Where's the rope?"

"*Rope?* What are you plannin'?"

Raven grinned, but now his gaze fell to the strands of hemp that had bound Charm's arm and he swore aloud. "You tied her up."

"Well, I . . ." Clancy tried to back away, but his shirt was still held.

"Goddamn you Clancy. How dare you tie her up?"

"But . . ." For a moment nothing but befuddlement showed on his expression. "*You* tied her up too."

"That was different," said Raven through his teeth.

"How so?"

"Cuz I l—" He stopped his words just in time. "Down on your knees."

"You're not gonna hang me, are y'?"

"Damn if you don't deserve to hang. After all you've done. I searched for her for six months . Six months! Nearly got killed more times than I can count. You know she carried a knife strapped to her thigh! And a derringer in her pocket. Shot the thing off right in my face. But I stuck by her." He shook Clancy by the shirt front. "And you know why? To gain her trust."

"You're right, pal," Clancy said, lifting one placating hand. "You deserve the prize. But think on it, old boy, I've done you a favor by helping old Jude find you. You couldn't be sittin' prettier, cuz you don't need t' settle for the measly reward. Not when the heiress herself is yers."

Goddamn, Raven thought, he himself was a bastard, but Clancy brought the whole misbegotten lot to new lows. "I should kill you, Bodine."

"Me?" Clancy squeaked. "What are you thinkin', boy? You don't have time to kill me. The girl's pretty enough to be a princess. If I was you I'd hole up with her somewhere private and have me an extended honeymoon. Then after a month or two of lovin' I'd head south to pick up her inheritance."

"Amazing."

"What's that?"

"That you've been allowed to live as long as—"

"Hey!" Clancy broke in, craning his neck to see past Raven. "She really is getting away."

Raven turned with a start, still holding Clancy's shirt. "Charm?" All that answered him was the sound of fleeing hooves. "Goddamn it!" he swore, and drawing back his fist, slammed Clancy into the safekeeping of oblivion.

Truth tumbled with lies in Charm's head. She was Charm Fergusson. But she was Chantilly Grady. She was Jude's daughter. But she was the child of the hat man, a monster from her darkest dreams who came only to torture her mind and body.

She shook her head, trying to flee from the doubts that hounded her. She knew nothing, except that she must escape, and lose the man that thundered after her, who planned to destroy her with her own ragged, unwanted emotions. Raven didn't care about her. He only saw her as a means to gain wealth. He was a liar. She knew that. She'd been a fool to believe a single word he'd spoken.

"Charm! Slow down before you break your neck," Raven yelled.

Beneath her, Angel galloped up a sandy incline, his speed

aided by hard years on the prairie and the light weight of his rider. But the night was dark, the terrain uncertain. Charm felt the gelding's shoulder dip and she grabbed for the saddle horn, but too late. Her mount's foot found a hole and she was flung aside as the earth pitched toward her.

"No!" Raven screamed.

But Charm merely hit the soft earth and rolled rapidly to her feet. She faced Raven in the darkness, seeing him fling himself from his saddle to race toward her.

"Leave me be!" she screamed.

"Charm," he breathed, slowing to a walk but still moving closer.

"Don't come any nearer. I won't be your pawn. I'm not Chantilly. You don't care about me!"

"Well, I care about *someone*," he said. "Someone who looks a hell of a lot like you."

"Stay back!" She felt as if her world was caving in around her, bringing reality to shattered ruins. "Stay back or you'll regret it!" she added and yanked the butter knife from her pocket.

"Good God, Charm!" Raven scoffed. "What the devil—" he began, but his words ended on a grunt of pain, and then he fell, crumpling to the ground like a limp rag doll.

Chapter 24

In the darkness, Charm could hear Raven's second gasp of pain. But she wasn't about to be duped again. "God damn it, Raven!" she yelled. "It's not going to work this time."

He didn't answer, but lay still upon the ground.

"Quit it. I hate it when you do this." Silence answered her. "I'm leaving. Do you hear me? I'm leaving." She stomped off a few steps before turning back. "Raven?"

Although she saw the movement in the grass near his leg, it took her a moment to realize it was a rattlesnake. In another instant she had reached Raven's mount and drawn forth the gun he kept there. Without hesitation she aimed, fired, and fired again. Raven's body jerked in unison with that of the dying snake's. In a heartbeat, she was beside him.

"Am I dead?" he asked, looking up. "Did you shoot me?"

"Don't be ridiculous," she said, the smoking gun held aloft.

"Is that a 'no'?"

"Yes."

"Yes, you shot me, or yes, it's a no?"

"Oh, for God's sake, Raven, shut up!" she demanded fretfully and all but tossed the gun aside.

"Charm?" His voice sounded weak. Worry seared her mind. "Will you call me Joseph?"

"What?"

"Maybe I've been Raven too long. No one ever calls me Joseph, except Clancy, damn his hide. And he tried to get me hanged."

Charm's throat felt tight. "I tried to get you hanged too," she reminded him hoarsely. Despite all her practical good sense she felt tears well in her eyes. People often died from rattlesnake bites, and she wasn't certain how many times he'd been struck.

"That's true," he said, gazing up at the night sky with solemn thoughtfulness. "What is it about me that makes my friends try to kill me?"

Charm wiped her nose on the back of her hand. "I can think of a half dozen things. Do you want to hear them now?"

"No," he sighed and let his eyes fall closed. "I'm rather tired right now."

"Raven!" Her voice was panicked.

He forced his eyes open. "Didn't you promise to call me Joseph?"

"No."

"Oh. Well, call it a dying man's last request."

Her hands gripped his embroidered vest in a hard clasp. "You die, I'll never forgive you, Raven Scott."

"Joseph," he corrected through clenched teeth. "Joseph Neil. My father's surname was Neil. Mother's was Scott. Took hers instead. Pathetic attempt at revenge." His eyes fell closed.

"Joseph!" she cried.

"Ahh, that sounds much better than when Clancy, damn his hide, says it." He paused, drawing a slow breath and opening his eyes. "I'm sorry I lied about my arm, Lucky

Charm. Wanted to reach River Bluffs before your aunt's wedding. Paid extra to get you there for the festivities. Didn't care how you felt about it." He exhaled a heavy breath. "Bastards run in my family. But hell, might as well tell it all now. Truth is, I didn't have the strength to let you go. I thought you'd be too afraid of me if I were hale. Let you think I was disabled. You can hate me if you like."

"I do hate you," she said on a sob. "Don't die."

His eyes fell closed again.

"Raven!"

He became immediately alert and found her face with his gaze. "You know, if you decided to suck out the poison, you'd get to cut me."

"What?"

"You'd get to cut my leg. Two places. Might be your last chance."

"But . . ." Charm shot a frantic glance toward his wound. "All I have is the butter knife I stole at dinner."

He winced dramatically. "Better than a stick. Still, sounds rather . . . tedious. There's a knife in my saddlebag."

She was gone in an instant and back even faster, but his eyes were closed again. "Raven?"

"You have the worst memory known to mankind," he scolded softly. "Can't even remember the name of the man who loves you."

"Loves . . . me?" she breathed.

He didn't respond.

"Loves me?" The words were barely forced from her lips. "Are you talking out of your head?"

"Yeah, I think so. Damn, this hurts like hell. I thought rattlers were supposed to be fair fighters. Give a warning before they struck."

"Did you say you love me?" she murmured.

"Aren't they supposed to give a warning?"

"What?" She shook her head.

"The rattler," he babbled. "Supposed to fight fair."

"Maybe it was a male," she reasoned. "Did you say you love me?"

"What do you mean maybe it was a male?"

"What did you say . . . you know . . . earlier?"

"I said it hurts like hell."

"Before that," she demanded, gripping his vest again as she leaned closer. "What'd you say?"

"Charm . . ." His face, she noticed, was very pale. "I'm not feeling so . . ."—he shivered—"good."

She scowled, loosening her hold on his vest. "Are you all right?"

"That would depend on your . . ."—he shivered again and for a moment she thought he might retch—". . . definition of all right."

Charm clenched her fist, panicked and guilty at her own delay. "What do I do?"

"Remove my pants," he said through his teeth, the pain obvious on his tense features. "Unless you'd faint at the sight of my overwhelming . . . good looks."

She tightened her fists, suddenly wanting nothing more than to run away. "I've already admired your . . ." She glanced nervously downward. Where exactly had he been bitten? Was it really possible to suck out the poison? And what if the whole process caused him to pass out? How would she get him on his horse?

"Admired my what?" he asked, squeezing his eyes closed.

"Your good looks."

"Listen, Charming, you've admired a hell of a lot more than that."

She had no time to blush. "Where were you bitten, Raven?"

He didn't answer and his breathing sounded ragged.

"Raven!" she called frantically.

"Charm!" he said with a start. "It's in my pocket."

"What? What is?"

"Your Bible. In my vest pocket. If I don't make it, take it with you. Go to St. Louis. River Bluffs."

"What are you talking about? Of course you're going to make it."

"Promise me you'll go there, Charm. Find Eloise Medina. Show her the Bible. Tell her your story. She loved your mother. She'll love you."

"We'll go together," Charm said hoarsely. The panic was bitter and new, not for herself now, but for this man whom she had fought so long.

"Promise me," he grunted. "Or I won't let you cut open the bites."

"I promise."

"Thatta girl." He paused as if gathering strength. "Do you really care about me, or do you just want to see me bleed?"

"Damn it, Raven!" she said with a sob. "Tell me what to do."

He arched his back suddenly, and his body stiffened as he sucked a gasp through his teeth. His hands gripped the sparse grass beneath him, and his chin thrust upward until finally the spasm passed and he relaxed marginally. "Two spots, I think. Cut crosses in the wounds. Suck out the poison." He shook his head weakly. "Not a job for a lady, Charm. We could just wait for Clancy, damn his hide. He'll come, you know. 'Course, I'd prefer the company of the snake," he added, but she was already slicing his pants from the bottom up. Even by the uncertain light of the moon she could see the edema. Grasping his right boot she pulled and pried, finally yanking it free from his rapidly swelling foot.

"Where do I cut?"

He didn't answer. Charm scrambled forward to shake him. "Raven! I can't find the wounds. Where do I cut? Raven!" Her voice was a sob. "Don't die. Not now. You said you love me, didn't you? Didn't you?"

There was no answer. Her mind reeled and her hands trembled, but there was no time for weakness or delay. She needed light, immediately.

At the bottom of the hill, she'd seen a few scrubby bushes growing. She scurried down the incline now. There was very little wood to be found, but she gathered what she could into her arms and speedily returned to Raven's side. Dried grasses were easier to procure, and she found matches in a saddlebag.

It took her several minutes of fanning and prayer to produce even a tiny flame. She hovered frantically over it, feeding it carefully until she was out of chafe, but still the smallest branch refused to ignite. "Save me, oh God," she chanted desperately, and then, seeing Raven's pant leg spread wide, suddenly gripped the thing in her hands and tore it away. In a moment, it was in small pieces and was being consumed by the starved little blaze that crackled so near her patient. Now the first branch caught fire. Finally, she was able to direct her attention to his swollen leg.

There were two wounds, boasting four holes each. It took almost more courage than Charm had to cut them open. But she did so, slicing a cross into their centers before lowering her mouth to the oozing lacerations.

She didn't know whether the venom had remained near the surface or if it was dangerous if ingested, but she had little time to consider these things, for the blood was flowing quickly now. Perhaps it would wash the poison from the wound, she reasoned; she watched fretfully as his life blood drained into the sandy soil beneath them.

Why didn't it stop bleeding? Had she cut too deeply? Or had the venom perhaps, somehow affected his body's ability to clot the wound? Whatever the answer, she could wait no longer. Tearing a strip of cotton from her petticoat, she wrapped it snugly just below his knee. Still the blood came. She bit her lip and prayed frantically, then tearing off another square of cotton, pressed it firmly to the wounds.

It seemed like hours before the bleeding subsided. Raven's face looked pale and drawn, but his breathing sounded fairly normal and when she pressed her ear to his chest, his heart seemed steady and strong beneath the hard mass of protective muscle. Charm stayed as she was, resting her ear against his pectoral and absorbing strength from that sound until she felt him tremble. She wrapped him in blankets and fed the fire. Soon it was bright and hot, but still Raven shivered. Charm stretched out against his side, sharing her body heat and praying for help.

There was no way of knowing how much time went by before a rustle of sound caught her attention. She sat up quickly, holding her breath. "Clancy?" No one answered. Her gaze darted through the darkness, seeing nothing unusual. "Who's there?"

The silence was suddenly terrifying. Anyone might have found them, what with the gunshots and fire. What had she done with Raven's gun? Her neck felt wooden as she turned to search, but it was nowhere to be seen in the failing light of the fire. Only the knife was in sight. She gripped it quickly in her right hand, feeling a small bit of courage galvanized by the feel of its cool handle against her palm.

Another whisper of sound alerted her. She remained as she was, kneeling beside Raven, her knuckles white against her feeble weapon.

They seemed to appear from nowhere. Two Indians, with hair as dark as the night that surrounded them, and faces unlike anything Charm had ever seen. Fierce and arrogant, as if chiseled from the very stone of the earth. They stared at her unblinking, watching with silent scorn.

Charm's fist ached with her tight grip. Her heart thudded painfully in her constricted chest.

One man spoke, his voice low and incomprehensible as he lifted a hand toward her with a grimace of a mocking smile.

"Stay back." She forced the words steadily past lips frozen with fear. Her right hand rose slowly, bearing the knife higher as her chin lifted in unison. "You touch him, I'll kill you. I swear I will."

They watched her in silence again, their expressions unreadable, and then one jolted toward her.

She rose to a crouch, snarling her feeble retaliation. But the Indian stopped some six feet away, and throwing back his head, laughed aloud. Behind him the other man joined in his mirth. "Little Cougar Mouse," he said roughly. "Stay with your mate."

The closest man turned, laughing again. And suddenly, like a chilling wind, they were gone, faded into the darkness.

Charm's breath came in great gasps. She felt suddenly dizzy and her stomach roiled. The knife slipped from her hand and she slouched to the ground. The whinny of a horse seemed dim and inconsequential. They were leaving, she thought vaguely, but suddenly the reality of the situation came home with a painful jolt. They were leaving with *her* horses.

"No!" she cried, scrambling to her feet. She couldn't get Raven to a doctor without a horse. "No!" Dropping to her knees, she scrambled frantically around in search of the revolver.

She felt it before she saw it and yanked it from beneath the blanket. In a moment, she was running. "Leave them," she screamed, but already Raven's gelding was fading into the darkness, galloping away behind the first spotted pony. Charm turned frantically toward Angel, whose reins were held in the other Indian's hand.

"Leave him." Her tone was hoarse and shaky. "Or I'll shoot." Her arms felt strangely stiff as she raised the gun. "I swear I will."

Silence filled the spot, and then the Indian laughed. Light as the wind, he leaped to his own pony's back, dragging Angel along behind him.

"No!" Charm screamed, but the Indian kept riding, forcing Angel away. She aimed without taking a breath. The trigger squeezed beneath her finger. The gun exploded. There was a yelp of surprise from the thief as his fingers were burned by the passing bullet. The reins were severed. The Indian pony reared, but Angel, free and loyal, whirled about with agile grace to thunder back to camp.

Silence again, except for thudding hooves against prairie grass, but in a moment the Indian had regained control of his mount, and sat in silence, as if testing her mettle. "Cougar Mouse deserves warrior in her teepee."

"Leave now and I'll let you live," Charm said, but her voice wobbled, and the revolver shook in her clammy grip. She'd never shot a man before, but when he turned his pony toward her, she cocked the pistol. "One more step and I'll kill you. I swear . . ."

"But she choose weak man instead," he said, and was gone, like a breeze. Simply gone.

Charm remained exactly as she was for a moment of eternity. Waiting. Watching. But no sound could be heard. The gun wobbled more dramatically in her hands and finally dropped uselessly toward the earth.

"Damn!"

She spun weakly around, startled by Clancy's voice.

"Cougar Mouse. Pretty and mean!" He grinned, little more than his teeth visible in the darkness as he looked down at her from his horse. "Two of my favorite characteristics. Would you really of shot him?"

She pointed the revolver directly at his head. "Drop your gun."

"Me?"

She narrowed her eyes, feeling weakness sweep away beneath the onslaught of rage. Clancy, damn his hide, was supposed to be Raven's friend! "Drop the gun or you'll see daylight through your chest."

Bodine pulled his revolver from its holster with careful fingertips. "Bad day, Miss Charm?"

"Now get down."

"I . . . Listen." He shrugged. "I was just passin' by. Wanted to make sure you was all right. And . . . you are, so I gotta go."

"Down." She cocked the pistol. "Now."

"Oh. You want me to get *down*." He smiled ingratiatingly and dismounted. "Anything for the pretty lady with the gun."

"Drop your horse's reins."

"You're not thinkin' of takin' ol' Mac are you?"

"Raven's hurt."

"Yeah." Clancy nodded, still holding his reins. "I saw that. Them rattlers sure can make a mess of a man, can't they? It's sure enough too bad, but—you wanted to leave him. I guess now's your chance, huh?"

"Do you know anything about snake bites?"

"I know it ain't my first choice for Saturday night entertainment."

"Move. Back to camp. No." She motioned him away from his horse. "Leave your mount and walk."

Beside their camp, Raven was still bundled in his bedroll, trembling visibly. Charm fell to her knees by him, touching his cheek with her palm as Clancy dropped down beside her with a shake of his head.

"Looks mighty bad. 'Fraid we'll have to leave him."

"Leave him?" she breathed, feeling the bitter edge of panic rip at her gut. "What are you talking about?"

"'Fraid there's no hope. We might just as well ride on without him."

For a moment she'd forgotten all she'd been taught of men, but she remembered clearly now. "I've already shot one snake tonight." She leveled her gaze and her gun on him. "Shall I make it two?"

Clancy opened his mouth to respond, but something in her expression must have changed his mind. "You . . ."— he shook a finger at her—"you got yourself a way with words, Miss Charm."

"Get him on your horse."

"But—"

"And make sure he doesn't fall."

Clancy scowled at her. "It wasn't so long ago you was

tryin' to kill Joseph yerself. Can I ask . . . what went wrong?"

Charm drew a deep breath and narrowed her eyes, feeling a thousand emotions jumble in her chest. "He can't die now. Not after . . . what he said."

Chapter 25

"We'd best stop. Joseph needs the rest," Clancy said.

"I can go on," Raven insisted, gritting his teeth and holding himself stiffly upright in Clancy's saddle. He'd been conscious for several hours but looked pale and strained. His leg was swollen and red from his foot to his thigh where his pants abruptly ended.

"No use trying to impress Miss Charm with your manly fortitude," Clancy said, shaking his head. "She's already seen you swoon."

"Don't touch the reins," Raven warned, irritably knocking Bodine's hands away, "I'll handle the horse."

"You don't know nothin' 'bout horses," Clancy responded before turning his attention to Charm. "He never did. Why, I remember when he was a lad, fifteen, maybe sixteen, he took a shine to Nora May Bentley. Pretty little thing she was. Anyhow, Joseph lost his head and decides to go see her. So he hops on this big old ornery bay I sometimes let him ride, seein's as he was like a son to me."

Clancy reached for the reins again, but Raven managed to

jab a sharp elbow into the other's ribs, prompting a grunt of wounded noise.

"Shut the hell up, Bodine."

"Yep, like a goddamn son," Clancy said before continuing with his reminiscence. "Anyhow, off he goes, ridin' hell-bent, only old Bay didn't feel like leavin' the barn and when Joseph leaned over Bentley's barbed wire gate, Bay decides it's high time to come home." Clancy chuckled, rubbing a wounded rib. "Left poor Joseph hangin' on the wire like a fresh-washed Sunday shirt. It was old man Bentley hisself that brung him home. With his arms all scratched up. And his pants! He had him a hole right . . ."

Raven must be feeling better, Charm deduced. This time when his elbow thwacked back, he almost unseated Clancy.

"Damn you, Joseph," swore Bodine, righting himself. "I'm just tryin' to entertain yer bride, seein' as how you ain't up to the task. . . . Hey! Fort Pierre finally, and none too soon. I been worried sick about you, Joseph. Feared you'd swoon on us again. I'm afraid he's never been real strong, Miss Charm. But I hope you won't hold that against him, cuz he needs somebody to look after him, now that he's left my nest."

"You got any relatives I should inform of your death, Bodine, or did Charm shoot the last one of them?" Raven grumbled.

Clancy chuckled. "We'll have to find him a good doctor, Miss Charm, and let him rest up fer a spell. But I'm sure that won't be no hardship, considerin' you two ain't had no chance to do no spoonin' yet."

Fort Pierre was small and bustling with the hectic life Missouri River travel had brought it.

Raven stopped the gelding at a tidy-looking boardinghouse. Clancy slipped over the animal's tail and hurried to help Charm dismount. For a moment fear accosted her, but she stifled it before sliding down on her own and hurrying to help Raven dismount.

His knuckles looked white against the saddle horn. His teeth were clenched as he swung his leg over the cantle.

"Are you all right?" Charm asked, catching his arm as he jolted to the earth.

Despite the pain obviously caused by the movement, his gaze turned abruptly to hers. "Do you care, Charm?" he asked softly.

Breath jammed in her throat, but fear was suspiciously absent. "What did you say before?" she whispered. "Back by the fire. What did you say?"

The whole world seemed to have gone silent as they stared at each other, but suddenly Raven turned his attention abruptly away. "Don't you have somewhere to go, Bodine?" he asked stonily. "Somebody's grandmother to swindle, maybe?"

"Matter a fact I . . . don't." Clancy shrugged with a grin. "Guess I'll just stick with you kids."

For a moment, Charm thought Raven would say more, but he turned stiffly to hobble up the steps toward the door.

"How are you feeling?"

Charm stood beside Raven's bed. Beside her, to Raven's grinding irritation, was Clancy, looking freshly washed and characteristically handsome.

How did Raven feel? Like an overblown idiot. His leg was stiff with swelling and pain, and his head ached as if a Sioux raiding party were bolstering their courage there with fire water and war drums. "Fine," he lied. He thought he did it quite well, considering his exhaustion and his irritation over his companions' long absence. Not that he hadn't wanted them gone. Charm did need clothing, but the idea of Clancy accompanying her on a buying spree somehow set his teeth on edge, regardless of the good that would come of it.

Raven did his best to concentrate on his mission. He'd sent a telegraph to River Bluffs, estimating their arrival time as best he could, and he'd purchased two tickets for the *Yankee Belle.* It would leave early next morning, and he had more plans to make, but his thoughts were confused by the sight of Charm in a newly purchased gown. It was pale green, like the color of aspen leaves in the early spring. It fit snugly across her breasts and abdomen before flaring away from her hips. A less disciplined man might imagine Clancy watching her as she turned for his approval. "I hope shopping was to your satisfaction, Charm."

She bit her inner lip. "You were more than generous."

"I think a bride at least deserves a decent trousseau." God, she was beautiful, standing there very still, her small face solemn.

"Damn right," Clancy said, breaking the mood with his usual aplomb. "I tried to talk her into buying this little lavender gown, but seems yer bride's too modest. Fit her like a glove." He shook his head with a grin, as if just the thought made him happy.

Raven clamped his teeth, and decided to wait to kill him.

"Cut down to . . ." Clancy raised his hand to his own chest to indicate the low décolleté, then broadened his grin and shrugged. "Anyhow, it looked damned good. But she didn't want to spend any more of your money." He chuckled. "Lucky fer you, I'm the kind of pal I am, Joseph, and knew when t' spend it." He lifted the bundles wrapped in brown paper, then shook his head again, looking perplexed. "Told her you was flush." He turned his charming grin to the girl. "He's not much of a detective, though I did my best t'teach him. But he's got him some luck with the cards. Ever seen him gamble, Miss Charm?"

Her face looked strained as she watched him, Raven noticed, and felt his gut tighten. If Bodine had touched her, he'd take him apart piece by piece and enjoy every minute. Perhaps it had been a bad idea to ask Clancy to accompany her during shopping, but he'd needed his old partner well out of the way to achieve his ends.

"Are you all right, Charm?" Raven asked.

"Yes." Her eyes were a cool green this evening and very wide. He could easily fall into those eyes and found, not for the first time, that he wanted to. Wanted to let go of all the restraint he had maintained for so long.

There was tension in her tone, and distance in her manner. It shouldn't bother him, but somehow the world seemed cold and rather empty when she held herself apart from him. "Scared?" he asked softly.

For a moment he was certain she would deny her feelings, but she drew a soft breath through her strawberry lips and graced him with the suggestion of a self-effacing smile. "Yes."

For a moment nothing ached but his heart. Truth and a smile, from a woman who shared little of either.

"I won't let anything happen to you." His own words were very quiet, and seemed foolish, since she was, after all, the one who had saved him. "I'm sorry we'll have to stay here. The doctor thought traveling would be a bad bet in my present condition."

"I don't mind," she said, looking younger than he knew her to be.

The room was very quiet for a moment—then, "She's too good for you, Joseph."

"Go away, Bodine."

"Oh! Almost forgot. Got something for you too." From the bundle of packages, Clancy selected one flat parcel and tossed it to the bed. "Can't hardly go runnin' round with your . . . leg hangin' out." He laughed.

"Don't think I'll be running for a while." Raven turned his gaze languidly to Clancy's. "But I suppose some thanks are in order."

"Never mind," Bodine said, laughing again, "since it was your money. So, what should we do now? Hey, how about a little game of chance? Just the three of us. Five-card stud?"

"Bodine."

"Yeah?"

"Get the hell lost," Raven said flatly.

"I'm not askin' to share your bed, Joseph, just her

company, and only for a while. Is that so much to ask from yer best friend?"

"Remind me to expand my circle of acquaintances."

Clancy chuckled. "What do you think, Miss Charm, a little poker?"

"I'm . . . I'm afraid I'm quite tired." She looked nervous and had erected that careful wall she could put up so efficiently.

The room seemed suddenly very still, as though she had said something so scandalous that it shocked them all speechless.

Clancy whistled low. "Lucky man. Well . . ." He tossed the remainder of the packages to the bed. "I guess it's good night, then."

Surprisingly, he actually exited without any further ado, splashing the room into absolute silence again.

The two stared at each other. Charm blinked. Raven cleared his throat. "He didn't touch you?"

"No!" She said the word very quickly and raised her gaze abruptly to his. Raven felt the contact as a sharp jab to his heart. "No," she said, more slowly now. "He was a perfect gentleman."

Jealousy was an ugly emotion and very bitter. "Let's just say . . . gentleman," Raven corrected, taking a deep breath and keeping his tone even. "The word 'perfect' makes it all a bit unbelievable."

She smiled. And here he'd thought the sun had already set. But no, the room seemed suddenly filled with light.

"Clancy's not as frightening as I thought."

I love you. The words almost escaped him, but he held them back, knowing better. Love was a strangling bond and rarely returned. He knew that well, had learned it at his mother's expense. "Actually, he is."

She drew a soft breath between her perfectly white teeth. He watched the inhalation, knowing it shouldn't be fascinating. "What?"

Raven scrambled to remember his line of thought. "I said, actually Clancy *is* that frightening. Don't trust him."

She stared at him for a moment, then shrugged lightly, lifting one shoulder in a delicate expression. "He cares about you in a way."

"Really? What way might that be? The kind that gets me hanged?"

She laughed again and took a step forward. What the hell was he supposed to do now, with the pain spreading upward from his leg and downward from his heart to converge at his groin in a cacophony of agony? Don't come any closer, he wanted to warn, because he couldn't be responsible for his actions if she came within reach.

"You know . . ." She was standing at the edge of the bed. *His* bed. Raven could feel himself begin to sweat. "All my life I've been warned that men want only one thing."

There was, it seemed, just enough room for her to settle her hips lightly beside his on the straw tick. Good God!

"I think Jude was wrong all along," she murmured.

"About what?" To Raven's ears, his tone sounded rather strange. Tight somehow.

"About men. I think he was wrong." She reached out, touching his stubbled cheek. Despite what he'd said to Clancy, despite his own admission that he was only accompanying her for the money, she believed he wanted more. *Needed* more. Needed *her*. Or did she only want to believe? "I think . . . I think I can trust you."

"With what?" Raven asked breathlessly.

With my heart, Charm thought, but habit and caution kept her from saying it. She took a deep breath. "I know it's not . . . I know it's not a real marriage." She scowled and looked away, unable to hold his gaze.

He said nothing, and she felt her tension increase. With all her heart she wished he would deny her words, say she was wrong. Their union *was* real. Very real. The kind that held two people together for eternity. The kind a woman could depend on, to protect her, to cherish her, to allow her

to cherish in return. The silence was sickening. All certainty
fled. He didn't care for her, never had. "I'm sorry about
everything," she whispered. "I didn't want to trick you into
marrying me. I was just . . ." Why didn't he say something? Why did her chest feel so tight? She squeezed her
eyes closed for a moment, then pursed her lips and set her
resolve. She was being an idiot. Obviously he didn't share
her feelings and resented being trapped here with her. Jude
had been right; women *were* fools when it came to men.
Charm straightened her back. "We'll have the marriage
annulled."

Raven tightened his fists. "It . . . can wait."

She swallowed, wishing she were a thousand miles away
and that she'd never met this man. "I think it would be best
to take care of it right away."

"Traveling might be safer for you as a married woman,"
Raven said. "And more respectable, of course. No one need
know that we don't . . ."

His words stopped abruptly. She waited, holding her
breath, feeling frozen with fear. "Don't what?" She couldn't
stop the whispered question.

"Don't share a bed," he answered huskily.

"But there's only one." She watched his nostrils flare and
his fists tighten. What did it mean?

"Neither of us wanted this marriage, Charm. There's no
reason to pretend otherwise."

Never had she experienced pain quite like what she felt
now. It reverberated from her heart, hindering her every
breath. What a fool she was. "No. Of course not. I was
simply afraid Jude would shoot you."

His nostrils were still flared, though his fists had loosened
a smidgen. "I appreciate what you did, but there's no reason
we should both suffer the rest of our lives because of Jude's
irrationality."

Suffer the rest of their lives! "No. Of course not." She
turned away, hoping to reach the door before she fell apart.
"I'll look immediately into getting it annulled."

"Charm!" His hand caught hers suddenly. "Not tonight!"

Did she imagine the sharp edge to his words? And if she didn't—what did it mean?

"Please." He loosened his grip abruptly, as if feeling foolish for his act of drama. "Don't bother. Not tonight."

There was something in his tone, *something*, but she didn't know what.

He dropped his hand away as suddenly as he'd grabbed her. "If you're afraid that I'll . . . that I'll take advantage of the situation . . ."

"No." No, she certainly didn't think that. After all, he had fought to keep from being bound to her. There was no reason to think he would allow himself to be trapped now.

"Then why not rest tonight?" His fingers had curled against his palm, not quite forming a fist, but almost. "You must be tired."

"Yes. I am." Exhausted. Tired enough to die. To want to die. To wish she'd never been.

"Why not lie down, Charm? I won't . . . I won't touch you."

"No." She turned away from the bed. "I'm sure you won't. I just think it would be best to resolve this . . . situation immediately." She was almost to the door, had almost forced her legs to carry her that far.

"Charm!" His voice was strangely husky, and she turned, locking her gaze on his face. It was shadowed by dusk and whiskers, making his thoughts unreadable. "Please. Not tonight. We've shared a bed before, with no harm to anyone."

She hesitated, trying not to fall under his dark spell. How could he know the harm he had caused her? How could he know she had almost learned to trust, only to find that trust led to a pain she'd never anticipated? But he'd never said he wanted to marry her. Indeed, he'd always been honest in his wish to be rid of her.

"Just tonight." His voice was not demanding, not frightening.

She tried to reach for the door, but her fingers refused to move to the handle. "I suppose I shouldn't leave you alone," she whispered.

"No."

She glanced at the floor and then toward the portal she had almost reached. "I can . . . I can nullify the marriage tomorrow."

He said nothing, but she could feel his tension, and she drew in a shaky breath, wondering how to hold back the tears. Wondering why they were there, behind her lids, filling her head.

"Charm, what's wrong?"

"Nothing." Her answer hadn't sounded quite right. She cleared her throat. "Just tired."

"Come and lie down."

She hesitated for several moments, torn between the desire to run away and another desire, something stronger, something unthinkable. "Perhaps I should sleep in the chair."

"You mean snatch."

"What?"

"You don't sleep, remember?"

"Oh." She felt worn and frazzled, weary beyond the boundaries of her body, and without thinking, she could remember how his hands felt against her flesh. How they had soothed the ache from her muscles and lulled her into blissful sleep. "Yes."

"So couldn't you risk not sleeping in bed, since you'll be able to keep an eye on me all night?"

She opened her mouth to object, but he hurried to override her words. "I'm hurt, Charm. What could I do?"

He'd confused the issue. The question was no longer what *he* would do, but what *she* would do. She finally lay down without a word. The room was quite dark now, the ceiling blank and white.

"I thought you trusted me."

She didn't look at him. All the reasons someone might try to hang him were rushing ruthlessly back into her mind. "What do you mean?"

"You didn't take off your shoes. Planning on a speedy retreat?"

She squeezed her eyes closed. "Leave it alone, Raven."

"*Raven* again." Silence followed. "Charm?"

She couldn't answer, and fought back the humiliating agony of tears.

"Charm." He was closer suddenly. "What is it? Have I done something wrong?" Damn! She was crying. "Charm."

She felt his breath against her cheek, and there was nothing she could do but turn into his arms.

"You're crying," he said, sounding shocked.

She tried to bury her face against his neck, but he held her back and brushed his fingertips across her cheek. The wetness smeared warm and salty to her lips. His fingers skimmed across them, and she shivered with feelings so deep they nagged at her soul. She must run away, she must! For now he would learn the truth. She'd committed the unforgivable sin. She'd fallen in love.

"Why?" he whispered. "Why are you crying? Please." The single word was little more than a warm breath against her face. The kiss, feather soft, felt no more substantial. "Don't cry." He kissed her again, beside her mouth. "Tell me what I did." His voice was husky, and he kissed her eyelid now, which was wet. "I'll undo it, Charm. I swear I will."

Never had she felt anything that ripped at her soul like the feel of his kisses against her love-starved skin. She couldn't move away, though she knew she should.

He kissed the bridge of her nose, where a tear had made an erratic escape. "What have I done, Charm?" His question sounded anguished.

"Nothing."

He kissed the corner of her mouth again, but suddenly he stiffened. "Clancy, damn his hide! What'd he do?"

She failed to immediately follow his line of thought.

Raven jerked away, rage possessing him. "I'll kill him!"

"No." She reached for him in desperation. "Clancy didn't do anything," she whispered and leaning forward, kissed his lips.

It was a magic never before experienced by either of them. It seared them like lightning, burning their flesh, confusing their thoughts, and suddenly they were clasped together in each other's tight embrace, feeling the heat and raw energy sizzle around and through them. Their tongues met, clashing in a gentle joust of sensation. Raven pulled his mouth away but only for a moment, and now his kisses rained across her cheek to find her ear. Charm shivered, feeling the tingling trail of his caresses curve across her ear in tiny nibbles of desire.

She was breathing hard. Her eyes were closed and her back arched. Every nerve was vibrating for his attention, and now his kisses fell lower, down the length of her throat to her collarbone. She shivered again, and when his lips reached the tiny hollow in her throat, she gasped. His fingers touched the buttons at the back of her gown, peeling it open. His lips left her flesh.

"No," she moaned.

"No?" he breathed, sounding hopelessly weak, but pulling his hands away with great effort.

"No!" she repeated, but drew his face back to her and kissed him with all the passion that smoldered within her. "Don't stop. Please."

For just a moment he waited, staring into her eyes before he pulled her into his embrace again. Nothing was held back now. Sheer desire took control, desire for touch, for feeling, for unity.

Her dress fell away from her shoulders. Raven followed its exit with kisses, running the length of her right arm, down to her shivering fingers, then back up, over the delicate, cringing bend to her shoulder. Charm drew it toward her ear, unable to bear the titillation, yet certain she would die if it stopped. And now he kissed the rounded swell of a breast. Never had she imagined she would burn so. Never had she thought she would need to feel his flesh against hers as she did now.

Her hands were trembling, but moved slowly along his sides to hug him to her. And then she kissed his chest, between his left nipple and the empty chain. Her hands slipped lower, and she closed her eyes, feeling the heat of his flesh sear her senses. She pulled him closer, pressing her half bared bosom against the solid mass of his torso.

Raven's moan was like a tonic, splashing hot excitement into her already overheated system. She tilted her chin up, kissing his chest again. His second moan was accompanied by the hard grip of his arms about her. Charm felt the backwash of her own warm breath against her face and knew she was far past control, deep into the raging flood of desire. But his head was thrown back now, and she could feel the steely tremble of his arms about her. Such strength there, and yet she made him shake. She kissed his nipple, and the tremor seemed to rip from his body directly into hers.

"Charm!" His voice was ragged, barely coherent, but she gave him no time to say more. Taking his nipple between her lips, she sucked it gently into her mouth.

His breath came in fire-rapid gasps. "Charm," he moaned again, and she pulled back finally, aching with a new, indescribable need. Somehow she had become planted on top of him. Though a sheet still remained between their lower bodies, she could feel the raging heat of his desire against her. She pressed into it, forcing a moan from them both. "Charm," he repeated, but she could see no reason for talk. She rocked against him again, a little harder now and slower.

Whatever he'd planned to say was lost. With a groan of savage desire he pushed her upward and kissed her. Rolling her onto her side, he yanked the sheet from between them. Somehow her gown too was pulled upward, and now, with a suddenness that should have been frightening, his engorged heat was pressed between her legs, against the steamy core of her being.

He kissed her breasts where they swelled taut and aching above her corset. Charm moaned and rocked up against him, and somehow, with the ease of oiled perfection, he slipped between the separate legs of her pantalettes and inside. Their gasps came in unison as both bodies jolted to a rigid halt. He was just within the hot gates, not too far surely to draw out and say it had never been.

"Charm!" Her name was no more than a hoarse plea on his lips, but what he pleaded for she couldn't guess, for at that moment she lost every vestige of control, and tipping her hips forward, pressed him deep inside.

There was a harsh rip of pain and pleasure. He gritted his teeth and she did the same, pressing in for more, and for a moment he obliged, rocking against her, thrust for thrust, before pulling out with a ragged curse.

"Raven!" she gasped, destitute.

"Damn it, Charm!" He was breathing like a running stallion, harsh and loud and hard. "This is no way to do it."

"No?" Her own breathing sounded no more sedate.

"Not with you," he moaned, pulling her back into his arms. "I need to caress you. To kiss—"

"Kiss me then," she ordered, and pushing him back into his pillow, pressed her lips to his lips and her hips to his.

His tongue touched hers. Their lower bodies jolted and suddenly, whether planned or not, he was inside once again, past the linen gown, the cotton pantalettes, and deep into the forbidden Eden.

If he tried to stop again, Charm never knew it for she was far beyond noticing anything but the need to fill the void. She pushed against him, welding them together with hot pleasure, pumping their desire to fiery heights until in a raspy shriek of surprise she climbed over the need and into the long soft folds of satisfaction. With a shiver that met his, she fell against his chest. Their hearts thrummed in tandem and their rapid, uneven breathing melded until finally, exhausted and sated, she drifted into the cumulus softness of sleep.

Chapter 26

"Wake up, Charm," Raven whispered. "We have to get you out of those clothes."

She didn't stir, but remained as she was, looking young and tousled and innocent. Raven settled back on an elbow, watching her sleep. Although it had been several hours since they'd consummated their wedding vows, he remained sleepless, for the enormity of the act kept him far from the sweet gates of slumber. Good God, what had he done? Slipping stiffly from the bed, he padded naked across the floor to the window. The night was silent and moon-shadowed, casting soft shades of blue across the room. Raven drew a deep breath and turned to see how that same moonlight caressed the girl's sleeping features.

What had he done? He'd married her—that's what. But it wasn't his fault. He hadn't meant to do it. It was simply that the options had been very unsavory. Marriage, or marriage with a leg wound. He'd chosen marriage—and look, he had the leg wound anyway.

Still, he'd kept his integrity. He'd planned to do right by the girl, which meant, of course, annulment. After all, he wasn't husband material. Look at his father. Or rather, don't look, because he'd never had a father.

And this woman—this . . . *girl* had not had a mother nor a true father. But still . . . Raven wandered close to the bed, leaning over it slightly to look into her face. Her hair was in wild disarray. It seemed to be everywhere, covering the petal-soft flesh of her shoulders, caressing the pillows. Her nose was very small, and her lips . . . her sweetly pinkened lips were upturned even in sleep.

Her childhood had been somewhat similar to his, and yet she was different. Not like him. Not like his father. But loyal, even to a man like Jude. Hell, she was even loyal to *Angel*.

Something inside Raven's chest ached. Perhaps, he thought, if she could tolerate such obvious imperfections in others, she could also tolerate his. Maybe she could even love . . .

Raven pivoted away with a sneer. He didn't need her love. He didn't *want* her love. But . . . At the window he turned back. The distance between them now seemed vast and painful. For a moment he wanted nothing more than to take her into his arms again, to beg for her love.

God, what was wrong with him? What had happened to his pride, and how the devil had he gotten himself into this predicament? He'd not only married her, he'd *bedded* her for Christ's sake.

Something in his chest swelled, but he deflated it with firm practicality. She hadn't planned to marry him any more than he'd planned to marry her. She'd only agreed, in fact, to save his hide from her crackpot father. Who was, in fact, not her father at all. Which was a lucky thing, or their children would be in dire danger of inheriting the old man's derangement.

Children! Raven almost moaned aloud. The fact was *he* was the deranged one. He was over the edge. Out of his mind! Insane! He couldn't marry. Never. He'd always known that, ever since the moment he'd realized his father wasn't coming back. For thirteen years his mother had suffered the humiliation and hardship of abandonment, and no matter how big a rat Raven knew himself to be, he would not put Charm through that.

He sighed and swept his fingers through his hair. True, she was beautiful, and true, she had a heart as soft as featherdown beneath her steely facade, and true also, he did love . . .

Raven jerked his mind abruptly into submission. He'd wake her immediately, apologize for his weakness, and explain the situation. In truth, it wasn't too late to annul the marriage, for surely no baby had been conceived by their one small slipup. Surely not. But what if one had?

He could feel sweat form on his brow. How long would it take to learn if a new life had been created? Four weeks at most. Probably far less. And it would take nearly half that time to reach St. Louis. That meant he could make certain she hadn't conceived before he delivered her to her aunt. He could then take care of business and collect his reward with a clear conscience.

Raven scowled. When had he developed a conscience? It was a damned nuisance of a thing, he reasoned, but looking at the girl again, he knew it was she that had changed him. Pacing forward now, he bent to shake her, ready to inform her of his plan.

But apparently their physical union was just what she'd needed for her insomnia. She slept on, only moaning softly in her slumber, and lifting one delicate shoulder in response to his touch. The movement urged her breasts even higher above the harsh stiffness of her corset, and seemed to cause Raven's breathing to come harder.

How could she sleep in that thing? It must be torturous. And her shoes! They'd never been removed. Somehow that knowledge made Raven feel even more like a dog.

Settling onto the mattress, he took her left foot in his hands to undo the ties. The second shoe and her stockings followed, but still her lovely, spring-green gown was crumpled about her waist.

"Wake up, Charm," he whispered, leaning across her body to settle his weight on one palm. "Let's get you undressed."

She smiled, a sleepy expression of childlike happiness that shadowed a dimple into one cheek, but did nothing to wake her. Such beauty! He was momentarily mesmerized by her, left speechless and breathless; he could no longer try to wake her. Perhaps, in fact, he should consider it a personal compliment that their lovemaking had helped her find the blissful sleep that the hat man had stolen from her as a child.

Her gown came away with little effort, and though the corset was more difficult to maneuver in the semi-darkness, he finally managed it. Now she lay in nothing more than crotchless pantalettes and the heavy silky veil of her luxurious hair.

Raven blew out a sharp breath. Well, his job was done. He could sleep now. Seconds ticked away as he stared at her. He could sleep, he repeated to himself. But . . . he wasn't sleepy. Not the least bit. In fact . . . He reached out to gently touch her cheek, then followed her satin skin down her throat.

It seemed no crime to kiss her neck, and then, when she didn't resist, there was no reason not to let his caresses slip lower, over the steep crest of a breast and down. Her belly was smooth against his lips, and when he kissed the tiny indentation at its center, she moaned softly, shifting her slim legs slightly so that he could see the dark mound of hair peeking out between them.

"Charm," he breathed, and somehow, like forbidden magic, he was stretched upon his side, with his arms about her luscious body and his kisses finding her mouth.

She came awake not with a start, but with a tiny whimper of desire, and suddenly he was within her inviting core and she was squeezing him with feverish vigor, arching against his need. He was a weak-minded fool, Raven told himself, but right now, at this moment, he was a fool in heaven.

*   *   *

Charm awoke slowly, without her usual jab of momentary terror, but with a niggle of soreness. She bent a leg and winced before pushing it back down and setting the bedsheet askew.

"I just covered you."

She opened her eyes, and he was there, settled into the room's winged chair with nothing but a blanket between him and mind-numbing nudity. Her gaze flitted to his bare chest, then hurried to his face only to find *his* gaze was a bit to the south of her shoulders.

"But on the other hand," he said huskily, "I can't begrudge your restlessness."

It took her a moment to realize she'd uncovered her bosom. Almost regretfully, she slipped the tangled sheet up above the point of his interest. His gaze rose slowly, but the fire in his eyes failed to be extinguished.

"Good morning." Did his voice always have the rich flavor of hot coffee or was it different now? Was everything different?

"Good morning." Her own tone seemed pathetically pale next to his, and though she tried, she found she couldn't hold his gaze.

"Did I wake you?"

Somewhere in the depths of her foggy memory was a recollection of kisses on her belly button. Yes, it seemed he had awakened her. She blushed, clasping the sheet tighter to her chest and trying not to look at his face, but his chuckle was throaty and pulled her gaze irresistibly upward.

"I guess I did," he murmured, apparently sharing the very memory that caused the heat in her cheeks. "I hate to say it, but . . ." He smiled at her, and she realized, perhaps through years of study, that there was no longer tension in his face, only quiet good humor. "We'd best be going."

"Going?" The question was surprised from her. "Where? What about your leg?"

He rose with surprising suppleness. "I think you healed me."

Her blush turned to a raging flame but she kept her gaze on his now.

"I've gained passage for two on the *Yankee Belle*. It leaves for St. Louis in a little over an hour."

"But . . ." She scowled. "You told Bodine we'd not be leaving for . . ."

"If Clancy, damn his hide, knows we're going, he'll come along." Raven watched her expression carefully. "Personally, I don't think we need his company, Charm," he said, and crossing the distance between them, bent to kiss her. "Do you?"

She shook her head and murmured, "Not at all."

Raven sighed. "You can't imagine how happy I am to hear that. Now come on, sleepyhead, get up." Taking the sheet in one hand he tried to tug it from her grasp, but she kept a tight hold. "Charm," he cajoled with a grin. "Quit trying to distract me." He tugged again, but she held firm.

He gave her a quizzical expression and settled onto the mattress, letting his blanket fall away in soft folds that threatened to reveal everything.

"So . . ." He yanked gently at her sheet again, watching as it sprang back beneath her tight fist. "As I see it, there are two possible reasons for this little battle over the bedsheet. Either you're begging for my attentions yet again." He raised his dark brows and canted his head hopefully at her.

She said nothing, but darted her gaze to the bright light at the window before dragging the sheet closer to her chin.

"Humm," he said, noticing her white-knuckled clasp. "Or, perhaps you're embarrassed." He paused again, watching her.

Heat seeped steadily toward Charm's ears before draining downward to inflame her body.

"But what could you possibly be embarrassed about?" Raven asked, looking puzzled. "Certainly not by this." Leaning forward, he kissed her bare shoulder. The caress sparked like a crackle of lightning from the point of contact off in a thousand directions. Her gasp was soft and breathy.

"Or this," he said, kissing her throat. Despite herself, Charm's head fell back slightly.

"Or this." Feather-soft caresses touched the hollow of her throat, the ridge of bone below it, the point of her shoulder, and then downward, over the quivering length of her arm to her fingertips. Shivers of raging desire flamed upward until her breathing came in short gasps and her grip on the sheet loosened. Their gazes met, smoldering. "Or this," he murmured, and leaning forward kissed the peak of one breast revealed by the traitorous sheet.

A violent quiver shook her body, and now there was no stopping him, no wanting to. The linen fell away. His hands slipped beneath it, pressing it downward, over her hips, along the length of her quaking legs.

"Surely you could never be embarrassed about this," Raven whispered huskily and kissed her thigh just beside her curly tuft of burnt cinnamon hair.

"Raven!" She sat up with a jolt, her heart thumping like the engine of a runaway train, her breathing just as harsh.

"What?" he asked, apparently trying to emulate her shocked tone.

"We can't . . ."

"Can't what?"

"We can't . . ." She'd found the sheet again, and though she dragged it back to her chin, she feared, without looking, that it had snagged on something and hadn't quite covered the intended body parts.

"We can't?"

"No," she breathed, vaguely remembering a shotgun wedding and talk of an annulment.

"You're right. No time," he sighed and with a simple jerk of his wrist, whipped the sheet effortlessly from her hand.

She gasped, shocked to learn that the snag retaining the sheet had been his fingers.

But before she could make another move, his arms were around her and she was scooted up against the warm, bare expanse of his chest. "There's no need to be embarrassed," he whispered and kissed her until she melted like hot wax in his embrace. "But feel free to blush anytime. It's very becoming."

"Raven," she breathed weakly, but he stopped her words with another kiss.

"You're a shameless seductress," he scolded blithely and dropped her feet to the floor. "Trying to sway me from my righteous promise to return you to the bosom of your family."

"I . . ." She blinked at him, feeling lost, but he shushed her with a finger to her lips.

"Don't think you can tempt me with your wanton ways, girl," he warned, his expression somber now. "I'm made of sterner stuff."

Baffled, she pushed against his chest, trying to get away, but he held her tight against him.

"Still trying to tempt me, aye?" he asked. "Well, you can't." He pulled her even closer. "I'm incorruptible." He kissed her, the caress hot and deep and slow. "Pure." He kissed her again, deeper still. "Immovable in my quest for justice."

In that moment his shielding blanket gave up the good fight and slipped with a rush to the floor. Against her hip, she felt the hot, sharp thrust of his manhood, impatient and ever ready.

"Well . . ." He grinned, looking into her eyes. "Maybe not immovable. Try to dissuade me."

"You're terrible," she breathed, finally realizing the jest.

"Yes." He nodded. "You're right. Please talk me out of leaving."

"You're despicable," she scolded, pushing hard against his chest and finally gaining her release.

"Try to dissuade me, Charm," he pleaded, following her like an infatuated hound.

"No!" she exclaimed, backing away.

"Oh, come now. Try to tempt me. Entice me. Seduce me,"

he begged, and then, when she least expected it, he made a wild grab for her.

Charm shrieked, but the scream was caught on a giggle as she sprang for the bed. She stood in its center now, her legs spread and slightly bent as she prepared to fly in any direction. Raven grinned. Who would have thought he would ever see her thus?

"No need to act coy, girl," he said, twirling his imaginary moustache like a depraved villain. "I know you want me."

She lowered her gaze to his jutting manhood and actually gasped, whether from real shock or in feigned surprise, he wasn't certain. But he took no time to dissect the truth and leaped to the bed just as she launched herself from it with a scream.

"It's no use—"

"Hey!" came a shout with a sharp rap to their door. "What's going on in there?"

Charm and Raven froze like recalcitrant children, staring at each other with wide eyes.

"What's the trouble, I say?"

"Nothing," Raven answered, finding his voice and his sense of humor. "No trouble. My wife just saw a . . ."—he shifted his gaze to the real reason for her gasp and raised his brows—"a mouse."

There was a pause. "Are you all right, ma'am?"

For a moment Charm failed to answer, but she somehow managed to cover herself with a blanket.

"Is that true, ma'am?" the harsh voice demanded, giving another rap to the door.

"No!" she called out.

Raven sent her a warning scowl.

"It was a *rat*." A grin lifted the corner of her mouth and her gaze slipped with shocking boldness down over his naked form. "A big one," she added, before lifting her eyes to his.

"You're certain you're all right, ma'am?"

"Yes," she answered, not breaking eye contact. "I'm sure."

"I could get rid of that rat for you."

"No!" they shouted in unison, tearing their gazes from each other to snap them to the door.

"No," Raven repeated, clearing his throat and yanking a blanket from the bed to cover his much maligned manhood. "That won't be necessary. But thanks for your concern, sir."

"Well, all right," said the stranger. In a moment he was gone.

Charm lifted a sheet from the floor and stifled a giggle behind it.

"You," Raven said, pointing at her, "are dangerous. A killer woman."

"And you're the devil's spawn," she quipped, raising her lovely shoulders in a quick shrug.

Raven watched the movement. He realized with some chagrin that he was holding his breath, waiting to see if the wayward blanket would bless him with abandonment.

"Don't look at me like that," she warned.

"Like what?"

"Like . . . like that." She waved vaguely toward him.

He grinned, raising his gaze. "I'll give you ten minutes to get cleaned up and dressed. If you're not ready in that time, I do more than look."

"Ten minutes! I can't—"

"Nine minutes and fifty-five seconds."

"I'm . . . filthy."

"Better wash. Nine minutes and fifty seconds."

She made a disgruntled sound in her throat and shook her head at him. "You'll have to leave."

"Nope. Nine minutes forty-five, and I watch."

Heat rose in beautiful living color to her cheeks. "Forget it."

He took a step toward her. "Then get in bed."

She held out a restraining hand. "Don't you dare come closer."

"Nine minutes thirty-five seconds."

"Raven!"

"Call me Joseph."

"Joseph! I can't." Her gaze flitted frantically away. "I really can't."

"Nine and a half minutes." He grinned. "The boat won't wait, Lucky Charm, and neither will I."

"It's . . . it's broad daylight." She sounded fairly frantic now.

"I know."

"It wouldn't be right. Me unclothed, washing in front of . . . No! Absolutely not!"

"Drop the sheet."

"Joseph!"

"I will if you will."

"There's no way I'll . . ." Her words came to an abrupt stop as air left her lungs in a slight whoosh of sound. "What?"

His grin broadened. "At the count of three, we'll drop them together."

Her lips moved but no sound came forth.

"All right?"

She paused, then nodded stiffly, her upturned little mouth pursed with prudish seriousness.

"One. Two. Three," he counted and let the blanket fall.

Her gaze did the same while her sheet remained pulled to her chin.

"You cheat," Raven complained, placing his fists on his hips.

Her eyes were wide, her mouth formed into a cute little circle of awe. "I know," she breathed.

He growled and started toward her, but she backed quickly away, tripping on her bulky tail before righting herself with a start. "I'll do it! I will." She waved toward the bed. "You just . . . you just go sit."

He raised his brows in distrust but finally nodded and bent to retrieve his blanket.

"No deal," she said sternly.

Raven remained half bent, only lifting his gaze to stare at her. "I beg your pardon."

"Leave the blanket or the deal's off."

He opened his mouth for a retort, then snapped his teeth back together and strode obediently toward the bed. Strange, how self-conscious he felt with her gaze hot and steady on his naked body. Self-conscious and aroused. The bed ropes groaned beneath his weight.

"I'm ready," he said.

Charm clasped the sheet tighter to her chest, took a deep breath, felt each nerve tingle at the sight of his boldly nude form and dropped the sheet.

His nostrils flared. His eyes narrowed slightly, and though she dared not stare at his nether parts, she could sense a tightening of his already granite-hard body.

Somehow the air had disappeared from the room, leaving it stifling and hot. Turning her back to him, she moved stiffly to the pitcher and poured the water with some difficulty into the basin. Washcloths and towels would be in the commode upon which it stood, she knew. But she lacked the courage to bend down and get them, and so she stood frozen in place like the proverbial pillar of salt.

"Eight and a half," Raven said from behind her, but his tone was husky, she noticed.

So it was not all such simple sport for him after all, Charm deduced. Encouraged by that knowledge, she retrieved the linens and straightened without breathing. Dipping a cloth into the water, she dripped it wringing wet over one shoulder.

The world was absolutely silent. She dipped the rag again, then draped it over her opposite shoulder and let the water bead cool and soft down her back and over the flared sensitivity of her buttocks. Once again she doused the cloth, and now the water skimmed like gentle fingers over her waist and down her thighs to converge at the vee between them. Glancing breathlessly over her shoulder, Charm settled her gaze on Raven's face.

He sat perfectly still. With his hands making fists and every muscle standing in hard ridges of discipline.

She drew a shaky breath. With almost unconscious method, she stroked the cloth down her belly to her thighs.

"Charm," he said gruffly. Without warning, he launched himself from the bed to turn her in his arms.

Their gazes caught like living sparks and their bodies trembled in unison. Her chin tilted slightly upward and against her hip his manhood quivered with excitement.

"Charm," he breathed again, leaning closer.

"Seven and a half," she murmured just before their lips touched.

Raven stopped an inch from her mouth, every nerve taut with anticipation. "Damn the time."

Her breathing was hard, but a tentative grin surfaced. "Seven twenty-five."

"You're an evil woman."

She lowered her lids slightly, employing the expression she had used so often with gamblers in the past. "And you're squelching on a deal, Joseph. I still have over seven minutes left."

As he removed his hands she thought that she felt them tremble. Her grin tilted up teasingly. "Back on the bed."

"Charm . . ." His hands were fists again. "If you lift that rag again all bets are off."

She raised one brow at him. "What? The poker-faced gambler brought low?"

A muscle in his cheek flexed. "Not *low*, Lucky Charm."

She chuckled, letting her gaze drop for a moment before raising it to his face. "I thought you were in a hurry to leave."

The muscle flexed again. "I changed my mind."

"Clancy *will* make a lovely addition to our journey."

It took him a moment to absorb her meaning. His fists gripped hard against nothing, causing his knuckles to go white with the pressure. He took a deep breath—then, "I'll wait in the hall," he growled, and grabbing blanket and a brown paper package, stiffly retreated.

"Damn him!" Raven entered the room and slammed the door shut behind. "Damn! Damn! Damn!"

Charm turned abruptly toward him, her fingers falling away from the buttons she'd just fastened. "What . . . ," she began but stopped when she noticed his pants. They were black worsted, expensively tailored . . . and five sizes too large.

"Well . . ." She cleared her throat and tried not to grin, but his bare chest, perfectly muscled and proportioned, made the ridiculously oversized trousers even sillier.

"He did this on purpose," Raven declared flatly.

Charm shrugged, letting her eyes go wide and innocent. "It's better than getting you hanged."

"I'm going to hang *him*," Raven vowed evenly.

She pursed her mouth. "One minute thirty seconds."

"Damn," he said again. Storming across the room, he retrieved the remainder of his clothing.

Chapter 27

"But we can't leave Angel."

"You're being ridiculous," Raven countered. "We can't take that tatter-eared mongrel on the *Yankee Belle*."

Charm lifted her chin slightly. "He saved your life."

Raven snorted. "He didn't save my life. You did. He's just a horse. And an ugly one at that."

"He *did* save your life," she argued. "He could have run off and kept running. But he came back to us."

Raven deepened his scowl. "We don't have time for this, Charm. We're leaving the horse and that's . . . ," he began, but lifting his gaze, he saw the earnest appeal in her emerald-bright eyes.

It was neither easy nor inexpensive to convince the *Yankee Belle*'s first mate to accept a lop-eared horse into the cargo room on such short notice. And yet he finally agreed, a fact which Raven could only attribute to Charm's charm.

In the end, she insisted on seeing to Angel's well-being herself. The *Belle*'s mate left to see to his own business. Surprisingly, there were two other horses in the cargo space, which the animals would share with the roustabouts. Beautiful, blooded stock with muscular thick-maned crests, they gave deep-throated snorts upon Angel's arrival. Apparently the highbred steeds were as unimpressed with their companion's appearance as Raven himself was. Nevertheless, Charm was relentless and begged a passing roustabout to see to Angel's welfare.

"Please take good care of him," she pleaded, settling her bright gaze on the gelding's lumpy head as if it were carved from purest gold. "He's got a kind heart."

"Yes, ma'am," the dark-skinned roustabout said respectfully. Although his was the lowest position on the steamer, there was a tender expression in his black eyes that suggested he would follow through with his promise.

"You're certain he'll be safe here?" asked Charm.

"Quite safe, ma'am. I'll see t' thet m'self."

"Those cages . . ." She scowled at the rows upon rows of empty squares made of wire and wood. "They won't come clattering about and scare him?"

Raven watched her in silence and almost smiled. The killer woman sometimes forgot to hide her tender heart and allowed the world a glimpse of her true self. But in this case her worry was misplaced, for despite the thrumming of the engines and the frenzied bustling all about them, Angel looked very near sleep. Still, Charm fussed over him as if he possessed the finest of blood.

"Them's cages for bringin' cats west," explained the roustabout. "To get rid of rats. But they're all empty now and tied real secure. No harm'll come to yer hoss."

Finally, after a few additional questions and as many heartfelt assurances, Charm was convinced to move up the stairs to find her own quarters.

The *Yankee Belle* was an impressive vessel and one Raven had had the privilege of traveling on before. Well over two hundred feet long, she boasted three ornate decks that loomed in scrolling elegance above the dark water of the muddy Missouri River. The oaken flooring resounded solidly beneath the couple's feet. From the stern they could see the huge paddle gleaming with whitewashed brilliance in the morning sun.

Glancing quickly about, Raven assured himself of Clancy's continued absence before noticing Captain Josiah Fields. In his late fifties, Fields was still an impressive man. He strolled on the upper deck now with an elegant lady on his arm. Raven could only hope that she was the captain's wife to whom he was well committed. Glancing at Charm now, he thought it might have been wiser to choose a less prestigious vessel, lest the Captain's attention be drawn to Charm's charms. But in a moment, Raven shook away the thought. Chantilly belonged here amidst the wealthy.

The room they were shown to was clean, attractively decorated, and intimately small. Raven guided Charm inside with his hand set to the small of her back. She felt tense, he noticed, and watched her step stiffly in to eye the single bed.

"Cozy." He grinned, feeling that now familiar grip on his heart as he looked at her. But in a moment he found the ability to pull his gaze away and deposit her bag on the floor. Unfortunately all of *his* assessable clothing was on his body, and mostly very embarrassing. "Good thing we won't need much room."

She remained as she was, affording him the lovely view of her posterior, the dramatic curve of her waist, the swell of her buttocks, the smooth length of her bare nape beneath the burnished chestnut knot of hair. Such a pretty nape. He leaned forward, kissing the delicate skin beneath her hairline.

Charm jumped, pivoting quickly about, her eyes wide and her face pale, as if unable to imagine who might have touched her.

Raven lifted one palm upward in a sign of peace. "Just me, Lucky Charm. And I don't bite."

She nibbled the inside of her lip, looking inexplicably nervous.

"Scared?" he asked softly.

"No!" Her answer was quick and terse.

Raven watched her carefully. "There's no need to fear me, Charm," he said and took a step forward.

"I don't!" She backed rapidly away.

He stopped, enforcing patience. "Then what is it?"

"You can't stay in this room!"

He scowled, forgetting to control his expression for a moment. "And why would that be, Charm?"

"Because . . ."

He was reminded of how she had looked on their first encounter, haughty and defiant. "We're not really married." Her voice sounded tight.

Raven could feel the tension seep from her body into his. "Exactly what do you mean by that?" he asked evenly.

"You know what I mean! It's not a real marriage! It's all a sham."

He remained silent for a moment, tightening his jaw and waiting for discipline. He had tried to disavow his feelings for her, but there had been no hope of that, and when he'd touched her the last time, he had fully given in to his desire, hoping against feeble hope that some small part of his love would be returned.

But now her expression warned him of the truth, so he kept his own features and his tone carefully smooth. "And what do you call last night?"

"A mistake!" Her answer came very quickly. She turned now, striding the few paces to the wall. "Oh . . ." She laughed, but the tone was very tight. "It was pleasant enough. But surely you don't think I'll be bound to you for eternity because of one rash moment."

Raven squeezed his fists, tamping down the blistering memories of passion and more. Damn her! Damn her for being the better gambler, for holding all the cards. "I seem to remember two rash moments."

She laughed again. "Don't be silly. You know exactly what I mean."

"No. I don't think I do."

Her face was pale and he wondered if she'd quit breathing. "*You* said we'd have it annulled. I thought we both understood the situation."

"Well . . ." His teeth hurt. "I'm rather slow on the uptake sometimes, Charm. Perhaps you'd better explain the . . . situation." Involuntarily he took a step forward.

She bumped sharply against the wall, holding her breath and jamming one hand into the pocket of her gown. "Don't come any closer!"

He stopped abruptly. It seemed he'd heard that warning a thousand times. If he'd learned anything, he'd learned that it was unwise to crowd her. Yet, every fiber in him wanted to shake her until she admitted the truth—that she'd felt the same internal storm as he, that she loved him, would never feel complete without him. She must feel it! She must!

"Damn it, Charm!" he swore, advancing.

"I'm warning you!" Her voice was scratchy, and the terror in her eyes was apparent.

It cooled something inside him slightly, allowing his fists to loosen a bit and his breathing to slow. "You slept in my arms," he said quietly. "You *slept*." He forced himself to move backward, toward the door, toward clearer thought. "Whether you want to believe it or not, you trusted me, Charm. Me, and nobody else."

Outside the door Raven drew a deep breath and swore in silence. An annulment! Dammit! Of course, he'd planned to annul the marriage, but it had seemed different when it was *his* idea. And besides, that was before. Before he felt her beneath him. Felt her quiver of . . . Damn! His strides were quick and steady now, bearing him as far away as the confinement of the steamer would allow. He needed air, needed space, needed . . . pants, he realized suddenly, and seeing one of the *Belle*'s mates, stopped him to ask how he might acquire a change of clothing.

"I'm surprised at you, Joseph, wantin' to get rid of my gift," Clancy chuckled from behind him. "And they look so fine on you."

Raven turned. Although every bit of good sense in him said to greet Bodine with feigned good humor, he could not oblige. Sweeping his hand upward, he grabbed the other's throat and propelled his thrashing body through the scattering crowd to the railing behind. "Get the hell out of my life, Bodine," he growled.

"Joseph! Joseph!" squeaked the other, his hands clawing at Raven's grip. "You think I'm following you? I didn't know you was on this boat."

Raven vaguely heard the squawks and gasps of the crowd behind him, but for once his patient self-control had snapped. He squeezed his hand. "You used to be a damned good liar, Clance. And not a bad swimmer. Hope you've been practicing that skill." He pushed backward.

"While we appreciate the spot of entertainment, gentlemen," said a carefully cultured voice from behind, "I fear there's insufficient room for fisticuffs aboard my vessel. Therefore . . ." The sound of a handgun cocking was perfectly clear to Raven's ears. "I must insist that you continue your dispute on land."

It would take little more than a shove to propel Clancy over the side, just a push and a curse, and it would feel so good. But Raven had spent his life controlling his fondest desires and did so now. He eased his hand open and backed away, though he found it impossible for a moment to unclench his teeth.

"Mr. Scott, isn't it?" asked Fields.

Raven nodded, not taking his eyes from Clancy.

"Yes. I thought I remembered you. A gambler, I believe, but not usually so . . . disruptive."

"This man tried to kill me!" croaked Clancy dramatically.

Fields turned slowly. "And who might you be?"

"Clancy Bodine. And he tried to kill me."

Fields's blue eyes turned to Raven again. "Was that indeed your intent, sir?"

"He's a madman," said Clancy, apparently appealing to the appalled crowd. "You'd best throw him off."

"And your story?" the English captain asked Raven.

"He seduced my sister," Raven lied smoothly. Perhaps Clancy's mere proximity brought out the liar in him. But whatever the reason, he hardly had time to launch into a litany of all the crimes Clancy had perpetrated against him in the past. And saying he had abducted the woman whom Raven had abducted first didn't seem to be the perfect plan. Besides, he couldn't say exactly why Clancy was there, although he could easily assume it was for no good. So Raven puffed out his substantial chest, looking affronted. "And now he hopes to steal the affections of my beautiful wife." He glanced about the crowd. Beautiful women were a rare and precious commodity in this part of the world. Rare, precious, and carefully guarded. "I suggest you ask your captain to refuse passage to this scandalous woman-izer," he said, remembering the captain's stunning companions from the past.

"Womanizer!" Clancy's tone was amazingly sincere, considering he'd never spoken an honest word in his life. "Ask Joseph here how he come to marry the gal."

Raven squeezed his fists and remained still. "That's none of your affair, or anyone else's."

"The hell it ain't," argued Clancy. "He screwed—"

Raven's fist hit Clancy squarely in the jaw. There were gasps and shrieks of dismay, but no one was more surprised than Raven. He'd always thrown his punches carefully, not like an undisciplined schoolboy.

"Use that word in reference to her again and I'll kill you, Bodine," he said softly. "I swear I will."

Clancy remained upon the floor, his jaw slightly ajar and his expression astonished. "You're in love with her!"

Every muscle in Raven's body vibrated with need. It would feel good to hit him again. "Get the hell out of here."

"You are!" Clancy said and throwing back his head, laughed aloud. "Who would have thought ten years ago that the bitter little Raven boy would fall for a—"

Raven lunged, but in that moment his arms were caught by burly men with dangerous intent.

"Cool down, boy," the larger of the two giants warned, "or we'll cool y' down."

The crowd milled nervously.

"Now folks, the show is over," said Captain Fields seriously. "Go about your business, and we'll be underway in a short while."

There was the shuffling sound of regretfully departing feet. Raven, however, barely noticed, for his attention was riveted hard and fast on Clancy's surprised features.

"Now gentlemen," said the captain softly. "It's like this, either you learn to get along during this little journey, or you both disembark here. You understand me?"

Raven gritted his teeth but forced his fists to loosen and his muscles to relax. Clancy, on the other hand, scrambled to his feet with his usual easy grin.

"Of course we do, Captain. Me and Joseph, we're just havin' us a little fun. We're pals really. Go way back."

They were surrounded by silence, and then, "Good, then I trust you will do more talking and less swinging. Yes?"

"Of course," Clancy said with a shrug, but Raven remained mute, still feeling the bitter burn in his gut.

"Yes?" the captain asked again.

"Yes," replied Raven finally, not taking his gaze from his adversary.

"Good," said Fields. "Then I'll buy you each a drink and give you one last warning. Disturb the peace on the *Yankee Belle* again and you'll find the journey back much more tiresome and damp than the journey out."

"Yes sir," said Clancy with an effusive smile.

Raven only managed a nod.

The table between them was too narrow for Raven's peace of mind. Clancy sat across from him, placing his whiskey glass against the bruise on his jaw and shaking his head. "Tell me the truth."

Raven swished the amber liquid, which he'd not yet tasted. "Why?"

"For old time's sake." Clancy fingered his jaw, then winced.

"*That's* what I did for old time's sake," retorted Raven, impassively nodding toward the other's bruised chin. His temper had cooled, though the tension was still there, lying just beneath his skin, waiting, contained, but not controlled.

"Do you love her or is it just the money?"

The tension increased a half-turn, though Raven was hardly surprised by the other's knowledge regarding Charm's true identity. Clancy was a lot of things; stupid wasn't amongst them. Still, it wouldn't hurt to pretend he didn't understand the other's meaning. "What money?"

Bodine grinned. "It's not like you to underestimate me, Joseph. If you'd been thinkin' clear you would have at least disguised the girl."

"What the hell are you talking about?"

"Once I knew you'd left the room, it was easy to figure where you was headin'. All I had to do was ask around about a young beauty and her baggy-legged escort." He chuckled. "When you was workin' fer me, you wouldn't a made such a mistake." He shifted the whiskey glass to his jaw again. "She's sure distracted you. Must be a hell of a—"

Raven rose without thought, without time for intent, but Clancy lifted a hand and stifled his grin. "God, I love to see you riled. You this coolheaded during poker now too?"

There were few things he could have said that would have been more sure to settle Raven back into his seat, for coolheaded thinking was something Raven valued above most everything else. Something he seemed to have lost and needed to retrieve.

"I know she's Chantilly Grady, Joseph," Clancy said now. "Suspected it soon as I saw your interest in her, of course. But once I started talkin' to Jude . . ." He grinned. "The old man can't hold his liquor worth a damn. You'd be surprised at the stories he'll tell when he's drunk." He paused, studying Raven intently before continuing. "'Course . . . he didn't touch nary a drop once we was on yer trail. Sober as a toothache. Just like you when the stakes is high. Yep." Clancy leaned back in his chair, drawing a deep breath and grinning. "The things he told me would make yer head spin."

Though Raven wanted nothing more than to learn all he could of Charm, though he felt like shaking the stories from Clancy, control was of the utmost importance now. He swirled his liquor again and tried to pretend he didn't care. "The money's mine, Bodine."

Clancy cocked his head and grinned. "Not if I get her there first."

The grin Raven offered was less congenial and far more predatory. "You think they'd pay *you* for returning *my* wife?" He laughed, thinking Clancy would understand only one thing. Greed. "Not likely, old man. She's mine—lock, stock, and inheritance."

Clancy remained silent for a full three seconds and then, "Damn! You're even slimier than I thought. God damn! I've always admired that about you, Joseph. Now me, I'm slimy, but you *know* I'm slimy, while *you*, you've got just enough clean to make a body wonder. Goddamn! So what's she worth?"

Raven smiled, slowly, calculatingly. "It's none of your affair."

"Damn! That much! Damn!" He smacked the table with the flat of his hand. "And you played it so damned close t' the vest. I was honestly believin' you cared fer her."

"Of course I care for her." Raven carefully raised a brow, keeping his expression very solemn, just as he would have if he were lying. "I adore her. Who wouldn't? Tender little thing that she is."

Clancy's gaze fell to Raven's chest. He knew a wound was hidden there. He laughed. "Damn me, if I didn't raise you right. Well, Joseph . . ." He lifted and drained his glass in a sort of toast. "You win."

*   *   *

On the deck above, Charm lurched away from the rail. She'd regretted her behavior in their room, but the old terror had tormented her for a time, gripping her in its terrible grasp and forcing her to say what she had said.

But another fear had driven her from her haven. Fear of loneliness, of failure, of losing the one person whom she could trust, if she but dared take the chance. And so she had flown across the deck in search of him. She'd reached the rail only moments before, just long enough to hear his words. *Tender little thing that she is.* He lied of course, easily telling Clancy and herself that he did not care for her. She was, after all, only a means to an end.

The words of tenderness. The gentle hands. They were all a ploy, nothing more than a trick to gain the trust of the bloodthirsty killer woman. She felt sick to her stomach. She had to get off, get away!

"Hey!" She could hear Clancy's voice clearly, then the scrape of his chair as he rose to his feet. "Wasn't that your blushing bride now?"

Raven's curse was just as clear, but already she was running, racing toward freedom. Faces blurred as she fled, down the steps, toward the exit. But the ramp had been lifted and the steamer was moving.

No! She glanced frantically toward land, but already she heard the thunder of feet behind her. There was no time to lose! She scrambled up the railing, ready to jump, but suddenly she was plucked down and swung away in Raven's tight grip.

"Let me go!" she screamed, thrashing wildly.

"What the hell do you think you're doing?"

"Let me go," she said, her voice huskier now.

"Settle down," Raven ordered, his arms tight bands around her, pinning her arms to her chest and her back to his torso. "I'm not going to hurt you. Let's go to the cabin. Discuss things."

"Go to hell!" she spat, flailing.

"Not right now."

"Let me go or I'll scream."

"You already did that. Do it again and you'll have men crawling all over you, Charm. Asking you questions, closing you in. But in the end they'll learn the truth. I'm your husband." His voice was little more than a whisper in her ear, but it seemed to boom like a death knell. "I've got my rights. So we might just as well go to the cabin and talk." He paused, loosening his grip marginally. "I won't touch you, I promise."

She fought to control her breathing, to push down the panic and bitter bile of betrayal. "All right." Her tone was steady. Her feet were lowered to the floor. She turned stiffly.

His face looked strained and she wondered if their fight had wounded him more than she knew. She hoped so and concentrated now on remembering exactly where the rattler had bitten him.

"Are you all right?" he asked, his voice deceptively soft. The bastard!

"Damn you," she said evenly.

"I think I am damned." His tone was cooler now, more controlled. "Are you ready to go?"

"Yes, I'm ready," she said. Drawing back her foot, she slammed the sharp toe of her shoe directly into his snake-bite.

Chapter 28

Pain shot through Raven's leg in flaming tendrils, streaking upward and outward. He gasped, and for a moment thought he might pass out. But gradually the truth of the situation came home to him.

She was getting away! In fact, she had thrown herself at the railing like a harried cat, claws outstretched, and was just about to fling herself overboard.

"Good God!" he cried, and jolting himself painfully into action, grasped her about the waist to drag her down again. She fought like a sacked bobcat, but he held on, feeling the blood drain from his face as her heels and fists found tender areas.

"Are you finished?" he asked finally when her thrashing subsided.

"No!" She swore, and kicked him again.

"So this is your blushing bride?" asked a carefully cultured voice.

Raven winced mentally. Charm slowed her agitated movements, pushing wild strands of hair aside to peer through the disheveled curtain at Captain Fields's impassive features.

His grey hair and beard were neatly trimmed, and his blue eyes showed a spark of sharp intelligent interest as he watched them. "She has a fondness for the water, does she, Mr. Scott?"

"I'm afraid there's been a small misunderstanding," Raven said, squeezing her middle as an unobtrusive warning for her to cease and desist. "Mrs. Scott has a bit of a temper."

"Truly?" Fields asked, somehow managing to act as if such a fact came as an utter surprise. "And what has she taken exception to? Nothing I've done I hope."

"No, sir," said Raven, and tentatively set Charm's feet to the gently shifting floor of the steamer. "It's just a spat. You know." He tried a careful smile, but everything from his ears on down ached. His greatest desire was to throttle the girl. If she got them tossed off the boat after everything he'd done to get them this far, he would. "A lovers' quarrel."

"I see."

Raven desperately hoped the good captain would leave now, for Charm hadn't hit him for several seconds. It was a record not likely to be outdone in the near future.

"Perhaps if you tell me what has caused this disagreement, I could help find a satisfactory solution." Fields paused, templing his fingers, and perhaps noticing the peculiar stiffness with which Raven stood, suggesting an ache in areas better left unmentioned. "Before she does you further bodily harm."

"It's nothing. Nothing to concern—" began Raven, but Charm interrupted with a sharp jab to his ribs.

"Devil's spawn!"

"I beg your pardon?" said Fields, not even raising his brows.

"She said, endless fun," Raven lied. "Endless fun, that's what we have together. She loves to—"

"He's the devil's spawn," she hissed. With the uncanny

accuracy of a side-kicking mule, she jabbed her elbow into his still-healing chest wound. Pain again, sparkling outward in slicing shards. Raven gritted his teeth and held on.

"Perhaps you should release her," suggested Fields.

Raven smiled through his aching teeth. "What's that?"

"I think she's airing a bit of her temper now, Mr. Scott. Please release her."

And let her drown herself in the muddy waters below? Not likely. When she died, Raven fully intended to orchestrate the act himself. "I think it best to keep my hands on her for a moment, Captain."

"Were you aware that I'm the sole owner of the *Yankee Belle*?"

"Really?" Raven asked, wondering irritably what the hell that had to do with any of his myriad pains and grunting softly as Charm's heel found his instep. "How . . . interesting."

"Yes. And therefore, while on this vessel I give the orders." Fields paused, settling his blue eyes on Raven's face. "Let the girl go."

There was nothing Raven could do but release her. He loosened his arms slowly, waiting for her to run. But she did not. Instead Charm straightened to push a few strands of hair back into her failing knot.

"Thank you, Captain." Her voice, Raven noticed, had taken on that husky tone it sometimes did when pressured.

"You're quite welcome, madam." Even though he stood absolutely straight, with his shoulders drawn sharply back and his hands clasped behind his hips, Captain Fields barely equalled Charm's height. Still, Raven got the distinct impression that Fields was the kind of man who did not need great physical stature to make him irresistible to women.

He turned now, his steely gaze sweeping the crowd that had gathered. A few of the faces Raven had noticed during his earlier fight, Clancy's irritating visage included.

"It seems Mr. Scott has again gifted us with a diversion,"

said the captain evenly. "But the entertainment is over now. Please disperse."

Every man, woman, and child remained exactly in place, as if certain war would break out again, and loath to miss a single blow.

"Please disperse," Fields repeated more coldly. The people finally snapped their jaws back into their proper positions and began to wander off, while throwing hungry glances back over their shoulders. Clancy, of course, didn't budge.

"Have you got a stake in this, Mr. Bodine?"

"Yes."

"No!" Raven exclaimed in unison with Clancy's affirmative.

"Yes, indeed I do," argued the other stoutly. "The lass is the daughter of a very dear friend of mine."

The captain turned slowly toward Charm. "Is that true, Madam?"

She raised her chin a notch further. "Between the two of them, sir, they've not spoken an honest word since infancy, I'm certain."

"I'm wounded," declared Clancy. Raven only glowered.

"I hadn't met either one of them before a month ago."

"I see. Then you are not wed to Mr. Scott?"

Here she paused and scowled. "Against my wishes, I assure you."

"I can see this is a tale not easily unwound," said Fields, still looking at Charm. "Perhaps we should retire to my quarters and discuss this."

"I really don't think that's necessary," began Raven, but Fields fixed him with a steady stare.

"It wasn't a request, Mr. Scott. Madam . . ." He lifted a hand, and to Raven's surprise, Charm quietly acquiesced, letting the man touch her back as he escorted her away.

They stepped into a sitting room of sorts, uniquely decorated with mismatched items from a hundred different lands. An intricately woven rug. A basket made from a strange manner of dyed reeds.

"Sit down, please," said Captain Fields.

Good God, how had it come to this? Raven wondered. "I'm sure you have more important things to do," he said. "We really shouldn't bother you."

"No, you shouldn't," agreed the captain, "but you have." He settled his gaze on Raven, who held it easily. "Let us not forget that you are, essentially, my guest, Mr. Scott."

Raven sat finally, knowing a threat when he heard one.

"Now." Fields paced the length of the room once before turning to look at each of them in turn. "Where do we begin?"

"I wish to obtain an annulment." Charm's voice was the first to enter the fray. Raven swore in silence. "Can you help me achieve that end, sir?"

"An annulment?" Though his expression showed little change, Fields's tone evidenced his surprise. "Forgive me for seeming indelicate, but, an annulment implies the absence of certain . . . rituals." He paused. "Have those . . . rituals been neglected?"

"No!"

"Yes!" Charm snapped, and glared at Raven.

Double goddamn! If he could just get her alone. Explain things. "I fear my wife is understandably angry," said Raven. "It seems she overheard my conversation with Mr. Bodine here and misunderstood . . ."

"I'll have an annulment, Mr. Fields," Charm said evenly.

"Perhaps we should start at the beginning," suggested Fields.

"Let's do," said Clancy, settling back in his chair.

"At the beginning," Fields repeated evenly. "And you start, madam."

It seemed to take forever to wind up the tale. Although every word spoken was surprisingly honest, discounting a few embellishments on Clancy's part, Raven found he sounded like nothing more than a gold-digging scoundrel. He resisted wriggling in his chair like a recalcitrant boy and took a sip of the spiced coffee a servant had brought in.

"So, in truth, you're uncertain of your own heritage, madam?" Fields asked now, still standing rigid with his arms behind his back.

Charm's eyes showed every bit of uncertainty that was in her soul. For a moment Raven would have given anything just to have taken her in his arms.

"It no longer matters." Her voice was very soft. Despite everything, Raven could hear no tension in it. Perhaps he should be grateful she had learned to trust as much as she had. Or perhaps it would never matter, for her hatred of him was something that could no longer be overcome. "I wish to return to my father."

"To Jude?" Fields, it seemed, had not missed a word.

"Yes." Charm remained very still, her slim hands clasped in her lap.

"And renounce your fortune?"

"Who can say if there is a fortune?" She quickly raised her gaze to the captain's. "But if there is, it's brought me nothing but trouble thus far."

"She's right," said Clancy, shaking his head like some worldly schoolmaster. "You've treated her shamefully, Joseph."

Shut the hell up, Raven wanted to say. Instead, he remained silent, watching Charm's somber face. If he could just hold her. Just for a moment.

Fields paced again. "One has a responsibility to one's family, though, madam."

She pursed her funny little mouth, painfully reminding Raven of a thousand different events that had shaken his world over the past weeks.

"My responsibility is to Jude," she said softly. "And to myself. I want an annulment."

All eyes watched her.

"I fear I can't help you on that front, madam," Fields said

quietly, "but I can, at least, give you some time to yourself, to think things through. I've a stateroom that adjoins mine. It would be an honor if you'd use it."

"But . . ." Every fiber in Raven's body screamed foul. He needed to see her alone. She was his *wife*, for God's sake! "We don't wish to trouble you, or *Mrs*. Fields," he said, thinking quickly.

The captain's gaze turned smoothly. If Raven weren't mistaken, there was, quite suddenly, a spark of laughter in it. "There is no Mrs. Fields."

Damn, damn, damn! "Then I fear it would hardly seem proper—" Raven began in his most formal tone.

"On the contrary," Fields interrupted, the shimmer of good humor hidden as he turned away. "It will be nothing but proper. I will consider Mrs. Scott's safety my personal responsibility, and will, if even remotely possible, grant her fondest desires. Mrs. Scott . . . ," he went on, extending his arm to her, "if you'll accompany me, I'll show you to your quarters and send a roustabout round to retrieve your possessions."

"Charm!" Raven stood suddenly, though he knew better, knew he should remain as he was, retain some pride.

Fields turned with her on his arm. "Yes, Mr. Scott?"

"She's my wife." They were, despite it all, the only words he could think to say.

Charm's smile appeared suddenly, slightly tilted, showing tiny dimples with her perfect insincerity. "I'll be certain to correct that problem at the earliest possible moment," she said, and turning smoothly, disappeared through the doorway on the captain's capable arm.

Dinner was excruciating. Perhaps fifty passengers crowded the dining area. Five shared the captain's table—Mr. Phelps, a man of obvious affluence, Fields, Clancy, Raven, and . . .

Charm! Only by the sheerest will power was Raven able to keep his gaze from welding to her. But in truth there was no need to look, for he'd relegated every detail to his memory. She sat at the captain's right, laughing her low lilting laugh now and then, and flirting. Not with words, or in any other concrete way, but flirting, nevertheless, to Raven's way of thinking.

Somehow she'd coaxed her hair to the top of her head, from where it spiraled down in intriguing curlycues of feminine appeal. Her face seemed to glow in the light of the falling sun, and her dress . . .

Raven swore in silence, forcing himself to keep his gaze from her, to remember his pride. But where the hell had she gotten that damn dress? It was lavender, sprigged with a design of delicate apple blossoms and cut so low that every time she drew a breath, Raven held his.

"Don't she look grand in that getup?" asked Clancy, leaning closer to Raven's left side. "Now you gotta agree, Joseph, there's an example of money well spent."

It took a moment for Raven to understand Bodine's meaning. This was the gown Charm had refused to buy, but Clancy had purchased anyway. It set his teeth on edge knowing she'd decided to wear it now, with another man, even if that man was over twice her age and a picture of proper etiquette.

Clancy chuckled. "Told you it fit her like a second skin, didn't I? That you'd thank me for my farsighted friendship someday? I'll tell you." He chuckled again. "When she first tried it on, I feared she'd bust right out of it, but you know, it's surprising how them seams hold all that . . . Joseph, you been smoking? I think there's steam coming out of yer ears."

"Captain." Raven sat very still, lest he do something he'd later regret. Murder for instance. "If it's not too much to ask, I'd like a few moments with my wife." Despite his best intentions, his voice sounded taut.

Fields lifted his gaze. "That would be up to the lady, sir."

"Charm?" Raven said, but though he did his best to manage politeness, his tone was tighter still.

"Yes, Mr. Scott?" She lowered her chin slightly, dimpling.

Raven swore again, silently, first at Clancy, out of habit, then at himself for being such a besotted, weak-kneed fool, and then at her, for having the spirit of a devil cat and still making him want her. "Would you accompany me for a stroll around the deck?"

"Oh." She'd gotten a fan from somewhere. Probably Clancy had purchased it with the gown, for it too was of lavender hue. It also possessed slightly more fabric than the bodice of the dress. "Thank you ever so for asking, sir, but . . . no . . . I think not."

His teeth hurt. "Charm!" The single word sounded a bit more like a threat than he'd planned.

"I'm available, Miss Charm," said Clancy cheerfully, "if you're looking for an escort and Joseph here ain't up to snuff."

"Why, Mr. Bodine!" She tilted her mesmerizing face downward, fanning herself and sounding like a simpering southern miss. But simpering southern misses didn't generally carry knives in their garters and derringers in their pockets. Yes, Raven thought stiffly, his Charm was decidedly unique. "How gallant of you. But no, I think I'll retire to my room."

"Charm!" Raven stood when she did, aware of the interest he drew from every man present. "I'd like a word with you."

"The lady said no, Mr. Scott." Fields's tone was low. Although they didn't move, Raven had the distinct feeling that the two large servers, who were standing very near their table, were suddenly very tense, as if waiting for their captain's command. "And on the *Yankee Belle*, a lady's wish is gospel."

"To hell with the *Yankee Belle*," Raven said through a congenial smile. He held Fields's gaze but was aware of two more large bodies shifting closer to the captain's table.

Four big men against himself, Raven thought. True, the odds weren't good, but they were stimulating, and would, perhaps, relieve the burning frustration that seized him.

Fields watched him with his all-seeing eyes. "Were I you, I wouldn't chance it, Mr. Scott."

Raven smiled slowly, feeling the pump of excitement in his veins. "And why is that, Mr. Fields?"

"Because it would be extremely painful."

"But . . ." Raven let his gaze skim to the two pair of toughs. They were slightly bigger than he'd first thought. He turned his attention back to the captain. "She's my wife."

Fields nodded once, as though in concession. "But it would be a very long swim before you saw her again."

With a half grin and a shallow nod, Raven removed his coat before hanging it carefully upon the back of his chair. His vest came off next, drooping a little where Charm's bible rested in its pocket. "I'm a hell of a swimmer," he said evenly. "Clancy here taught me."

"What are you talking about?" Charm asked. Her simpering mannerisms were suddenly gone, replaced by her characteristic, steely tone.

"I believe your young Mr. Scott wishes to fight my men for the honor of a few words with you," offered Fields.

Charm's face went absolutely pale. "That's insane."

"Tell you what, Fields," Raven said quietly. "I'll make you a bet."

The captain's arms crossed slowly against his chest. "I've been known to make a wager or two, Mr. Scott."

"I'm saying I can take out three of them."

The captain smiled with a tilted nod, as if admiring Raven's bravado while doubting his ability. "And if you do?"

"Then I stay on the *Belle*."

"It's a bet."

"But if I take out all four . . . ," Raven said, his tone carefully flat, "then I get ten minutes alone with my wife."

There was an interesting light in Fields's eyes. "That decision would still have to be up to Mrs. Scott?"

"This is insane," she repeated, her voice louder and more harsh.

"You needn't say yes," Fields assured. "The decision is yours."

"Stop this. Right now."

"But the wager's already set, madam."

"Raven!" She appealed to him suddenly, her tone sharp. "Stop it!"

"I'd think you could spare ten minutes," Raven said evenly, "if I whip 'em all." Brawling brought out the white trash in him and jumbled his speech to his native level.

"Raven!" she pleaded as their gazes locked.

"Yes or no, Charm?" he asked quietly.

Her lips moved soundlessly for a moment, but finally emitted a plea. "Please don't," she whispered.

"Yes or no?"

"I'll talk to you," she promised.

Raven found a smile, welcoming her expression of horror, yet knowing he was a fool to hope she was worried for his safety. Still, perhaps he should take advantage of her moment of weakness and try to speak to her immediately. He found, however, that his fighting blood was up and that he welcomed the opportunity to battle against flesh instead of her impenetrable defenses. "It's a wager then, Captain."

"Good." Fields rose abruptly, motioning to someone unseen. "I'll see you safely to your quarters then, madam. And you . . ."—he nodded toward Raven with a spark of respect in his eyes—"you and my men will go directly to the hold." He stepped away from the table, offering his arm to Charm as he did so.

She was holding her breath.

"Oh, and Mr. Scott . . ." Fields turned with a hand on Charm's fingers. "I will join you very shortly. Don't start without me."

*   *   *

Charm turned abruptly in her doorway to glare at Captain Fields. "This is barbaric! Why are you letting them do this? They'll kill him."

The captain smiled. "Be assured that I won't let it go that far."

"Please." Her voice sounded strange. "Stop the fight."

He watched her closely, his gaze thoughtful. "I don't remember your Mr. Scott being such an impetuous man. But perhaps it will rid him of some pent-up frustration, yes?" He smiled, reaching for the door handle. "And besides, this little contest will give you time to consider your wish for an annulment. Oh!" He turned abruptly back toward her. "And about your fondest desire." He laughed. "It seems derringers are in rather short supply on the *Yankee Belle*, but perhaps at our next port."

"Please stop them," Charm pleaded suddenly, gripping his sleeve in stiff fingers. "Please."

He watched her. "You're an interesting and alluring woman, madam. If I were a younger man I'd envy your Mr. Scott. As it is . . ."—his eyes sparkled mischievously— "I'll simply pray for him." He left then, closing the door behind him and speaking quietly to someone on the far side.

Charm stalked her narrow room like a caged cat, trying to calm her breathing, to think rationally, but the entire situation was insane. She had to stop them! The truth came rather belatedly, but when it did she rushed to the door, seizing the handle before coming to a halt.

The fact was, Raven didn't love her, had lied to her repeatedly, was using her. He deserved to have the tar beaten out of him, and if he did, she didn't care. She swore she didn't but jerked open the door even as she made that vow.

A large, ham-shaped face turned impassively toward her from the hallway. "Mrs. Scott." His tone was deep and thoroughly respectful, his nod shallow and slow.

She took a swift, frightened step back. "Who are you?"

"My name's Ralph, ma'am."

"I want to go to my husband."

"I'm afraid the captain wouldn't like that, ma'am, seein's as how yer man's . . . ahhh . . . occupied just now."

She lifted her chin and swallowed hard. He was, she thought, the biggest lump of human flesh she'd ever seen. "I said, I want to see Raven."

Ralph looked at her as if to say that perhaps she should have thought of that sooner, but he said nothing to that effect, instead merely nodded toward the room behind her. "The captain thinks you'd be safest here."

"I told you." She narrowed her eyes, feeling her heart pound wildly in her chest and trying to look dangerous despite the fact that the top of her head failed to reach Ralph's collarbone. "I don't give a . . ."

Ralph loomed closer, causing her to scurry back. "The captain says you stay put," he all but grunted. "So you stay put."

"Oh." She swallowed and retreated another pace, letting her eyes fill with a fear that was painfully real. "I suppose you're right. After all, a fight is no place for a lady. I might faint or . . ." She kicked him with all the strength she had before pivoting away.

There was a yelp of pain, but as she flew toward the stairs, she could already hear the giant's limping steps following her. Despite his bulk, he was quick. Charm felt his blunt fingers graze her back. She shrieked, dodging to the right before grasping her skirts and sprinting for the stairs.

"Hey!" yelled the giant, thundering after.

Her lungs burned with panic. She was almost at the bottom. One more step . . . But suddenly her toe snagged in her petticoat and she tripped. Hands grabbed her and she screamed, righting herself to spin around and deliver a quick knuckled jab to the giant's eye. He grunted in pain, thrusting his fingers over his abused face. There was no time for guilt, only time to flee, to save Raven. She lurched away . . . only to smack gracelessly into another man's chest. A scream ripped from her throat, but already Clancy was steadying her.

"Hey, Miss Charm. It's all right."

"Clancy," she breathed, feeling weak with relief. "Take me to him."

He scowled. "To Joseph?"

For a moment she considered hitting him too. "Of course to Joseph! I have to stop this," she gasped.

"Truth is, miss, he sent me to make certain you stay put."

Charm opened her mouth to protest, but Clancy held up a calming hand. "Seein' as how you're so set on goin' to him, I'll sure . . ." His fist hit her chin dead center. She fought for clarity, but darkness filled her head and she fell into the waiting arms of the giant behind.

She woke with a start just after dawn and dragged herself groggily to the door. It was locked. "Let me out!" she shouted. Trying the handle again, she nearly fell into the arms of the ham-faced Ralph. She stumbled forward, finally finding her balance and skidding to a halt. "Where is he?" she asked, straightening dizzily.

Ralph, she noticed, had a black eye. He didn't back away but looked as if he wished to. "Who?"

Charm doubled her fists. "Where?"

"Mrs. Scott," said a voice from her opposite side.

She turned with a start to recognize Mr. Phelps, her table companion from the evening before. Having already sized him up, she saw no need to waste her time now. Paunch and ego were his outstanding characteristics.

Charm scowled. In the hazy light of dawn, she regretted many things, not the least of which was her foolish flirting of the night before. But anger and bitterness showed no favors when it picked a fool, and she'd felt unusually secure under the captain's protective regard. Secure enough to hope to make Raven share some of the agony she felt at his betrayal.

"You look very lovely this morning, madam."

She scowled, far too preoccupied to act coy. "I'm busy just now."

"Is something wrong?"

Obviously something was wrong. She narrowed her eyes a bit more. "Do you know where my husband is?"

"No, I'm afraid I . . ."

"Then Ralph will have to tell—"

"Mrs. Scott," the captain called. Charm turned abruptly toward him. "Up so early to terrorize poor Ralph?"

"How is he?" Her head hurt and her vision was slightly blurred but she managed the question.

"Would you care for a turn about the top deck?" asked Fields.

"Patronize me once more and I'll pop you in the eye too," she warned. "I want to know where he is."

The captain actually laughed. "Come along, madam. We'll converse as we walk."

She took his arm with a scowl before pacing along beside him, her own strides consistently outpacing his.

"Beautiful, isn't it?" he asked, gazing out across the wide, muddy Missouri to the endless green of the rolling riverside.

"How is he?" she asked again, still scowling.

The captain kept up his leisurely stroll. "*He*, madam? Oh, of course, the young man from whom you'll soon obtain an annulment. I'm really not certain."

"What do you mean?" She found with some surprise that she'd pulled the captain to a halt. "What do you mean you don't know?"

He watched her quietly, and if his eyebrows weren't raised they might just as well have been. "I mean I haven't yet seen him this morning."

"Then he's . . ." She drew a deep steadying breath, knowing she should attempt to act cool and aloof, but failing to do so. "He's still on the boat?"

The smallest piece of a smile showed on Fields's square face. "Your Mr. Scott seemed to have a good deal of energy to expel." From the second deck a mate waved to him.

Fields nodded in reply. "For a while I thought you'd be obliged to speak to him." His eyes were sparkling again, as if the demon had escaped captivity. "But Eli falls hard."

Her grip tightened on his arm. "What do you mean by that?"

"I'm sorry, madam, much as I enjoy the company of a beautiful companion, the *Belle* claims my heart. I must go."

"But . . ."

"Perhaps I'll see you at breakfast."

She stood numbly staring after him, but in a moment, she realized she was alone and unhindered. She raced to the room Raven and she had shared for less than ten minutes. It stood empty, showing no evidence that he had ever been there.

Only she and Phelps breakfasted at the captain's table that morning. Though she knew he watched her, she easily ignored him as she waited, breath held for some news of Raven's well-being or whereabouts.

None came. But two of the toughs from the night before finally appeared. One man's skull was bandaged, and the other sported an eye the color of rotting crab apples.

Their wounds served to remind Charm of several things. Raven was a very capable man. He could care for himself. And he didn't want to see her. Therefore, she should be grateful for her time alone.

By suppertime, however, she felt as if a large man had been beating her with a broom, not terribly hard, but very steadily. Her muscles ached from tension, and her head throbbed with a rhythmic pain in her temples. Yet she hadn't allowed herself to search for him. She hadn't cried. And she hadn't promised the captain every penny she might someday inherit if he would just allow her a few minutes in Raven's arms. All in all, that was the best she could say for the day.

She sat now, keeping her gaze on her plate and flatly refusing to ask the captain about Raven's well-being again. Mr. Phelps sat down to her left, but she only raised her gaze when Clancy appeared, pulling a chair out to accommodate his lithe frame. She was holding her breath again.

"And where is our bold Mr. Scott, tonight?" asked Phelps expansively.

"Joseph?" Clancy chuckled. "I suspect he's tendin' them busted ribs.

"You know, Captain, I think I was meant to be a sailor," Clancy rambled. "Cuz this life on the water suits me fine. Just rollin' along, games of chance anytime you please. Good food. . . . Damn, you look pretty tonight, Miss Charm. Yellow suits—"

She rose abruptly.

"Where're y' goin', Miss Charm?" he asked, but there was no point in answering as she sped away.

There were more than fifty staterooms on the *Yankee Belle*. Charm began her search on the top deck. The first door was locked. The second opened to an unoccupied room. The third door resisted but finally opened, granting her a bird's-eye view of a man and woman passionately occupied upon the bed. The woman screamed, the man swore, and in less than two minutes Charm found herself confined to her room with Ralph stationed in the hallway and the captain reprimanding her.

"Mrs. Scott, although I admire your spirit, I fear I must insist that you . . . act like a lady." He raised one grey brow.

"Where is he?"

Fields watched her before drawing a deep sigh. "Did I misunderstand, or did you tell me you wished for an annulment?"

"Tell me where he is or I'll search every room from top to bottom."

The captain all but rolled his eyes. "Much as I hate to deliver this news, I fear your husband doesn't wish you to know his whereabouts."

"Then if you'll excuse me," she said, smiling primly. "I have things to do." She took a step forward.

"Ralph," said the captain.

Ralph, too, stepped forward, though he looked leery.

"I can't have you terrorizing my passengers, Mrs. Scott."

"Then tell me where he is."

"I can tell you he's well."

"Well?" she asked breathlessly.

Fields smiled. "Well enough. And now I must go."

She was shoved gently but firmly inside and the door closed behind her.

The second day was worse than the first.

She knew she should be content. In fact, she knew she should be overjoyed that Raven could no longer bother her. But instead she paced, not sleeping, barely eating, wanting only to see him, to read the carefully guarded mannerisms that were his alone. To know he was safe and whole. She knew she was a fool. She knew he didn't love her. And yet . . . she loved him. Despite it all there was nothing on earth she could do to change that.

Although Charm was allowed to leave her cabin, she was followed by the dogged Ralph and not permitted to tear doors from their hinges in her search for Raven.

Days passed in slow, weary succession. Nights dragged along as if pulled through eternity by the languid tide of the Big Muddy, and still Charm saw no sign of her husband. Much of her time she spent with Angel, gaining solace from his appreciative presence and feeding him tidbits she'd taken from her own plate. But during the sleepness nights, she would often pull forth the intricate miniature of Caroline Grady to pore over every detail.

Was this really her mother? Had this woman with the soulful eyes and solemn expression held her as a child? Loved her? Cherished her as only a mother can? Charm tried to remember, and sometimes she thought she almost could, for there, at the dark fringe of her memory was a woman with gentle hands and emerald eyes. Her mother? Charm didn't know, and now, on the fifth day since Raven's fight, she wasn't certain it mattered. For love was a precious, fleeting thing, and once gone could not be regained, but only mourned.

She was sitting at the supper table, staring at her place setting and ignoring her companions when Fields's voice broke in. "Mr. Scott! So you've decided to join us."

Charm's breath ended sharply as her gaze lifted with guileless speed. He was there, whole and live and real, causing the ache in her body and soul to become an indescribable cramp. There was a healing laceration on his left cheek and a yellowish bruise adorned his brow, and yet, despite it all, he was, she thought, the most beautiful thing on earth.

Their gazes fused, and though his face showed no expression, the intensity of his eyes spoke of something just beyond her immediate comprehension. But in a moment the light shifted from his gaze and he withdrew seemingly into himself as he was seated.

"I've come to a decision." His voice was very quiet.

Although Charm struggled to appear calm, her lungs ached with her suspended breathing and her nails pressed painful depressions into her hands.

"I've decided to grant your wish," Raven continued.

Her lips felt stiff but managed to move. "My wish?"

"Yes." He nodded once, his expression perfectly implacable.

"Well, Mr. Scott," said Phelps, his words slightly slurred. "Good of you to join us after your daring battle. And *Mrs.* Scott, more enticing than ever," he crooned.

Charm failed to hear him, so focused was she on the dark features of her husband. "My wish?" she asked again, her chest painfully tight.

"An annulment," Raven said flatly.

Chapter 29

Charm had eaten none of her prairie chicken pie. The watermelon, sliced to look like a rose, sat untouched upon her plate. Her wine glass, on the other hand, had been drained several times. Probably a sort of celebration for her victory, Raven deduced, fingering his own glass.

His ribs burned like hell and his face still stung, but it was her presence that caused the most persistent ache. Over the past five days he'd convinced himself he could live without her. But as Clancy had stated sometime earlier, he'd always had a colorful imagination.

She sat between Bodine and Fields now and was dressed conservatively in a fine russet gown. Her tiny matching hat sat at a careless angle and complemented the glistening auburn highlights in her dark, upswept hair. But it made no difference what she wore, for every man there wanted her. Even the captain, Raven was sure, despite his goddamn fatherly demeanor. But he was far preferable to Phelps, the pompous, wealthy ass, who didn't bother to hide his lust.

"Do you play poker, madam?" asked the pompous ass now.

"Poker?" Charm lowered her eyes. Her cheeks were flushed with a bright hue that matched her solemn, upturned mouth. She swirled the contents of her glass before raising her eyes. "No, Mr. Phelps. I don't play." She stared at him point-blank, concealing nothing with her expression, and in that moment Raven knew she was truly intoxicated. "I distract."

Phelps laughed, the sound rusty and deprecating. Raven considered hitting him, but thus far, throwing punches during this journey had done little to ease his frustration.

"I'm sure you do, madam. Do you mind if I call you Charm?"

She took another sip of her wine. "You may call me Miss Grady," she said in a flat tone. In one breathtaking sweep of her eyes, she riveted Raven with her gaze. "Chantilly Grady, for that will soon be my name, won't it, Mr. Scott?"

Raven said nothing. Damn him for being a weak-kneed, besotted fool.

"Isn't it, Mr. Scott?" she repeated.

"Perhaps you should see her to her room, Captain," Raven said quietly.

"I don't want the captain to see me to my room." She smiled, very sweetly, so much so that few there would recognize the deception she was able to carry off.

"I'd be honored to escort you to your quarters, madam," said Phelps, leaning back in his chair.

Raven let his gaze skim slowly toward that man. "I don't think so," he said evenly.

Phelps raised his brows before draining his glass. "If I understand the situation correctly, it ain't your decision, Scott."

"Clancy," Raven said softly.

With an obvious start, Bodine chimed in. "I'll take you back, Miss Charm."

"Well . . ." She smiled again, and Raven watched, trying to loosen the tightness of his muscles. "I'm ever so flattered. All you gentlemen willing to put yourself out just for little ol' me."

She should have brought her fan, Raven thought, for it would be the perfect time to flutter it in front of her mesmerizing, conniving little face. Damn him for loving her despite it all. And damn her for not caring. True, she'd tried to come to him during the fight, but he knew better than to think it was out of concern for his well-being. Clancy had told him how she'd battled Ralph. Little Cougar Mouse, Bodine had called her.

Despite Raven's ravenous need to see her, he had refused her company for he was not quite ready to allow her to gloat. Neither had he been ready to see her face and again twist the facts to convince himself there was some concern there for him. He'd been a fool to think he was ready now.

"Perhaps we should gamble for the honor of her company," suggested Phelps.

Clancy's brows rose happily, but one glower from Raven and he cleared his throat. "Bad idea," he said with a shake of his head.

"On the contrary," argued Captain Fields, his steady gaze finally leaving Charm's face, "it sounds like a fine way to decide this little dispute. Shall we give it a five-hundred dollar cap?"

"Why limit the pot?" asked Phelps. "I think you do the lady an injustice." His salacious gaze moved to Charm again. "Surely she's worth more than five hundred."

"No one will be impoverished on the *Belle*," said Fields. "Five hundred is my limit. Is everyone agreed?"

Goddamn Fields right along with Phelps. Raven rose stiffly, wanting to pummel them all. "I'm afraid I'll have to decline."

"Really?" Phelps asked. "Too bad. But if the stakes are too high I'll just see her to her room myself."

Goddamn right the stakes were too high, and if Phelps touched her, he'd tear the sweating little lecher limb from limb. "You've convinced me," Raven said evenly.

* * *

The card table was round and accommodated the four players easily. Charm sat beside Captain Fields, who had lost his stake sometime before. Clancy, too, was out of the game, leaving only Phelps and Raven.

The two sat now, eyeing each other and sitting very still. Charm watched them. The insanity of the situation was not lost on her, even though she was drunk. She knew she was drunk. In fact, she was thrilled by the fact, for it would dull the pain of her loss. But why hadn't it yet?

An annulment. A few simple words spoken. A few simple lies, and Raven would be gone from her life. He'd collect his reward, if indeed she was this Chantilly Grady he took her to be. He'd take his money and run, happy to be rid of her and the trouble she caused. After all, everything he had done had been to obtain the reward and nothing else.

"Shall we bet it all, Mr. Scott?" asked Phelps. He spread his pudgy fingers over his winnings and nodded to the hand they'd just thrown in. "And call it quits? After all, our funds look to be relatively even and the lady must be growing weary of the wait. Such a pretty thing should not be delayed so long." He sent her a tilted leer. "Isn't that right, my lovely?"

She'd been collecting weapons again and had quite an array now. A butter knife and a sharp stone in her pocket, a hat pin in her chapeau, and her favorite, a silver serving fork, which was stuck into her garter. It was a most unsatisfactory place to keep it, she mused now, wishing she could reach it. Still, the soothing memory of it allowed her to smile into Phelps' chubby face.

Damn him for being a horse's egotistical ass. Damn Fields for putting her in this position. And damn Raven, for not loving her.

"You flatter me, Mr. Phelps," she said, finding, to her surprise, that she didn't fear him, only detested him. But it did nothing to brighten the depression that pressed her down, so she lifted her smile a half notch and lowered her eyes.

"No flattery at all," Phelps chuckled. "What do you say, Scott, do you dare bet it all?"

Charm could feel Raven's gaze on her. She met it with chill breathlessness, hoping her expression showed no more emotion than his.

"Yes." His tone was flat and ultimately steady. "Let's call it all quits."

Fields dealt the hand, and though Charm told herself there was nothing more at stake than a walk to her cabin, the tension burned her mind. If Raven won, she would be afforded a few moments of his company. A little while during which she could breathe before the roiling undertow of loneliness smothered her.

They received their cards.

"We bet it all then?" asked Phelps.

Raven shrugged, looking unconcerned. "If you like."

Phelps's face appeared jovial as he asked for one card, but beneath the ruddy color, Charm could see the tension.

And Raven? She turned her gaze to him and found his eyes, dead level and sharp as a wolf's on her face. They smote her like a blow. She drew in her breath, fear and excitement sparking at his expression of possessiveness.

He held the winning hand. He knew it and she knew it, and now, with the look of a predator, he eyed his prey. But she was no more than that to him. A challenge at best. A meal ticket at worst. She raised her chin, pride and pain mingling as she met his gaze with passionate anger.

"How many, Mr. Scott?" asked Fields, and suddenly, like a light going out, Raven doused the emotion in his eyes and shrugged. From his hand he pulled forth a couple of cards.

"Two," he said evenly.

The room was still, and if anyone present breathed, it was only Raven.

"A pair of nines," said Phelps tersely.

Raven's eyes met hers again, but flatly now, without

feeling. "Guess it's not my game," he said. Turning his hand up, he showed a worthless collection of random numbers.

Charm felt the blood drain from her face. He'd lost . . . intentionally.

"Well . . ." Phelps's smile was sloppy. "I'd call this a fine evening. A fine evening indeed." He pulled the pile of chips toward him but stood before stowing them away. "Perhaps you'd be so kind as to see to my winnings, Captain. I have a lady to escort to her cabin."

He'd lost. Charm felt suddenly numb, as if every nerve had been severed, as if the sun had fled her universe, leaving her in darkness.

"Come along, my lovely." Phelps extended an elbow.

Like one in a trance, Charm took three steps forward to lift Raven's discarded cards. Two queens. She felt sick to her stomach but lost control of her expression for only a moment. Wordlessly, she replaced the cards, and then lifting her chin, turned to leave the room.

Phelps was beside her in a moment, taking her arm in his clammy fingers. She didn't resist, for there was no point. Raven hated her. Hated her so much that he would give away thousands of dollars to avoid her presence for less time than it took him to consume a meal.

Her shoes rapped against the floor. She noticed their hollow sound, but failed to comprehend what Phelps said, despite his constant string of chatter.

"Shouldn't we go in before we're spotted?"

They were at her door, she noticed suddenly. "What?"

He leaned closer. "An evening of stimulating sport, topped off by the titillation of you." He chuckled and pressing nearer, kissed her neck.

"What are you doing?" Some of the numbness faded as she turned about to bump up against the door.

He grinned, or more correctly, he leered. "Just getting started, my lovely. Shall we go in?"

"No." Charm said the word blandly, though panic was beginning to rise. She knew the moment his anger was ignited. It showed in the narrowing of his eyes, the tightness of his smile.

"A little late to cry off now, madam, after all I've gone through to win this night for us."

"For us?" she breathed, still reeling, it seemed, in the turmoil of her own emotion.

He chuckled again and stepped closer. "It's not that I don't appreciate the chase, but the game is over. And I've won the prize. You can drop the act."

She lifted her chin slightly, trying to concentrate. "And what act would that be, Mr. Phelps?"

He let his head drop back slightly, as though he found her words very amusing, but in an instant, he held her right arm in a meaty fist. "That act, my little dove," he ground out, squeezing hard. "Acting like you don't want me when I know damned well that you do."

"Let me go!" Full-blown panic came late but was blinding in its intensity. The knife was in her pocket, but she couldn't reach it.

"Let you go?" he asked, then laughed, reaching around her to push open the door. "After I'm through, my pretty little tease."

He pushed her forward. She fell against the bed, ready to scream, but suddenly she was jerked around and his mouth was on hers. He was pressing her back against the mattress as he knelt between her legs. Bile rose in her throat like a tide of loathing. She pushed against him with all her might. Despite the drink and her own terror, she was still strong. Phelps fell backward, momentarily thrown off balance and striking his head on the edge of a trunk.

He rose with a lurch. Drawing back his arm, he crashed his fist against the side of her head.

Charm whimpered in reeling shock, cowering away as he raised his hand again, but in that second the door crashed open. Phelps staggered about, staring at the man silhouetted against the vague light.

"Who's there?"

"Hit her again, Phelps, and I'll break your neck," said a gravelly voice. "Right here. Right now."

"Scott!" Phelps's tone held none of the even certainty of Raven's. "What the hell are you doing here? She don't want you!"

"Maybe not." Raven didn't move, nor did the steady tone of his voice change. "But I want her. So if you leave now, I'll . . ."—his head tilted slightly, showing a sudden glint of white teeth in his dark silhouette—"I'll only break your legs."

"Goddamn you cocky bastard!" roared Phelps. Bolstered by the intoxicants of liquor and victory, he rushed forward, head low and fists doubled.

Raven's knuckles caught him in a neat uppercut to his jaw, slamming the heavier man back into reverse. But he stumbled only a few steps before steadying his weight and leveling a glare at Raven's dark form.

"You're gonna regret that, boy," he growled, pulling a handgun from his pocket, but already Raven was driving himself forward.

The impact of his body knocked Phelps flat onto his back. The gun exploded nearly in Raven's ear, but rage possessed his senses. He slammed his fists into the other's belly again and again, oblivious to the empty clicking of Phelps' derringer.

"Hey!" someone shouted from behind. "Hey!"

"Joseph! Don't kill 'im!"

"Scott! Quit. Quit now or my boys will have to stop you."

Sanity washed back in cooler shades of temper. Raven rose slowly, barely feeling the deep stab of pain in his ribs as he pulled Phelps to his feet.

Four large toughs leveled guns at him, but Raven only lifted one bloody corner of his mouth. "Shoot me if you like, but he's going over the side."

"Shoot him! Shoot him!" croaked Phelps, still holding his useless gun and staggering in his opponent's grip. Raven merely turned, meeting each tense gaze in the light of the lanterns before stepping forward, dragging Phelps behind.

The rail wasn't far away. There was a gasp of terror and outrage from Phelps. "Shoot him!" he screamed again, but the last word was no more than a moan as he was yanked from the floor and heaved, like a sack of rotting potatoes, over the side. A shriek issued upward, followed by the sound of an overweight body meeting water.

Raven turned, not waiting to see if Phelps surfaced. He was surrounded now by onlookers. Clancy, Ralph, Fields, his four goons, and a bevy of bleary-eyed passengers in nightshirts who stared from him to Charm with loose jaws.

Absolute silence held the place.

"He was staring at my wife," Raven explained casually. As a unit, the men turned to gaze at Charm, and then, like so many leaves in the wind, they scurried into their prospective rooms.

"You came." Charm's words were barely audible, but Raven turned, sensing her presence more than hearing her voice.

Her face was pale and her dark hair tumbled about her shoulders like a tide of silken waves.

"I tried to let you go, Charm. To let you walk out of there with another man. But it seems I'm not as strong as I once thought. Still, I'll do my best."

"Raven," she breathed, and though it took every ounce of strength he had, he managed to turn and walk away.

Chapter 30

"Raven, please," Charm called through the solid door that stood guard between them. He'd refused to talk to her on the previous night, and he refused again now. "Let me in."

"She's beggin' again," said Clancy from the far side of the door. "God, Joseph, I hate it when she begs. It sounds so damn pathetic."

"Go away, Charm," Raven said quietly.

"I need to talk to you, just for a little while."

"I'm sleeping."

She scowled, then slammed her palm against the door. "At least you could have the decency to make your lies believable."

"It was the best I could come up with on short notice."

"Why won't you let me in?" she asked, feeling like a fool with her ear pressed to the portal.

"Because I'm weak."

She knew what he meant. Somehow she knew, and somehow it made her chest ache with hope and longing, but she pretended she didn't understand, perhaps just to hear his voice again. "You bested three out of four, Raven. I don't think that means you're weak."

There was a moment of silence, and then Clancy's quiet, chuckled rejoinder which she couldn't quite hear.

She remained as she was, listening, imagining how Raven would look. "Please let me in."

Still no response.

"Raven!" She kicked the door, losing her carefully contained patience and hurting her foot. "Clancy! Let me in."

"He's sleeping."

"Damn it, Clancy! He is not sleeping."

"Well, he says he is."

"Let me in, Clancy, or you'll regret it. And I mean it. I still owe you for hitting me, you know."

There was a moment of silence again, a prelude to Raven's rumbled question, which didn't quite meet her ears.

Clancy's response was quick as he tried to explain his reasons for striking her. "She was determined to come to you, Joseph. And you'd said not to let her. What else was I supposed to do?"

"You hit her?" Raven's voice was not so quiet now.

"I wouldn't call it 'hit' exactly. 'Tap' maybe. I tapped her. Real gentle like, and just on the jaw."

She could not quite make out Raven's growled response.

"You told me to keep her safe," Clancy objected quickly. "And I was scared she'd go attackin' one of Fields's hired bulls. Get herself really hurt."

Another rumble from Raven.

"Well, you wouldn't go sayin' she's just a girl if'n you saw Ralph's eye. Looks the color of rotten meat. And don't think I ain't seen yer chest. Now, don't go givin' me them looks. You didn't see her with them Injuns neither. Cougar Mouse they called her, and got the hell outta there. And me, I didn't see no reason to get myself killed so I just popped her on the jaw a little. Just a little—"

"Oh, for heaven's sakes!" stormed Charm, having heard

enough. "Let me in!" she ordered, kicking the door again so that it reverberated under her assault.

"Shall I assume my door has done something to offend you, Mrs. Scott?"

"Captain." Charm turned to him in a fresh state of near panic. "Raven won't let me in."

"Then may I suggest that you go to bed? After all, you've been here since dawn. It must be quite fatiguing, battering innocent doors."

"I don't want to go to bed," she all but growled. "I want to talk to my husband."

Captain Fields shook his head. Taking her arm in a firm grasp, he turned her away from the abused portal. "It seems, to the dismay of this door and my entire crew of passengers, that your Mr. Scott has decided you need more time to learn your own mind."

"Well, he's wrong." She stopped, pulling Fields to a halt with her. "I know my mind. I know exactly what I want."

He watched her intently, then nodded. "Good. That's fine." He urged her down the stairs toward her own cabin. "But he wants you to meet your aunt, realize what you've missed, claim your rightful inheritance . . . Need I go on?"

"If you want to be punched in the nose," Charm mumbled irritably, but her lips quivered when she said it and for a moment she feared she might cry.

"Charming. Tell me, was this Jude quite sober when he named you?"

"My mother named . . . ," she began, then stopped. "Who cares who named me? I can be charming if I want to be, but there's no point now, because I'm not even allowed to see him." Her eyes had filled with tears, but she sniffed and held them back.

Captain Fields watched her, then shaking his head with a soft sigh, opened her cabin door to shove her gently inside. "Take heart, Mrs. Scott, for I fear no man could hold you at a distance for long. Now go to sleep."

"I don't . . ."—the door closed in her face—"sleep," she finished wearily.

Charm paced the room for about fifteen seconds before she came up with a plan. It wasn't a great plan, but it was sound, serviceable, and acceptably diabolical. In less than five minutes she'd found a roustabout, bribed him with two bits, and hidden around the corner to Raven's room, where she held her breath and waited.

The roustabout rapped perfunctorily on the portal she had kicked only minutes before. "Mr. Bodine, I was t'tell y' there'll be a poker game startin' in a couple a minutes. You's invited."

"Poker game?" Clancy's enthusiastic voice responded. "Who's playin'?"

Charm held her breath. She'd neglected to go into much detail and hoped that for two bits, the roustabout could formulate a viable lie.

"Some of them rich gents from N'Orlens. You know, the ones that smoke them fat ceegars and mess ashes all over the *Belle* when they gets drunk."

Drunk, rich gamblers. There was nothing Clancy would like better. If only Raven didn't find the temptation too much to resist. She heard a murmuring from the room, and though she failed to make out the words, she knew the outcome in a few moments when Clancy opened the door to step into the hall. Slipping into his coat, he whistled a few tuneless bars and strode off in the opposite direction.

Charm glanced carefully about her, and then, quick and furtive as a cat, slunk into Raven's room. In a moment the door was closed behind her and they were face to face.

"Raven." His name slipped from her lips, and though she'd carefully planned what she'd say to him, the words were stuck now, jammed in her too tight throat.

He was beautiful, dark and alluring and whole. His brown eyes were warm and steady, his massive chest bare above the sheet as he reclined upon the corn husk mattress.

"I . . ." Her chest ached, and more than anything in the world she wanted to hold him. "I needed to see you."

"Charm . . . ," he began, shaking his head, but she stopped him.

"Please don't send me away. Not right now. Not yet."

For just a moment she could have sworn she saw the light of hopeful passion in his eyes, but finally he shook his head.

"You don't understand, Charm."

"What?" She could hear the tension in her own voice, could feel it like a cold draught of air, freezing her hope, her chance at life. "You don't care for me?"

He said nothing.

"Don't you?"

The tension seemed tangible.

"You're an heiress to a great fortune, Charm. You're not going to want me tying you down. You'll be flooded with suitors and balls and—"

"Say you don't care for me at all then. Say it, and I'll walk out of your life right now," she said, tears welling. "I'll go to my aunt, drown myself in suitors and champagne." She paused, holding her breath and failing to notice the tear that slipped over her lower lashes. "I will."

He looked pale suddenly, and against the bedsheet his hands formed into fists. "I don't care about you, Charm," he intoned into the silence.

For a moment her body went absolutely tense, and then, letting her air out in a sudden rush, she threw herself against his chest.

Without thought, his arms wrapped about her and his eyes fell closed. She felt like heaven, like food to a starving man, but reality was a hard thing for him to ignore, and it nudged him finally, so that he pressed her away a gentle inch.

"Did I misunderstand myself?" he asked quietly. "Or did I just say I didn't care for you?"

"You did," she whispered, and in that moment he felt her fine, slim body shiver against him. "But you made fists. You always make fists when you lie."

"I do not."

"Yes you do," she sniffed.

"Charm . . ." He tried to push her away.

"You saved me," she said, refusing to let him go but drawing back slightly so that she was looking into his eyes with an earnestness that made him ache. "You came when I needed you. I know you don't want to believe it, Raven, because I've been so difficult. But you care for me a little. And maybe, someday . . ."

He saw her throat constrict and the tears well up again.

"Maybe some day, if I try really hard you'll . . ." She stopped speaking, and another tear fell, following the salty course set by its predecessors.

It made his chest ache. Against his will Raven lifted his hand to gently swipe it away. His fingers were shaking, he noticed with some despair. "Don't make me say it, Charm," he whispered. "Leave me some pride."

Her emerald eyes looked frantic. With hope? he wondered but squelched the thought, refusing to allow himself to believe.

"Why? Why pride?" she asked. "What good has it done us so far?"

He watched her closely and realized with rare clarity that she was right. Pride was a fool's excuse to fail, but he was scared, more scared than he'd ever been in his life.

"Just for this moment," she whispered. "Just for now, let's be honest."

"You want honesty?" he asked suddenly, his muscles painfully tight. "Then I'll tell you honestly. I'm a selfish bastard, Charm. Just like my father. Not some—"

"I love you."

Her words slashed across his senses, rattling his world to a halt.

Neither breathed. Her face was very pale, and against his back her hands shook.

Never in Raven's life had he been more frightened than

now. He swallowed hard. "I love you . . . more than life itself," came his broken response.

For a moment she stared at him with her soul in her eyes, and then her head fell against his chest and she hugged him with quaking fierceness.

Time halted, binding them together like lost children.

"Were you aware that my ribs are cracked, Charm?" Raven asked finally.

"Oh," she breathed and eased quickly away, wiping at her cheek with a hand that still shook. "I'm sorry."

"That's all right," he said and managed a grin.

She smiled back tentatively, making his chest hurt with the familiar pain. "What can I do to make it better?"

"Charm—" he began.

"Shh." She leaned forward, carefully avoiding his ribs as she set a finger to his lips. "Perhaps there might be something I could do."

"Charm . . ."

"There must be something, Raven. Bandages, ointments," she whispered. Leaning forward, she kissed him.

Every ounce of good sense fled, and for a moment Raven was kissing her back, but he pressed her away finally, employing every bit of quivering self-control he could dredge up. "Damn it, Charm," he rasped. "What the hell are you doing? This doesn't change anything. You think love makes everything right? Well, it doesn't."

"Then why did you make love to me the first time?" she whispered.

"Because I'm a weak-willed fool."

"I don't believe you."

"I am, but I'm not going to ruin your life. I'm not going to."

She bit her inner lip, and in that instant, he saw the light of hope flare boldly in her eyes. "Where does it hurt?" she whispered huskily.

It hurt in his soul, every time he looked at her, every time he thought of her turning away from him. "Dammit, Charm, this is no game."

"You think I believe this is a game? You think I'm not scared too?"

She was. He knew it. But she was braver than he. Women just were. His mother had been.

"I'm scared too, Raven. But what if we don't take the risk? What then?" Her fingers slipped, feather soft over his cheek, as if memorizing each line.

"Where does it hurt, Joseph?" she whispered again, and now she kissed his cheek, the corner of his mouth, the base of his throat, where his pulse leaped to meet her lips.

"Charm." He barely forced her name out on a warbling breath.

"Lower?" she whispered, and now he felt her kisses rain across his chest, eliciting a moan from his own body even before her tongue teased his nipple.

"God!" Raven groaned, gripping the bedsheet with frantic fingers.

The door swung open. "There ain't no . . . Hey!" said Clancy, coming to an abrupt halt. "What's going on here?"

"Save me, Clancy," pleaded Raven pathetically.

Clancy shook his head. "You crazy?"

"Clancy!" snapped Raven.

"All right. All right. Come on then, Miss Charm," said Bodine, approaching the bed. "Let's leave Joseph alone with his insanity."

Charm lifted her head and smiled. Raven loved her. She wasn't about to give up now. "Back off, Clancy!" she said sweetly. "I've got a fork in my garter."

"A fork? In your garter? Really?" He sounded intrigued. "I think she's threatening me, Joseph, but I'm not certain."

"Get her off me, Bodine. Don't let her scare you."

"Her bark is worse than her bite?"

"No," said Raven. "Her bite is pretty much deadly, but if you don't remove her soon, it'll be too late."

"Too late for what?"

"Just—" Raven drew a deep breath and closed his eyes. "Get her off."

"Come on, Miss Charm," coaxed Clancy again. Taking her arm, he tried to pull her away. Charm, however, had latched onto the sheet beneath Raven's body and held on tight.

Clancy pulled again, then straightened. "Damn. Tough as a coon in a trap. I think you're stuck with her, boy."

"Get her up," ordered Raven.

"I'm not leaving you." Charm had lifted her body slightly from his, so that she could look directly into his eyes. "It doesn't matter what you do. I'll be back if I have to break out your window and tie myself to your bed. If I have to scream down the boat until the captain insists that you take me in."

"Good God, Charm!"

"I mean it, Raven. I won't leave you."

"She's just a pretty little mosquito, ain't she?" asked Clancy, chuckling.

"Can't you do anything more constructive than make inane comparisons?" asked Raven woefully.

"Nope. Don't think so."

"I'm not leaving, Raven."

He rolled his eyes. "All right. Just . . . Sit up."

She did so, slowly, carefully, still gripping the bedsheet in white-knuckled hands.

He took another deep breath. "You wanted the truth, Charm. So I told you the truth. What more do you want?"

"You."

Raven sighed and ran his fingers through his hair. "You don't know what you're saying. My father—"

"You're not your father."

"Well, I'm not any goddamn saint, either."

"I don't want a saint, Joseph. I want you."

Raven scowled and exhaled again. "You don't know that, Charm. There'll be other men. Men better suited to—"

"You think I haven't met other men?"

"I know the kind of men you've met, Charm. I don't mean that kind. I mean decent men, men with upbringing, character, means."

"Rich men, you mean?" she asked.

"Yes." He nodded. "I suppose."

"Like Phelps?"

Raven gritted his teeth. "Goddamn it, Charm. You're not listening."

"Neither am I leaving," she said flatly.

"All right." Raven lifted his hands in defeat. "But I set the rules."

She smiled, just a little, because the joy that swept through her was consuming. "Yes, Raven."

"First . . ." He pointed his left index finger. "You don't sleep in here."

"I don't sleep. I—"

"Well, damn it all, you don't snatch in here either!" he stormed. "And that's final!"

"But—"

"No buts. I've already confused you enough without having all that . . ." He waved again, trying to find a decent way to voice his thoughts. But he could think of none. "All that . . . sexual . . . stuff to worry about."

"But—"

"No sex!" Raven insisted. A man passing in the hall tripped as he went by. They could see his startled expression as he continued on, trying to appear nonchalant. "Good God, I think I'm losing my mind."

"I think so too," said Clancy.

"You can stay," said Raven more evenly. "And we'll talk." He sighed. "For a while. But when I say to go, you have to go. All right?"

She smiled again, then shrugged. "All right."

In the end, Charm spent almost every waking hour with Raven, time they spent talking of their pasts, their hopes, what made them solely unique. She propped him against his pillows, fed him roasted buffalo meat and lemonade and laughed at his protests when the icy liquid dripped onto his chest.

"Cold?"

"Good God, Charm, are you trying to give me a heart attack? It's bad enough that you sit so damn close."

She laughed again, thinking the sound very low and strangely familiar now, for he had been complaining constantly about her blatant attempts to seduce him. "Shall I lick it off?"

The air left his lungs in an audible hiss.

She lifted one corner of her mouth. "If you don't say something, I'm going to assume that's a yes."

"You're an evil woman, Charm."

"Fie, sir," she said, adopting that odd southern accent she sometimes did when flirting. "Do you forget I am your wife?"

"No." His tone was suddenly hoarse. "I don't forget." Their eyes met in a melding stroke of fire.

"Raven . . ."

He cleared his throat quickly and shifted back into his pillows. "I think you'd better leave now, Charm."

"Already?" She sat straighter, feeling honestly unable to leave, for the loneliness without him was oppression, and the time with him so breathlessly precious. "Please let me stay a while longer, Raven. I'll be good."

He drew a deep breath through his nostrils. "I'm afraid Jude failed miserably with you, Charm. You don't know how to be good. But God knows I'm a calf-eyed weakling where you're concerned."

"Thank you." She kissed his cheek. "You won't regret it."

"Yes I will."

"No." She set his lemonade glass on the nailed-down commode before shoving her hand into her pocket. Her pilfered butter knife was in the way, so she pulled it out to place it casually on the bed. It was joined a moment later by her stone.

"Now I know why I shudder every time you reach for your pocket," he said, and she laughed.

"Don't be silly. I'll probably never try to kill you again."

"I feel so much better now."

She chuckled, then dug back into her pocket. "Here," she exclaimed, pulling forth a deck of cards. "I'm going to teach you to gamble."

"Ahh." Clancy stood in the doorway, which Raven insisted on keeping open. "Seems to me Joseph already knows how to gamble."

"Well . . ." Charm shrugged. "Then he can teach me what I don't know."

Clancy winced. "I think I'll leave."

"Good idea," said Charm.

"No!" said Raven. "Clancy . . ."

But Bodine was already gone.

Two hours later he returned to find Charm stretched out beside Raven on the narrow cot. Her slim arm was stretched lightly across his chest and her youthful face was peaceful as she slept.

"Thought you was gambling," Clancy commented wryly.

"She won," Raven said with a sigh.

Chapter 31

The *Belle* arrived at the St. Louis harbor in the early evening of the sixth day of June.

"Well . . ." Fields stood very straight on the steamer's freshly whitewashed ramp. "It's been . . . interesting having you with us, Mrs. Scott."

Charm laughed aloud, looking very young and newly confident as she linked her arm through Raven's. "Perhaps we'll see you again, Captain."

He raised his brows as if loath to admit such a possibility, but in his eyes was the sparkle of youth that Charm could coax from any man. "The *Belle* and I will retire from the Missouri until high water next spring," he said. "I'll not risk her hull on its shallow bottom, but if you ever need a ride down the mighty Mississippi . . ." He paused, his eyes laughing. "Try gaining passage on the *Evening Star* instead."

Charm chuckled, unoffended by the captain's reluctance to see her again. "When we travel next," she said, "we'll want it to be with you. Perhaps . . ."—she glanced first at

Fields, then at Raven—"for our thirtieth wedding anniver-
sary?"

The captain bent down toward her. Retrieving her hand,
he kissed it gallantly. "I only hope our Mr. Scott can survive
your adoration that long."

Raven eyed the sprawling city of St. Louis. It was
bustling with river-front life and seemed little changed from
the last time he'd seen it. Although he would have preferred
to hire a decent-looking horse for the carriage they rented,
Charm insisted Angel's feelings would be hurt if he weren't
allowed to pull them to River Bluffs.

Miraculously, the homely gelding was a decent, if not
elegant, cart horse. He stood now, munching oats from a
feed bag and waiting as his mistress finished her meal inside
the restaurant. They'd left the *Belle* several hours before. In
that time, Charm's smile had faded and her face paled.

Reality, it seemed, had finally set in, and now that they'd
left the relative security of the steamer, Raven deduced that
doubts were assailing her. He'd been right to try to keep her
at arm's length, for less than five miles from town there was
an estate, a stately, aging plantation, spared by the war and
peopled with a bevy of loyal servants. It would be her home,
her life, with no place for a backwater bastard who sported
the ridiculous name of an irritating black bird.

Something twisted in his gut. He ignored the bitter ache,
glancing at his mother's ring on her finger and feeling the
comfortable bulk of her small Bible inside his vest pocket.
How would he ever live without her? But no. This was
hardly the time to worry about his own needs.

"You all right, Charm?"

"Yes." She glanced up, not quite able to match her tone
and expression to her words. "I'm fine."

"Scared?" he asked, raising his brows at her.

She honored him with a laugh, though it was a bit tight.
"No."

He forced a smile for her lie and managed to refrain from touching her hand. "It'll be all right."

She sat very still, looking strangely small and fragile. "Tell me about my family."

He was her family. And she his. His hope. His life. Or rather, that's how he wanted it to be. "They'll think you irresistible, Charm." Just as he did. "No need to worry."

She tried a tilted smile and another lie. "I'm not—" she began, but a fleeting figure caught her attention, and she gasped, cutting her sentence short.

"What?" Raven was on his feet in an instant. "What'd you see?"

"I thought . . ." She blinked, calming her breathing with an effort. "Nothing. It was nothing. I . . . I was just imagining."

Raven turned his head slowly, scanning the crowd around him before returning to his seat, every muscle tense. "Imagining what?"

"Nothing." She smiled again and laughed, seeming to think herself silly. "You're too jumpy." Reaching out, she took his hand as he had wished to do only moments before. "You've no need to worry. They'll think I chose well."

Raven skimmed the room again, noticing every shadow. "I've not the faintest idea what you're talking about?"

"My aunt. She'll think you irresistible," she said, using the same words he had.

"Charm." Raven forced his attention back to her face with a scowl. "You forget that I've already met your aunt." In fact, surprisingly enough, she *had* thought him irresistible. And though he wasn't easily charmed, he had found an honest kindness in her that appealed to the homeless boy in him. "I thought we agreed not to tell her about our . . . situation."

"Our *marriage*, you mean?" She grinned, but behind her eyes there was worry. "*You* agreed. I didn't."

Raven watched her, reading the nuances, judging her thoughts as best he could. "What did you see, Charm?"

"Nothing."

"Try a better lie."

She pursed her fine mouth with a shrug and looked at the table. "Well, if you're not going to give up, the truth would be easier."

"All right. The truth then."

She smiled. It almost reached her eyes. "I thought I saw my father."

"Jude?" he asked in surprise.

She raised her gaze rapidly. "I miss him, Raven. I'm sorry."

Sorry! Good God! That's all he needed to add to the list of problems between them. Her guilt. "I don't see a need for an apology on that front, Charm."

"You're not jealous?" she asked, wanting nothing more than to lean forward just a few inches more and kiss him.

"God, Charm, you make me sound like an ogre. Jealous of your father."

"Well . . ."

"Are you two at it again?" inquired Clancy, returning to their table.

"At what?" asked Raven, not looking up.

"If you two break into a kiss right in front of God and everybody, I won't be escorting you to River Bluffs."

Raven scowled, pulling his attention from Charm with some difficulty. "How do you know the way?"

For a fraction of a moment Clancy was silent, then, "Hell, what kind of detective do you think I am? Can't find an estate half the size of Kentucky? We goin' or you two have better things to do?"

"We do," said Charm, "but he won't."

"Yeah." Clancy sighed. "Well, he's always been a little daft."

"To think I spent most of my life worrying about men taking advantage of me, and now when I want one to, he won't."

"He's a dolt!" agreed Clancy.

"And not very considerate," added Charm.

"And—"

"If you two are done assessing my sundry shortcomings, maybe we could go," interrupted Raven.

"I was just beginning to have fun. Haven't used my best insults yet," complained Chancy. "You don't plan t' go there yet tonight?"

"Yes, I do," said Raven as he rose to his feet. "Eloise will be married in two days."

Clancy scowled. "A terrible time to go bustin' in. We'd best let the excitement die down. Relax in old St. Louis awhile. I'll show you the sights."

"I've seen the sights."

"It'll be dark before we get there. And besides, maybe yer little Cougar Mouse ain't seen the town."

"I haven't," said Charm, her wide eyes finding Raven's. "Couldn't we stay, just a few days?"

Her voice was very soft, and when she asked liked that, there was little Raven wouldn't have done to please her. But the truth of why she wanted the delay was not lost on him. She was scared. Scared of learning her heritage, meeting her family. Scared of the truth. It wasn't the thought of being with him that caused her allure for St. Louis. It was fear, and until she overcame that fear and faced the truth of who she was, he'd never be able to force himself to leave her, knowing she was better without him.

"Best to get it over with, Charm," he said evenly. "No point delaying just because you're frightened."

Her gaze was very steady. "I think you're the one who's frightened, Raven."

He narrowed his eyes at her, silently questioning.

"Scared to believe that I love you just for you."

No. The truth was, he was scared to believe she didn't. But people very dear to him had a tendency to disappear from his life and never come back. "Let's go," he said. "Before I prove the extent of my shortcomings."

*   *   *

The country beyond the bounds of the city was lush and
fertile. Overflowing since the war with unfurling crops and
majestic oaks, it glowed in the last rays of the evening sun,
washing the rolling vista with a rosy glow.

Clancy drove the carriage, leaving Raven to sit in the
back seat next to Charm. Her thigh lightly touched his, her
arm brushed his chest as she pointed to a hawk that soared
overhead or to a willow that grew at a crooked angle above
a meandering stream.

"Couldn't we stop, just for a few minutes?" she asked.
Her eyes were the same shade as the whispering leaves. She
shifted them now from Raven's face to the cool shelter
beneath the willow.

Raven mentally sighed. He'd given ten years of his life
just to spend an hour beneath that tree with her, but there
was no place for weakness in the world of a bastard son.
"You're not two miles from your home, Charm. You can
come here anytime you want."

"*Our* home," she corrected, but her tone was tight, and he
wondered if she too doubted. Doubted whether she'd still
want him after the truth was revealed.

"It'll be over soon," he said, more to himself than to her.

They rattled along, watching the evening sky turn to
purple and fade above the surrounding woods.

"Damn," Clancy said suddenly.

"What is it?" Raven's voice was harsh, making him
realize his own tension.

"Horse is lame."

"What are you talking about?"

"I think the horse is lame," repeated Clancy, pulling
Angel to a halt.

"He's too ugly to be lame," insisted Raven. "Trot him out.
Let me see."

"You don't know nothin' 'bout horses," argued Clancy.
"He's lame, I tell you. We're gonna have to go back."

"Go back! Are you crazy?"

"No. I ain't crazy," said Clancy. "I ain't the one who won't . . . you know . . . with your own wife, when she's sittin' there lookin' so . . ." He waved one hand and turned in the hard seat to gaze at Charm. "Damn, she's pretty. Why don't we sit down here for a spell while I gaze at her and you tell me how you two met?"

"Get going," insisted Raven.

"Listen boy, I don't take orders from"—Clancy started to argue, leaning across the seat, but just then a rifle exploded from the nearby trees.

Clancy jerked like a wooden puppet, body instantly stiff and eyes widening in shock and pain before he fell beside the suddenly rocking wheel of the carriage.

Angel reared. Charm screamed. The unseen rifle spat again. A bullet bored a hole through the back of the carriage.

"Get down!" Raven roared, but Charm was frozen with fear, rising up in the buggy. "Down!" he yelled again, and pushing her to the floor, launched himself to the ground, grasping for Clancy's arm.

"Go on!" Bodine screamed. "Go back! Go!"

"Get in!"

The rifle exploded again. Angel lunged, spurting forward in a wild flight, but somehow Charm reached the lines and pulled him in a tight, rocking circle back to her companions.

Another crack from the rifle. Angel screamed and reared.

"Go!" Raven yelled at her. "Go on!"

"No!" she sobbed.

Death cracked from somewhere behind them. With a lurch and a curse, Raven yanked Clancy into his arms, and then, running beneath his burden, raced for the carriage. Clancy's back hit the floor with a jolt. Raven vaulted over Bodine's body and onto the seat.

Charm slapped the reins against Angel's back. A bullet followed them, soaring between their heads. Far behind, a horse raced toward them and another rifle screamed.

Charm yelled to Angel, calling his name, and they sped ahead.

"God, Joseph!" Clancy's words sounded feeble above the rattle of the wheels and the racing panic of their own hearts. "I'm sorry. Didn't know her then. Didn't mean no harm."

"Shut up!" Raven ordered, dropping to the floor to clasp the other to his chest. "Save your strength. We're almost there. There'll be a nurse there. Hang on!" he groaned, teeth gritted in anguish.

"Don't . . ." Clancy rasped, gripping Raven's coat. "Don't go, Joseph! Please."

"I'm not leaving."

"No. I gotta . . ." Bodine grimaced, stiffening again.

"You're all right," promised Raven but Clancy was gone, limp in his arms.

"Turn there. Left!" Raven yelled. Charm pulled Angel about. The carriage careened on two wheels before righting itself and bouncing along behind the racing gelding. One more rocking turn and there was River Bluffs, towering against the night sky.

The carriage slammed to a halt. Raven jumped out, lifting Clancy from the floor to hurry him to the house, but Charm was already at the door, yelling for help. People appeared all around them, jabbering in the uncertain light of uplifted lanterns.

"He's shot!" Raven yelled. "Where's Eloise?"

"Here." A reed-slim woman scurried through the crowd. "Bring him in here. In here!" she ordered, and Raven followed, bearing Clancy's limp body to the dining room table.

"Sara, fetch hot water, bandages. Where's Ty? Someone send Ty for Dr. Wells. Nel, in here quick!" ordered Eloise, and then she was peeling off Clancy's coat.

"You're Caroline's chile, ain't y'?" asked a rusty voice.

Pushed aside as Eloise labored over Clancy, Charm turned woodenly. She struggled to find reality as her gaze fell on the wizened black face set on a bent and ancient body. "What?"

"My fine, little bright-eyed Cari. You're her gal, ain't y'?"

Charm managed no words and the old woman shook her head. "Ain't no reason fer y' to answer. I see her in yer eyes. I see the lovin'. And the hurtin'. Cuz I's Cora, and I knowed yer ma good as anyone. Come along."

"But . . ." Charm felt lost. Cora. Caroline. Eloise. Did the names trip memories in her mind? Or did she only wish it were so? "Raven might need . . ."

"You're pale as a ghost," Cora chided. "And I ain't havin' no chile of Cari's faintin' down here midst common folk." The old woman wagged her frizzled head and spoke firmly. "Come now."

Charm followed like one in a trance, not thinking, not feeling, only moving up the stairs, through the huge, old manse.

"Yer mama's room," explained the old woman, lifting her lamp in a feeble grip.

Charm peered in, feeling goose pimples trip across her flesh.

"Thet's right, it was hers," said the crackling voice. "My sweet Cari's. Go on in. Lie down. Out of harm's way," she croaked, shifting her gaze about the room. "I'll call y' if'n you're needed," she said, and closing the door, left Charm alone.

The room was blue and white with a canopy bed and double doors that opened to a high porch. She was in her mother's room. Perhaps. Dear God! An inexplicable loneliness swelled within Charm. She swept toward the door, needing Raven.

"Chantilly?"

The name came from the porch. Charm turned with a start, breathing hard, hearing the voice as if from the depths of a nightmare. "Who's there?" she gasped.

A man in a tan hat stepped into the flickering light of the lantern. Her father! Randall Grady! She knew him immediately. Recognized the face, or the voice, or the evil aura. She wasn't sure which, but suddenly memories flooded her senses in a confusing backwash of terror.

"You're dead." Her words were barely audible. "Raven said so. Jude killed you when I was ten."

"On the contrary, my dear . . ." Grady stepped forward with a smile. Although Charm knew she should run, she was frozen in place, like a child with no hope of escape, only able to follow him with her eyes as he moved toward the door. "Jude, as you so charmingly call him, didn't kill me. I owe him a great deal." He removed his hat, and Charm saw now that he was no longer handsome, for his nose was strangely bent and his face scarred. "Yes, I'll have to be sure to repay your Jude somehow, for you see, your dear Aunt Eloise didn't recognize me. Of course, she was only a child when I wooed your mother. Once I heard the old woman was gone I knew it was my chance to return. There'd be no one here to remember me. Except maybe a darkie. But they hardly count. I think old Cora distrusts me," he said with a laugh. "Crazy old bat. She'll be the first to go once I marry."

He took a step toward Charm. She retreated, stiff with terror and dark, rising memories. "What do you want?"

Grady shook her head as if she should not have to ask. "The money, my dear child. Always the money. It was supposed to be mine all along, you know. But your mother was foolish enough to get herself disowned." He laughed again, but the sound was low and frightening. "I did my job too well. She was infatuated and wanted nothing but to leave with me. And then you came along."

Charm backed stiffly toward the wall, remembering him reaching for her as a child. Remembering screams as a cigar burned into her thigh.

"And suddenly little Caroline wasn't so tractable. Thought she had to protect you . . . from me!" he tsked.

"You killed her," Charm whispered, shaking with the rush of memories.

"You were perhaps four when she tried to leave me."

"You killed her," she whispered again.

"Yes." He nodded. "But your Jude saved you from the same fate. It took me years to find you again. Years of planning. But I realized finally that you were my ticket to wealth. Surely the old woman would pay to see you safely brought here to River Bluffs."

His face tightened with hatred. "Yes. I owe your Jude a great deal. But first I must get rid of you, for our lovely Eloise would grant you half her fortune. I can't have that. Not after all these years. I fear I need it all. And once you're gone I will."

She backed away again. "You're crazy," she murmured.

"Perhaps."

"Eloise will never marry you after this."

"I might be crazy my dear, but I'm not stupid. Eloise knows me as Benjamin. Very biblical, don't you think? I'm quite frail now you know. Beaten down by years and the injustices of life," he said dramatically, then shrugged, easily dropping his act. "Eloise has a weakness for weakness. No. I'll climb down the trellis. They'll never see me in the darkness, and never consider I might be capable of scaling the wall to reach your room.

"Of course, this is hardly how I would have preferred it," he went on. "Did you know I promised Mr. Bodine a great deal of money to keep you away? Actually, I thought you must already be dead, for I searched for you at great length. Now it appears your brave father figure must have changed his name. It *was* Neil. Lucas Neil, I believe. All those years inquiring about the wrong man. And you . . . *Charm* . . . isn't that sweet? But how I ramble on. The fact is, Mr. Bodine came inquiring about the reward, but my dear Eloise had already hired Mr. Scott, so I enlisted Bodine to see to *my* needs. I couldn't have you barging in before the wedding." He shook his head. "I really thought Bodine would have enough stomach to kill you, but you can't trust anyone these days."

"You . . ." Charm scanned the room, desperately trying to think. "So you had him shot?"

"Mr. Bodine? No. It's funny how things happen, isn't it? Scott sent a telegraph telling us of your impending arrival.

All I had to do was hire a few men to watch the docks, make sure you didn't show up at the last minute. How they managed to shoot Bodine instead of you is a mystery to me." He laughed again. "But life goes on. Except for you." Suddenly there was a gun in his hand.

The door sprang open.

"Charm!"

Grady fired. Raven launched himself forward, blocking the bullet's path and falling with it planted in his body.

"No!" Charm screamed, crumpling beside him. "No."

Grady pointed his gun at Raven's head. "Always have a champion, don't you, my dear?"

"No!" Charm cried, desperately covering Raven's chest with her arms. "Please! Please no. I'll go away. I promise. I've never come back. Never. The money's yours."

Grady shook his head. "I wish I could believe you. But I fear I don't trust in the fruit of human kindness."

"Then . . ." She shifted in front of Raven, trying to shield him with her body. "Get rid of me instead. He's no threat to you. Please. Let him live. I beg you."

"So brave," Grady jeered. "Your mother's child. But now you die."

Footsteps charged up the stairs.

Grady swung his weapon toward the door and fired. Jude's gun exploded at the same time. Both bullets hit their targets. Both men fell. Jude's gun spilled to the floor.

Grady struggled to his elbows. There was an insane light in his eyes as he aimed at Charm again.

Desperately snatching up Jude's gun, Raven fired. There was a gasp of dying pain, a spastic jerk. Grady died, leaving the room in stunned silence.

"Raven?" Charm's voice wavered. "Raven!"

Blood oozed from his chest, seeping through his shirt and into his vest.

"Please, Raven, don't die. Please." She cradled him in her arms, rocking steadily like a child with a broken doll. "I couldn't live. Not now. Not without you." Silence answered her. "Please!" she gasped, letting her head fall to his shoulder.

His hand lifted slowly, patting her back. She drew away shakily, tears smearing her vision.

"Raven?"

"Charm." He opened his eyes and moved his fingers to her wet cheek. "I love you, killer woman. More than life."

"Don't leave me, Raven. I'm begging you. I'll do anything." Her tears fell upon his shirt, diluted by the blood there. "Stay with me. I'll never try to kill you again."

"Promises, promises," he said weakly and let the darkness take him.

Chapter 32

"Dear God!" Eloise gasped from the doorway.

"Evil. The evil one is dead! I feel it." Cora shrieked.

"Benjamin," Eloise said, rushing to Grady, but there was no life left there.

"He tried to kill her. Just like when I found her." Jude's voice was cracked and weak. "She was so tiny. So frail. But she's safe now. Safe."

"Kill her?" Eloise straightened, turning her head woodenly toward Jude. "Who are you?"

"Help the boy."

She shook her head, dazedly stumbling toward Jude. "You've been shot."

"Goddamn it, woman!" Jude exclaimed, pushing her hands aside to drag himself toward Raven. "Goddamn it!" he grumbled, finally grabbing Raven by the jacket. "I gave you the best I had, boy. Don't you leave her now."

"Jude!" Charm sobbed, trying to pull him away, but he pushed her aside.

"You hear me, boy? Don't you got no guts at all?"

Raven lay pale and silent.

"Boy!" Jude roared. "She deserves more than this. And so does yer mama!"

"Jude! Please!" Charm pleaded.

"Goddamn!" Jude yelled, shaking Raven with ferocious rage.

"What the devil are you doing, old man?" Raven asked, weakly lifting a hand to swipe at Jude's arm.

"Raven!" Charm breathed.

Jude went pale before finding his voice again. "Joseph. Abigail'd never fergive me if I let you die now."

"What the hell are you talking about?"

"Don't speak," Charm pleaded as Jude tore Raven's shirt open. "Please. Rest. Get a doctor. Somebody please. Get a doctor!" she yelled. But Jude only smiled and scoffed. "He ain't gonna die."

Raven scowled at him. "Can't I enjoy this little bit of sympathy from her? What the devil's wrong with you? And how the hell do you know I'm not going to die?"

Jude actually laughed now, though blood oozed through the hole in his pant leg. "'Cause she's a good-luck charm, boy. And now she's yours. And anyhow . . ." He reached inside Raven's vest to draw forth a punctured book. "Her goddamn Bible stopped the bullet. Must be an old wound that started up bleedin'."

Charm breathed a disbelieving whimper of laughter. Then she sobbed. "You're going to live, Raven," and fell to his chest.

Raven patted her back tentatively, waiting for her next words.

She drew away finally, a frown dissected by the salty tracks of tears. "You weren't faking again, were you?"

"Now, Charm . . . ," he said soothingly, trying a smile, "you promised not to try to kill me."

"Were you faking?" She settled back on her heels to swipe shakily at her tears and stare at him.

"Here now," said Eloise, pressing Charm aside, but her

gaze was caught on her niece's face. "Good Lord! Chantilly! You've got her eyes. But . . ." She drew herself from her reverie with a stern hand. "Later. Later. Things to do now."

"How's Bodine?" Raven asked.

"Got a hole in his arm and a bump the size of a watermelon on his head. Says you rapped him against the floor of the coach."

"Ingrate," Raven snorted.

"Relax now, while I see to your chest."

"Oh hell, he's fine," Jude scoffed. "It's my leg that . . ."

"Will you back off, old man," Raven said. "Who the devil do you think you are to barge in here and—"

"Your father." Jude's face was suddenly as pale as dawn. "I think I'm your father."

The wedding took place on the lawn of River Bluffs. Guests milled, drank punch, and gloried in the gossip of St. Louis' most notorious couple.

But the couple, notorious or not, had slipped away after cutting the cake. Now they lay beneath the gnarled branches of a maple that leaned over a sleepy curve of the Mississippi.

"So . . ." Chantilly Charm raised her gaze slowly to Raven's. "Have I convinced you of my love?"

"With that little hen peck?" he asked, keeping his expression sober. "It'll take more."

"Really?" She raised her brows at him. Leaning forward in their hidden hollow, she placed her lips up to his and her hand, feather soft, upon his chest. It was several minutes before they drew apart.

"Now?" she asked softly.

"I'm . . ." Raven began breathlessly, "I'm beginning to believe. Try me again."

She smiled, showing the shallow, twin dimples in her cheeks. "You're shameless."

Raven felt the now familiar ache in his chest. Unable to

resist, he pulled her into his arms once more. "Lucky Charm," he breathed against her hair. "You would have given your life for me."

Her arms tightened around him, squeezing him to her. "In a heartbeat."

Raven kissed her ear, loving her with aching intensity. "It's difficult not to believe under those circumstances."

"So you finally agreed to make an honest woman of me?"

"What are you saying?" Raven asked, pushing her to arms' length. "I had *already* married you."

Charm tilted her head at him. "Because Jude threatened you with a leg wound."

A frown crossed Raven's brow. "The old bas . . . ," he began, but shifted his gaze to Charm and softened his words and expression. "The old goat."

Charm, however, was not to be fooled by such poor camouflage of emotion. "He looked for you for years, Joseph. Tried to find you."

Raven lifted an arm to pull splayed fingers through his hair. "But he failed."

She touched his cheek. "He loved her so. I know now how it tormented him when he couldn't find Abigail. And you."

Raven scowled.

"He made mistakes. Horrible mistakes. But when he couldn't find you he tried to make up for it. Saved *me*, kept me safe. Even after he saw the ring you gave me and he knew you were his son, even then when he was scared to admit the truth to you, he was too loyal to leave, and he followed us. I couldn't have asked for a more faithful father, Raven." She smiled. "He's not perfect, but he saved me from Grady. And I think, in a way, he thought maybe he could make up for the wrong he'd done by caring for me."

Their private little alcove was silent for a moment. But there was no longer any reason for Raven to hide his thoughts from this woman who owned his heart. "Mother had left him a note."

"But you know Jude can't read," soothed Charm. "He explained it all. His attempt to reach the neighbors with the letter. His fall in the river. The note was washed away. He almost lost his life."

"Still . . . ," Raven began, but Charm placed a finger gently on his lips.

"He used to tell me stories of my mother." She smiled. "Or so I thought. My mother with the golden hair and laughing eyes. My mother who would sing 'Old Dan Tucker.' " She watched Raven's face and laughed, remembering the first time she'd heard that song from his lips. She shrugged. "But now I find it was *your* mother he spoke of. *Your* mother he mourned, that I heard about all those years."

"Charm . . ." Raven pulled her closer. "I've been a selfish, whining child. I'm sorry."

"No." She shook her head. "I'm not sorry. I feel as if I know both of them now. Like they're watching us," she added, biting her inner lip and feeling somewhat silly for her sentiment. "From above. And smiling."

Raven watched her, the way her mouth tilted, her dimples winked. "I understand now."

"What?"

"How much a person can love. How much Mother loved Jude."

Charm shrugged. "He's a lovable man."

"He's a bas— An old goat."

"Eloise likes him."

"Eloise is driving him insane. And Clancy too. Won't allow them so much as a glass of punch."

"Jude has never looked healthier."

"Not even a cigar." Raven winced, commiserating.

"He said he wanted to see his grandchildren."

"Children," Raven said as an eager light gleamed in his eyes. "We'd best get right on that," he said, and kissed her. "For my dear old pappy's sake, of course."

"Of course," she sighed, melting into his embrace.

Their kiss was long and sweet and languid before Raven drew back, eyeing her from close proximity. "Charm?"

"Umm?" she replied contentedly.

"Tell me that's not our cake knife I feel in your pocket."

Author's Note

I hope you've enjoyed reading *The Gambler*. Charm is a character I've wanted to write about for a long time, a woman who has suffered abuse and is still able to open her heart to happiness and peace. I have many friends who have lived through similar kinds of abuse, and I know there are thousands of others who still suffer. I hope this book can remind them that there is hope, that there are people who are able to love and help them forgive.

Thanks to everyone who has taken time to read *The Gambler* and understand Charm's quirky ways, and thanks to all of you who have written to me in the past. Your letters mean more to me than I can express in words. God bless you all.

Lois Greiman
PO Box 16
Rogers, MN 55374-0016

If you enjoyed this book, take advantage of this special offer. Subscribe now and get a

FREE
Historical Romance

No Obligation (a $4.50 value)

Each month the editors of True Value select the four *very best* novels from America's leading publishers of romantic fiction. Preview them in your home *Free* for 10 days. With the first four books you receive, we'll send you a FREE book as our introductory gift. No Obligation!

If for any reason you decide not to keep them, just return them and owe nothing. If you like them as much as we think you will, you'll pay just $4.00 each and save at least $.50 each off the cover price. (Your savings are *guaranteed* to be at least $2.00 each month.) There is NO postage and handling – or other hidden charges. There are no minimum number of books to buy and you may cancel at any time.

Send in the Coupon Below

To get your FREE historical romance fill out the coupon below and mail it today. As soon as we receive it we'll send you your FREE Book along with your first month's selections.
